CHASING TAILS

R. LINDSAY CARTER

ROCK AND FLOWER PRESS

First Edition Paperback

Cover design by Angelee van Allman

ISBN
Hardcover: 979-8-9859072-5-4

Paperback: 979-8-9859072-8-5

Ebook: 979-8-9859072-7-8

www.rlindsaycarter.com

CONTENTS

Dedication ... VII

Chapter 1 ... 1

Chapter 2 ... 11

Chapter 3 ... 19

Chapter 4 ... 29

Chapter 5 ... 37

Chapter 6 ... 42

Chapter 7 ... 54

Chapter 8 ... 69

Chapter 9 ... 77

Chapter 10 ... 88

Chapter 11 ... 99

Chapter 12 ... 105

Chapter 13 ... 112

Chapter 14 123

Chapter 15 138

Chapter 16 147

Chapter 17 157

Chapter 18 167

Chapter 19 175

Chapter 20 180

Chapter 21 190

Chapter 22 197

Chapter 23 208

Chapter 24 215

Chapter 25 223

Chapter 26 229

Chapter 27 234

Chapter 28 242

Chapter 29 247

Chapter 30 254

Chapter 31 265

Chapter 32 273

Chapter 33 280

Chapter 34   287

Chapter 35   294

Chapter 36   303

Chapter 37   312

Acknowledgments   322

About the Author   325

Books by R. Lindsay Carter   326

Connect   327

To Dante
You are everything I wanted and dreamed of in a boy, minus your horrible kitchen etiquette, your penchant for sticking your tail under my foot, and your loud mouth. Never change.

CHAPTER I

The blood of a thousand hunters ran through my veins. Every hunt, every chase, was as natural to me as breathing. And this time was no different.

A cat's senses were her best friend. Our ears could locate the faintest of noises, our noses were sharp enough to detect scents unnoticed by most, and our eyesight, while not amazing in the middle of the day, could nonetheless spot miniscule details that other species may miss. In this moment, I was busy putting all my senses to use.

I was a bounty hunter, after all. Tracking was my profession and I reveled in it.

It was autumn in the Oracune Region, a season always welcomed after the long summer of heat. The days slowly grew shorter, but not so short that I missed the sun yet, and the trees were either secure in their green finery if they were of the coniferous variety, or a riot of reds and oranges if they were deciduous. In the Oracune woods, it was not unusual to see the fiery shades intermixed with the evergreens, as was the case in this particular patch of forest through which Grimm and I now stalked our rather elusive prey.

Wet maple leaves squelched under Grimm's feet, an unwelcome distraction to my tracking. I tried to ignore the din as I swiveled my ears about, but the excess noise of the abundant leaves made catching pertinent sounds an extra tricky task. I folded my ears back in mild frustration.

"Have you caught his scent yet?" I asked my business partner, whose massive black canine body dwarfed my petite feline frame.

Grimm bent his head to the ground, using his superior nose to suss out our quarry. "Not yet. He's a sneaky one."

I scanned the ground, looking for any possible tracks in the thick detritus. "Why don't we split up? You go that way and I'll try this direction."

Grimm snorted, leveling me with a yellow-eyed gaze. "Do you really think you'll be able to out-track me? If I recall, I'm the one who always finds the werewolves."

"You find them easily because the idiots can't help but give themselves away by howling at the moon," I retorted with a return stare of my bright blue eyes. "And this isn't a werewolf, in case you hadn't noticed. I have just as much chance of finding him as you do."

"Very well. Call me if you find him." Grimm, loath to argue with me, trotted off in the direction I had pointed him, his tail waving low as he sniffed the ground.

Once he and his distracting footsteps were far enough away, I trained my ears forward, sure that I had heard something unusual amid the relative peace of the woods. This particular patch was very familiar to Grimm and me, as it happened to be located just an hour's walk from home. Grimm and I had explored these woods between bounty jobs multiple times over the last two years, and they felt as much our territory as the cottage did.

Usually, we had to travel long distances for the sake of the chase. I should have been thankful to hunt my quarry so close to home this day.

There. I froze as I caught a faint scent against a twig. I approached cautiously, keeping my body low to the ground. Yes, that twig had come into contact with our prey. The scent was fresh. He was near.

A small scratching sound caught my attention. I focused first my ears, then my eyes on the location, my pupils enlarging to accent my vision.

There he was. My heart rate quickened in my chest.

I took a moment to recall all the previous times I had successfully caught my quarry; werewolves, vampires, cannibals, thieves, and basic ne'er-do-wellers had all fallen to me. I was good at my job. One of the best. This time would be no different.

I crouched, wiggling my shoulders until I was in the perfect position, and then I sprang gracefully into the air to pounce upon my current objective.

Victory was mine.

"Got you!" I declared as my front paws landed just inches in front of the tiny gray mouse. He let out a squeak at my landing but followed it up with tagging my paw cheekily with his own miniscule appendage.

"Grimm, I won!" I called out to my partner. Lucky, the mouse, jumped up onto the back of my neck, his favorite riding spot ever since I had rescued him from the Addelboro Correctional Facility about six months prior.

Grimm came into view, grumbling in a wolfish way. "I think you cheated. You sent me away because you knew he was here."

I lashed my tail at the accusation. "I did not! It's not my fault my excellent feline senses are more attuned to hunting small rodents. Small and stealthy versus big and bulky, am I right?"

Grimm approached us and blew out a large breath, disturbing some of the downed leaves on the ground before him. He nudged my side with his nose, unbalancing me in the process. "Very well, Cress. If that's what you have to tell yourself to be content, I'll allow it."

I lowered my head at his statement. "Content" was a word of some dispute these days. Up until March this year, I had been free to pursue whatever bounty came my way, because only a handful of people knew that I was more than a mundane woman. My mother had drilled the importance of this charade into me from a young age. All would be well as long as the secret of what I was stayed exactly that: a secret. After all, my lineage was unique in the magic world—I was a cat who could transform into a woman at will.

And my lineage also held the legacy of my family, which kept the world safe from an ancient malignance: an immortal witch with a penchant for world domination. Annie Coddle.

Not that I was doing it directly, of course. No, my ancestor, Glivver, who happened to be Annie's familiar, had banished the witch and spelled up a simple prophecy:

"By Glivver's blood the witch is bound,
By Glivver's word the witch must obey,
So long as the daughters of Glivver remain,
So long as the cat that walks as a woman lives,
The witch Annie Coddle can never return."

Each cat of my particular lineage had held her end of the prophecy with no issues. It wasn't until it was my turn that everything went sideways. A little over a year ago, I had faced off against Annie and came out the victor. It wasn't a clean defeat, however. Annie got the last laugh.

But even then, I held out hope. After all, Annie had been badly beaten by me, and, while I figured she would do her best to try to get back at me, she was still marooned in a prison dimension, one that sucked up magic like a sponge, which would make it difficult for her to gather enough magic to do anything harmful. As far as I was concerned, she was stuck there indefinitely, especially after I stymied her latest attempt at escaping.

I had assumed the worst was over. I could still live my life with my feline side staying privileged information. I could still go out on any hunt I desired, my secret safe.

But my carefree days came to an abrupt end when my father, who hadn't known of my existence, was suddenly on the chopping block for a crime he did not commit. I was hired to apprehend him; instead, I helped him. And in the process I inadvertently exposed myself to a shady organization that would stop at nothing to end my line. Because their only goal was to bring back—wait for it—Annie Coddle.

I always assumed that Annie worked alone, but I was wrong. She had an entire cult at her back. Even their organization's name, the Annie Coddle Fanclub, was problematic. The ACFers, as I called them, were a fanatical bunch, and they wouldn't stop until Annie was back, for reasons that escaped my logic.

So, no thanks to some mishaps along the way in helping my father, the ACF now knew I existed, just like Annie did. Even worse, they knew my name.

I was anonymous no more.

The result of this was that I had been effectively grounded from being a bounty hunter and forced to go into a form of hiding. Hiding meant not showing myself around town or farther out by myself, human or otherwise. The closest I could get to Knobby Hill as a solo human was the local veterinarian's farm, just a mile and a half away from my residence. I could no longer stop by the Hunter's Guild or the town board in search of bounties without Fleurette as a chaperone.

My life had shrunk to a very small existence.

But unlike my mother, Belinda, who relished doing nothing all day, I needed stimulation. Hunting was in my blood, which is why I chose the profession of bounty hunting in the first place. The ultimate rush was tracking down dangerous criminals, werewolves, and other wayward supernaturals. That had been stripped from me for the last six months. Now, I was reduced to play-hunting with Lucky for thrills.

So, to get back to Grimm's word choice, was I content? No. I was incredibly bored.

But Grimm was determined to keep me occupied as best as he could, and Lucky was game, so long as our hunting was less bloodthirsty and more like playing tag. He had nothing to worry about from me; ever since befriending the little guy, I had sworn off hunting mice all together.

Still, as much as I appreciated my partner's attempts at entertaining me, this dull life was definitely beginning to grate on my nerves more with each passing day.

"I miss bounty hunting," I moaned for the hundredth time. "You know what we haven't hunted in a while? A vampire. Man, I could really sink my teeth into one of those right about now."

Grimm let out a canine chuckle. "Better than having one sink its teeth into you."

"Remember the last one we took down together?" I asked, looking off into the distance.

"How could I forget?" Grimm shook his shaggy black body. "It had been hiding under the roots of an old tree, coming out at night to stalk its victims. All it took was for you to be the bait as soon as it was dark enough. I still get shivers thinking of how it crept up on you, and you turned at the last second and staked it without so much as a quiver of fear." His tone was filled with admiration.

"Yeah," I said fondly. "We sure suckered that sucker."

We fell into silence. It was all well and fine to think of past escapades, but with every hour the awkwardness and frustration at not being able to act upon my desires grew.

"Have another go at it?" Grimm asked, looking from me to the mouse. Lucky raised up on his back legs. He never spoke to us, but he had his own way of communicating. This body language meant he was happy to hide again for another round of hunting.

I weighed my options. It was still just shy of noon, if I had to guess. It was either stay here and hone my skills in some little way, or go home. And what to do at home? Fleurette was busy filling orders for the approaching Samhain holiday. Fal and Wren, Fleurette's wards, were at school. I couldn't even visit my parents because, due to the unknown nature of the ACF, my mom and dad had been whisked away into hiding shortly after being reunited.

I never thought I'd miss my mother after the blatant animosity I had felt for her this spring, but Freya's furs, I desired to see her again. And my father, too, who I barely knew. We had just connected before GOGS, the society that looked after my kind, decided he and Mom should go into hiding.

I was sure my parents did not miss me. They were probably treating this whole event like one long second honeymoon.

After consideration, there was nothing to do at home besides take a lengthy nap. Playing hunt-the-mouse was the better option after all.

"Sure," I conceded, trying to sound upbeat about it. "Grimm, you and I will go over this way. Lucky, go hide."

Lucky, the good sport he was, instantly scampered off through the leaves. I admired his plucky attitude.

I turned and led Grimm over to the edge of a shallow ravine. The valley of this natural ditch contained a superficial creek that was dry in the warmer months. As it was early in the wet season, the creek was just a trickle. Still, it was picturesque, and would make for a nice resting spot while we gave the mouse enough time to find a hiding place. The banks sloped gently, allowing for an easy walk to the bottom of the ravine.

We reached the bottom and waited. Grimm glanced at me and cocked his head to one side.

"Cress, you have that manic look upon your face again." Grimm licked his lips, a gesture that was almost anxious.

I made an effort to force my ears back into the forward position. But my tail had a mind of its own, and it lashed from side to side as I tried to calm my thoughts.

I stretched my legs forward in pretend nonchalance. "I miss my job. I wasn't cut out to be a do-nothing house cat."

Grimm lowered his head in acknowledgement. "I know, CC. Fleurette is doing her best trying to gather information. It's too risky to go out as a human, what with that organization knowing who you are now."

I'd heard it all before. ACF could track me down now that they had my name. I was too noticeable with my unique appearance. I needed to stay hidden so that my lineage was protected. Blah, blah, blah.

The problem with that last line of rationale was the fact that my lineage was already endangered. Annie's last laugh, remember?

In order to pass the legacy on, I had to do two things that every single cat before me had done: find my one true love, and have a kitten with him. My future daughter would be the next to bear the burden and prevent Annie from returning.

There was just one problem with this plan.

Annie had cursed me to never fall in love with a man. Without my true love, no daughter. Without a daughter, my lineage effectively went extinct.

It's not to say that we weren't still trying to find a workaround for the curse, but it was a terrible blow all the same. And now, we could add another blow in the shape of a cult actively seeking me out to downright kill me.

It was a case of six of one, half a dozen of the other. And all in my disfavor.

Couple this knowledge with my inability to live my life the way I wanted to, and yeah, it made for some depressing days at times.

It was a good thing I had such a supportive family and business partner to get me through those darker moments.

I could feel myself slipping into one of those moods now. They came at more frequent intervals than before. And Grimm, who seemed attuned to my emotional states, could feel it coming too.

"Chin up, Cress. As soon as GOGS find where the Fanclub is now hiding, we can get back to our livelihood. It can't be that much longer, right?"

I loved that he was trying to buoy me up. The problem lay in the fact that his topic of choice was not the way to go about it. I had begged—*begged*—to go and help hunt for the members of ACF. Fleurette was hesitant but willing to allow me, but unfortunately the other members of GOGS put it to a vote and I lost. They said it was too risky to chance myself, the whole "protecting the cat's lineage" thing again. After all, they reasoned amongst themselves, they had to do everything to safeguard the legacy, since that was their sworn duty. Even if it meant death for GOGS members.

And it seemed like they were holding to that bargain. Not only were they having trouble rooting out the nefarious organization, but ever since I had literally sunk the ACF's secret headquarters, certain members of GOGS had been found dead, about one per month. At first we couldn't say that the two things were connected, but as time passed, it wasn't looking good. It had us all on edge.

I closed my eyes, hating that I might be letting my canine friend down with my pessimism. "Right. Come on. Let's go find ourselves a mouse."

Grimm flattened his upper body, sticking his rump into the air in a classic play pose. He looked to the top of the ridge, eager to scamper up the embankment, but froze. He let out a quiet warning growl.

My hackles rose at the sound. "What is it?" I asked in a quiet tone.

Grimm's nostrils flared as he pointed his muzzle to the top. I took his cue and stuck my own tiny pink nose into the air, scenting. A faint odor, slightly musky with a hint of magical spiciness, wafted through my olfactory organs. Something was up there.

We were not in suspense for long.

At first I thought the vibrant leaves had come alive, because the creature blended in so well with the fiery colors. But then my cat eyes discerned a head with big ears and a pointed muzzle, followed by a graceful body and a very fluffy tail. A fox.

The appearance of the fox would have been less concerning, had it not been for the mouse that dangled from its mouth by its tail. Lucky let out a squeak of fear as he writhed about like a worm on a hook.

The fox regarded us as a whole from the top of the ravine, before fixing its amber stare upon me.

"Hello, Cousin," it said.

CHAPTER 2

I bristled as soon as the fox addressed me with my mouse dangling from her teeth.

"*Mine!*" I snarled, racing up the incline to fight this beast. "I'll kill you if you've hurt him!"

To my surprise, the fox gently placed Lucky on the forest floor before I reached her. Lucky instantly regained his footing and ran to me. The fox sat down on her haunches, her tail fluffed out to the side. I stopped short, staring at her with a healthy balance of distrust and curiosity as my mouse cowered against my front leg.

"I wouldn't dream of hurting him, Cousin," she practically purred at me. "I only thought I'd join in the fun. It looks like I won that round."

"Who are you?" I asked, narrowing my eyes. I had seen foxes in the distance before, but they never wanted to have anything to do with Grimm or me. They tended to be a secretive lot, choosing to stay solitary for the most part, even from other foxes. This one was suspiciously gregarious.

The fox yawned, showing off perfectly white and pointed teeth. Up close, she was only a bit bigger than me, although certainly fluffier. Her fur was a beautiful russet with highlights of red, orange, and gold that caught the dappled light and made it dance. The white of her muzzle and cheeks swept south over her chest, and her legs were almost black. She was a striking creature, I'd give her that.

She fixed an almost bored gaze upon me. Her eyes, darker than Grimm's but still of amber hue, disconcerted me. It took me a moment to realize why: the pupils were slitted, like mine, instead of round like Grimm's. That, and they held a keen intelligence, one I rarely saw on wild animals.

She spoke to me, "Now, now. I've traveled a long distance to make your acquaintance. It would be nice if I could be greeted in a mannerly way for my troubles."

By this time, Grimm had joined us at the top of the ridge. He was in full angry-Lycanhund mode, complete with a menacing posture and raised hackles. "You threaten a creature in our care and then have the gall to accuse *us* of no manners?"

The fox turned her full attention to my partner. She stood gracefully, nimbly stepping closer to him without a trace of fear as she gazed up at his face. "Oh my. Aren't *you* a striking specimen?" The purr in her voice was back. Grimm deflated and froze at her words. "I'll be very happy to get to spend time with you."

Her previous mannerisms had already begun to grate on me, but her sudden interest in Grimm was too much. I growled my frustration. "You won't be spending time with either of us! Why don't you leave us alone now?" I backed up my words with a bit of a hiss and a threatening posture.

The fox assessed me with cool eyes, clearly not afraid of my display. "Oh, Cousin. That's no way to treat a guest."

Her name for me further confused me. "Why do you insist on calling me that?"

She actually laughed, a high keening sound that made my ears flatten. "Doesn't that cute little kitty nose work? Can you not smell me? You and I are alike, *Cousin*."

As if to prove her point, her scent wafted on the breeze over to me, engulfing my senses in that heady smell of magic. I flinched back at the power of it. Grimm, from behind me, gave an odd whine before sneezing. The fox's eyes flashed with a coral light that took over the normal amber color, and I could almost see an aura of the same hue emanating from the creature's body, creating the sense that she was much grander than physical perception led us to believe. And as this vision swarmed my senses, I could swear she fanned out not one, but multiple tails behind her, all of them basking in the supernatural light of her aura.

As quickly as I sensed this overwhelming display, I blinked and she was just a fox again. I wondered if I had imagined the whole thing, if not for the smug air the vixen emitted.

"That's right. I am more than meets the eye, just as you are. You hide the body of a human under your fur. In a fashion, so do I." She sat again, graceful and poised like a queen on a throne.

I blinked in confusion at her. What did that mean? "What *are* you?"

The fox made the keening laugh again. "A fox, am I not? Oh, Cousin, I am so glad I chose you for help. It will be such fun."

I did not like the sound of that. "Fox, I don't know what game you are playing at, but I'm not interested. Go away and leave us alone."

Grimm backed up my sentiment with a small snarl. The fox blinked as if bored by his display, which took the wind out of his sails.

"I suppose it is time for me to go. See you around, handsome," she directed this last part at Grimm, who cocked his head to the side. She glanced over her shoulder at me. "Until next time, Cousin."

I hissed at her, tired of her presence. "I doubt that."

The fox sprinted away at a rapid pace, letting out another unsettling laugh as she disappeared from view.

"That ... that wasn't normal, right?" I asked Grimm once she was gone.

"Definitely not," he answered.

After that bizarre encounter, Grimm and I—and Lucky—decided it was time to go home. Not only had the strange fox quashed any hope of a frolicsome mood, but the entire atmosphere of the day had changed. The October weather, having played nicely all morning, allowed clouds to move in, chasing away the shy autumn sunshine. I smelled rain in the air.

We took our time walking back, though. I wanted to clear my head of magical foxes, but it was all my mind fixated on.

I wracked my brain of my supernatural knowledge. While this world was filled with many mundane people and creatures, there were just as many magical beings out there. Off the top of my head, I could think of witches, elementals, and projectionists. Magic users who could manipulate anything from crystals to the weather. Enchanters. Seers.

Animals were certainly not left out of the list, either. I'd heard stories of kelpies, sasquatch, and thunderbirds. Grimm certainly had magic in his blood. Even *I* was considered a magical creature.

So, what other magical species existed? Shapeshifters were at the forefront. Each shifter could change into one type of mammal, the wolf being the most common. I had inadvertently met a river otter shifter in the spring. I did not have a chance to converse with her in her animal form, seeing as how I had to pretend to be fully human the entire time she was near me. Perhaps shifter animals smelled potently of magic like the fox had, but I somehow doubted it.

Grimm and I were not the only magical animals to exist in the Oracune Region, so surely there were other creatures with magic about. However, try as I might, any knowledge of magical foxes eluded me.

There was someone who might know more on the subject, I surmised, as we exited the woods onto Rabbit Hole Road, heading east. Fleurette, my best friend and an exceptional witch, seemed to be a fount of knowledge. Like me, she was forced to keep a part of herself a secret. Her classified aspect had to do with the extent of her magical prowess. She posed as an ordinary minor witch, an herbalist—they were a dime a dozen. Her natural plant magic backed up this claim, and she made a good living selling plants and small potions in town. But I knew she actually was much more powerful than she let on. She hid her true power from the world, worried that it would draw negative attention to her. After all, her mother had disappeared when Fleurette was a child, and Fleurette and her father feared that it was because of her mother's own magical aptitude.

That was the theory until Fleurette's mom turned up like a bad penny and appeared to be in cahoots with ACF.

Meanwhile, Fleurette covertly continued her studies, gaining knowledge with a genuine thirst as her magic levels climbed. She excelled at research, and was the most well-read witch I knew. If anyone knew something about magic foxes, it would be her.

I would ask her as soon as we made it back home. I wouldn't have long to wait; already I could smell the familiar scents of the cottage ahead. We were almost to our destination.

Not a moment too soon, either. The rain started, just a tiny drizzle as we reached the small porch, but with a promise of more volume to come.

At the plum-colored front door I paused to let Lucky off of my back, and then I performed my one bit of inherited magic. With a small amount of concentration, my whole body shimmered, became amorphous, and transformed into that of a human woman, all within less than a second. With a height advantage and grasping appendages, I scooped up my mouse and opened the door with ease, letting myself and Grimm inside.

A welcoming wall of warmth hit us as soon as the door opened. When the temperatures dropped for the season earlier in the month, Fleurette had pulled out a small contraption called the everlasting flame and placed it on a table at the back of the room. The magical appliance was an empty fireproof vessel with a powerful charm inside. One simply had to activate the charm to produce a small but powerful flame, which would burn steadily for as long as the owner kept the charm activated. The vessel itself never became hot enough not to handle, but gave off a constant, pleasant heat, enough to warm the entire house.

It was my favorite object when the weather cooled.

I closed the door behind me, trapping the luscious heat inside. The air was thick with autumnal smells: cinnamon, pine, pumpkin, and countless herbs for magical potions and spells. Fleurette must have been busy in her tiny workroom. The holiday Samhain was a big deal, especially to witches, and it was one of Fleurette's busier times, aside from spring when her plant magic was utilized to its fullest for market season.

A small wooden box perched on the windowsill behind the loveseat by the door. It was filled with fluff and chewed up papers, the perfect nest for a little mouse. When he wasn't hanging out with us larger animals, Lucky enjoyed sleeping in this box. He ran down my arm now, as I held it out like a miniature rodent highway directly to his abode. He plopped into the fluff and buried down with mousy contentment as I walked further into the cottage.

"Fleurette?" I called out. The cottage was small, so my shout was probably unnecessary, but sometimes my friend became caught up in her work and didn't hear me enter our shared dwelling.

No answer.

Grimm whined. I frowned at him, unsure what his noise meant. I hated that our communication was limited when I was in my human form.

He padded forward, leading me toward the kitchen. As I approached, I heard what had troubled him.

Sobbing. Wren.

Alarmed, I rushed into the kitchen. Seeing no one there, I followed the sound into the dining room, just to the right. I stopped in the doorway, to take in the scene. Fleurette sat turned away from us at the table, with Wren sitting in a chair facing her. They both leaned toward each other, their upper bodies entwined in an embrace as Wren's shoulders hitched with her crying. Rupert, Fleurette's crow companion, perched on Wren's chair, watching the two silently. He gave a small, mournful caw at our appearance.

The sound alerted Fleurette, who swiveled her head to glance our way. Her eyes were red. Wren obviously wasn't the only one crying.

My heart leapt for my throat. Wren was still a child and crying was not all that unusual for her, but what alarmed me more was that her sobbing was coupled with the fact that she should have still been in school. Why was she home?

Added to that, Fleurette's reddened eyes sent my pulse into overdrive. My friend was not prone to suffer from hysterics. As a matter of fact, I had never seen her so distraught before. Something very bad must have happened.

"Fleurette?" My voice was pinched in my throat.

She and Wren parted, although Wren still looked miserable.

Fleurette dabbed her eyes on her sweater sleeve before giving me her full attention. "Cressida, I'm sorry."

CHAPTER 3

My alarm climbed higher. Thoughts of my parents or Fal in danger raced through my imagination. "Sorry for what? What's happened?"

She must have seen the panic in my face and grimaced. "Sorry for appearing this way."

I pushed on. "Is someone hurt? My parents? Fal?"

She waved a hand to dismiss my fears. "No, they're safe. It's another GOG."

Now that I knew my family was okay, I let go of my fear with a relieved sigh, settling my heart into a more normal pace. Having grounded myself, I rushed to comfort my distraught friend. "Oh, Fleurette. I'm so sorry."

She let out a hitched breath. "I had just gotten back from picking up Wren from school. Apparently she fell asleep in class and had a doozy of a nightmare. They asked me to pick her up early."

I frowned. That would explain why Wren was home. I turned my attention to the girl. "Wren, are you okay?"

She squeezed her eyes shut and shook her head, her chest beginning to hitch uncontrollably again. Fleurette leaned forward to once more offer her comfort. I rushed to her side and crouched by her chair, placing a hand on her back. Grimm leaned into her on the other side.

I turned my eyes to Fleurette. She sighed. "As soon as we walked through the door back home, I received a message on my mirror." Her voice turned soft. "It was Maurice. He was found this morning. Same as the others."

I sucked in a breath through my teeth. Maurice was Wren's personal GOG teacher, coaching her in her special brand of magic over this last year. He had lived with his father—also a GOG—one town over.

Wren harbored a small schoolgirl crush on him. She had only turned thirteen a month prior, after all—the time in a girl's life when hormones had a mind of their own. No wonder she was grieving so.

It did not help that she and her brother had also lost both of their parents to a tragic demise when she was only eleven. Death of loved ones left indelible scars on children, no matter what.

I rubbed her back in soothing circles. "Wren, love, I'm so sorry. Is there anything I can do?"

She released Fleurette and wiped her eyes on the back of her hand. She had cut thick bangs into her long dark hair as a thirteenth birthday present to herself, and this whole time her eyes had been hooded by them while she kept her face tilted forward in misery. She now lifted her head, displaying her glassy hazel eyes. "No, but it's okay," she told me with a watery smile. "I can't help but feel responsible, though."

I shook my head, dismayed at her words. She had been the physical hand in causing her parents' death, even if she had no control over her actions at the time. She suffered from nightmares for the next year over that fact, and it had taken a good amount of therapy to convince her that she was not a murderer. I hated that the processes seemed to have reversed with Maurice's untimely death.

"Why do you feel that way?" Fleurette asked her, clearly in agreement with me.

Wren looked at her guardian, fear flitting through her eyes. "I ... dreamed about him. I saw him. Not alive." She shuddered at her own words. I noticed she had skirted around mentioning the word death.

I exchanged glances with Fleurette before she brought her attention back to the girl. "Was this today?" she asked gently.

Wren nodded. "I didn't mean to fall asleep in school," she explained. "I haven't been sleeping well this week."

"Why not?" I asked. Wren and I shared a history of nightmares, but I thought they had been getting better.

"Bad dreams. But not the same as I was having. These are ... disjointed, more feeling than action. And I can't sleep after I have one. So I just stay awake until it's time to get up."

I grasped her hand. "Why didn't you tell me? You know I'm always happy to sleep in your room with you."

She shrugged, not meeting my eyes. "I dunno. I know you've been unhappy with things lately. And I didn't want to add to your burdens. Besides, I'm too old to need ..."

"A living safety blanket?" I finished for her once she had trailed off. She gave me a quick smile and a nod. I pursed my lips. "Wren, you aren't too old. It's not babyish to need a little help sometimes. And that's what the adults in your life are there for. To help you. Both me and Fleurette."

"My two weird moms?" Wren joked anemically.

"She's right," Fleurette butted in. I looked at her askance. She rolled her eyes. "Not about the mom thing. If anything, we're more like two weird aunts. But I agree with the notion of us helping you. I wish I had known you were being plagued with bad dreams again. And I'd like to hear more about your dream at school, but not now. For now, I'm going to make us all a pot of tea to help everyone relax. I know I could use it."

While Fleurette bustled into the kitchen, Grimm and I led Wren into the sitting room. The girl had grown considerably in the last six months, and I was surprised to discover that she was now a good inch taller than me as we walked side by side. I plopped the two of us down on the loveseat, cuddling her shaken form. Grimm leaned his weight into our feet.

I wasn't sure what to say. How did one help a grieving young teen?

I opted for something that would allow her to take the lead, if she wanted. "You know you can always talk to me, right?"

Wren nodded, resting her head against my shoulder. I gave her an affectionate squeeze.

She sighed. "I don't want to talk about him just yet."

"I understand. When you're ready, okay?"

"Okay."

Fleurette walked in, balancing a tray with three steaming mugs in her hands. She set the tray down on the low table, handing Wren a mug first and then one to me. I took it gratefully, freeing my arm from Wren's body to firmly hold the hot vessel.

We sipped in silence, each of us wrapped in our own thoughts and emotional fortresses, stocking up on weapons and preparing for the personal battle that always takes place after a traumatic experience. The tea, however, was a wonderful herbal blend of Fleurette's creation that calmed the nerves and dulled the sharp edges of grief, at least temporarily. Battle could wait.

Beside me, Wren's head began to lull once she was finished with her cup. Fleurette noticed too and took the mug from her grasp.

"C'mon, sweetheart," she murmured to Wren. The girl obediently sat up, although she appeared quite woozy.

Wren turned to me. "I love you, Cressida."

My heart expanded. "I love you too, Wren. You look like you need some sleep."

"Mm-hm. I'm going to go take a nap." With that statement, she stood and carefully made her way to her bedroom. Fleurette followed her.

I could hear the sounds of Wren crawling into bed, thanks to my sensitive ears. "Fleurette?" I heard her say with a sleepy voice, "You know I wouldn't mind having two weird moms, right? If that would make you happy? Not with Cressida, but with someone else."

Fleurette's answer was very quiet. "I know."

Wren's voice continued, "I love you, Fleurette."

"I love you, Wren. Get some rest."

It was obvious Wren passed out after this brief but touching conversation. My friend returned, retaking her seat across from me.

I eyed her suspiciously. "What did you put in her tea?"

Fleurette looked half-exhausted herself. "Nothing soporific, if that's what you're accusing me of. That was purely Wren running on physical and emotional fumes. I did slip a small charm in her tea to give her dream-free sleep, I admit. The poor girl deserves that much at least."

I nodded. "It's troubling, isn't it?"

Fleurette let out a bark of a laugh, although there was no humor attached to it. "Which part?"

I scrunched up my lips. "All of it." I sighed, setting my mug back on the tray now that the warmth had seeped out of the porcelain. "The dreams, for sure. I wish she had told me she hadn't been sleeping well."

Fleurette gave a small nod, as if to herself. "I as well. She's my ward. I want to be able to protect her from these sorts of things.

But she feels like she's growing up and doesn't want to be babied. I can understand that too. But a prophetic dream? I don't like the sound of that."

"About Maurice, of all things too. How many deaths does that make?"

Fleurette thought for a moment. "Six. And he was the closest to us, both geographically and emotionally."

I had not known Maurice well, having only met him a couple of times. He was younger for a GOG, only slightly older than Fleurette, and quiet but incredibly passionate about his studies on the art of projectionism. That was Wren's magical gift, a type of magic so rare that she was probably the only projectionist alive at the moment. Maurice may not have been a projectionist himself, but his profound knowledge made him the obvious choice as a mentor for Wren, and she had grown as a magic wielder under his tutelage.

And now he was gone.

Fleurette huffed a breath. "I don't get it," she said. "I thought I was getting an idea for who would be targeted. The murders seem random, but up until Maurice, the people targeted were older GOGs, those who had been around for over twenty-five years."

It was true. Until Maurice, the ages of the departed had been between sixty-two and eighty, and the deceased members had been from all over the western portion of Vinland, although most had been stationed within the Oracune Region.

The problem was, GOGS was highly secretive. Only other members knew about it. I was the first of my line to learn of its existence. That pointed to one thing: a spy in their midst.

Fleurette let out a fresh sob, her emotions working up again. "And Maurice only lived one town over. It's so close to home. I need to get Dad to safety. He fits the pattern. He could be next."

Lyle Williams was the local veterinarian in Knobby Hill. He was also Fleurette's father, and, although he was a mundy, he was an honorary member of GOGS.

I got up, rushing over to her and nearly tripping over Grimm in the process. I pressed her head into my midsection, gripping her by her shoulders. For once I was taller than her, and it felt good to give my friend the comfort she needed. "Now, now," I soothed. "We don't know how they are targeting GOGS. Your father could be safe. After all, none of the members killed had even helped us escape this spring. And the one person who did help us, we already got into hiding once the killings started."

I was referring to Melokuhle Ndou, the GOG who helped me and my great-grandmother escape the clutches of the ACF last March. Once members began dying after our venture, he was the first person whose safety we feared. At my insistence, the society helped get him into hiding, with his cat Mitzi as well. After all, Mitzi had close ties to my own great-grandmother. I wanted to keep her just as safe as Melokuhle.

I understood Fleurette's fear for her father, though. He was the last family member she had a connection to. And as a mundy, he had no way of keeping himself safe from magical attacks. And we simply didn't know how people were being picked for assassination. It was for this reason that my parents had been relocated almost immediately after the events of March, even before people began dying.

Fleurette patted my back and let go of me. She looked up with appreciation. "You're an amazing creature. Thank you."

I grinned. Her words jolted me into remembering the weirdness of earlier today. "Speaking of amazing creatures ..."

But Fal burst through the front door at that moment. His ear-length black hair was wet with the rain and stuck to his scalp at odd angles. He took off his sopping rain jacket, hanging it to dry on the hook next to the door. Only then did he turn and see the two of us.

"What's happened?" he asked immediately.

I gazed at him with something akin to sisterly love. Fal had always been a good kid, but he had really blossomed over this last year, and he was an incredibly kind and sensitive young man. The concern he held for his guardian proved that.

Fleurette sighed. "Fal, come sit. I have some disturbing news."

The teen crossed the room to take the unoccupied chair next to Fleurette's. At seventeen, he was all legs these days, and he now topped even Fleurette's height by a few inches. He flopped into the chair, a concerned look upon his face.

Fleurette repeated the story of Maurice and Wren in a calm and caring manner. Fal had not been close to Maurice like Wren had been, but he was appropriately sad to hear of his passing. But he was more troubled by his sister's dream.

Fal was the only other person beside the two of us who knew that dreams could be more than they seemed on the surface, especially when it came to Wren. And he was very, *very* protective of his little sister.

"There must be something we can do!" he exclaimed, running a hand forcefully through his drying hair.

Fleurette turned her palms up. "What do you propose, Fal? You don't have the ability to go into her dreams and keep her safe. The best I can say for now is that I can give her a potion to keep her dream-free. It will hopefully be enough until we have more answers. In the meantime, I will be consulting with GOGS to see what else can be done."

Fal picked at a cuticle on his finger, listening to his guardian. "I hate this."

"Hate what, Fal?" I asked.

His foot tapped on the wood floor, a nervous staccato that reflected his inner turmoil. "I hate that even now, we can't be safe. There's always one thing or another! I just want to protect Wren. She's gone through so much."

"As have you," Fleurette stated kindly. "Safety in this life is never guaranteed, even for those living a charmed life. The only thing we can rely on is our will to keep trying." She stood up. "Let's get some dinner started, shall we? We'll let your sister sleep as much as she needs. Healing happens when the mind is at ease. What do you say?"

Fal stood, uncertainty shining bright in his eyes. He nodded, once again trusting Fleurette to help him.

It was only after dinner, when Fal had left the cottage to retreat to his own personal outbuilding bedroom, that I felt the timing was right again to ask Fleurette about the fox.

We once more retired to the sitting room, both of us weary from the high stress and emotions of the day. The sun had long since set, and the rain pounded in full force upon our cottage, making the room feel extra cozy with its dry warmth. Grimm was curled up against my body, barely fitting his great mass next to me on the loveseat. I draped my left arm over his back, absentmindedly stroking the long fur under my fingertips.

"Fleurette, we had an odd encounter in the woods today."

She had been sitting with another cup of tea. I could tell she had lost herself in the trappings of her own thoughts more so than the physical world. At my words, though, she snapped back into the present with a sharp look. "Oh?"

I nodded. "It was a fox. But not just a fox. Do you know of any supernaturals that look like foxes?"

She mulled it over with a small frown. But before she could answer, a loud thump sounded on the front door. We froze.

Grimm recovered first, growling softly as he lifted his head to peer at the door. Goosebumps rose on my arms. Thoughts of slain GOGs flashed rapidly in my mind, the killer in each case never identified, the cause of death unknown. Was Fleurette next? Was there a murderer outside our cottage?

Fleurette snapped out of her inaction. She stood from the chair and made her way quietly to the door, pausing in front of it. I too stood, nimbly stepping to her back with Grimm at my heels. I crouched to remove my only weapon, an enchanted knife named Hail Mary II, from my boot. I held it up, poised to throw it if we were attacked at the front door.

Taking a deep breath, Fleurette opened the door, and then jumped back. Her action surprised me, nearly making me throw the knife from sheer nerves.

"What is it?" I hissed.

Fleurette looked at me, but there was no more terror upon her face, which set me at a margin of ease. Instead, she seemed confused, and when I finally got up the nerve to peer around her, I understood.

On the darkened stoop, lying in a limp heap, was a naked woman.

CHAPTER 4

The woman was clearly unconscious, the subtle movement of her torso giving a hint at her breathing. She sprawled as if she had collapsed upon our stoop, with her head closest to the door. Her legs hung uncovered off of the small porch, shining and beaded with the downpour of rain. It was clear that she didn't have a stitch of clothing upon her, but her long black hair fanned out in wet clumps, covering the entirety of her face and parts of her upper body, a rather crude charade at modesty.

Grimm whined.

Fleurette gathered her wits and turned from the door to grab the nearest throw. Blankets were a hot commodity in the fall, with a throw living on every single stick of furniture, seemingly. It only took her a second to have the blanket in hand, at which point she fanned it out and over the prone form, covering her nudity.

"Help me get her inside," Fleurette directed me. She did not wait for an answer from me, but promptly bent down and began scooping up the woman's top half, tucking the blanket under her as she did. I got over my shock at the circumstances and, pausing only to tuck the knife back into my boot, I maneuvered myself around the woman until I was able to pick her up by her legs. It was awkward, but we managed to carry her into Fleurette's bedroom at the far end of the hallway. Grimm followed in our wake, intrigue and concern etched into his countenance.

Fleurette took the majority of the woman's weight while we hoisted her onto the bed. Once she was positioned with her head on the pillow, Fleurette switched out the now-sodden blanket for two new ones, a necessity for warmth and for modesty. Then she smoothed the long hair out of the stranger's face for our first glimpse at her features.

The woman looked serene upon the bed, her eyes closed peacefully. Dark eyebrows and eyelashes adorned her oval face, as well as a long straight nose and a narrow mouth. Her complexion looked rather sallow, especially in the low light of the bedside lamp. As if reading my mind, Fleurette turned up the lamp's intensity to help chase away the shadows. In the brighter light, there was a hint of a very old bruise upon her right cheek. This was the only imperfection upon an otherwise porcelain complexion, which made guessing her age rather difficult, although I estimated her to be Fleurette's age, or perhaps slightly younger.

"Who is she?" I asked Fleurette, who had continued to gaze at the woman as she crouched by the bed.

She straightened and glanced at me. "I haven't a clue. I've never seen her before. Have you?"

Living in a small town, one got to know most—if not all—of the other folks residing within. This was less true for me, considering I only went to Knobby Hill for business reasons and I otherwise stayed away from most people, but Fleurette was well known, and had worked plenty of farmers markets and the like over the years. If she didn't recognize the woman, she must not have been a local. So, the question was, how did she get here?

I shook my head in response to Fleurette. "Never seen her before. She does look vaguely familiar, though." It was the shape of her closed eyes. I knew one other person with a similar facial structure.

Fleurette stood. "I'm going to make something to help her wake up. Yell if you need me."

I sighed, sitting on the edge of the bed close to the woman's feet. I shook my head, ruminating. More mysteries. And here I thought this day was over.

Grimm padded forward as Fleurette exited, placing his paws on the mattress near her torso and hoisting his upper half up to inspect the woman. I let him, as I knew he would do nothing to harm her. He sniffed at her form before cocking his head to the side. I watched him, intrigued. I was a pro at reading his moods while I was human, given it was the only way to communicate while I was in this form. He turned his head and looked at me. His yellow eyes were alert and curious. He gave me a whisper of a whine, indicating a hint of worry.

Interesting. Grimm's concern could just be for her well-being. After all, an unconscious naked lady wasn't an everyday occurrence, and certainly something to be concerned about. I had noticed that her frame seemed a shade too thin to look fully healthy, and before Fleurette had covered her up I spied some scarring and very old bruises on her legs, specifically her upper thighs. She had clearly had a rough time of it in the past.

But his curiosity—that piqued mine. What smells did she give off to elicit such a reaction from him? I'd have to shimmer into cat form to find out. Too bad the timing wasn't right, because I had the feeling Fleurette needed my help in my larger, more dexterous body.

So, I stayed glued to my spot, watching the mystery woman until Fleurette quietly bustled back into the room with a small ceramic pot in one hand and a steaming mug in the other.

She set the mug down carefully on her nightstand before walking to the corner of the room, where an old wooden chair stood. She hoisted it one-handed and placed it by the bed before sitting in it. Then, ever so carefully, she maneuvered the pot until it was in front of the woman's face.

"Stay alert," she told me in quiet tones as she watched the unconscious woman. "This may have a powerful effect."

Fleurette gave the pot a little shake. The contents within were apparently in powder form, because the movement produced a tiny cloud from the pot. Like smoke, the cloud traveled closer to the woman's face before disappearing into her nostrils on an inhale. Fleurette swiftly extracted her arm, along with the pot, and placed it down next to the mug.

Nothing happened.

"*Chikushou!*" the woman practically screamed as she sat straight up, her dark eyes wide yet unseeing. She let out a string of more indecipherable words with anger lacing each syllable as she flailed her arms about, disrupting the blankets Fleurette had placed upon her and exposing her upper half once again. She finally seemed to regain control of her appendages because her hands went straight to her nose, batting at the underside as if to dislodge whatever it was she had breathed in.

During this chaos, Grimm had backed away with his tail practically tucked behind his legs and his ears forward, and Fleurette had been forced back a bit in her chair to avoid being smacked in the face. Me? My first instinct was to grab onto her legs to prevent them from thrashing as wildly as her arms had. They bucked weakly a couple of times under my hands, but otherwise stayed still.

All the while, the woman spoke in a foreign language, at first with complete abandon. As her body calmed, so did her speech patterns. After less than half a minute, she stilled, resting back against the pillows. Her chest heaved with uneven breaths, as if she had just run a mile. She closed her eyes again, briefly.

Fleurette took the opportunity to readjust the blankets, covering the woman's nudity back up. The gesture seemed to revive the stranger, for she opened her eyes to watch Fleurette. She asked a question, her voice a deeper timbre than I would have imagined it sounding given her physique. While whatever she said sounded calm and rational—unlike her crazed rambling from before—we still could not understand a word of it.

Fleurette shook her head, a concerned smile marking her face. "I'm sorry."

The woman closed her deep-set eyes again. She paused, ran a hand up her face and through the top of her hair, and opened her eyes again, fully intent on Fleurette. "I apologize. Do you understand me now?" Her words were laced with an accent.

"Yes, of course! You speak our language." Fleurette's smile widened.

The foreign woman nodded, giving Fleurette a small smile of her own. "I am not as skilled in your language, but I have been taught from an early age."

"You speak it beautifully."

"Thank you. I am sorry I spoke Tyonoshimese just now. I awoke confused. I am better now."

Fleurette looked gracefully chagrined. "Yes, sorry about that. You had us worried when you wouldn't wake up, so I gave you a little waking powder. It ... isn't pleasant, I'm afraid."

"I understand. You are the resident witch, yes?" The woman studied Fleurette with renewed interest.

I had remained invisible during this entire conversation, noting the way the two women interacted together with perfect amiability, despite the oddness of the meetup. But now I witnessed Fleurette become aloof at this last question, putting up a wall that diminished her natural friendliness. She also didn't answer right away, despite the eager look in the other woman's eyes.

"In a manner of speaking, she's the town's herbalist," I responded for Fleurette, my innately guarded nature coloring my words. "And who might you be? Why did you come here?"

The woman turned her head to stare at me, her nearly black eyes turning from narrow to wide open once she took me in. "You are who I came to see! But forgive me, my manners are lacking. I am Inaba Kokoro." She gave me a small head bow before turning to Fleurette and doing the same to her.

"Inaba, what do you mean, you came to see me? Or us?" This whole thing was becoming more confusing by the second.

She shook her head. "Inaba is my marriage name. Please, call me Kokoro, as that is my given name."

Fleurette nodded in understanding. "In many cultures, including Tyonoshima, the family name comes first. It's the opposite of what you've known, Cressida." Fleurette turned her attention back to the woman, her aloofness vanishing once more. "Kokoro, my name is Fleurette. It is a pleasure to meet you. I too am curious by what you said to Cressida. What did you mean?"

Kokoro watched Fleurette for a moment, her eyes dancing with wonder. "My apologies. I am not making myself understood. I think I am still a little confused from the powder. And I have not had the use of my body in a long time."

I blinked. The use of her body? "What in Gaia's great greenery does *that* mean?"

Fleurette shot me a small frown. "Hush, Cress." She turned and smiled again, clearly trying to set her unexpected guest at ease. "Take your time. It's normal to feel some bewilderment after inhaling waking powder."

Kokoro bobbed her head in acknowledgement. I simply rolled my eyes at Fleurette's overly nice temperament. She was a naturally kind person, don't get me wrong, but right now she was laying it on rather thick. It made me wonder why, given that this strange person had seemingly dropped out of nowhere and hadn't given us any solid reasons as to why yet.

Fleurette's syrupy demeanor helped set the woman at ease though. "Let me try to make sense." She turned to me, her mouth set in a kind smile that lit up her sallow face. "I came looking for you, because you are the cat that walks as a woman."

My stomach bottomed out in a rush of dread at those words. Despite the seemingly kind package the message had been delivered in, I instantly felt unsafe. No one was supposed to know what I was. How could *she*?

Was it worth denying? I gaped at Kokoro, my mouth working like a landed fish's as I tried to come up with something, anything to say.

But she must have seen that her words had negatively affected me. "I am sorry! I was not told by anyone. You are safe. You see, I have no magic of my own, but I was born with a gift all the same. I can see the magic in others. I can sometimes taste spoken spells. And written words make music when I read them in my head."

I scrunched my brows down. "Say what?" Her words made no sense. Taste spells? Hear writing? I began to suspect this woman might have escaped from a mental facility.

But Fleurette only nodded as if Kokoro's statements made all the sense in the world. "You are a synesthete?"

I blinked deeply as I looked at her. "A what?"

She returned my stare. "Synesthesia is a rare condition in which the senses overlap, or get muddled. People can hear colors, taste sounds, or any other odd combination. Each synesthete is unique."

Kokoro nodded, following along with our side conversation. "Yes! That is the term. For me, my strongest gift is seeing the inner magic each person possesses. Sometimes magic has a color when it is used, but magic inside a person has no color. But I see them anyway. Each magic is like an aura. Greens for earth. Red for elements. Blue for healing. Purple for enchantment, turquoise for spells, yellow for mind. I see black if someone has wielded dark magic, death magic. And if their magic is just a part of them, like shifters, they glow white. Innate magic, I believe would be the term?" She turned to me. "You are very white. That is how I knew you were the right person."

I took a deep breath. That was not what I was expecting, but I believed she was telling the truth. "What about Fleurette? What does her magic look like?"

Kokoro glanced back at my friend, who looked a tad un-comfortable at being put on the spot. Kokoro did not seem to notice, however, since she watched Fleurette as if in a state of rapture. Still staring both at and around her, the woman said in a breathy voice, "You are amazing. I have never seen such bright colors before. Mostly shades of green, but with flares of purples, turquoise, blue, yellows. You are like a living meadow filled with bright flowers, but all made of shifting light. You are the most beautiful person I have ever seen."

Fleurette had the grace to actually blush, no small feat given the tan shade of her skin. In a small voice, she said, "Thank you."

"Okay, so you knew what I was by my color. But how did you know to look for me?" I tried to steer this conversation back into important matters.

Kokoro looked puzzled for a moment, before her face smoothed out again. "Oh, that is easy to answer. She told me she would search for the cat that walks as a woman. She led me to you. She said you would be able to help me."

"She?" I asked, the confusion clear on my face. "Who did?"

Kokoro smiled. "My fox."

CHAPTER 5

I bristled immediately at Kokoro's words as my distrust snapped back into place. "*Your fox?*" I fumed at her. "You mean to say *you* are the fox?"

The words of that loathsome fox came back to me. *I am more than meets the eye, just as you are. You hide the body of a human under your fur. In a fashion, so do I.* So this is what she meant. She was a shapeshifter, like me.

Kokoro cocked her head to the side at my words, reminding me of Grimm. Then she shook her head in negation. "No, I am not a fox. I *have* a fox."

I sighed. More mind games. "You change into the fox, correct? You are a shifter?"

Again she shook her head. "I do not change into the fox. She is her own self, and I am too. When she is out, I am in her, but not in control. When I have my body, she is in me."

That did nothing to clear things up for me. But Fleurette nodded with sudden understanding. "Fox possession. Kitsune."

Kokoro whipped her head over to look at Fleurette. "Yes," she stated, clearly impressed. "She is kitsune. You are very wise. Many people have not heard of them."

I raised my hand. "Me. I'm one of them." Although now that I thought of it, the name was familiar. "What exactly is a *kit-soo-nay?*"

Kokoro turned back to me. "It is a fox. But one with special powers. My fox is very old, old enough to possess me. She has helped me. She has led me to you." She yawned, her jaw cracking.

Fleurette immediately fussed over her unexpected guest. "I'm so sorry, we should let you rest. Here, I made this tea for you—" She handed the mug over to Kokoro, who took it graciously, smelling the contents with a small smile. "It should be cool enough to drink. You can sleep in here tonight. I'll get you a gown to wear. And the bathroom is just next door, if you need it."

With this small speech, she shooed me from the bed as she walked over to rummage in her wardrobe for a nightgown. I hopped down from her bed, shooting a look at the stranger, who pretended not to notice as she sipped her tea. I still did not trust this situation. The woman knew things she should not have. And that fox … I was unsure what her game was as well. And were they one person, or two, sharing bodies? I shook my head.

Fleurette clearly trusted her, to give up her bed. And I had never seen her act so flustered, as I watched her barge about the room. Something was up.

But I temporarily washed my hands of it. It was late, it had been a long day filled with emotions, and I was tired. I motioned for Grimm to follow me, and we made our way back to the sitting room.

I needed canine cuddles. Grimm knew this about me, and jumped up on the sofa before I had even shifted. Once I was my true self, I wedged my body into the cradle of his neck and front legs for maximum comfort. I instantly began to feel soothed.

"What do you make of her?" I asked him after a moment.

Grimm sighed. "Perplexing. What did you talk about?"

I relayed all the confusing details as best as I could, given the fact that I hardly understood much of anything. When I told him about the kitsune, he thumped his tail.

"I knew she smelled of the fox. There's no mistaking that scent."

"But *is* she the fox? Or is she separate?"

He placed his great head down on the loveseat, stretching his neck to the side. "Separate, I think. I can smell the fox, but I can also smell her, and if I try really hard I can isolate the two. She's human. Her skin is not fox-scented, but the smell is ... inside of her."

His analysis set me at ease more so than Kokoro's words had. Perhaps she really wasn't the fox, after all. Still, it was an odd situation, one I was not familiar with.

Whatever the circumstances were, they could wait until tomorrow.

I had gone to sleep on the loveseat without saying anything to Fleurette, as she was still in her room. Normally, Fleurette would have used the sitting room to sleep if her bed was taken up, but this time she did not show.

All the same, I was awakened in the dead of night by a visitor.

A small, furry visitor with a pointed snout.

It was an abrupt transition from sleep to wakefulness. One moment I was dead to the world, dreaming of swirling autumn leaves that danced in front of me, only to watch them drown one after another in a dark lake that smelled of decay. The next moment, I was awake, staring into the amber eyes of the fox.

"I told you I'd see you again soon, Cousin," the fox practically purred.

My fur stood at the intrusion. "What do you want?" I hissed.

Her tongue poked out, delicately licking her nose. "Nothing more than your help. Your Lycanhund can assist me too, if he likes. I appreciate a big, strong male."

I flattened my ears and sneaked a glance at Grimm. He too was awake, and stared raptly at the fox, his ears pricked forward with interest. The sight shot a bolt of consternation through me. I wasn't sure why, but her flirtatious manner bothered me, and the thought of Grimm responding positively to that kind of attention made me want to bite something.

I quashed this desire for the sake of diplomacy and gave my attention back to the vulpine creature. "What makes you think I'm interested in helping you?"

She flicked an ear. "Just a guess."

"Why are you here? Talking to me? Shouldn't you be possessing your human?" My irritation for this intrusion was taking over any civility I owned.

"I am already possessing my human. She is here, with me. She and I are permanently linked until I have finished helping her, or until I choose to leave her before then. My human was exhausted, however. She fell asleep easily. It can be very tiring to have one's body back after such a lengthy time. I wanted out, so I took over. That is all." She yawned, showing off her impressive teeth.

"Just like that? Well, fox, I'm tired as well, so why don't you leave us alone?" I tried to snuggle back into Grimm's side. His head was still raised, so the position wasn't quite working.

She stared at me, her pupils large and rounded to let the moonlight in. I squirmed under her scrutiny. "Very well," she finally conceded. "Have a good night, Cousin, Grimm."

Before I could say anything else, she flitted away, not as a normal fox, but almost like a wisp of air, supernaturally fast, back to the hallway and the bedroom.

I shook my head to dislodge the unsettled feeling she had left me with. "What do you think of her?" I asked Grimm, who was still staring at where she had disappeared.

He settled his head slowly. "It's interesting, that's for sure. I know how bored you've been. This may just be the excitement you're looking for."

I buried my nose into the fur of my tail. Grimm had a point, but I wasn't sure this was the kind of excitement I'd had in mind.

CHAPTER 6

I awoke while it was still dark out, but my internal clock told me it was early morning, with dawn not far away. I was not the only one awake, either, as evidenced by the low voices coming from the kitchen.

I stood from my position against Grimm's stomach. He let out a grumble but stayed put, content to keep sleeping until the sun made more of an appearance. Stretching fully with a giant yawn, I hopped down from my bed, intent on investigating what was happening in the next room. From the sound of the voices I discerned it was Fleurette and Kokoro. Knowing that my secret was already out with the strange woman, I decided to saunter into the kitchen as I was, furry and small. Perhaps they wouldn't notice me right away and I could do some investigating on Kokoro.

No such luck, as Fleurette spotted me the moment I entered the kitchen. "Ah, Cress," she greeted me. She was still dressed in the same sweater and long skirt she had worn the previous day, albeit with a bit more of a rumpled look. Her hair, a lovely mass of honeyed brown curls and waves, was tied back in a quick ponytail to keep it out of her face. She looked tired.

Kokoro, on the other hand, was much refreshed from the last time I saw her. She was also less naked, as she was wearing one of Fleurette's favorite sweaters and a borrowed skirt. The sweater was perhaps a bit too large, and the skirt swept the floor—Kokoro was a couple of inches shorter than the skirt was intended for—but she did not seem to mind the fit. She turned and smiled at me upon Fleurette's greeting.

There was no point in being rude and keeping my cat form, now that they knew I was there. Still, I almost felt the urge to do just that, to spite Kokoro.

My good graces won out.

With a quick shimmer, I regained my human form. "Good morning," I said to the room. My stomach growled audibly. "What's for breakfast?"

Fleurette put down the mug of tea she had in her hand. "We just got up ourselves. I was going to let the tea wake me up a bit more before I put any thought into food."

Kokoro beamed at me, the motion crinkling the corners of her eyes. I hated to admit it, but it was becoming harder to be annoyed with her, despite my natural inclination to distrust her because of the whole fox thing.

"Miss Creh-seeda, *ohayo*," she said with a small head nod.

I had no idea what the word meant, but I hoped it was a nice greeting. Her mispronunciation of my name irked me, however. It happened on occasion. "Kokoro, good morning. But it's CREH-sih-da, not creh-SEEDA, and you can drop the 'miss.'"

She nodded again. "My apologies. Are you well this morning?"

Was I? Perhaps a bit wary and irritable. "I think so, yes."

My tone of voice must have been guarded while I talked to her. Her smile faltered. "I understand you have no trust in me. Now that I am rested, I would like to tell you my story. Then, maybe you will trust me."

I stared at her. She seemed to be pleading with her eyes for me to allow her this small favor. She gave off an impression of desperation. "Of course. But first, food."

She grinned widely, showing off slightly crooked white teeth. "Thank you."

Fleurette heard my response, and thrust a mug of tea (no sugar with extra cream) and a plate of buttered toast into my hands. "Already got you covered. Let's go sit in the parlor."

From behind me, Kokoro said, "I must use the bathroom. I will join you shortly."

Fleurette shooed me into the sitting room, where Grimm still lounged on the loveseat. He flopped his tail at seeing us, his own lazy way of greeting. I settled down next to him, placing my warm mug on the side table to focus on my toast. I switched the lamp on as well, since it was still quite dark in the room, and I wanted to see my food. The lamp hummed with the free electricity.

"So," I said as I took a giant bite of toast, "where did you sleep last night?"

Fleurette looked away, hiding behind her hair. "I originally took the chair in my room. But it was too uncomfortable, so I laid on the bed."

I coughed to dislodge a crumb I had swallowed too soon. "You shared the bed? With her?"

"Shh, keep your voice down!" Fleurette furrowed her brow at me. "It wasn't like that. She was under the covers. I stayed on top. And we talked."

"Mm-hm. Might I remind you that we don't know this woman?"

Fleurette sighed and sipped her tea. "Talking is how you get to know a person, in case that fact slipped your mind. I feel like we understand each other. She had a terrible upbringing, with a family that did not understand her, and a husband that didn't love her. My childhood was good, but I feel like most people these days don't understand me."

A tiny squeak in my left ear alerted me to Lucky's presence at my shoulder. The smell of food had obviously roused him from his nest. I broke off a corner of my toast and passed it to him absentmindedly as I mulled over what Fleurette just said, trying not to feel a slight sting of hurt at her words.

I finally spoke up. "*I* understand you. Fal and Wren understand you. Do we not count?"

Fleurette shook her head. "No, that's not … it doesn't matter. Nothing untoward happened last night. I was being friendly. She needs that. Now, be nice; here she comes."

Kokoro came out of the hallway and stopped short upon seeing Grimm. Her dark eyes grew wide. "Your dog has innate magic as well?"

I glanced at him. He lifted his head from his paws to gaze into my eyes. "Is he white like me?" I asked, intrigued.

She nodded. "Only a small amount, though. Not bright and shining like you."

Grimm was a Lycanhund, a special canine bred for hunting werewolves. And yes, they did have a small amount of magic naturally in their blood. It helped to neutralize the power of a werewolf, as Lycanhunds were bred solely to hunt the supernatural creatures. Other than that, Grimm couldn't *do* anything with this magic, per se, but the magic gave the breed an unnaturally long life, as well as a certain protection against illness and injury.

I explained this to Kokoro, who listened attentively. Once I was done, she remarked, "He is a very beautiful dog. I would like to paint him one day."

Grimm, who couldn't understand much of human language, seemed to catch the gist of that statement. He stretched out his legs and wagged his tail, threatening to upset my plate with the strong gesture.

"You paint?" I asked.

She looked down at her tea, her smile slipping. "My one joy in my past was art. I was considered to be very talented in my country." Her words held no hubris, just simple fact.

Once Kokoro had settled into one of the wingback chairs, and Fleurette the other, the mood further sobered. Kokoro shifted in her seat with an awkward pause, before she began speaking.

"I know I came with no warning last night. I am sorry for this rudeness." Fleurette opened her mouth to dispute this claim, but Kokoro held up a hand. "Please, I would like to tell you where I came from and why I am here."

Fleurette bowed her head in acquiescence. Kokoro nodded with a small smile and continued, "As I said last night, I am from Tyonoshima. My husband Inaba Ebiru was a powerful businessman in my country. I was forced to flee Tyonoshima because I killed him."

She paused. I glanced at Fleurette, who seemed rather shocked at this admission.

"Would you please explain what happened?" Fleurette asked with what I could discern as a forced calm.

"My husband was not a kind man," Kokoro replied, frowning. "I never loved Ebiru. I was forced into marriage with him. My family would not let me out of the contract, as my marriage would bring much prestige and honor. You see, my parents were ... how would you say it? Old-fashioned. For most Tyonoshimese, women are equal to men. But not for a select group; they still think in the old ways. To my family, my life was not important. I was only good for one thing."

"Marriage," I filled in the blank for her.

She nodded. "My goal in life was to give him heirs. Sons. But secretly, I rebelled. I took potions to prevent my body from conceiving.

"My husband did not know about the potions, but he was angry at me always. In public, he treated me like I was his doting wife, rather indifferent to me but never unkind. In our home, I was lucky if he ignored me."

"What did he do to you?" Fleurette asked, her voice soft and kind.

Kokoro blinked, her eyes shining. "He would use me. I never lay with anyone before my husband, and I never wanted to lie with him. But he was the will of the house, and he never let me say no. At first, if I did not fight, he would be done quickly and nothing more. But after he grew to hate me for being barren, he would hurt me ... during. Little pinches on my arms and thighs. Sometimes a strap to my backside. Eventually he started to burn me with incense. My screams seemed to make him more excited."

"Great Freya," I murmured. The man sounded like a monster. It also explained the bruises and burns I had spotted last night upon Kokoro's body.

Fleurette was equally horrified. She leaned toward the other woman, resting a supportive hand on her arm. "You don't have to say any more if you don't want to."

Kokoro wiped a hand across her face but shook her head. "I must." She took a cleansing breath. "I was trapped with him for ten years. His abuse increased each year, but he never marked me where others could see. It was important for him to appear normal to the public.

"During all of this, he never let me know about his business. We were wealthy, and we lived in a great mansion with many servants and guards. Our gardens were grand. The estate was entirely contained in a high rock wall, with a single large gate at the front for an exit, always guarded. Ebiru would leave for days on end, or he would have his employees come to the mansion, where I was forced to wait on them for public meals. Always with contentment upon my face, or my punishments would be worse in the night."

She took another breath. "I was a prisoner in my own home. I was not allowed to leave the rock walls of the estate. I had but one servant I trusted, and she was one that came from my family when I married. It was she who would go to collect my potions and deliver them in secrecy. And then, she was gone. Just over one month ago, about."

"What happened to her?" I asked, mesmerized by the story.

Kokoro shook her head. "I do not know. One day she was there, the next my husband announced he had hired a new girl to be my servant. I did not trust her, like any of the other servants Ebiru had hired, but I was desperate to replenish my monthly potion. It was almost time to take it, you see."

I thought I knew where this was going. Kokoro proved my assumption correct as she continued her story. "I asked if she could keep a secret, and she assured me she could. I told her I needed her to deliver a potion from the local witch. I did not tell her what the potion was for. But she was not trustworthy. She told my husband."

I sucked in a breath.

"When he found out, he cornered me in my room. He beat me, all of me, for the first time. He left welts on my back, legs, arms, even my face. I thought I would die. He did not stop for a long time. When he was done, he left me on the floor. I could not move for a time after that." She touched the side of her face where the last yellowings of the old bruise resided, her eyes faraway. "When I could move again, I made my way to the garden, to a creek that ran through a corner of the property. I thought I could slip under the wall here, to escape before he finished killing me, but the opening for the creek was too small to slip through. I sat by the water, crying. I was about to give up. I thought to throw myself into the creek, even though it was not deep enough."

Kokoro's face morphed from despondency to contentment. "And then *she* showed up."

"The fox?" Fleurette hazarded a guess.

Kokoro nodded. "She found me there. I knew as soon as I saw her that she was not a normal fox. First, because the wall kept most wildlife out, and second, because she shone with a vibrant display of colors from her vast magic. She was kitsune, the most powerful of foxes. There are people in my country who revere them as gods. After seeing her, I understood why.

"She somehow communicated with me once she approached. Not with words, but I understood her perfectly all the same. She told me she was very old, and wanted to leave this world for her home, but first she needed to earn another tail."

"Another tail?" I repeated, dumbfounded.

"Yes. Kitsune can have more than one tail. They earn them by doing good deeds. A fox with nine tails becomes a *tenko*, a celestial fox, which can then ascend to the heavens. My fox claims to have eight. Her last good deed will be helping me," Kokoro explained with patience.

I ruminated on that thought. The fox I saw looked normal, but then again there was that moment yesterday, a moment of extreme magic, and I could swear she had flashed me more than one tail.

Kokoro went on, "When my fox told me that she could help me, I chose to accept rather than end my life. In that moment, she possessed me. She ... jumped into me, somehow."

"And then what happened?" I asked.

"She took over my body, tucking me into hers. I could see through her eyes, but everything was ... muted, like I was under-water. I could talk to her, but she did not always listen. She could communicate with me as well, but she chose not to for the most part. My clothes were left behind there by the creek, and she took me outside of the rock wall for the first time in ten years."

"How?" Fleurette asked, as engrossed in the telling as I was.

Kokoro shrugged. "No walls can keep a kitsune out. It is one of their magics. But she took me on a run, and I had never felt more free than in that moment. All too soon, though, she reentered the wall, and let herself into the house.

"She took me directly to my husband's office, where he held a meeting with his workers. Then she gave me back my body. I stood there, just outside of the door, naked, afraid, but curious too. I listened to the meeting. And I finally learned more about my husband's business."

She shivered at the memory. "The only thing I knew about his work is that he manufactured items for other businesses. But while I listened, he spoke of murdering his competitors and creating a new order in Tyonoshima with what he called 'the chosen ones.' He spoke at length about a new business venture that would ensure their place in this upcoming utopian world. He asked his worker how the rods were coming, and the man answered that they were complete. Ebiru congratulated him and spoke of shipping them within the week. He said he would personally see to them arriving safely in the Oracune Region."

The Oracune Region. Where I happened to live.

Kokoro paused. "And then, a servant caught me listening at the door. He raised an alarm, and all the men came out of the office to see me standing there, guilty of listening to their meeting."

She grimaced, lowering her head until a curtain of her long sleek hair covered her from my view. In a small voice, she said, "Ebiru ... his eyes, they were full of anger, a murderous intent. He planned to finally kill me, I knew. I had heard too much. I knew he wished to kill certain people, important people. He turned to his employees and bade them all a good night, and then he grabbed my arm—hard—and led me to our bedroom.

"Once inside, he shut the door to our room, and I knew I was about to die. Only ... the fox took over."

"How?" asked Fleurette.

Kokoro gave it some thought. "She did not take my body, but instead she filled me with strength. Strength of mind, of intent, and of body. When my husband began to approach me, he expected me to cower and take my death. But I stood my ground. When he lashed out with a fist, I stopped it with my bare hand. When he could not move his arm from my grasp, I saw real fear for the first time in his eyes. It empowered me even more, and I allowed the fox to take over my mind and use my body for revenge."

She seemed anything but empowered now. "When I awoke, I was covered in blood. But not mine. The fox had exacted her vengeance on my behalf. He ... he ... I could not look at his body. I could only retch." She looked at us both pleadingly. "I did not mean for it to happen! I only wanted to be free of him."

Fleurette once again reached out a comforting arm. "And you *are* free of him. You are not to blame. A man who keeps a wild animal caged cannot fault it if it mauls him in a bid for freedom. You did what you had to do."

Kokoro smiled meekly, but the expression did not reach her eyes. "I am not free, however. Ebiru's men soon came looking for him. The fox took over so that we could easily flee, but I overheard them say that they knew I killed him, and they would kill me just as brutally. That, and they said I had stolen something from him."

"What did you steal?" I asked.

"Nothing!" Kokoro's face screwed up in frustration before smoothing out again. "I could not have stolen anything, I had no clothes, no pockets. I have been naked since my first change. Until now. They spoke of an engine missing, something that would have powered up a gate instantaneously. Ebiru supposedly had it in his pocket. They said I must have stolen it. The fox told me these men will not rest until I am dead. They will continue to hunt me down."

"How is it you are here and not in Tyonoshima?" I asked.

She leveled her gaze at me, still distraught. "I needed help. I could not expect it from Ebiru's family, nor my own. They would have given me up or killed me themselves. But the fox, she knows things somehow. She knew I had a cousin in the Oracune Region."

My heart skipped a beat. "Gavin." Gavin St. Cloud, my once-upon-a-time work nemesis but now cautiously a friend. He was instrumental in helping me with my father this spring. He had told me that his mother was from Tyonoshima.

It was no wonder Kokoro had looked familiar to me when I first saw her.

She looked amazed for just a moment. "Yes, his name is Gavin. My fox told me he could help, that he was honorable, not at all like my parents. So, I let her run to the shipping port and hide on the very ship my husband was using to transport the rods he had talked about, whatever they were.

"I spent the entire two weeks at sea as the fox. She hid very successfully below deck and ate rats when she was hungry. I mostly slept. When the ship finally arrived in Dogwood, she slipped off easily and made her way toward Knobby Hill, which is where my cousin lives. But once we got close enough, she told me she knew of someone else who could be of even greater help, and she decided to change direction. She told me of a cat that walked as a woman, and her friend the resident witch. She said the cat would be a great ally and that she would be my ultimate protection."

"But how?" I asked. "How could she know of me? Very few people are aware of my existence."

Kokoro only shook her head. "I do not know how she knows. But she has not been wrong yet. Here you are. And now I know my cousin truly exists as well.

"By the time I arrived here, I had been inside the fox for nearly three weeks. I did not know it then, but being away from my body for so long had some negative effects. I took one step and fell asleep. When I awoke, I was in your bed." This last line was delivered in Fleurette's direction.

She turned back to me. "And now, I am here. The fox has faith in you. The men will not stop looking for me. According to her, they must be stopped. She has chosen you as my protector. Now that you have heard my story, will you help me?"

This last line was directed squarely at me.

CHAPTER 7

All eyes swiveled my way, including Grimm's. Talk about being put on the spot.

"Um," I hedged, squirming in my seat. "Listen, Kokoro, you seem like a nice person. I'm just not so sure about your fox."

Kokoro's eyes, normally a brown so dark as to be indistinguishable from the black of the pupils, flashed a coral shade as her brows lowered. The unnatural color faded as quickly as it came, but it left me uneasy, as if the fox within her was displeased by what I had said.

I hastily added, "Give me today to think about it."

Her shoulders slumped and she broke eye contact, but she nodded. "That is acceptable."

Fleurette, however, scowled at me, but she said nothing about my lack of decision. Instead, she glanced at her wrist, noting the time. By now, the room had filled with the subdued light of morning.

She sighed as if disappointed, and finally said something. "That is your right, Cressida. Give it some thought today. While you make your choice, I think I will take Kokoro to town to talk to Gavin. I have some potions I need to drop off at the apothecary store." She turned to Kokoro. "On the way back, I'd like to take you to see my father. Your color is better than last night, but I would feel better if you saw a physician. Dad is a veterinarian, not a human doctor, but he can at least give you an assessment. Taking you to the town doctor may raise too many questions, and the last thing we want is to bring attention to your whereabouts."

Kokoro acquiesced with a nod. "Do you think it is wise to involve my cousin?"

Fleurette nodded. "At the very least, I think you should meet him. He is your family, and the fox said you could trust him. He was her first choice, after all."

I sighed, patting Grimm's back absentmindedly. I had no desire to see Gavin; even though we were no longer enemies, I still wished to stay away. There was a small matter of him and me sharing an impromptu makeout session during our mission, and while that was enough canoodling for me, thanks to my curse, I had the feeling that he would still like to pursue a romantic entanglement.

"I'll meet you at the farm," I said. I was planning on going there today anyway. Ever since being "grounded" from bounty hunting, I had started to help Lyle as a veterinary assistant whenever he thought he needed it. Earlier this week, he had asked me for assistance with his nanny goat, who had started limping and was not allowing Lyle to investigate the issue on his own.

A thought occurred to me. "What about the kids?" It was a school day, after all, and they would be due to get up any moment now.

Fleurette checked the time again. "I'm going to let them stay home today. Maurice's death is reason enough, and I want to make sure Wren is okay after the shock of yesterday. Are you sure you won't come with us to town?"

I nodded. "Quite sure. I'm just going to get some breakfast for Grimm and Lucky and then head over to your dad's. You two have fun, though!"

I must have said that last bit with just a hint of sarcasm, because Fleurette scrutinized me with a look of disappointment that she never reserved for me. I chose to ignore the look, however, bouncing into the kitchen to escape any more unwelcome moods from my best friend.

Lyle's farm was, as usual, a diverting distraction from my worldly issues. Grimm and I had a routine there now, and since we had some time to kill before Lyle was free, we began it with gusto.

First, we checked on Humbert, my aging horse employee. In the before times, when we were in between jobs and hanging out at home, Humbert usually stayed on Fleurette's property, free to roam about when he wasn't resting in her tiny one-stall stable. With our profession on hold for the foreseeable future, however, we thought it best to place Humbert in a more reliable and permanent environment, and Lyle happened to have pasture to spare, plus a barn big enough to shelter the enormous horse.

With the fickle weather once more temporarily cooperating, we found Humbert sunning himself near the fence.

"Hey, Humbert. How's life?" I greeted as I jumped up onto the nearest fence post to be closer to eye level with the beast.

Humbert let out a horsey snort. "Hello, Mistress. Hello, Master. I'm well, but I sure am tired of this place. When will we go out for a job?"

I shared a look with Grimm. For the past few months, Humbert had grumbled about the lack of work. I couldn't seem to get him to understand that there wouldn't be any work, not anytime soon, at this rate. The old horse enjoyed pulling the wagon immensely, even if he was beginning his twilight years. I didn't want to completely demoralize him.

"Well, Humbert, we're still working on that. But I promise, you'll be the first to know when we have another job. In the meantime, hang tight. It's not so bad here, is it?"

Humbert scratched his neck on the fence post I sat on, causing it to wobble enough to nearly dislodge me. I didn't think he noticed my tenuous grip on the wood. "No, I suppose not. The other horses aren't unkind, even if they don't stay with me. More than anything, I'm bored here."

You and me both, buddy, I thought, but I kept that to myself.

The brief patch of sun disappeared once more behind a rain cloud. Fat drops began to fall from the sky. Not wishing to become drenched, I said my goodbyes to Humbert. "I'll check back in with you later," I promised, and then we were off to our next station, the barn.

The barn used to be Mom's old haunt. She slept out there every night, and enjoyed lounging about on the hay bales if the outdoor weather was not amenable to sunbathing. With my dad back in the picture, I wondered what she would decide to do for a new home. If—when—my parents came back, I doubted my father would want to live in a barn.

Mom also used to control the rodent population, which should have exploded in her absence. The only reason it didn't was because Mom's job had been reassigned to a new barn cat, a small but scrappy silver tabby named Gin. Gin used to live on the streets of Dogwood, but had been captured and brought to Addelboro at the same time as me, heavily pregnant and terrified. After our harrowing escape, Gavin had kept her and her offspring in his room at the Hunters' Guild until all the kittens had found homes to go to. Gin was unhappy at being constrained to such tight quarters, so Lyle readily agreed to relocate her to his barn—with the stipulation that she be fixed. Knobby Hill did not need more kittens to add to the population, as cute as hers were, and Lyle did not want to attract the attention of any roaming tomcats. Once she was back up and running, however, Gin's hunting skills really shone.

Gin was sometimes hard to track down. While Mom could be counted on to be inactive, Gin was more like me, with limited moments of downtime.

Luck was on our side, however, as she had just settled into a grooming session when we entered the barn. Before understanding that it was Grimm and me, she arched her back, her eyes wide. She settled as soon as our scent hit her nostrils.

I took no offense. Gin was still mostly feral. She allowed Gavin to pet her, but only on her terms, and while she was always glad to see me and Grimm, she was not an overly friendly cat in general.

"Hello, Cressida, Grimm," she greeted from across the barn.

I walked closer, sniffing cautiously until she sat on her haunches. It was her signal that she was agreeable to affection. I only had one other cat that I was friendly with—my mother—but since we were both magical, it was nice to have a mundane cat as a friend. I rubbed my head against Gin's chest, letting out a comforting purr. Gin returned the favor.

"Nice to see you, Gin. How are you?"

"I live in a warm, dry barn that smells of hay and horses. There are plentiful rodents for me to hunt and I don't have to compete with any other mouths to feed. I am very well, thank you."

I marveled at how far Gin had come from her days as a scrawny street cat. She may never drop her aloof nature, but that was a part of her charm.

Another part was her frankness.

"I hope you don't plan for a long visit. I yearn to check out a section of the barn that has suspicious sounds coming from the timbers. I suspect there might be rats about."

I kept my ears perked forward. "I wouldn't dream of keeping you from doing your job. We just wanted to say hi while we wait for Lyle to be finished with his appointments."

Gin flicked the tip of her tail. "This man, Lyle, the one who sometimes feeds me. You told me he is a nice human, like Gavin."

"He is indeed. He cares very much about animals."

Gin licked her paw. "Yes. I can sense that about him. He wants very much to make friends with me. Gavin gives me pets sometimes. While it is terrifying to have a human touch me, his touches feel very nice, and I sometimes crave them. But Gavin rarely visits. I think I'd like pets from Lyle, since he is around more often than Gavin."

"Please do!" I agreed with enthusiasm. "Lyle is very gentle. I didn't allow humans to pet me for a long time. Once I did, I realized what I was missing out on. It would make Lyle happy as well."

"And human happiness is important?"

I thought about that. "Mutual happiness is important. As long as both parties are content with what is happening, it doesn't matter what species they are."

"I see," she answered, her eyes glittering. "Well, I shall give it some thought. Perhaps some rat tracking will help my decision. See you around."

She scampered away, already focused on her task. I envied her ability to go after her project with such ease and determination.

I did not have long to ruminate on such thoughts. Lyle wandered into the barn, dragging his lame goat along with him by a rope around her neck. Both man and goat were rather wet, thanks to the persistently foul weather. I thanked Freya that the barn was nice and weatherproof; Grimm and I were nearly dry again after our own outdoor excursions.

Lilac the goat was a reluctant patient. She twisted and turned, trying to be free of her bonds as Lyle tugged on her leash. She was not going to make this easy for him.

I shimmered up before Lyle noticed me. The subtle glow must have caught his attention. "Oh good, you're already here," he called out to me.

"Just catching up with Gin. She says she may let you pet her."

"Come and hold Lilac's head, my dear. No—like this. Good. So, I may get to pet the elusive Princess Gin?" Lyle moved to the back end of the goat, getting in position to lift the leg in question.

Lilac twisted her head to try to escape my headlock. I only held on tighter. I could be just as stubborn when I wanted to be.

Lyle grunted as the goat kicked out, nearly connecting with his shin as he struggled to hold her. He grabbed for the wounded leg, trying to hold it steady so that he could diagnose the issue. Still, she battled for complete control of her body, letting out a bleat of anger at being pinned down.

"Damnit, Lilac," Lyle swore with a heavy sigh. He straightened, clearly not being able to help her, as worked up as she was. He looked at me, assessing. "Cressida, can you talk to her? I can't get a look at her hoof without her kicking me in the face."

I pursed my lips. "I can try. But you know she doesn't like to listen to me."

He nodded and wiped the sheen of sweat off his dark brow. "I know. But anything will be an improvement over this." He grabbed the rope again, making sure she wouldn't escape at the first chance.

Lyle was one of a handful of people who knew about my true form. While he was a mundy, he was also an honorary member of GOGS, thanks to the connections his missing wife and daughter had supplied to him. Given that he had seen me shift plenty of times, I wasted no time in shimmering down into cat form.

I looked at Lilac head on, focusing on one horizontal pupil since she had a hard time seeing me with both at once. "Listen, Lilac. Your owner is a professional animal healer. You are injured. He needs to examine your injury to make it better. Could we speed this process up by, I don't know, *cooperating*? Just for a while?"

"I *don't* want to be held down, and I *don't* want him touching my hoof! You can just bugger off, you pesky ball of fur." Lilac grumbled in her throat, a sound reminiscent of Grimm. I looked over at him where he lay placidly, yellow eyes watching Lyle and I struggle. It gave me an idea.

I narrowed my eyes. "Look, you capricious, demonspawn knockoff. You don't want to be held down? I can nicely hold your head while Lyle nicely inspects your foot to remove the pain, or I call over my friend Grimm, and he can hold your neck in his jaws—they can subdue a werewolf by the way—and wrap his legs over your back until you can hardly breathe. So, which will it be?"

The goat gave a bleat of alarm. While Grimm was probably the gentlest dog I had ever met—when he wasn't grappling with a supernatural criminal—he truly was scary to behold, and most animals regarded him with a healthy dose of fear. Lilac was no exception.

"Fine, you flat-faced muskrat. You win. Tell my owner the pain is between my toes. Be nice about it!"

Satisfied, I transformed back to human. I once again tucked Lilac's head into the crook of my arm and gave a quick flourish at the rest of her body to Lyle. "Your goat is quite the temperamental ninny. But she'll behave herself, at least temporarily. She says the pain is located between her toes."

Lyle grinned, instantly setting to work by lifting up the affected foot. "Thank you, sweetheart," he told me as he bent to examine the digits. I smiled. Lyle was probably the only man who could call me "sweetheart" and not gain my wrath.

He grunted and squinted his eyes as he carefully pried the two toes apart. A moment later he smiled as he held up the culprit: a small, sharp piece of gravel had become wedged into the fleshy section between the goat's toes. He dropped her leg.

"She can be temperamental, for sure," he agreed, giving her a loving stroke down her tan back. He motioned for me to let go of her head, which I willingly did. He removed the rope from her neck and Lilac pranced away and out of the barn, with no sign of pain visible. Lyle sighed. "She's been a bit angrier ever since her sister died. Goats don't enjoy living solo. She's lonely. I suppose I need to get her a companion to make her happier again. I've just been so darn busy."

A companion. That one little word made my heart give a funny lurch, like a sad memory. My curse would not allow me to find a companion, a true love. As time passed I was slowly getting used to the idea, despite Fleurette's optimism that we'd find a solution, but the pain crept up here and there.

And it was not just me who was without a companion. Fleurette herself had been single since I had met her two and a half years ago. And Lyle had not had a partner ever since his wife Althea vanished when Fleurette was only eight years old.

What Lyle did not know is that I met Althea for a brief moment when I was escaping from the underwater dungeon of Addelboro Correctional Facility. He also did not know she was willingly working with the ACF. I promised Fleurette I wouldn't tell him.

The problem was, I was wracked by guilt every time I thought about that promise. It somehow seemed incredibly wrong to keep this information from a man I viewed as a father figure. But every time I thought about telling him, my mouth seemed to glue itself shut.

Fleurette had been in quite a mood when she demanded that promise from me. I often wondered if she had somehow laced it with magic. It would explain my inability to let it slip out.

Still, I hadn't promised not to skirt around the issue, and I could not help but give into my naturally curious state about this topic. "Lyle, what about you? Are you lonely?"

He glanced over at me. "I have my daughter, I have you, I have my animals and my work. Your mother, up until recently. I stay busy. What do I have to be lonely for?"

I side eyed him. "Work is not a suitable substitution for human affection."

He chuckled. "No, but it's a handy bandage."

"And just how long has this bandage lasted?" I asked him with full skepticism in my tone.

He did some mental math. "Twenty-four years." He sighed, running a weathered hand through his short salt-and-pepper curls. "The truth is, Cressida, that Thea leaving without a trace really did a number on me and Fleurette. I thought I had a happy marriage. But I must have been wrong. Her leaving put us through hell, but we came out the other side eventually. Still, you can't go through a traumatic event like that and not get left with a few scars. For Fleurette, she vowed to be a better person, a better witch than her mother. Me?" He looked away across the barn for a long moment. "For a very long time after, I had no interest in relationships. I threw myself into being the best damn mundy veterinarian, and everything else, other than my daughter, took a backseat. And I've been doing it that way for so long that I don't see myself changing now. I'm too old for romance anyway."

"Well, I don't think that last point is true," I argued. He gave me a small smile tinged with melancholy. "Listen, sorry to pry. I'm learning to live with the thought that I'll never have love either. Hearing some different perspectives is helpful to me."

His warm brown eyes softened. "I heard. Chin up. Have faith in my daughter."

I snorted, eyeing the familiar figure of Fleurette as she came into view through the barn doors. "That daughter? The one who's approaching us with a woman who has a fox inside of her? Sometimes I wonder."

Lyle looked confused for a moment, but regained his composure once he saw his daughter. "Hello, my dear!" he called with affection.

Fleurette led Kokoro into the barn. They both had umbrellas to stave off the rain, which they shook at the doorway before folding them. Kokoro glanced side to side furtively, perhaps on edge by the new surroundings. Fleurette hovered close to her, introducing her to Lyle, who was quite adept at putting people—as well as animals—at ease.

"You're here a lot sooner than I expected," I told Fleurette.

She nodded. "We stopped by the Bounty Hunters' Guild, but Gavin wasn't there. He must be out on a job." She sighed and shook her head. "We left a note for him in his mail cubby."

"Hmm." I was desperately hoping that Gavin would be able to keep Kokoro under his wing, rather than leaving that to Fleurette. I did not count on him being absent.

In Kokoro's presence, I once again became aloof. Fleurette, on the other hand, was completely at ease with her, staying by her side as Lyle listened to a truncated version of her story and as he performed a cursory exam upon her.

This was a side of Fleurette I had never seen before. Sure, she was always incredibly considerate and willing to help those individuals in need—case in point, myself and the Ramberts—but she had never *doted* on us, or clung to us like we were the most precious person present.

It made me realize that Fleurette was all in on helping Kokoro. And that realization made me ... nervous.

Lyle finished with his assessment. "Miss Inaba, you are a little malnourished, but otherwise in good health. My daughter makes a healing tonic that I fully recommend. I use it on the regular with my patients that need a boost, but its healing properties work on humans as well as animals. Fleurette, do you have any on hand?"

Fleurette nodded. "I have some at the house. I'll give one to her as soon as we get home."

I looked through the barn door, noting that the rain had tapered off significantly. "We should probably head out now, to beat the weather. Unless you need more help, Lyle?"

He shook his head. "I'm good. I'm going to be seeing some regular patients soon anyway. Thanks for your help, Cress." As Fleurette and Kokoro began to leave, he said to me in a lower voice, "And take care of my daughter. This is not an everyday thing for her."

"You got it." Lyle clearly picked up on Fleurette's unusual behavior too. It must have made him as nervous as it did me.

Back outside, the four of us trekked down Lyle's generous driveway to Rabbit Hole Road, taking this route back to the cottage. It was a short trip, as walking goes, with only a mile and a half between houses.

Kokoro was quiet, introspective. "Miss Williams," she finally broke the silence, almost hesitantly, "thank you for taking me to meet your father. I admit, men make me very nervous. I never wished to have a relationship with one. But your father is a good man. I felt at ease with him. Perhaps it is his magic at work."

Fleurette turned quickly to look at her. "Please, call me Fleurette. I'm pleased you liked him. He *is* a good man. But Kokoro, my father doesn't have any magic. He's mundane."

Kokoro stumbled on a small rock. "My apologies. But my gift has never failed me. It is very faint, true, but I see traces of yellow upon him."

I thought back to last night when she was describing her unusual gift. "Mind magic?" I asked.

She nodded. "Yes. Just little wisps. Many mundane people actually have traces of magic in them, but they are not aware. Mind magic is the most common. I don't think he knows he has it. But it was enough to comfort me."

"A touch of charisma," Fleurette murmured, almost to herself. "I'll be damned. Kokoro, you mentioned you saw yellow in my aura. Is it the same for me?"

Kokoro gazed at Fleurette, that same expression of wonder filling her face as she did. "I see just a hint. The same yellow, like lemons, fresh and appealing. It is not enough to sway me, only put me at ease, like your father."

It explained so much, honestly. I had always felt like I belonged with both Fleurette and Lyle. It had never crossed my mind to consider a slightly magical charisma was at work.

"I like that," my friend said. I observed Fleurette give the other woman a wide smile. "I do hope you are comfortable around me—us. I'm so sorry you had such a traumatic experience before."

Kokoro glanced down at her feet. "Thank you. My entire upbringing was centered around how to be a good wife. Other girls around me relished in the task, but I felt ... hollow. Men did not attract me. Only ..." she trailed off, hiding her face within her silky black hair.

Fleurette did not pry into what Kokoro decided not to say. She only placed a soothing hand on her shoulder. "I understand."

When we entered the house, the kids were in the sitting room. They had not gotten a chance to meet Kokoro yet, so Fleurette made introductions.

Kokoro bowed her head at Fal first. "You are Fleurette's son?" she asked shyly, not making eye contact with the teen.

Fleurette and Fal exchanged glances. "Not exactly," Fleurette explained. "He is my ward, but we aren't related."

"Not to mention that Fleurette would have been an incredibly young mother for this to be true," I muttered.

Kokoro looked abashed upon hearing me. "Yes, of course. How foolish. It is only that your colors are very similar to each other." She bravely peered closer at Fal. "You are much more blue, however. An equal mix of blue and green, like a warm sea, and with the same meadow-flower wisps as Fleurette, but not as many."

Fal quirked a dark eyebrow. "I'm sorry, I don't follow."

Before anyone could explain, Kokoro had moved on to Wren with a mien of delight upon her face. "Ah, I have never seen colors like this before! You must have rare magic, indeed."

Wren opened her mouth with a gasp, unsure of what to say.

Fleurette answered for her. "Yes, Wren here is a projectionist. She is likely the only one in the world right now. She is incredibly talented." Her pride in Wren was heady. Wren beamed.

"A powerful witch, a healer, a projectionist, and a cat that walks as a woman," Kokoro mused out loud. "My fox did choose well."

My heart did a freefall at her statement. The walk home with her had been rather pleasant, to the point that I had forgotten about the fox. But hearing her say those words, I fell back into my previous mode: severely cautious.

I was beginning to like the woman herself, though. She was kind, soft spoken, and honest. Her previous life had done a number on her, clearly. She was the type of person I would normally be happy to help.

But what if her persona was her way of manipulating us? She clearly wanted something from my little family, and I was not convinced this entire thing hadn't been an act to get her way. She already had Fleurette convinced, and both Fal and Wren seemed taken with her instantly. Perhaps she was the one with the mind magic.

I needed to get away from her, at least for the time being. A head clearing was in order.

"I'll be back for dinner," I said to the room at large. They barely noticed me, which made me feel all the worse. I grabbed Lucky from his box behind the sofa and motioned for Grimm to follow, making yet another hasty exit for the day.

CHAPTER 8

True to my word, I returned as the sun began to dip below the tree line, indicating that dinner was near at hand. I had taken the hours in between to get my nervous energy out by running, climbing trees, and hunting Lucky with Grimm. I tried to talk with my partner about what was bothering me, but I had a hard time formulating coherent sentences, and Grimm simply said he was here for me if I needed an ear. In the meantime, he would do his best to distract me from my inner turmoil, as always.

Now, back at the cottage, I did feel better after having exerted myself all afternoon. The fox had deeply unsettled me, despite our brief encounter. I still didn't understand why exactly, but I also needed to step back and give Kokoro a chance. Even if I was still unsure if she truly was separate from the fox.

I found my family in the kitchen, with our guest among them, who was chopping carrots. Fleurette smiled at my return and motioned for me to take a turn at the stove, stirring the onions that hissed and steamed as they sauteed in butter. I took over for her, my stomach coming to life at the decadent smells that teased my nostrils. Fleurette moved on to measuring out flour for biscuits.

I stayed introspective all throughout the cooking process and into eating. The five of us sat around the table, with Grimm consuming his own meal near my chair. I watched as Wren and Fal asked questions of Kokoro: her childhood, her favorite foods, what Tyonoshima was like. Each question from the youngsters was delivered with animation, an excitement to get a glimpse at another culture. And Kokoro, to her credit, answered each one with vigor, never straying into melancholy at the way her life had turned out, although she did skirt around the sadder topics. She was a natural with the kids.

Fleurette was also unusually quiet during the meal, but she watched the interaction between Kokoro and Wren and Fal with a look of contentment upon her face. I noticed that each time her eyes met with the other woman's, they sparkled in a way I had never witnessed before.

After we had finished eating, Fleurette took charge. "Fal, Wren, it's your turn to clean the kitchen. Cressida, let's go practice."

Fal groaned and Wren sighed heavily, but they departed to do their chores. I too let out a sigh. Practice was not my favorite thing to do.

"What shall I do?" Kokoro asked, her voice small.

Fleurette considered her question. "Would you mind helping the kids in the kitchen? Just for a while. It won't take us very long."

Kokoro nodded, ducking her head slightly in a tiny bow of subservience before following Fal out of the dining room.

"I need to stop her from the constant bowing," Fleurette murmured once the other woman had left the room. "I know it's a cultural thing. She's been programmed to be submissive to those 'above' her, but she should know that we are all equals. It's sad."

I happened to agree with her on that front.

The greenhouse out back was our practice room. It was fairly hidden from view, so I felt comfortable changing forms at will.

We had been working on strengthening my ability to stay in my shimmer form, which was an amorphous, in-between state of being. Normally, I was only in this form for a split-second as I transformed, but over a year ago, when I encountered Annie Coddle for the first time and she had tried to kill me, I was able to hold the shape for a matter of minutes. That was apparently a onetime thing, though. Even though I had been practicing for over a year now, I was only up to five seconds. Still, this was an improvement over the two second record from six months ago, and a lot could happen in five seconds during a fight.

Once I entered the greenhouse I expected to launch right into the training. But Fleurette had other plans.

"Cress, how are you doing?" she asked me as soon as she closed the door behind her.

I was taken aback. "I ... um, doing well, I guess? How are you?"

She observed me. "You haven't exactly been yourself ever since Kokoro showed up. Have you given her request any thought?"

"It's pretty much all I've been thinking about," I admitted. "But I assumed you wouldn't want me taking on any missions. I can't bounty hunt, and I can't help find the ACF, so why would this be any different?"

Fleurette frowned. "You're right. There are too many op-portunities for you to get snatched while bounty hunting. And actively searching for the members of ACF is too risky, the GOGs agreed. But this is one woman who has had a terrible life up until now. And her fox *chose* you for assistance. It sounds like the fox knows what she is doing. I think you should help her."

"But we don't know Kokoro, not really. What if she *is* the fox, and she's just lying about it? According to everything I've heard and read, foxes are tricksters. Any story about them tells you that. Why would kitsune be any different? What if this was one big trick? How do we really know she is telling the truth?"

"Well, we don't. But Cress, I just have a feeling about her. She needs help. I don't think she's lying." Fleurette's eyes softened as she gazed out of the greenhouse windows in the direction of the kitchen.

I sighed. "I wish I had the same faith in the situation. Look, I'm still thinking about it, okay? I just need more time."

Fleurette nodded. "Fair enough. Now, I suppose we should get some practice in. Unless you want to try that new thing I talked about."

I shuddered. Back in March, we learned two new aspects about my strange magical heritage. First, it was possible for me to take a living thing into my interdimensional pocket and bring it back out unscathed. Lucky was proof of that, after I inadvertently transformed from human to cat while he was in my jacket pocket. The change had put him to sleep, and he was fine after being in there for a couple of hours.

The second thing I learned was that I could effectively steal someone's magic while I was between forms. The shimmer was the closest I could be to a true familiar's form. In this state, I could easily suck up residual energies, such as the lightning spell Annie had tried to kill me with, and the fire magic of the elemental goon Hobbs at Addelboro. After his fireball passed through me, I was able to wield his magic for a short time after, which came in handy as we made our escape from the doomed prison.

Fleurette, bless her heart, had glommed onto these two notions with astonishing glee. She wanted me to have a full bag of tricks, so that if my life was ever threatened—and let's face it, it seemed to happen at least every six months—I'd have a bigger arsenal with which to defend myself. She had brought it up back in late spring, volunteering as guinea pig to both go into my interdimensional pocket and hopefully let me borrow her magic in the process. I had declined with fervor. I had no clue just what my pocket was like. It was possible that Lucky had truly lived up to his name and that anyone else would not be so fortunate.

I refused to budge from my stance. And that had been that.

"No, I still have not changed my mind on that one," I told her.

"Oh, Cressida. You worry too much. I'm sure I'd be fine. And I'd like to know just how to transfer magic to you. How else can we make it work? I don't have the type of magic that can just pass through you, like the fire and lightning did."

"Gee, that's too bad. But my answer is still no."

She sighed. "Very well. Let's get to work on your shimmer stickiness, then. Shall we try for six seconds?"

I grimaced at the thought.

It was night number two of Kokoro—and the fox—staying in Fleurette's room. And, just like last time, Fleurette was conspicuously absent.

I tried not to let my friend's mysterious actions bother me. She was a grown woman. Clearly she felt something for the other woman to want to help her. Nevertheless, I still had trouble sleeping.

The wall clock in the sitting room showed midnight, the face illuminated by a beam of moonlight. I turned my body ninety degrees in an attempt to get more comfortable, but it was futile.

Finally, after another half-hour of restlessness, I decided a midnight stroll might be the ticket to getting some sleep later.

Grimm had no sleep issues, and his soft snores next to me indicated that he was well and truly asleep. I chose to let him be. Misery may love company, but he did so much for me on any given day that I wanted to keep my gloom to myself this once.

I nimbly jumped down from the sofa, shimmering at the front door to let myself out as quietly as possible. I successfully navigated out the door and shut it without disturbing my partner. I gave myself a mental pat on the back for that.

Once outside, I transformed back into a cat. The grass was incredibly wet, thanks to the frequent downpours. Luckily, no rain plagued me at the moment. I could deal with wet feet over a wet body any day.

"Hello, Cousin."

A screech of alarm left my throat as I launched myself into the air. I flailed midjump to position myself for a safe landing. As soon as my feet hit the ground, a wave of foolishness washed over me at my reaction. It was swiftly followed by anger.

"What do you want?" I spat at the fox.

She cocked her head to the side. "You asked me the same question last night. My answer remains the same. My human told you her story. You told her you would take the day to consider. It is now night."

She wasn't wrong. I had deliberately avoided giving Kokoro an answer for the rest of the evening. When I turned in for the night without saying anything to her, a look of sadness passed over her face. I admit, it had made me feel like a bit of a cad.

Perhaps that was why I couldn't sleep.

Perhaps I needed to get to know the fox better to finally decide. It might take a load off of my shoulders.

I started off simply. "Do you have a name?" Referring to her as "the fox" was getting old.

She stretched her legs out in front of her, sticking her tail straight up into the air. "I do not. I've lived nearly one thousand years, but no one has granted me a name. Not even Kokoro. Such a shame, really."

"Then what do I call you?"

"Whatever you would like, Cousin."

Carte blanche on a name? It almost seemed too good to be true. I would consider my options. But first, I needed some answers to pertinent questions.

"So, spill. How did you really learn of my existence?"

She sat back down after her stretch, regarding me with intelligent eyes. At least her pupils were more rounded at the moment, thanks to the darkness of our surroundings. "Because I am omniscient," she answered plainly.

"Come again?"

"Omniscient. I am all-knowing, within a certain geographical bubble, so to speak."

I flicked my ears back a bit. "Uh-huh. I'm not buying it."

The fox laughed, that high sound still grating my every nerve. "Whether or not you 'buy it' is not my concern. I am old. I have many tails. When I reached my seventh tail one hundred years ago, I was granted this new power. But you want proof? Fine." Her pointed snout clicked shut as she stared me down enough to make me want to squirm. "I knew about Kokoro's cousin because *she* knew he existed. I am able to access her thoughts and memories in this way, and my omniscience fills in the blanks. As soon as I was most of the way over the Serenic Ocean, knowledge of *you* popped up, even though Kokoro had no knowledge of you. And I know everything about you. I know you are the last in line of Glivver's descendants. I know you are cursed; I can see that gaping dark hole in your soul. I know you kissed Kokoro's cousin and now you want to forget that it happened."

I flinched. The less people who knew about that, the better.

She continued, spurred on by either my reaction or my silence. "I know Grimm is incredibly loyal to you, and you don't deserve his devotion."

I bristled. She was walking a fine line now.

"I know you think you don't need anyone else, but you are nothing without the people you call family!" she finished with a flourish.

That was it. I was done. I had reached my boiling point. "Get out!" I practically screamed at her.

She stared with level eyes. Her tail twitched from side to side. "I also know that if you don't help me, you will regret that decision. Are you sure this is your answer?"

The anger flared deep within me, pushing away any logical thoughts. "Yes! I want nothing to do with you. Fleurette will understand. Time to go, *Kitty*." The name flew from me, unbidden, but it was perfect. A shortened version of *kitsune*, with a feline twist that sounded almost insulting when compared to the supernatural fox.

I hoped she choked on it.

Instead, she preened. "You throw me away in the same breath you name me. Very well. I know more about Fleurette than you do. She will not soon forget this, or forgive you for it. But ultimately, it is your choice. Until we meet again, Cousin."

And then, like a wisp of orange smoke in the wind, she was gone.

I blew a breath of relief out of my nose before turning to go back to the house.

I'd done it.

Good riddance.

But at the threshold, I paused. I had let my anger get in the way of making an educated decision. I was leaning in that direction anyway, but I couldn't help but feel a little bad for Kokoro. Perhaps she truly was separated from the fox—Kitty, I reminded myself—but she made her bed by pairing with such a loathsome creature.

I was sure Fleurette would understand.

CHAPTER 9

The start of the new day came upon swift wings in the form of Fleurette, who startled me awake with a hand on my furry back. I blinked sleepily at her, seeing only the general outline of my witch friend in the gloom of the sitting room. My internal clock told me it was morning, but, given the lack of light, it was no later than seven.

"Cress, do you know where Kokoro is?" she asked me with quiet urgency. "She's not in the bed."

I shimmered immediately, filling the space next to Grimm and giving my human body a good stretch and a yawn before answering. "She's gone."

"Gone?" Fleurette repeated, a note of hysteria creeping into the single syllable. "What do you mean?"

I rubbed Grimm's head, which had made its way into my lap. I gave a sigh, guessing that perhaps Fleurette wasn't going to be as understanding as sleep-deprived me had assumed. I reached over and turned on the lamp, squinting at the flare of brightness before turning back to Fleurette. "I mean, she left. The fox and I had a conversation, and at the end I told her I wouldn't help her. So, she left, and obviously took Kokoro with her."

Fleurette regarded me with a stony face. I could swear I saw a sheen to her eyes, a sign of barely controlled emotion flitting through her countenance. "You told the fox you wouldn't help Kokoro? How could you?"

That last line had been as accusatory as they came. I frowned. "Listen. Kokoro is nice, but Kitty—the fox—is manipulative. I mean, you were bending over backwards for a person you only knew for a couple of days! Kitty is up to something, I'm sure of it. I want no part in that."

Fleurette brushed a hand over her eyes, her exasperation plainly showing. "Cressida, can you even *begin* to comprehend what you've done? Kokoro is innocent in all this. She came for our help. And I wasn't 'bending over backwards' for her. I was genuinely caring for her. Showing her that the life she previously lived was not normal. I ...." She blew out a breath. "Do you understand that your family members have a true love, a person that is a soul mate? All other relationships pale in comparison. It's why you have a hard time being intimate with any other potential mate. Well, humans don't often get that experience. It's rare. But from the moment I met Kokoro ... I felt something. Something I had never felt before." Her face fell.

I stared at her. " Oh? Ohhh."

She shook her head. "I can't say that the feeling was returned. I was hoping to spend more time with her to see if she even leaned that way. But she's gone? Really and truly?"

I dropped my eyes. "I'm sorry, Fleurette. I didn't know."

She straightened, all emotions leaving her face. "Well, I have things to do today. If you'll excuse me."

She walked stiffly out of the room, her last words like an icy jab at my heart. I sat there, fully assimilating this new information, which ultimately did not take long. And the results? My mental reflection upon the whole situation and Fleurette's crushed behavior left me feeling about two inches tall.

Fleurette ignored me for the rest of the morning. The weather outside matched my own mood: dreary. These factors, both external and internal, did little for any motivation I might have had. I decided a day sleeping on the couch was needed.

I told Grimm about my last conversation with Kitty, and I likewise explained Fleurette's reaction to finding Kokoro gone. He mulled these over.

"Fleurette is receptive to Kokoro?" he asked.

I twitched an ear back. "More than that. It's deeper than an attraction. She felt like they could possibly be soul mates, based on how Kokoro made her feel."

"Ah. Lifelong companions, then?"

"Yes."

"Like us?"

I stared at him. "Nooo ... not exactly. We're business partners. And best friends."

He huffed out a sigh. "I fail to see the distinction. Partners, companions, friends. They all relate to each other, do they not?"

He had a point, and his words made me feel strangely happy. It was nice to have a companion like Grimm, even if he was a dog. Still, he was way off the mark. "Take my word for it, buddy. The complexities of human courtship go way over your head. Just chalk it up to the fact that Fleurette could see herself possibly marrying Kokoro one day, but I messed it all up."

"I'm still not sure I understand why you hated the fox so much," he said. "She seemed nice enough to me."

"That's because she flattered you. She manipulated everyone around me. How could I not hate her?"

"Flattery isn't the worst thing out there. I found it rather nice."

"Of course you did. That's the whole point. No, I can't trust that creature farther than I can throw her. I'm glad to see the last of her. I feel badly about Kokoro, though. I wish I could have helped her separately from the fox."

Grimm made a small snort out of his nose before sticking his snout into my fur. "Understandable. But things will work out. I just have a feeling."

We stayed on the loveseat, sleeping all morning. Close to noon, a loud knock sounded on the door, waking both of us with a start. Grimm gave a small growl, but I told him to stay put.

"I got it," Fleurette called from her workspace. She made her way to the sitting room without a glance in our direction, opening the door as we watched.

A scent of familiar cologne wafted in, triggering memories of a night of dancing and intrigue. I knew who our visitor was instantly.

"Oh, Gavin! Please, come in," Fleurette greeted as she swept to the side of the door.

"Hello, Miss Williams," Gavin St. Cloud responded as he came into view. He closed the blue umbrella in his hand, giving it a shake on the porch before placing it in the holder by the door and shutting the door firmly behind him.

"I believe we're past such niceties. Call me Fleurette. What brings you here?"

Gavin's eyes swiveled about the room, landing first on Grimm, who tensed beside me, and then locking in on me. "I didn't know you had a cat," he said.

Fleurette waved a dismissive hand. "Oh yes. Her name is Pita."

I stared at her. Pita?

Fleurette added, "It's short for 'pain in the ass.'"

Oh.

Gavin chuckled before turning his attention to Fleurette. "Is Cressida around?"

Fleurette shook her head and motioned for Gavin to sit in one of the chairs while she took the other. "She's out on an errand and I have no idea when she'll be back."

A hint of a buzz issued from his vicinity, and he gave a small frown. "Is that so?"

Fleurette nodded. "Is there something I can help you with?"

Gavin returned the nod, settling into his seat across from where I rested. "I'm surprised Grimm is here without her. Those two are usually inseparable," he commented.

Fleurette cleared her throat. "Grimm doesn't like the rain," she lied smoothly.

From my seat, I could definitely hear the tiny vibration emanating from his pocket. It was his pocket watch, the one that detected lies. Gavin had to know that Fleurette was lying through her teeth, yet he made no move to extract the watch or to call out Fleurette on her behavior.

Instead, he stared at me. "Your cat seems so familiar," he murmured, then shook his head and turned his attention to other matters. "I received your note. I just got back to town a couple of hours ago. Is my cousin still here?"

Fleurette looked at me with narrow eyes, an accusing glare if I ever saw one. "I'm afraid not. Cressida told me she left in the middle of the night."

Gavin blinked, oblivious to the look Fleurette had just given me. "The middle of the night? That's odd."

Fleurette sighed. "It's ... complicated."

"I wouldn't expect anything less from this household." He made a little hum in his throat, not waiting for a reply from Fleurette. "Anyway, the fact that she's not here doesn't surprise me. I met her already."

My friend placed full attention back on Gavin. "Is that so?"

He nodded. A contemplative look flitted across his face as his gaze fell upon me. He opened his mouth to speak, stopped, and fished his watch out. He placed it on his lap, opened toward him. Fleurette's eyes darted to it, but said nothing.

Apparently, this was the point at which Gavin wanted full honesty.

"Early this morning, I was camped on the side of the road, having taken a nap in my MC. I was awakened by a flash of light. I thought it was an oncoming vehicle shining their lights on me, but nothing was out there. When I got out of my MC to investigate, there was a woman in the bushes, with just her head peeking out. I thought it was the ghost of my mother at first; she looked so much like her. She said she was my cousin, and that she was in trouble. She was making her way to the coast because that is where the fox said her salvation would lie. And then she disappeared from my view, and I saw a fox slink away. Am I crazy?"

"Not at all. There's something you should know, Gavin. Your cousin has been possessed by a fox, a kitsune. It happened back in Tyonoshima. Are you familiar with them?"

Gavin shrugged, turning his head to look at Fleurette after a quick peek at his watch. "A little. My mother told me about them. Kitsune help people in order to gain tails. Once a fox has nine tails, it can ascend to a new celestial plane of existence. The older the fox is, the more tails it usually has. It also must choose harder tasks in order to gain its last couple of tails. How many does her fox have, do you know?"

"Eight, I believe. She just needs to earn the last one. Saving Kokoro was her task to do this."

"And she came to you for help?"

Fleurette waffled her hand. "She came specifically for Cressida. Which is why I'm a little put out that Cressida denied her."

"So, then, what was Kokoro's new plan?" Gavin asked, his eyebrows drawing together in concern.

"I'm not sure. I suppose the fox plans to take on the men chasing after Kokoro herself. I'm just worried that the fox alone won't be enough to protect your cousin."

"Agreed." Gavin steepled his fingers over his mouth in thought.

"Gavin, what happens if a kitsune fails to help someone?" Fleurette asked, leaning forward.

Gavin pondered. "Nothing good, I'm afraid. My mother explained that a fox will lose a tail if they fail to help the person promised their assistance. But this fox possession also worries me."

"Why?" Fleurette leaned further forward.

"*Kitsunetsuki* can end badly. Only powerful, old foxes can possess people. But it's taxing to the human's system. So, if one is possessed for too long of a time, the person can go insane, or become sick, or even die. But also, if the fox fails to help their host, and leaves their body prematurely, the person *will* die."

I opened my eyes wide. Fleurette sucked in a breath before responding. "Wait. So you're saying that if Kokoro's fox can't help her within a short time period, Kokoro might lose her mind, or die?"

Gavin nodded grimly. "Yes."

"And alternatively, if the fox fails to ultimately protect Kokoro, and the fox cuts her losses and gives up Kokoro's body, Kokoro *will* die?"

"Also yes. Unfortunately."

Fleurette took an unsteady breath. "So, the only way Kokoro gets out of this alive and unharmed is for the fox to help her in a timely manner. Which might prove difficult, considering the creature was actively seeking help."

Gavin grimaced. "It would seem that way. What exactly is the trouble that Kokoro is in? Did she tell you?"

"Kokoro mentioned that some people are after her because she murdered her husband, who was some Tyonoshimese bigwig, and she was accused of stealing something important. She said the fox by herself was not enough to save her from them. She came to Cressida for assistance, but Cressida would not help her." The glare was back in my direction. I stared right back at her. How was I supposed to know that Kokoro could die without my help?

Gavin turned to look at me again; apparently, I was a common focal point. "That seems unlike Cressida," he mused.

"I agree. It's the reason why Kokoro left suddenly. I'm not at all happy with Cressida right now."

Gavin snapped his watch shut. "Ah, that explains the fibs you told me earlier."

Fleurette only stared.

Gavin held up his watch, pinched between two fingers. "It tells the truth. I would have thought Cressida had mentioned my watch to you. It certainly tripped her up enough times."

Fleurette gave a ghost of a smile. "I can imagine. I'm sorry for not being truthful earlier. But the fact is that Cressida is indisposed at the moment. That's all I can say."

Gavin waved a hand to dismiss her apology. "No harm done. You were truthful in the parts that mattered most to me. And Cressida mentioned that there are secrets she must keep. I assume you are also privy to them?"

Fleurette cautiously nodded.

Gavin grinned, showing his teeth. "Then say no more! I've gotten used to Cressida's ways after all the hullabaloo this spring. I won't pry."

"Thank you, Gavin." The mood turned somber once again. "Listen. I've become very fond of your cousin within the small amount of time she was here. And after everything you've just told me about fox possession, I'm worried sick about Kokoro, frankly."

Gavin slapped his hands on his thighs. "I'm worried too. Which is why I came here. I want to track her down and help her in any way I can. I don't have much in the way of family, and I'd like to get to know my cousin. I was hoping to get Cressida to help me, but I guess I'll have to do this on my own." He made to stand.

Fleurette rose quickly, a light in her eyes. "Gavin, would you accept the assistance of someone else? Like me?"

He looked askance for just a moment before smiling at her. "I would be honored. Thank you, Fleurette."

She nodded with affirmation. "I just need to gather a few things. Will you give me a couple of minutes?"

"Of course. I'll go and get Scarlet started. I won't leave without you." He grabbed his umbrella from the stand but paused at the door. "Oh, I nearly forgot. This letter came for Cressida at the guild headquarters. I saw it sticking out of her mail cubby as I left to come here, so I thought I'd drop it off." He pulled the letter from his vest pocket and handed it to Fleurette.

"Thank you," she said, turning it over with a small frown. "I won't be but a moment."

Gavin nodded, opening the door and shutting it politely behind him.

As soon as he was gone, Fleurette rushed over to the loveseat, stooping until her face was close to my body. "You don't have to transform," she said in a rush, "and I don't really want to have a discussion about it. I've thought long and hard about what happened earlier. I'm sorry I've been angry at you. You had every right to follow your gut and deny the fox your help." She gave me a little half-smile. "And I have every right to follow mine, and right now it's telling me I need to do what I can to help Kokoro. I can't just let her go. So please take care of the place, and let the kids know what's happening. I love you, Cress, and I hope to be back soon."

She stood and bustled out of the room to gather some items for the trip. I ignored her wish that I stay as a cat, jumping up from my seat and transforming quickly. "Fleurette, wait—"

Fleurette emerged from her workspace with a basket in her hand. "No, Cressida. My mind is made up. You do so much to risk yourself for the sake of our world. This time, it's not your battle. It's my turn to go on an adventure now." She placed a hand on my cheek, cradling it in a sisterly gesture. "I love you, Cress. I hope to be back soon."

"I ... I love you too, Fleurette. Be safe." It was all I could manage to say, as my inner thoughts were a whirling mass that I didn't have the luxury of time to pick apart.

She smiled and grabbed her down coat off the rack by the door. She paused as she glanced at her basket and plucked the letter that Gavin had given her off the top. She handed it to me. "Be sure to open this, too. I'm frankly surprised you received anything, given that I suspended any correspondence through the guild. Don't forget."

With that, Fleurette brushed past me and headed out the door, shutting it firmly behind her. I heard her call for Rupert, who, judging by the loud cawing emitting through the walls, joined her and Gavin in their adventure.

All that she left behind was a concerned dog, a woman with a confused heart, and a letter marked with a big red "URGENT" on the outside.

CHAPTER 10

I sat back down on the loveseat, dazed. Grimm nudged my closest hand, and I petted his head, taking comfort in the silky feel of his fur. I stayed this way for a good minute, just processing what had happened.

I went through a mental checklist. Fleurette: crushing on Kokoro. Now gone in a hurry to save her. With Gavin, of all people. Gavin: concerned about his cousin, even though he only met her for a brief moment. Kokoro: will probably die if she doesn't get help. Cressida: a complete and total ass.

That snapped me out of it.

Right. First thing's first: the letter.

I tore the envelope and shakily removed a single piece of paper.

To Cressida Curtain,

This is an unusual circumstance I find myself in. I have knowledge of a secret organization that I believe you have interest in. I am aware that you faced wrongful imprisonment at the Addelboro Correctional Facility back in March. I would like to discuss and hopefully work with you to right this wrong. I am currently staying at the Belmont Inn in Knobby Hill. I plan to be at Fresh Gatherings (the tea shop on Verdant St) tomorrow, Friday October 15th, at 10 a.m. I would be most appreciative if you could join me. If not, please do not hesitate to call on me at Belmont Inn. I plan to leave soon, but if I must, I will stay in Knobby Hill longer than I originally planned. I do not believe it is in your best interest to pass up this opportunity.

   Best,

   N. Hoterson

I stared at the note, reading each word carefully, yet it did no good to increase my comprehension. This person knew about Addelboro? Surely that would mean that he or she also had information about the ACF. It was either that or their self-proclaimed knowledge of a secret organization referred to GOGS. After all, I did have two secret organizations to deal with. Hopefully a third was not an option, because it was becoming ridiculous enough as it was.

I shook my head to remove the dazed feeling. I needed advice.

After shimmering down into cat form, I immediately picked up a paw and began licking it, hoping that the repetitive action would soothe my frazzled nerves. Grimm stared at me, his sunflower eyes boring into my head as I temporarily ignored him.

"Alright, what's going on, CC?" he asked me.

I put my paw down and gazed at him with half-lidded eyes. "Too much, I suppose," I answered dazedly. I gave my head a brisk shake. "That letter, it's someone who wants to meet with me. They have information about Addelboro and a 'secret organization.' Does this sound too good to be true?"

Grimm let out a grumble deep in his throat. "Too much like a trap, if you ask me."

I sighed. "I thought of that too. But I'm inclined to at least meet with them. It's a public space, so how much trouble could I get into?"

"It's terrifying that you of all cats have to ask that." Grimm chuckled.

"Yes, yes. I dunno, Grimm. I think I need to do this. But I won't go without you."

Grimm cocked his head back. "You won't?"

"Of course not! I made that mistake once," I said, the memory of being captured by Gregory Elkins at the Equinox Ball surging through my mind. I had left Grimm at home that night. Perhaps things would have gone differently if I had taken him with me. "I plan to have you by my side through this entire thing, partner."

Grimm licked my face in one quick, sneaky maneuver. "That's all I could ask for, Cress."

At ten in the morning the next day, Grimm and I entered Fresh Gatherings, a quaint little tea shop in the heart of downtown Knobby Hill. Normally, dogs were not allowed within businesses selling food, but we were both fairly well known in town, even if we mostly kept to ourselves. Many of the owners did not care, given that Grimm had a standing reputation for behaving well.

Before I even placed my hand on the handle of the door, I was fretful. I had slept poorly due to nerves, and my agitation had stuck with me throughout the morning. I'd been on a self-imposed sabbatical for the last six months, and I feared it had made my already dubious people skills even rustier. I was also breaking Fleurette's rule about going into town by myself. And that wasn't even mentioning the fact that this Hoterson person (why did that name sound so familiar?) had knowledge of *me*, knowledge of things that happened that nobody of good standing should rightfully have access to.

This could be one of the stupider things I'd recently done.

The bell tinkled sweetly as I pushed the door to the shop open. I walked in, trying my hardest not to look like my heart was pounding or that I was sweating profusely despite the chill in the air. I foresaw another thorough grooming session in my near future. But pretending everything was A-OK with me, I stepped to the side to allow Grimm entrance, and then shut the door, eliciting the bell a second time.

Two tables contained single patrons, and both occupants looked up at the bell's jingle to see who had walked in. The first customer took one glimpse and then went back to his business. The second continued to stare with a small smile gracing his face, as if he recognized me.

This must be N. Hoterson.

I swallowed and approached this table, tucked toward the back of the cozy space. Grimm matched my steps, leaning slightly against my leg as a reminder of his support.

"Miss Curtain, thank you for meeting me," the man said as he stood in greeting. He held out a hand. "Nicomedes Hoterson."

I was surprised to see that Mr. Hoterson was young, my human body's peer at no older than twenty-five, if I had to guess. His honey blond hair was ear length but slicked back in a debonair style. His blue eyes twinkled as he gave me a handsome smile, showing off straight white teeth.

There was something familiar about his eyes and his smile, but my initial assessment was that I had never met this man before. Some people simply had familiar faces.

I took his hand, which compounded my awkwardness and deepened the flush on my face. He gave it a gentle shake before releasing it.

"Mr. Hoterson," I said politely, looking up into his face.

"Call me Nic, please," he replied with another winning smile. As soon as he said the words I felt a measure of relief, an odd ease that erased the worst of the nerves.

He glanced at Grimm and let out a low whistle. "You don't see many Lycanhunds wandering around these days," he said with a hint of reverence. "Is he friendly?"

I glanced at Grimm, who looked up to meet my eyes. He gave a small wag of his tail. "It depends on who's asking," I answered, looking back up at Nicomedes—Nic. "For you, he seems to be. Consider that a good omen."

Nic chuckled. "Oh, I will."

He motioned for me to sit, waiting until I had done so before folding his slim and well-dressed body back into his own chair. He smoothed the front of his button-down shirt before gripping the mug that rested before him. "Can I get you something to drink?"

I shook my head, my left hand automatically reaching out to settle on top of Grimm's head for support.

Nic nodded in understanding. "Of course you must be wondering why I wrote you. Shall we get right to business?"

"Yes, please," I breathed, feeling another wave of relief. "You must understand, Nic, that the contents of your note caused me quite a bit of alarm."

"I apologize for that, Miss Curtain. Or can I call you Cressida?"

I waved a hand dismissively. "Cressida is fine."

"Thank you. I had a feeling you wouldn't willingly meet with me unless you felt that the stakes were high. Is that a fair assessment?"

I tilted my head. "You could say that. So tell me, just how *do* you know about the things you mentioned?"

He chuckled. "Straight to the point. I like it. Did you know, Cressida, that this is not the first time I've seen you?"

"What?" I asked, gripping a hunk of Grimm's fur in consternation.

"Please, don't be alarmed," he soothed. I relaxed my grasp as Grimm licked my wrist. Nic continued, "I was at the Equinox Ball. I saw you from a distance, but I did not get a chance to introduce myself."

A stray memory found its way back home. "*Hoterson.* I thought your name sounded familiar. You were the man who told my partner about the study!"

"The very same. Your date that night was Mr. Shimada, correct? Except I'm quite certain that wasn't his real name." Nic maintained the same calm demeanor he had initially presented himself with.

I should have been scared. After all, Gavin and I had been asking all around that night about where the study was located in the mansion in which the ball was held. It was our mission to find a ledger from which we were hoping to gain my father's alibi, clearing his name of the wrongdoing he was being hunted for.

And then we had fallen prey to Gregory Elkins.

So yes, I should have felt some sort of consternation. But, surprisingly, all I did was wait for Nic to continue speaking.

"I suppose I should explain why I was there, and why I had such knowledge of Deerhorn Manor. You see, I'm an attorney. You've met the senior partner, Thomas Babcock."

Another puzzle piece slid into place. I remembered the letter I had received all those months ago from the law office that represented Lightfoot Shipping Industries. "The letter. It had the names of the lawyers on it. Babcock was the first. The second name ..." I failed to recall it.

"Brothers. Babcock, Brothers, and Hoterson," Nic filled in for me.

I nodded. "The Hoterson is you, then?"

He looked pleased that I was connecting the dots so easily. "The very same! I am the junior partner of the firm, fresh from college."

I gave him a once-over. "I could have guessed that."

He flashed me another smile. He had a dimple on one cheek that gave him a boyish flair. "I *am* incredibly young to make partner. You could say there was a tiny bit of nepotism involved; my grandmother is quite the matriarch of my family."

"Oh?" I said blandly. I was not familiar with the word nepotism, but I didn't want to let him know.

He seemed not to notice my ignorance, but he grew serious. "Unfortunately, since joining the firm, I've uncovered some rather ... unsavory activity. Which is why I'm here."

I straightened in my seat. Nic took a deep breath before asking, "Does the acronym ACF mean anything to you?"

I narrowed my eyes. Now was the time to keep my head, to not give away my playing cards too soon. "Yes."

He waited for me to expand upon my monosyllabic answer, but I simply stared back at him. Finally, he let out a small laugh. "Well, it means something to me as well. Lightfoot Shipping Industries is one of our biggest clients. Babcock wouldn't let me look at any of the files except one, which was as standard as they come. I knew there were more files for Lightfoot Industries, but I had no access to them. You can imagine how curious that made me."

I very well could imagine. The phrase "curiosity killed the cat" existed for a reason. I leaned my head forward, eager to hear more.

"The first chance I got, I snooped. The second file was rather ... illuminating. It talked of off-the-books deals. Retainers for people I can only describe as lackeys for shady dealings. And that's when I learned about ACF. And the silent partner."

I sucked in a breath.

He noticed. "I'm fairly certain you also know who the silent partner is."

Considering he had framed my father in order to discover the whereabouts of my mother—and in turn, to end the line of Glivver at long last—yes, I knew who he was. "Elkins."

"Very good, Cressida! Gold star to you."

I smiled.

Nic took a sip from his mug. "Lightfoot himself is just a pawn in all of this. He's straight as an arrow, businesswise. And he's rich as sin, and doesn't actually check in with his own business to verify anything because of that. But Elkins and some of his workers ... let's just say they run the real show. And Babcock was hired to help run *their* business, not Lightfoot's. That first file was just a front for use in the outside business world. The *real* file was the one I wasn't allowed to view. I found a lot of enlightening tidbits of information from that file. Including about you."

This was it. My pulse ratcheted up to an alarming rate at his words. "Me?" I squeaked.

"Nothing terrible on your end, I assure you," Nic hastened to reply. He must have thought my obvious fear revolved around him finding something nefarious about me. No, that was not my concern at all. My true fear lay in the direction of my secret heritage no longer being safe.

He continued, "C. Curtain was on file as being hired to apprehend one Roger Curtain back in March. Later, I ran across your full name on a list simply labeled 'interrogations, ACF.' And on the next page was a quick note that read you were missing but presumed alive. And that you were wanted on the spot, alive or dead."

I gulped.

"After all that, I did a little research and found your bounty hunting license through the Northwest Bounty Hunters' Guild. And here I am."

I blinked slowly, taking it all in. "But *why* are you here, exactly?"

"I suppose I didn't make that insanely obvious," Nic said as he rubbed a hand over his chin. "I've seen enough corruption in the last calendar year to last me a lifetime. I'm an honest man, Cressida. I don't want to work for the bad guys. But I also know too much to just up and quit. They'd be on me in a heartbeat. So, I'd like to take them down from the inside. Elkins needs to be stopped, at any rate. The files indicate that he is using the Lightfoot business to construct something major, and I have a feeling it's going to cause some damage to this world. Towers, of some sort. I'd like to get rid of them at the very least. Problem is, I don't have much experience with this sort of thing." He gave me a piercing look that gave my heart another jumpstart. "You, on the other hand, are apparently badass enough to survive interrogation at the worst defunct prison in the Oracune Region, and make it out alive while it sank. Hell, for all I know, you were the one to destroy the facility in the process."

"You might be onto something," I mumbled.

"You also seem to already have insider knowledge about the corruption. And if it means I have to permanently 'remove' Elkins? I'm not sure I could do it. I'm not a killer."

"Woah, woah, woah," I protested, my eyes widening. "Neither am I." I was slightly insulted that he would jump to that conclusion.

Nic studied me. "Are you not a bounty hunter?"

I frowned. "I apprehend criminals. I don't kill them."

"No? Does 'Jenson Hobbs' ring any bells?"

I blanched. The first name, no. I had never learned what the big, bald fire elemental's full name had been. He was too busy trying to fricassee me to offer it. But yes, Hobbs' death, while an accident, was inadvertently triggered by me.

How would Nic have known that, though? The only person who possibly would believe me responsible for his fate was Althea, who was about to end me before her sudden change of heart. Perhaps she made a note of it in the files.

Still, I had to set the record straight. "I did not kill him. He met with an accident."

Nic waved away my clarification, seemingly not too worried about my possible status as a murderer. "Nevertheless, you'd make the perfect colleague. So, what do you say?"

I worried at my top lip, contemplating my options. This could be my chance to root out Elkins and destroy his nefarious organization for once and for all. But then again, it was a terrible risk for me. If I was caught, I would have no hope of breaking the curse and passing on the legacy to my future kitten.

And that would mean that Annie would win.

Nic must have sensed my indecision. "Look, I understand your hesitancy. It seems like you've been keeping a low profile since March. Just as well, considering the people Elkins has managed to kill in the meantime."

I whipped my head up. "What people?"

Nic looked almost ashamed for having brought it up. "Just another ghastly secret I uncovered. A list of names of people on file, each with a short description of where they lived, how long they had been a member of GOGS—whatever that is—and two dates: the first being 'date contacted' and the second being 'date exterminated.'" He shivered.

"Do you happen to remember any of the names?" I asked, trying to keep my voice steady.

Nic shook his head, then reconsidered. "Actually, I do remember the last one. I used to know a guy by the same name. It was Maurice ... something."

A solid bundle of dread weighed me down. "How is he killing them?" The bodies of the deceased GOGs never had any wounds or marks to speak of. We still didn't know what exactly was killing them.

Again, Nic gave a little head shake. "I don't know. If I had to guess, though, it's through his special magical gift. Are you aware of it?"

I nodded, the dread being replaced by dawning horror. "Dreamwalking."

"See? You do have insider knowledge."

I ignored Nic, rearranging my scattered thoughts into a neater bundle to sort through. If Elkins was using his dream magic to kill people, it wouldn't leave a mark. I glanced up at Nic. "How much time was between contact and death for these people?"

He rested a finger horizontally on his mouth, recollecting. "About a week," he finally told me. "Why?"

The horror washed through me completely before coalescing into a steely resolve. Sweet Wren had had the nightmare on the same day Maurice had died. It was too much to be coincidental. "Because I know who the next victim is," I said with barely contained rage. "And I'm going to put a stop to him before it's too late."

CHAPTER 11

The plan was simple. As soon as the kids were finished with their school day at half past two, Grimm and I would leave with Humbert and the wagon, pick up Nic from the inn, and head out of town. Our ultimate destination: Oyster Bay, on the Serenic Coast of the Oracune Region. Nic explained that this locale was where Elkins was currently living now that his mansion had been compromised. It was a journey of approximately one hundred miles and would take us close to five days to complete with the horse and wagon. We were getting a late start today, but I was determined to push our drive until late into the night, if need be.

After all, Wren's life was at stake.

After the meeting with Nic, Grimm and I walked to Lyle's farm. Lyle was in the middle of an exam with a client, so we waited in the barn until he was finished. I also filled in the missing bits of my conversation with Nic for Grimm, who had a hard time fully following human speech.

"Do you think I'm making a mistake?" I asked him. In the heat of the revelations Nic had unveiled, I had allowed myself to run on instinct alone. I'd had to make some pretty heavy decisions without conferring with my partner, and on the walk to Lyle's the weight of those decisions was starting to pull me down.

"A mistake?" Grimm cocked his head to the side as he stared at me. "No. Why would you think that?"

I stretched upward against a hay bale, digging my claws into the textured surface before leaping onto the top. "I dunno. Trusting this Nic guy, I suppose. He's a complete stranger who knows a lot about what's going on. But my gut was telling me that he's on the up and up. What about you, Grimm? Did you get any indications that he's leading us into a trap?"

Grimm thoughtfully tilted his head down before responding, "None. He seemed sincere in his desire to take down the bad guys. I trust him."

"Good. You and I are on the same page. I suppose the only part I can't believe is the fact that we've been trying to locate Elkins and the ACF for half a year now, and this random guy just waltzes in and knows exactly where to take us. It's almost too good to be true."

Grimm snorted. "Perhaps the gods are finally taking pity on us."

"Oh please. As if the fate of one world is enough to interest them. There's plenty more out there if this one gets damaged."

Grimm grumbled deep in his throat. "Surely at least one of them would be concerned. Regardless, I don't think you are making a mistake. If Wren is in danger, you and I will do what is necessary to protect her. It's not like Fleurette is around to help out. This may be our only chance at taking out Elkins and ending the ACF for good."

"Thanks, buddy. You're right. And I'm so thankful to have you in my corner."

Grimm straightened and licked my chest. "Always."

As soon as I heard the tell-tale sound of the client leaving the property, I transformed and ran out of the barn toward Lyle's clinic, Grimm at my heels. Lyle was surprised to see me.

"Hello, dear. I wasn't expecting your help today. I only have one more patient to see, and it's an in-home visit." Lyle ran a hand through his closely cropped curls as he smiled at me.

I shook my head. "I'm sorry, Lyle," I responded. "I actually need to leave town today. Are you able to take in the kids for a while?"

Lyle frowned. "Why can't Fleurette?"

I nibbled my lip. "Um ... she's gone."

"Gone!" Lyle raised his voice in disbelief. Fleurette only ever went to town or, on the rare occasion, to the city of Dogwood. She was the definition of a homebody. "Where has she gone to?"

"Well, Kokoro left two nights ago because I didn't want to help her fox. Fleurette decided to go look for her with Kokoro's cousin, Gavin."

Lyle closed his eyes with a heavy breath. He opened and leveled them at me in a disapproving way. I squirmed under the scrutiny, feeling like a child who was about to be reprimanded.

"Cressida. Didn't I tell you to take care of my daughter?"

"I thought I was! I didn't trust the fox, which means I didn't fully trust Kokoro. I assumed I was doing the right thing," I said, a slight whine creeping into my voice.

Lyle sighed again and took a seat in his rolling chair. "Your heart was in the right place. Listen. Did you know the cottage belonged to my mother?"

The change in topic threw me for a second. "No, I don't believe I was ever told that."

Lyle nodded, his heavy brow pulled into a faraway look. "My grandparents built that cottage, and my mama was born there. She was an herb woman for Knobby Hill, same as Fleurette, but with only a quarter of my daughter's talent. She never ventured too far from town, and she never met anyone she liked enough to marry. That is, until my daddy moved to town and bought this place.

"Being neighbors and all, they got to know each other, and soon fell in love. They married and Mama moved here. But she kept the cottage and continued to tend to the grounds, stating that her magic worked best there.

"Mama and Daddy were a bit older when they met and got married. They weren't sure they'd be able to have kids. But I came along anyway. I think my mama was forty-two when she had me. Daddy was a bit older at forty-six." He chuckled. "Man, I cannot imagine having a thirteen-year-old at my age. No thank you."

I nodded, still unsure why he was telling me this story.

He continued, "Althea came into my life right as I moved home after finishing my degree. At the time, I didn't know why she moved to this sleepy town, but I didn't care. She swept me off my feet and I was a goner."

"Why *had* she moved here?" I interjected.

He smiled. "She was a GOG, of course. She'd been transferred here, since this area needed a representative. After all, there was a clear pattern of your ancestors slowly moving farther west as the years passed. Once we became a serious item, she was able to tell me this, since spouses usually become GOGs as well. And even though I'm a mundy, that's exactly what happened."

"Oh," I said, once again uncomfortable with the unsaid knowledge I contained about Althea. I allowed Lyle to continue his tale.

"My daddy unfortunately died just after we were married. Mama decided to move back to her cottage, and gifted me this house and property. By then, I was already establishing myself as the local veterinarian.

"And then Fleurette was born. We were over the moon. My mama became Gramma Betty, and she and Fleurette had the sweetest bond I ever did see. Those two were as thick as thieves. I think once Fleurette was out of diapers, she spent more time over there than she did here. So it was no wonder that Mama willed her the cottage when she died."

"When was that?" I asked.

Lyle stroked his five o'clock shadow. "Fleurette was eighteen. Mama lived a good long life, passing away at eighty-seven.

"And here's the point I was very slowly getting at. Mama was instrumental in filling in that mother role for Fleurette when her real mother abandoned us. When Mama died, a spark went out in Fleurette's eyes and never came back. She's had a good life, mind you, and having the kids and you around has really helped her. But she's been lonely, even with all of that. I can tell."

Lyle straightened and looked me in the eyes. "But the other day, when she and Kokoro came over, I saw my old Fleurette; I saw that spark again. I can't tell you how happy that made me."

"And I had to go and ruin it," I added miserably.

Lyle shook his head. "Don't be so hard on yourself, dear. You have a lot on your plate. And I don't think I made myself clear when I said to protect Fleurette. You thought it was a warning against Kokoro. I apologize for that. No, I wanted to keep that spark for Fleurette, and thought you wanted that too. I suppose all is not lost, though, if Fleurette's chasing after her."

"I suppose not. Lyle, I'm sorry."

"You're a good cat, and a good person, Cressida. You gotta do what you gotta do. I'll look after Fal and Wren, don't you worry. But didn't GOGS tell you no adventuring?"

I squirmed. "Yes. And I don't care that I'm breaking their ruling. Wren is in danger, and I'm the only one with the knowledge to stop anything from happening. GOGS doesn't own me. If they disagree with me, they can just shove it."

He chuckled. "I'm glad to see the spark is back in you too, sweetheart. You've been lost these last few months. I've missed you."

His words soothed the resentment I had felt ever since going into hiding. "You know what? I missed me too."

CHAPTER 12

The rest of the day was a blur of activity: packing the necessities for the long ride, hitching up Humbert to the wagon—he was beyond excited to be useful again—and, once they were home from school, telling the kids what was happening. I couldn't simply blurt out to Wren that her life might once again be on the line; she didn't need that added burden. And while Fal seemed suspicious, I couldn't disclose the truth to him either. He was simply too protective of his younger sister and would either insist on coming with, or he'd make himself sick with worry. Neither outcome was to anyone's advantage.

My hands may have been tied regarding telling Wren the truth, but I did raid Fleurette's stash of valuable potions, finding the one that allowed for dreamless sleep. I gave her instructions to take it every night while I was gone to ward off the nightmares, only going so far as to tell her that the dreams were a bad sign. Hopefully, preventing the dreams would be enough to keep her safe, but it was pure speculation on my part.

Fal wanted to accompany me immediately, but I drew him aside, deciding to at least drop a hint to him. "I need you here, Fal," I said in a low tone. "Elkins is at it again, and your sister needs protection. Your love for her saved her once; it can do so again. But not if you're with me."

"It's not fair," he grumbled, the age-old adage of children everywhere. He may have been seventeen and close to adulthood, but he still clung to some misnomers of youth.

"You're right," I agreed with a shrug. "But neither is the fact that out of all people, sweet Wren is being targeted, nor the fact that I'm cursed. It won't stop me from doing everything in my power to do the right thing for this world, however. You're young. Your time to help will come." I gave him a wry grin. "In the meantime, watch Wren like a hawk. Or a falcon."

Fal groaned at my pun, but he smiled nonetheless.

When I dropped them off with Lyle, I hugged all three of them, promising to be safe and to come home soon. I wished I could peer into a crystal ball to know for sure if I would keep my promise. But, instead, I had a lawyer to pick up.

Nic was waiting outside the inn when I pulled up at three in the afternoon. The storm that had passed through just days earlier was completely gone, and brisk October sunshine took its place. I counted this as a good omen for our journey. I hated driving in the rain.

He whistled as I pulled the wagon up to him, eyeing Humbert appreciatively. "You must have a thing for big animals," he said with a grin. He made a point of looking at Grimm, who had followed me on foot.

I suppressed a laugh; in my natural form, most animals were large animals to me. But I smiled as I jumped down to open the back doors of the wagon. "I didn't have much of a choice with Humbert here. He was about to be auctioned off to a butcher. I knew he still had plenty of life left in him, so I outbid the butcher. It was that or buy a regular-size, younger horse. I think I made the right choice."

"I'll say," Nic said. He stashed his luggage in the back then turned to look at me. "Is he up for the trek, though? It's quite the distance."

I bit my upper lip. The thought had crossed my mind as well, but Humbert had told me he would rather give it a go than waste away in Lyle's field. "He's not let me down before. He may be past his prime, but Humbert's got plenty of spunk yet."

Nic nodded, taking me at my word. He grinned at me. "A real animal lover, then. Not only are you resilient and pretty, but kind too? You're turning out to be quite the unicorn."

I blushed at the compliment, but at the same time it made me uneasy. Truth be told, I hated when men brought up how pretty I was. I may have been vain about my grooming habits, but otherwise I didn't care a whit about my looks. As long as I passed as a regular human, that was enough for me. Otherwise, my appearance was of no consequence to this journey, and bringing it up so nonchalantly was unnecessary. Would he be this flirty the entire time we traveled? The idea didn't sit well with me.

Still, I decided to give him the benefit of the doubt. If he came on too strong, I'd simply tell him to clear off.

Grimm took this moment to jump into the back of the wagon, breaking my inner tension. He enjoyed the physical exercise of walking near the wagon at times, but on other occasions he preferred to let Humbert do all the work. I shot him a smile—he responded with a tail wag—and shut the doors securely. I didn't bother to lock them; no one in their right mind would purposefully meddle with a Lycanhund.

Our cargo secure, Nic and I climbed up onto the bench seat, with Nic to my right. He glanced at me.

"Aren't you going to be cold?" he asked with concern.

I always kept my outfit choices simple: same trousers, leather boots, and dove-gray vest throughout the year, but I changed the linen shirt from short sleeves to long sleeves when the weather turned. I also made use of leather driving gloves in the colder weather, since my fingers tended to get stiff with cold. Otherwise, unless the temperature plummeted past the usual temperate climate measures, I didn't bother with a coat.

Nic, on the other hand, wore a plush down coat that also appeared to be waterproof, as well as gloves and a warm hat.

I shrugged. "I run hot. I do have a raincoat in the back if the weather turns. I'll be fine."

He raised his eyebrows at me, but didn't say anything more on the matter. He unfolded a map and angled it my way as I grabbed the reins.

"Here's us," he said, pointing to the small dot on the map marked *Knobby Hill*, "and here's our destination." His finger traced along a route that led to the Oracune coast and a small divot in the land marked *Oyster Bay*. "There's a travel inn past the Willmaunt River I've stayed at before. I figure we'll stop there for the night. But I need to grab a few things at my townhouse in Kousa. It's on the way to the inn, so it won't take much time."

At the mention of the town of Kousa, my anxiety flared for just a second. After all, my last time in that area involved being kidnapped and shipped off in a box to a defunct prison for torture.

I kept this to myself, however. "You aren't fully packed? I'm sure I have enough stuff for the both of us. Are you positive we need to travel through Kousa?"

Nic looked at me with an understanding smile. "Unless you want to go out of your way to travel to Dogwood, yes. Don't forget, we need to cross the Willmaunt River if we are to make it to the coast. Kousa has the nearest bridge, with Dogwood being the second closest. It's either that or be at the mercy of the ferries and their schedules."

I sighed with resignation. "Nope, you're right. Kousa, it is." I flicked the reins in my hand and urged Humbert into his plodding cadence.

The moment the wagon lurched into movement, I let out a sigh of contentment and settled in for the journey. I had missed this, taking my wagon out for a job. The last six months had been hard on me, harder than I had realized. Sinking my teeth into another expedition was just what I needed.

Of course, I still wasn't sure about my new companion. But I needn't have worried about Nic's flirtiness. His previous comment had slid by with no follow-up. In fact, we initially rode in silence, the restrained quiet of two strangers. But after a spell, Nic decided to break the peace.

"So, how long have you been a bounty hunter? You seem awfully young."

I side-eyed him. "About as young as a junior partner at a law firm?"

He chuckled, flashing his dimple again. "You got me there. I shouldn't judge."

I leaned back to stretch my spine a bit. It had been a long time since I had sat in this seat and my body was no longer used to it. "To answer your question, I've been a hunter for more than two years. It's the perfect job for me. What about you? Did you always want to be a lawyer?"

"Hmm." Nic took a moment to think. "My father was the one who pushed me into the field. He said it would be good to have a lawyer in the family."

"Is he one too?"

Nic shook his head. "No, he's ... independently wealthy. He dabbles here and there, but basically lives off of his investments."

My eyebrows shot up. "Does that mean you're set to inherit a fortune?"

Nic let out a bray of laughter, startling me in the process. "I would, if the old man ever dies!" He chortled. He looked at me, his dark blue eyes twinkling. "That sounds terrible. He's older than he looks, yet he still keeps ticking. I don't see him slowing down any time soon."

"I see."

He shot a glance at me. "What about your folks? Are they still around?"

Now we were headed into dangerous territory. I did not want to give away too much about my background, for obvious reasons. At the same time, I felt it was rude to not answer at all. "They're ..." Dead? Living on the other side of the country? For once, my gift of lying on the spot was on the fritz. "... on an extended vacation," I finished.

I quickly changed the subject. "Won't your partners realize you're missing?"

Nic made a dismissive sound. "Hollis Brothers has been on a sabbatical for the last few months, for health reasons or something. Babcock is currently in Dogwood. The goons that work at Lightfoot Shipping are up in arms and called him there earlier this week. Something about a fox."

My heart stuttered. "A fox?" I repeated with a timid voice.

Nic looked at me. I tried not to look shell shocked, despite the sudden racing of my heart. "Yeah. One of their ships from Tyonoshima just docked in the port at Dogwood, and apparently one of the workers saw a fox run down the gangplank and off into the shipping yard. They summoned Babcock, who seemed to think it was a big deal. Something about a Tyonoshimese associate being murdered and part of an engine being stolen. They seem to think the fox is responsible. I'm not sure; it didn't make a lot of sense to me."

My pulse pounded in my ears as Nic talked. My voice sounded frail as I asked, "Lightfoot Shipping has ties to Tyonoshima?"

"Oh yeah. Big ones. One of Elkins' associates did business with the murdered businessman. What was his name ... Inaba? Anyway, the dead guy was subcontracted as a manufacturer of magically enhanced metal, from what I could piece together. The towers I told you about earlier were basically made by the Tyonoshimese fellow, and shipped here on that boat." Nic glanced at me, assessing. "You seem a little pale. Are you okay?"

I tried my best to snap out of it. "Me? I'm fine. Foxes make me nervous, is all." I grimaced at the terrible lie.

He still watched me, a slight glaze of concern on his face. "You didn't happen to see the fox, did you?"

"The fox? No, I mean, if I had seen one, they live around here. One fox is the same as another. How could I possibly know if it's a foreign fox?" I made an effort to stop my word vomit. Nic did not need to know about Kokoro. My brain still tried to register the fact that once again, I had messed up. Kokoro and her fox happened to be mixed up in Gregory Elkins' business after all. And here I thought they were two completely unrelated issues.

I'd been given the chance to track down the ACF with Kitty's help. I could have worked with her to save Kokoro and take down Elkins all in one go. And I blew it.

Kitty was right. I did regret my decision.

CHAPTER 13

W e arrived in Kousa at seven in the evening. The sun had already set, but the small city provided plenty of light along the main road with tall black lamp posts. Even without those, I had my trusty lamp hanging on the pole near my head to help guide Humbert's way. We were well versed in nighttime travel.

The last time I had journeyed along this road was in an MC with Gavin, on my way to the Equinox Ball. At the time, I hadn't paid much attention to the directions, but I did recall that Deerhorn Manor was located on the outskirts of Kousa, not in Kousa proper, and that at some point Gavin had made a left-hand turn off the main road to drive to the estate. I gripped the reins tighter as we approached this same fork in the road, but Nic directed me to continue straight. The tension in my body eased instantly at knowing that I would not have to set eyes on the mansion.

Kousa itself was a charming little city with a vibrant downtown area. The local businesses had decorated for the fall season, with pumpkins and autumn leaf garlands adorning entryways and windows. Even more lights lit up this section of town, making for a cozy atmosphere within the surrounding darkness, much like reading with a light on under the covers.

Nic directed me to make a turn in the middle of this area, and guided me a few blocks north until we reached a block of three-story townhouses painted a uniform cream color and built in a similar architectural style as the buildings downtown . I stopped in front of one at his urging.

"I'll just be a moment. Would you like to stay here or wait inside?" Nic asked as he let himself down from the wagon seat.

I mulled it over as I removed my gloves, ultimately deciding to stay where I was. Grimm probably needed a break from the wagon, and I was reluctant to leave him out here on his own. Not because I worried about him getting into trouble, but I had learned in Dogwood that city folk could be less accepting of giant dogs roaming about on their own.

I stretched my back as Grimm did his business against a bush near the townhouse. It had been six months since I last sat in the wagon seat, and my body had apparently gone soft. I rubbed my behind, wondering if I needed to invest in some cushions since I was already feeling sore.

Grimm watched me, his yellow eyes practically glowing in the soft light of the lit windows surrounding us. "I must be getting old," I commented.

He sneezed theatrically, a sign that he did not agree with me.

A stiff breeze rolled across the sidewalk, and I shivered despite my usual resistance to the cold. Perhaps it would be better to wait in the relative warmth of Nic's house. Grimm seemed to be content to continue his wait in the wagon, so my concerns about his safety were unfounded.

I walked up the steps and to the door, planning to wait just past the threshold, lest I intrude too much. The door opened onto a short hallway painted a neutral cream color. Nic stood at the end of this hall, his back to me and two large duffle bags at his feet. He held something in his hands. Curious, I peered from the doorway, craning my neck to see what he was doing.

It was a message mirror, and he scrawled something upon it.

At this point, I felt guilty for spying, so I cleared my throat.

Nic jumped and clicked the mirror shut as he turned toward me, a look of surprise on his face.

"Sorry," I said bashfully. "It was cold outside, and I thought I could wait in the hallway for you."

Nic's face smoothed into a pleasant mien. He tucked the mirror into his pocket. "Quite alright. I did invite you in, after all. You just startled me. Shall we?"

Nic shouldered the bags and began walking toward me and the door.

"Can I help you with one of those?" I asked, standing in the way awkwardly.

Nic shook his head. "No, unicorn. I've got this. You just open up your wagon for me."

I stepped out ahead of him, leading him to the wagon and reopening the doors. He carefully pushed his bags deeper into the interior, mindful of Grimm's location.

We were off once more. Humbert lumbered along stolidly, his clip-clop rhythm echoing off the pavement beneath his feet. Within a short time, he took us to the bridge and began the trek over it.

The bridge was wide enough for multiple lanes, but we were the only travelers upon it. Willmaunt River was wide and deep, and from our high position I could hear the steady rush of its waters as it traveled south. I marveled at the strength that the sound conveyed as it surged below our feet.

Eventually, the bridge came to an end and the wagon once again rode over solid ground. Kousa claimed a small portion of the land on this side as well, but it was mostly residential sections, and soon enough even those petered out, and the friendly streetlights that had lit our way throughout the town also ceased to be.

It could be dangerous driving a wagon with so little light. Still, Humbert was a trooper and trusted me to guide him with the light of my lamp. He knew I could see better in the dark than he could.

Once we were past the outskirts of Kousa, the land on the other side of the Willmaunt River changed to open farmland, illuminated only by the waxing gibbous moon. Less than two hours later, the farms gave way to another woodland, although this one was younger and tamer, having been whittled away by the farms for wood over the years. Still, having been born and raised in a forest, I felt much more at home in this environment than I ever did in a field or city.

The main road took us into the heart of this woodland, and once the trees closed in on us, even the light of the almost-full moon couldn't help illuminate our way. All too soon, though, I spied light through the trees.

"That's the inn," Nic remarked, pointing at the glow in the distance.

Within minutes, Humbert had taken us to the yard of the travel inn. I steered him into the ample U-shaped driveway and halted him directly in front of the main building.

I inspected at my surroundings before disembarking. The inn to my right was a solid wood structure, built in a clearing in the woods. A wooden sign hanging above the entrance proclaimed the official name to be Douglas Inn, with a painting of an evergreen tree next to the words. Ahead of my wagon was a small parking lot, mostly filled with MCs, and beyond that was a stable for traveling horses. The entrance was brightly lit, as were most of the windows and the interior of the stable, making it a bright oasis amidst the gloom of the surrounding forest.

Nic took the initiative to slide down and off the wagon. I followed suit, tethering Humbert to the hitching post. Before joining Nic at the entrance, I ventured to the right side of the wagon and knocked a couple of times.

"Hang tight. I'll be back," I called out to Grimm within.

He acknowledged he heard me with a faint chuffing bark.

Satisfied, I walked over to Nic, who opened the door and held it gallantly for me. I entered, the lawyer at my heels.

I hadn't registered just how chilly the night had gotten until we were inside and the door closed behind us. Instantly, a dry warmth enveloped me like a cozy blanket. I took a moment to relish the feel of it before following Nic to the reception desk, where a young woman with a round face and strawberry blonde hair waited for us with a practiced smile on her face.

"Welcome back, Mr. Hoterson," she greeted Nic, glancing at me with a measure of surprise. If Nic truly were a regular here, he did not frequently arrive with unknown women, apparently.

"Good evening, Jacinda," he responded, flashing that charming smile at her. "We'd like two rooms for the night, please."

Jacinda's smile faltered as she checked an open book in front of her on the desk. She looked back at Nic with a troubled expression. "I'm so sorry, Mr. Hoterson. We are unusually full tonight. I only have one room vacant." She checked the book again. "It only has one bed, but the bed is large enough for two people." She smiled apologetically, but it was also tinged with conspiratorial cheek.

I blinked rapidly at this news. Did she really expect us to share a bed? I had only known him less than twelve hours.

Nic shrugged and turned to me. "What do you say? I promise to be a gentleman."

Sheer madness. I'd rather sleep in a bathtub than share a bed with a man I hardly knew, no matter how charming he was. Without skipping a beat, though, I replied smoothly, "Oh, that won't be necessary." I turned to Jacinda, smiling politely. "Mr.

Hoterson will take the room. I will sleep in my wagon, if that is amenable to you."

Nic touched my shoulder. "Are you sure? It's going to be chilly tonight."

I nodded. "I sleep in there all the time. Besides, I have Grimm to keep me warm." And this way I could sleep as a cat without fear of discovery. There was no way I could share a room, let alone a bed, with this practical stranger of a man.

Jacinda nodded. "Of course, miss. Normally we wouldn't let guests sleep in their vehicles, but given the circumstances ..."

"Excellent! It's settled," I declared, sealing the deal before Nic could further protest.

He only nodded, resigned. "Very well. You *will* dine with me for dinner, though, won't you?"

Now that he had mentioned it, I *was* incredibly hungry. It was past the time I normally ate, but traveling often made for strange mealtimes.

"Of course. I'm famished." Which meant that I wasn't the only one. I leaned toward the front desk receptionist. "Do you allow dogs inside?"

The dining room at the inn was surprisingly roomy, with multiple tables lining the walls, plus two larger tables and chairs taking up space in the middle. Like the rest of the establishment, this room did not skimp on light. A decorous wooden chandelier hung in the center, and sconces of a similar design lined the walls.

Nic led me to a smaller table off to the left. I sat first at Nic's insistence, and Grimm—who was allowed in given Nic's apparent influence—stationed himself by my side.

As soon as Nic sat opposite me, a buxom older woman approached our table. She was lacking the polite smile that Jacinda was so proficient at, but it was clear there was a family resemblance between the two women.

The woman grabbed a pen from behind her ear, causing part of her messy gray-and-blonde bun to unravel further. She took no mind of her hair. "What can I get you folks?" she asked, before doing a double take upon seeing Grimm. She watched him warily.

I studied the single page of the menu that had been on the table. The choices were few: simple travel fare for tired travelers.

Nic answered first. "The stew for me, please. And an ale. Cressida?"

"Does the stew contain onions or garlic?" I asked, looking up at the woman.

She stopped staring at Grimm and looked at me, frowning at my question. "Yes to both."

I nodded. I had thought of ordering a bowl for Grimm, but both ingredients were toxic to him. "Thank you. I'd like the stew as well, please. Could I trouble you for some boneless meat for the dog, though? I'll pay, of course."

"I've got it, Cressida," Nic butted in. He turned to the waitress. "As the lady requested, please. A good portion of stew meat scraps, perhaps?" He ended his request with his charming smile.

Our server's face bloomed with a smile of her own for the first time since meeting her. "Of course, sir. Won't be a problem. Miss, did you want an ale as well?"

I shuddered slightly, remembering the first and last time I'd had alcohol to drink. I vowed never again. "No thank you," I said carefully. "I'd like an herbal tea if it's no trouble." I smiled at her.

My smile did not have the same effect as Nic's. She only grunted before answering. "Coming right up."

Once she left, I had an opportunity to survey the room. Jacinda had been right; the inn *was* busy, if the activity in the dining room was an accurate indication. In a far corner, an elderly man and woman dined together, focusing on their food rather than chatting. Across from us on the far wall, four men crowded around a table, conversing in low tones. Behind Nic, another four men ate in silence. I could not see a single face from the way they were sitting, but I thought they might be related, as all four had the same shade of black hair. And as we waited for our food, three more men entered and sat at one of the central tables, closer to us.

This new table kept shooting us small glances as they ordered a round of beers. These covert peeks made me uneasy, although I couldn't pinpoint the exact cause of my consternation. After all, I was used to being the center of attention. My platinum blonde hair with the two black streaks at the temples garnered looks no matter where I went, and the large shaggy beast at my feet didn't help either.

I was more than thankful when our food arrived, taking my attention away from the oddness of the table near us, as it was making me feel squirmy. Nic, who seemed oblivious to the stares, thanked our server and dug in with obvious relish.

As soon as the smell of the stew hit my nose, I dug in too. It was thick, rich and meaty, with crudely cut potatoes, carrots, celery, and onions. It could have used a little more seasoning, but I was too hungry to care.

Nic paused his eating to take a drink from his mug. "Not a drinker?" he asked conversationally.

I paused my spoon and swallowed the bite in my mouth. "No, not really. I don't care for the way it tastes, or the way it makes me feel."

He cocked his head. "It's an acquired taste, for sure. But part of the appeal is the way it makes you feel." He thoughtfully studied me. "I hope it doesn't bother you that—"

The room plunged into darkness. Every single light powered off in the blink of an eye.

"What in the hell?" I asked, my heart leaping into my throat. My eyes, normally fine-tuned for night vision, were slow to respond after the previous brightness. Several voices made similar inquiries in the blackness around me.

"Cressida, are you okay?" I heard Nic ask me, his voice laced with worry.

The lights flickered, sending phantom images into my brain, before turning back on fully. Some of the folks in the room had stood up, looking ruffled over the unexpected blackout. Nic's hand was halfway across the table, as if he had been seeking me out in the darkness.

Nic retracted his hand and let out a shaky breath. "That was strange."

I also blew out a breath of nervous laughter. "What was that?"

"Seems like the free energy got disrupted for a moment."

I wracked my memories for a similar occurrence. None came to mind. "Has this ever happened to you before?"

Nic thought for a moment. "Not that I can remember. But I'm sure it has. Electricity can be a fickle thing. Now, what were we talking about before all that?"

Apparently, Nic was ready to dismiss the entire episode. It surprised me that he could be so cavalier about the electricity going haywire. The free energy, a gift from a dimensional traveler some one hundred years ago, was known for its untiring stability, as long as everyone used it prudently. There were laws in place about how much electricity each manufactured item could use, and these practices had led to there always being enough energy available at all times. A complete and utter shutoff of power simply did not happen, despite what Nic had said. But I rolled with his comment, not wanting to make a scene. Especially not with a close audience like we currently had.

So, what *had* we been talking about?

Oh yes. "You were asking me about drinking."

"That's right. I was just about to say, does it bother you to be in my presence while I drink?"

It was such a mundane thing to ask after the temporary excitement. "Not a bit," I assured him.

Nic nodded. "Glad to hear it. I'm not a heavy drinker or anything, but I like to unwind at the end of the day. I guess I assumed most young people felt the same way."

I shrugged. "Guess not. Um, do you know those men over there?" I asked, lowering my voice and quickly pointing with my head.

Nic covertly surveyed the room. "Never seen them before. Why?"

I glanced over at the group, inadvertently making eye contact with a shorter man with shaggy hair the color of straw. He had a scar that crossed his forehead in a diagonal line; it puckered one eyebrow up into a permanent quirk. There was no frown or smile on his countenance, just a passive stare as our eyes met. Despite the lack of expression on his face, I felt a wave of menace from the stare. Whether or not I imagined this, I broke eye contact first.

"They keep looking over here," I responded quietly as I finger combed my hair to hide the half of my face closest to them.

Nic chuckled. "Can you blame them? I mean, not to sound like a creep, but you're a very attractive woman. Even that old guy in the corner noticed you when we walked in."

Somehow, his response did not help me to feel at ease. I'd been stared at and hit on before. This was not the same. But clearly

Nic wasn't about to understand why I was rattled. Hell, I didn't exactly understand it, either. I decided to drop the matter with a shrug of my shoulders, finishing my stew quickly in relative silence.

CHAPTER 14

I decided to turn in for the night after our meal concluded. Over the past six months, I had spent less time than usual as a human, and I could tell that my resilience to the effects of longer periods of wearing this body had diminished because of it. I was tired and achy, and more than ready to call it a day.

Nic was understanding, even if he did not know the full reason for my exhaustion. He only insisted that I make use of his bathroom to complete my ablutions before I turned in. I humored him and took the opportunity to relieve my bladder in relative warmth instead of the cool wetness of the surrounding woods. After that, I puttered around in the bathroom until sufficient time had passed.

Nic also requested that he escort me to the wagon.

"I'll be fine. I have Grimm with me," I countered. Grimm, standing at my heels, puffed up his chest to look more commanding.

Nic eyed him with appreciation. "Of course," he said and splayed out his hands. "But I'd feel much better if I went out with you anyway."

"Suit yourself," I said with a shrug. Arguing with the man was proving to be tiresome. It must have been the lawyer in him coming out.

The wagon was parked next to the multiple MCs in the small lot in front of the stable. Humbert had been taken care of by the stable hand and was probably content in his stall. The lights in the parking lot still blazed brightly, which would have been annoying to sleep through, but my wagon had no windows save for the small hatch behind the driving seat, so the interior would be pleasantly dark.

"Have a good night, Nic," I said as I unlocked the back of the wagon and allowed Grimm to jump in first. I crawled in after him.

"Sleep well. We'll want to get an early start tomorrow. Will you be awake at six for breakfast with me?" His hand lingered on the open door that I was about to shut.

I chuckled. "I'm an early riser. That works for me."

The glow of the parking lot lights behind Nic meant that his face was in shadow, but my eyes could still detect that boyish smile he wore. "Until breakfast, then," he responded. He removed his hand slowly, as if reluctant to leave, before backing up and turning to walk back into the inn.

I latched the door, not waiting to watch him enter the building. I fished a key out of my vest pocket and locked the doors by feel, not bothering to turn on the lamp. Lastly, I made sure the hatch was open just enough for a small cat to squeeze through. Just in case.

All that was left to do was shed my human form and don one that was much more comfortable. With a quick shimmer, I was myself again, and I took a moment to bask in the feeling.

Grimm padded over to the mattress on the floor and sank down on it. I joined him, seeking out the divot created by his belly and legs, my favorite spot to curl up into for sleep.

His chest heaved and moved me like a ship at sea. "What an odd day," he commented. "What's the plan for tomorrow?"

I stretched out an arm with a purr-infused sigh, sinking into his canine warmth further. "Early morning start," I replied. "Let's get some sleep. I don't know about you, but I'm exhausted."

Grimm was not as tired as I was, however. "You've spent more time around Nic now. How are you finding him?"

"Hmm. He's nice. Polite, ever the gentleman. He did offer to share a bed with me."

"He *what*?" Grimm lifted his head up rigidly.

I placed a paw on his leg and pressed my claw tips ever so slightly. "Chill, buddy. It was only because there were no other available beds. Again, the chivalry thing."

Grimm flopped his head back down. "I'm not so sure that's what his intention was. Sounds more like he's looking for a mate."

I tucked my paw back in. "Humans usually require a lot more pomp and courtship before getting to that. I've known Nic for a day. I don't think he wants to marry me, for Freya's sake."

"That's the second time you've mentioned this concept in so many days, yet no one I know is married. Can you explain this 'marriage' thing again? And how do you know he doesn't want to do it? Doesn't that mean he wants to mark you?"

I flicked an ear in amusement. "I suppose it *is* akin to marking one's territory. Except it's a mutual marking, a 'hands off' to other potential suitors, and it's supposed to be permanent. Once a person marries, they should only ever mate with their spouse. And Nic just met me. Marriage happens when two people really get to know each other. Even then, not all humans go through with the ritual, instead choosing to be faithful to their partners without a wedding, but I think I'd like to get married ... eventually."

A small pang of pain rattled in my chest, a reminder of Annie Coddle's curse upon me. The pain had lessened over the months ever since my experimentation with Gavin had failed utterly, but I couldn't tell if it was a true diminution, or if I was simply used to the constant, dull pain. Either way, I had no inclination to go through testing the curse's boundaries again, as charming as Nic could be. Still, any time the thought of finding my true love flitted through my mind, the curse would give a little flair, a tiny hint that it was still alive and kicking, lest I get any ideas.

"Don't worry, partner," I told Grimm with a yawn. "I have no desire to make out with this one."

Grimm let out a chuff. "Thank the gods for small favors."

I was out like a light and dreaming.

My dreams were often about hunting rodents or running through fields. Sometimes my dream-self climbed trees to chase birds into the sky, as my paws ran upon thin air. Cat fantasies, all of them. On incredibly rare occasions, I dreamed I was human.

This night was one of those occasions.

I walked through a forest, a common event. But this wood had a different feel than the ones I was used to. The trees were ancient and draped in shrouds of moss and lichen. The forest floor was packed with bushes: salal and huckleberry, thimbleberry and salmonberry. The ground was covered in ferns and sorrel, the three-leafed plants resembling giant emerald green clover.

I would have been hard-pressed to push my way through this dense foliage, if not for the path I stood upon. The way forward was obvious, but I stayed still, apprehensive about where the path might lead.

But suddenly, with the extraordinary logic only beholden to dreams, I knew I was being hunted. A bloom of alarm unfolded in my midsection. I ran down the path, away from the feeling of sharp eyes upon my back.

As I hurried down the trail, the greenness of the woods desaturated until I stood in whiteness. The foliage had disappeared. I turned in a tight circle, trying to find the path again, but it had blended into the bland surroundings.

In front of me, a shape appeared. It was tall, humanoid, but vague, as if I viewed it through a thick membrane. All I knew was that it searched for me but could not get to me.

And then the screaming began.

I thought it was the being before me, screaming from frustration, but the sound snapped me from my dream, and the screaming continued.

Fear, my jumbled mind registered from the sound. *Pain.* Equine pain, I realized, now that I was awake.

"Humbert!" I cried out as I sprang up, shimmering instantly.

Grimm was also awake and alert, although I could barely see him in the darkness. I hurried over to the doors, fumbling in my pocket for the key. Like I was still stuck in my dream, I moved far too slow, but my fingers finally clutched it. I moved to unlock the latch.

The screaming continued. Human shouts of anger and fear joined the background noise.

The key finally turned and I flung both doors wide. Near-blackness greeted me, a far cry from the brilliant outdoor lights that had flooded the area when I had gone to bed. The inn windows were also dark, with not a single electric light to be seen. The only light came from the nearly full moon, which glowed with an unusual orange cast.

The free energy had been cut off again.

Wasting no time on such trivial matters, Grimm rushed out and I jumped down from the wagon to assess what needed to be done.

Grimm didn't wait for instructions from me. He didn't need any. I watched him race toward the stable, his black form a blur in the near darkness.

I made to follow him, but a shape loomed out of the shadows of the lot, no more than ten feet away from me. My mind flashed to my dream, that same feeling of being hunted. But this was no dream stalker.

It was a werewolf. Covered in gray fur and standing upright, it towered over my petite frame by two feet. Its eyes gleamed in the moonlight. And it had its sights set on me.

Grimm's snarls came from within the stable, along with scuffling; he must have already engaged in battle with someone or something. He would not come to my aid fast enough to stop this lycanthrope that leered menacingly at me. It was too near, and Grimm was too far away.

I was on my own.

But that never stymied me before.

I stopped and reached down into my boot, grasping Hail Mary II and crouching for the impending brawl. The werewolf let out a snarl in my direction before dropping to all fours and charging me. I waited until it was almost upon me, and then I threw myself to the side in a quick roll. I recovered my footing and raked the knife outward, catching the monster with a passing blow and giving it a shallow scratch along its back leg.

I prayed to Freya it was enough.

The werewolf stopped its trajectory once it realized its prey had outmaneuvered it. It turned, locking eyes with me, and roared in fury. Its muscled hind legs bunched to spring at me.

I threw Hail Mary II as hard as I could at the lycanthrope. The aim didn't matter.

The knife flew true and buried itself into the neck of the werewolf.

The monster flinched at the impact, reaching up a clawed hand to paw at the knife's hilt. It gurgled as blood trickled out of its mouth.

I stood then, watching as the massive beast collapsed and stilled. Then, the hairy body began to shrink, until all that stood in its place was a naked man, quite dead and covered with a scarlet splash of his own blood.

I blew out a breath and went to retrieve my knife. The charm was now depleted, making it an ordinary weapon once more, but it was better to have ordinary protection than nothing at all.

I refused to look at the man I had just killed. Normally, I did everything in my power to prevent a werewolf's death. After all, most werewolves were created by accident. Lycanthropy was viewed as a magical disease, easily infecting humans who came into contact with a werewolf's saliva. This malaise turned an infected person into a killing machine, even if normally the person was sweet and docile by nature. So, despite the necessity of this particular killing, I still felt a modicum of guilt as I grasped the handle of my knife and extracted it from the dead man's throat.

As soon as I had my knife back in hand, the sounds of battle once more reached my ears. The screaming of the horses had stopped, but people in the distance yelled or shrieked in fright. And from the stable I could once again hear the fearsome growling and barking of Grimm as he fought his own enemy.

A second werewolf, I wagered.

I started to run that way.

"Cressida!"

I stopped at the sound of Nic's voice from behind me. I turned as he ran over, his white shirt unbuttoned and flapping in the breeze, and his pants barely on. He must have thrown his clothes on quickly to venture out into the melee.

"Are you alright?" he asked me breathlessly once he reached me.

I nodded, then realized he probably couldn't see the gesture. "I'm fine. A werewolf attacked me. I think another is in the stable with Grimm. I need to help him!"

"Cressida, wait—" Nic began, but I had already turned to run into the stable, having waited too long already to check on my partner.

The stable interior was darker still than the open lot, but the small amount of moonlight that trickled in was enough to make out the fight happening at the end of the line of stalls. Grimm surged around the second werewolf, snapping and biting with intensity. The larger monster tried to claw and bite back, but Grimm was too fast.

Lycanhunds, bred for this specific reason, had a magic running in their veins that began to nullify the lycanthropy as they fought the werewolf. The longer the two factions warred, the weaker the werewolf became, until eventually it would give up the fight and turn back into a human against its will.

This werewolf must have been a particularly strong individual, because Grimm was having to work especially hard to best it, with the confrontation taking longer than usual. Even so, I could see that Grimm was slowly gaining the upper hand.

My partner was a marvel to watch, but I needed to be smart about this. I quickly backtracked out of the stable, intent on running to the wagon for the silver shackles I kept in there.

My fascination with watching Grimm's battle had distracted me. As I made it back into the moonlight, I nearly ran head-on into a third werewolf.

This one loomed in front of me, its too-long arms wide as if it meant to embrace me. I gripped the knife in my hand, prepared for the worst.

The werewolf suddenly yelped in pain as its body shuddered forward a fraction and its head tilted up to the night sky. Confused, I watched it slump in front of me and morph back to human, seemingly dead.

Once its body was on the ground, I looked past where it had stood. Nic was in the distance, his right arm raised as if he had just shot the beast. I heard no gunshot, nor did I see a weapon in his hand before he lowered it, but perhaps the near-death experience had deafened my ears temporarily.

I shook off the perplexity of the moment and rushed to the wagon for my intended mission. Grabbing the shackles, I sprinted to the stable, where Grimm had finally gotten the best of the beast, and he gripped the whining werewolf by the nape of its neck.

"Good job, Grimm," I praised as I clamped the biggest shackle around the neck, once Grimm had moved slightly for easier access. It was a maneuver we both had plenty of practice in.

Once the neck shackle was secure, I swiftly added the two wrist shackles, making sure to place them behind the lycanthrope's back. During this time, the monster went limp, passing out from the pain of Grimm's teeth in its neck combined with the contact with silver. With the final cuff in place, the werewolf began his transformation back to a man.

I breathed a heavy sigh once the creature was fully a naked human again. Grimm leaned into my side where I crouched, lending his silent support. I placed an arm over his back, cringing slightly as I touched a wet spot and hoping it was spittle and not blood.

At least I didn't have to worry about contracting lycanthropy. Having been born a cat and not a human, I was immune to the disease. Silver linings and all.

A dim light flickered overhead and then turned on, casting the room in a soft glow. I stood, taking in my surroundings with new detail.

Blood droplets tracked down the length of the aisle, ending where the naked man now lay. Upon further inspection, I discovered blood on his hands and surrounding his mouth as well, as if his werewolf counterpart had been busy clawing and biting some poor victim.

For a short moment I thought it might be Grimm's blood, but he seemed fine.

A horse whickered weakly from a nearby stall.

That was when I recalled that the horses had been screaming. They were silent now.

"Humbert," I breathed, and shot to my feet to check the stalls.

Most were empty. One had an incredibly frightened horse that rolled its eyes and tossed its white head when I came into view. It was seemingly unharmed, so I left it to go to the next stall, which had been bashed open.

I stopped in the shattered doorway, too overcome to move.

Humbert lay on his side, his back end facing me. Four deep gashes had been carved into his dappled flank. His chest rose and fell, but otherwise he was unmoving.

He let out a small groan, and that got me focused. I rushed in, careful of his legs. The front ones looked a bit battered, with ragged bloody scores crisscrossing their lengths. Skirting around them, I fell to my knees next to his great gray head.

His face had taken a beating as well. Bite marks appeared upon his lips, which bled freely. More scratches tracked across his long muzzle and up his forehead, dangerously close to the one eye I could see. This eye was open, and when he saw me, he tried to lift his head.

"Shh, it's alright," I soothed at the horse, cradling his massive skull in my hands to still its movement. Humbert obliged and rested again. His nostrils flared with each pained breath, and he let out a little grumble of distress as I stroked his forelock. This sound, while seemingly insignificant, shot straight through my heart. I choked back a sob as I ran my hands down his neck to try to find more damage.

The good news was that the lacerations on his side were the worst of his injuries. The bad news was that those by themselves were enough to cause me concern. Each breath he took opened the gashes slightly, enough to allow a trickle of blood to ooze out. It was obvious that while this wasn't life threatening by itself, it needed doctoring as soon as possible.

I sighed and pushed the hair out of my face, smearing Humbert's blood into it in the process.

I needed Lyle.

"How is he?"

I jumped at Nic's voice behind me. I turned to look at him. He had managed to button his shirt and tuck it into his pants. I pursed my lips. "He'll live if I can get a doctor to him, but I'm afraid he's officially out of the journey no matter what."

Nic hummed in his throat. "And what about you? And Grimm?"

I blinked. Other than a brief glance after his fight, I hadn't yet assessed Grimm's state. Now was the perfect opportunity, however. I crouched to his level to begin my inspection. Grimm wagged his tail—a bit morose, perhaps—but seemed in good spirits. Running my hands along both sides of his body did not reveal any wounds, just more flecks of spittle and a little blood that had transferred from the werewolf.

"He's fine, thank Freya," I murmured.

"And you?" Nic insisted.

I shook my head but smiled with weariness. "I'm fine too. No wounds."

"You sure?"

"Yes." I fumbled in my pocket, looking for my message mirror. "But I need to get Humbert a vet. I'm calling a friend."

"It's one in the morning," Nic pointed out.

"Doesn't matter." I pulled the mirror from my pocket. "Humbert needs help as soon as possible."

I opened the mirror case, writing quickly, "WEREWOLF ATTACK. HUMBERT INJURED AND NEEDS HELP. PLEASE COME ASAP. AT DOUGLAS INN ON RT 62, PAST KOUSA."

I only hoped that Lyle kept his mirror by his bedside so that the vibrations would wake him up.

A human groan came from the stable corridor. Grimm perked his ears and ran out of the stall. Nic and I followed.

The nude man stirred, flipping to his back as he moaned. Naked lycanthropes in human form were a hazard of the job, but it gave me ample practice in the art of not looking south of the belly button. I put these practices to use as I shuffled closer, getting a good look at the man's face for the first time.

It was the blond man with the forehead scar who made eye contact with me at dinner.

"What's this?" Nic asked.

I glanced at the lawyer. "This is the werewolf Grimm fought. Does he look familiar?"

Nic nodded. "I suppose you were right to be suspicious of that group after all."

He marched past me, walking up to the man. Nic's face hardened into an expression I had not yet witnessed on him: pure loathing. He held out his hand, palm out. A curious silver glow formed in his palm. "Scum," he said, his voice laced with poison.

The man fully opened his eyes. Alarm bloomed within them. "No, wait—"

The silver light shot from Nic's palm and hit the naked man squarely in the chest. Tendrils of silvery dust rose into the air upon impact. The man gasped, his muscles constricting as he curled in on himself, and then his whole body flopped once like a ragdoll before coming to rest.

"What did you do?" I asked with dawning horror. The man's eyes were open, lifeless.

Nic wiped his palm on his pants. "What needed to happen."

"You killed him?" I accused, my voice ratcheting up to a higher pitch. "Why would you do that?"

Nic scrutinized me, his expression neutral. "He attacked you. Tried to kill your horse."

"As a werewolf!" I yelled. "Everyone knows that the actions of werewolves do not reflect the actions of the humans they usually are! You can't condemn a man to death because of the werewolf inside of him."

"You did, though; you killed one of the werewolves yourself."

I scrubbed a hand down my face in agitation. "That werewolf was trying to kill me," I explained as calmly as I could. "It was a matter of self-defense. This man—he was neutralized. He couldn't do anything to harm us. He was locked in silver, for Freya's sake! Besides, I was hoping to ask him some questions. He could have been cured with a wolfsbane potion. How could you?" I blurted, losing my cool again. "You told me you're not a killer."

Nic shook his head, chagrined. "I'm not. But I don't count werewolves as human. I only see them as a threat to be wiped out. I apologize, Cressida. I didn't think; I only acted. I'm only trying to keep you safe."

A nervous guffaw slipped out of me. "I can handle myself, thank you very much."

Nic's face scrunched into a dubious look. "You can say that all you want, but you were two seconds away from getting mauled by that other werewolf out there. I killed him before he could get to you."

"With what, exactly? You have magic?" I had never seen the silver light before from any magic user.

Nic nodded. "Yes. It's rare. I can concentrate it in my palm, and with enough juice, it's deadly. But I can only use it if I think I'm in danger. My dad has a mild form of it, not enough to kill. But my mom is a powerful witch, so her powers must have amplified the gift." He looked sheepish. "I'm sorry I didn't mention it before. I'm not proud of it, and I didn't think I would need to use it while I was with you." He smiled, the dimple flashing. "Forgive me?"

The knot of panic and agitation loosened at the sight of his apologetic smile. Of course he wouldn't want to advertise the fact that he could kill with a bolt of magic. "Very well. I forgive you. But please rethink your stance on werewolves. I've hunted a lot of them, and most are incredibly remorseful for their crimes once they are in the right headspace again. They're people; they most likely didn't choose to become monsters."

Nic thought on my words. "Oh, my little unicorn. Kind to animals and werewolves alike. Now, I would normally agree with you," he said. "But in this case, there's something off about these particular lycanthropes."

"What do you mean?" I asked.

Nic ushered me to the stable entrance and pointed up into the sky. "It's not a full moon yet."

CHAPTER 15

I processed Nic's words as I stared at the moon.

It was true that people afflicted with lycanthropy could morph into werewolves for about three nights each cycle—when the moon was at its fullest.

But as I had noted earlier in the night, this moon was decidedly not yet full. It was missing a significant sliver on one side.

Werewolves could not change during gibbous moons. I knew that as a hard fact.

Except these three had.

I shivered at the unnatural turn of events. "How?"

"Are you asking me how they could change before the full moon?" Nic clarified. "It's unprecedented for sure. It's a Hunter's moon, so perhaps they gained extra strength this month."

I quickly flipped through my mental file about moons. The Hunter's moon was always the first full moon after the fall equinox. It was also strikingly larger than it appeared in other cycles. Many witches claimed that these factors made it one of the most powerful full moons within any given year, used to amplify their magical abilities temporarily. But could werewolves glean this much extra power as to allow them to transform days earlier than usual?

Based upon my time and experience as a bounty hunter, no.

"Nic, I've been hunting werewolves for the last two and a half years. Including during Hunter's moons. I've never seen this before."

"Well ..." Nic ran a hand through his hair, which was already unkempt from sleep.

I dropped my eyes from the moon, looking out over the courtyard of the inn. Now that the attack was over and the werewolves were dead, a hush had fallen. People stood in small groups, talking nervously as they stared at the two obviously dead men lying where they had fallen. No one wanted to approach them.

"We need to burn the bodies," Nic said, changing the topic. He too had turned his attention to the corpses.

"Why?" I asked.

He turned to me, incredulous. "To prevent their bodily fluids from infecting anyone else. Lycanthropy is highly contagious. How can you hunt werewolves and not know this?"

"I know how contagious it is!" I countered with a frown. "Again, though, Grimm and I capture them *alive*. I have never had to burn a body before."

"Hmm. Good point. I forgot about your secret weapon against the lycanthropes. Your dog is quite something, isn't he?" Nic rubbed his chin in thought.

I nodded. "It's not surprising, though, given that Grimm was bred to take them down."

More people emerged from the inn, looking fearful. Nic strode closer to the bodies, and to the groups standing around. I chased after him, knowing that he was still intent upon this gruesome task.

"Nic, wait." I grasped his arm, causing him to turn around. "It's not right to simply burn them. The authorities should be involved. Perhaps they can identify the men."

Nic smiled at me in a condescending manner. "Cressida, I understand that you are used to working alongside the authorities in such a manner. But here, in the middle of nowhere? People take matters into their own hands."

I frowned, annoyed at his words. "Do they, though? Nic, I'm known for my werewolf hunting skills. These small villages ask for me by name if they are having a werewolf problem. I think I know how things are usually done, even out 'in the middle of nowhere.'" I couldn't help the snark that filtered into my words.

If it was one thing that got my goat, it was being talked down to. Especially by a man. And doubly so for a man who did not have the same level of knowledge as me.

But Nic didn't seem to notice my rising irascibility. He only smiled kindly again, and rubbed my arm in a soothing fashion. "Oh, Cressida. Can you trust me on this one? I'd hate for anyone to become infected, given the amount of werewolf bodies here. It would be a mess, especially so close to the full moon time."

Dammit, he had a point. Besides, who knew how long it would take for any law officers to get here? I nodded, letting go of his arm. My temper cooled.

He brushed a strand of my hair from my face with a serene smile. "That's my unicorn. Kind, beautiful, *and* incredibly brave. You are a badass."

I blushed at the compliment, still uneasy at his words but warming up to them as well, despite myself.

Nic turned back to the crowd. "People, we need to burn the bodies to prevent spread. I'll need some strong individuals to carry them into a pile. We'll have to be mindful of their saliva. Do we have any firestarters among us?"

Two men volunteered their assistance, including the owner of the inn. No one seemed to possess the ability to conjure fire, but the innkeeper allowed Nic to use the everlasting flame located in the dining room to burn the bodies. The flame was enhanced to burn extra hot, so it would be able to handle the cremation with no issues.

I was not needed here. I went back inside the stable to check on Humbert, having no interest in the goings-on outside. Grimm, ever faithful, followed at my heels. I stopped at the stall door, noting that it had been badly damaged and would not close. Blast. I wanted to talk with my ailing horse employee in privacy.

I turned to Grimm. "Will you be my lookout? I need to talk to Humbert."

Grimm let out a whuff and stationed himself at the door, looking toward the exit.

I carefully approached the fallen horse, crouched by his head and shimmered.

"Humbert, how do you feel?" I asked him as soon as my feline body materialized.

"Well, Mistress, I hurt like the dickens. I should have fought the werewolf off, but I didn't have room to turn. I guess that's it for me. Sorry to have let you down."

I placed a paw on the bridge of his muzzle, gently so as not to hurt him further. "You've done nothing of the sort, and this isn't the end. I regret to say that you won't be able to pull the wagon for a while, but I'll get you patched up, one way or another. Hang in there, okay?"

"Yes, Mistress." He let out a blowing grunt of discomfort.

"Company, Cress!" Grimm said with a sharp bark.

I transformed immediately. Nic popped around the corner two seconds later.

"Did Grimm just bark at me?" he asked, then shook his head to brush off the question. "Cressida, good news: I've found a veterinarian to help your horse."

"You did?" My heart lifted at his announcement. Lyle still hadn't gotten back to me, and despite what I just told the horse, I worried about Humbert's health deteriorating overnight.

A tall, thin man with small glasses perched on his nose rounded the stall door. He looked a bit disheveled, probably woken from sleep due to the werewolves, along with everyone else. He carried a black bag in his hand.

The man entered the stall and crouched next to me. His eyes lit up as they met mine, an almost exuberant shine. But the rest of his face did not match, and he only gave me a pitying smile and held out a hand.

"I'm Dr. Orcutt. This is the patient, I presume?"

"Yes. Thank you, Dr. Orcutt. Cressida," I said, shaking his hand with appreciation.

He let go of my hand and placed his bag on the ground. The veterinarian found a pair of gloves in his bag and put them on, and then he began tenderly touching some of the wounds on Humbert's face. "Happy to help, young lady. It's a matter of luck that I'm on my way east to visit my daughter, and I needed to stop for the night."

Dr. Orcutt made his way down Humbert's body, noting the various injuries. The wounds on his side were still the worst of them, but half of the horse was hidden from view as he lay prone. With Nic's and my help, the three of us managed to get Humbert standing again. Luckily, no other injuries presented themselves, but his flank began freely bleeding with the change in position.

The doctor worked quickly, applying some healing pastes to the gashes and smaller wounds, and wrapping the horse's midsection to prevent further bleeding. I stayed and helped, mostly by holding Humbert's head still and murmuring soothing words to him to keep him steady while Orcutt did his mending. My assistance in this manner was purely ornamental; if Humbert had wanted to, he could have flung me across the room with his giant head. But my horse employee was a gentle soul, and he stayed still for me while the doctor tended to his wounds.

Nic bounced between checking on us and monitoring the disposal of the bodies in the parking lot. The air filled with the smell of charring flesh. Knowing what was making the scent, it mentally sickened me, but my body reacted traitorously to the smell, and my stomach grumbled loudly, much to my embarrassment.

Dr. Orcutt heard the noise. He patted my hand when I looked chagrined at my body's reaction. "Don't worry, my dear," he said with compassion. "It's a common response of the body to such smells. *You* may know it's human flesh you are smelling, but your body simply can't differentiate between that or a good steak."

By the time the vet had finished his ministrations, it was close to three in the morning. The excitement of the battle had worn down, and most of the inn's guests had gone back to bed. Only Nic and the two helpers stayed up to finish their task of lycanthropic cremation.

I walked outside for the first time since the doctor had joined me. I had gotten used to the scent in the air and thankfully no longer reacted to it. The bodies on the pyre were almost completely turned to ash.

Nic noticed me and approached. His shirt was liberally smeared with soot, as was his face. He tried to smile, but it came across as more of a grimace.

"We're nearly done here. How's Humbert?"

"Patched up. Dr. Orcutt wants him to stay here for a few days." I said, ending with a wide yawn.

Nic's face softened. "You should get some sleep."

I shook my head. "What about Humbert? What are we going to do?" I still needed to get to the coast to stop Elkins from hurting Wren. I couldn't afford to hang around here until Humbert had healed.

Nic looked beyond me. I turned to see Dr. Orcutt approaching us, his gait betraying his fatigue.

"Doctor, what's the word?" Nic asked him.

Dr. Orcutt removed his glasses and polished them on his sleeve. "The horse will heal, but he shouldn't walk anywhere for at least a few days. I unfortunately can't stay for that long, although I'm willing to stick around for most of the morning. But he's stable—pardon the pun—for the next few hours, at least. The stable boy said he'd keep an eye on him for the rest of the night."

I worried at my lip, trying to think through the tired fog. "I can't fault you for leaving, Doctor. I'm just grateful you were here in the first place. I'll try to contact my friend again and let him know. He's a vet, too."

Orcutt nodded in agreement. "An excellent plan, young lady. Now ..." He looked down at Grimm, who had stuck to me like glue throughout the last two hours. "What about the Lycanhund?"

I frowned. "What about him?"

"Was he injured in the fight? While I'm still here, does he need medical assistance?"

"Oh." I locked eyes with Grimm, who licked his lips anxiously. "I already looked him over. I couldn't find any wounds. I think he's fine."

Dr. Orcutt raised an eyebrow. "Are you quite sure? I could give him a thorough examination while you sleep. It's possible he received internal injuries."

The words alarmed me, but I rationalized them away. "I'd like to keep him close, if it's all the same to you. He'd tell me if he was in pain."

"Would he?" the veterinarian mused. "And what about the dried fluids on his body?"

"What about them?" I asked, trying to keep the edge of irritation from coloring my words.

Orcutt peered at Grimm through narrowed eyes. "Is it blood, or is it saliva? It's difficult to discern in this low light with his black fur. But if it's saliva, he could very well be spreading the disease to anyone he comes into contact with."

I suppressed the eye roll. "Doctor, I appreciate your concern, but the saliva on Grimm is the safest werewolf spit you'll find. Grimm's magic has by now nullified the lycanthropy. It's just normal drool at this point."

Dr. Orcutt pursed his lips. "I see. I've not gotten a chance to study a Lycanhund before, so I was not aware. Very well, then. But don't take his health too lightly. You say that your dog would let you know if he was injured, but dogs are notorious for hiding deadly wounds." He looked over at Nic with a serious expression. "It might be best if the dog were to stay behind with the horse to heal."

I laughed, a quick little chortle that was driven more by exhaustion and nerves than true mirth. Frankly, it irked me that the doctor would think that Nic had any authority over what happened with my partner. "Thank you, Doctor, but Grimm stays with me."

"Then I bid you a good night. Or a good morning, as the case may be." The vet tipped his head at us with a small smile and trudged into the inn.

Nic turned to me. "Get some sleep, Cressida. It will only be for a few hours before we leave."

"How exactly are we leaving? We've just lost our mode of transportation."

He sighed. "Leave that to me. You two get some rest. I'll wake you up when it's time to go."

There was nothing more to do than to send a quick message to Lyle, explaining that Humbert would need his assistance come daylight, but was currently okay. Lyle clearly didn't have his mirror on him but would hopefully see the message when he awoke in the next few hours.

Having done that, I wearily crawled back into the wagon, shutting the doors and locking them once Grimm and I were both inside. I transformed.

"Are you hurt anywhere?" I asked Grimm as soon as we could properly communicate.

"I'm fine, just like I always am. But thanks for asking. What a wild experience." Grimm nuzzled my head with his snout in affection.

I did a quick groom, despite my weariness. I had gotten a good portion of Humbert's blood on me while fixing him up, enough to leave an iron tang in my mouth as I licked my fur clean. "The doctor was worried about you. He thought you should stay behind."

Grimm snorted. "Not bloody likely! Did you tell him to piss off?"

I cuddled into Grimm's warmth. "Of course not. He *did* help us patch Humbert up, after all. I wasn't about to insult the man. Anyway, I'm too tired to think. Get some sleep."

Grimm lowered his head, resting it alongside mine so that our cheeks touched. With the warmth his shaggy body gave off, I swiftly fell into a dreamless sleep.

CHAPTER 16

An intrusive banging jerked me from my slumber. I panicked, jumping up with all claws out and sprinting from the sound. Only after I had crouched in the far corner of the wagon did I realize it was someone knocking on the doors.

"Cressida, are you up? It's time to get going!" Nic's voice filtered through the wood.

I willed my heart to slow to a more normal pace before walking over to the doors. As I passed Grimm, I noticed he was in a defensive posture, his head facing the sound. Apparently, he had been as surprised as I had been.

"At ease, soldier," I quipped before morphing into my human counterpart. I found the key in my pocket and unlocked the doors, carefully opening the left-hand side to peer out.

The sky was still a deep navy blue, with no hint of sun. "Nic, what time is it?"

"6:30. I know, I let us sleep in a bit. But I figured it was needed."

"6:30?" I repeated, my brain still not fully clicked on. "A.m. or p.m.?" This time of year, both options were depressingly dark.

"It's morning, silly. You didn't think I'd let us sleep all day, did you?"

I rubbed a hand down my face. "I honestly don't know what you're capable of. I've just met you, remember?"

He chuckled. "Go ahead and pack up your things. I took the liberty of grabbing you some breakfast. I already have everything I need loaded up."

I crawled down from the wagon. "Loaded up in what?" I asked, confused as he began to guide me away from my vehicle. Grimm jumped down and matched our pace, his steps more jaunty than mine. "The wagon's already packed, but we can't—"

"Not the wagon, of course," Nic interrupted me. "I was able to secure a rental MC for the rest of the journey."

I stopped walking. I had a small hatred for MCs, mainly due to the high-pitched hum that was clear as day for me, but imperceptible to humans. I wasn't thrilled by the prospect of riding in one. "You did?"

"I did." Nic gently nudged my arm with his hand to get me walking again. "It's a bonus, if you ask me."

"Why's that?"

He paused in front of a sedan style MC. Painted a shiny midnight blue, the vehicle sported four doors and a sleek cab devoid of sharp angles, the antithesis of my boxy wagon. As appealing as the design was, I hated it for what it stood for: the abandonment of my employee.

Nic opened the trunk, displaying his luggage inside. "What do you think? Not to belittle your wagon, but this baby will get us to the coast much faster. By the end of tomorrow, I calculate. Sooner, if we take turns driving."

"Oh, I don't know how to drive," I said, feeling suddenly small.

Nic stared at me. "No? Well, no worries. We'll spend a night camping. Hopefully it will be more restful than last night."

I nodded absently, his last words barely sinking in. Humbert was on my mind. I patted my vest pockets, looking for my message mirror. It should have been vibrating the moment I regained my human form if Lyle had messaged me back. I frowned at the implication.

Patting the pockets did not yield results, so I reached a hand into one to search for the magical item.

"What are you looking for?" Nic asked, noticing my increasingly frantic movement.

"My message mirror," I replied with a scowl. Still no sign of it, and I was running out of pockets to check.

"Oh! You left it in the stall. I checked it for you; your friend responded that he would be here around eight this morning."

"You read my message?" I asked, a trickle of displeasure coloring my words.

Nic guiltily looked away for a second. "I apologize. You were so tired; I figured I'd be doing you a favor. I made sure to place your mirror with my luggage so that you wouldn't forget it." He grinned apologetically.

I smiled back automatically. "Of course. No, you're right; it wasn't too personal a message. No harm done."

Grimm looked between us, his ears pricked up. I ignored him.

Nic patted me on the shoulder. "Well, we should really get on the road. Humbert will be in good hands; Dr. Orcutt said he'd stay until your friend gets here. Go get packed and you can eat in the car."

I heaved a sigh, still a tad bewildered by the rushed morning. I'd do as Nic said, but first, I needed to see for myself that Humbert was doing well.

He nickered at me when he saw me walk into the stall. The stable boy had moved him into a different apartment, one with a working door. The floor was covered in fresh straw, and Humbert munched on a mouthful of hay with contentment, his nicked lips working perfectly. I wished that I could speak with the old horse one last time before I left, but Dr. Orcutt was there, monitoring his patient.

"Cressida, good morning. I trust you got some sleep?" he greeted me politely.

I smiled at him. "As much as I could. I just wanted to see Humbert before we left. Thanks again for helping us."

He waved a hand, a smile of his own making his face look fatherly. "Think nothing of it, my dear. Happy to help."

I patted Humbert on the nose, careful to avoid the many healing cuts and bite marks. "So long, Humbert," I told him. "You'll be in good hands while I'm gone."

I absolutely hated leaving Humbert and my wagon behind. Sure, the horse was old, and the wagon even older, but they were an integral part of my identity. It felt wrong to just abandon them.

But we could not have stuck around at the inn waiting for Humbert to heal. I needed to get to the bottom of the killings before Wren became another victim. And Nic was right; the MC was a much faster alternative.

But even with the mechanized vehicle, going was slow. Once we got into the thick of the forest, the road quality decreased, and Nic was forced to drive only slightly faster than a horse could pull a wagon. I was honestly flabbergasted that such an important road would be so poorly maintained, but perhaps this was normal. After all, I'd never been this far west before.

Halfway through the day we reached the first hills of the Serenic Coast Mountain Range, a collection of incredibly ancient mountains that separated the expansive valley in the east from the Oracune coast to the west. I assumed that at one point these mountains had been a mighty sight to behold, but the eons had slowly diminished their stately nature to smaller, gentler peaks. Nevertheless, the chill increased as Nic drove us to higher altitudes.

On top of that, the weather decided to become fickle once again, and we went through bouts of rain showers. The biggest downside to my wagon was the lack of cover from the elements. Being inside the waterproof cab of the MC was admittedly a huge bonus.

I spent the time in a bit of a sleep-deprived fog. I was still exhausted from the excitement of the previous night, but napping was out of the question, as it was simply too uncomfortable to do in my human form. To add another stress layer to my fatigue-addled brain, I was also worried about Humbert, and made the decision to message Lyle for an update once we stopped for the night. Perhaps then my anxiety would simmer down a bit.

The windshield wipers let out a squeak as the rain cleared up into a fine mist. The noise startled me from my reverie, and I twisted forward in my seat.

Nic switched them off and sighed. "Apologies, Cressida."

"For the squeaky wipers? I wasn't sleeping."

"No, not that. This trip is going slower than I thought. I was hoping to reach the summit before we stopped today, but at this rate, it won't happen."

"It's fine." I gazed back out the window, watching the endless forest. Skeletal limbs draped with moss reached toward the road as we drove through. Evergreens in the fall weather always reminded me of specters, despite how green and alive they were. "As you pointed out, we'd be in the same situation in my wagon."

"True, but—"

I lurched forward unexpectedly as Nic slammed on the brakes, stopping the MC with a slight squeal of the tires. The seatbelt prevented me from traveling into the dashboard, but it painfully bit into my chest.

"What—" I began, but Nic pointed at the road before us.

Another MC blocked our path, all four doors open. I squinted. I could just make out the forms of people in the seats, although they appeared to be asleep. A chill passed through me. There was something unnatural about this scene.

Nic unbuckled himself. "Stay here."

I unlatched my own buckle. "I don't think so. I'm coming too."

I let myself out of the vehicle, opening Grimm's backseat door as well. Cautiously, the three of us approached the MC.

The smell hit me well before we came close to the vehicle: a metallic tang in the air that curdled into rust in my nostrils. Fresh blood.

We reached the back half of the MC, with Grimm and I peering in through the open right-hand door, and Nic taking the left. Both sides offered the same scene in the back seat: two men, their heads thrown back, their throats nothing but bloody, gaping wounds.

"Freya's furs," I muttered, covering my mouth with my hand.

Nic ventured to the front seats, in which two more dead men sat, also with torn-out throats.

Grimm growled deeply, as unsettled as Nic and I were.

"What could have done this?" I asked. "Werewolves?"

Nic pursed his lips as he stared at one of the corpses. "Not likely. The wound is fresh, and," he placed a hand on the closest man's chest, "this one's still slightly warm. This just happened within the hour, I'd say. Even enhanced werewolves can't be active during daylight hours."

I looked at the men, studying their faces. "Nic, these men were at the inn as well."

He glanced at me. "How do you know?"

"They were in the dining room, behind you in the corner. I didn't think anything of them at the time, except that they could be related, since they all had dark hair. I didn't get a look at their faces, however. But now I know why I thought that." I took another look at them. They all had frozen expressions of pain or anguish upon their faces, but their facial features were unmarred. Now that I saw them, I could tell they weren't related at all; they only shared similar coloration. "They're Tyonoshimese."

"It would appear so." Nic ran a hand through his hair.

As I stared at the fresh corpses, my mind whirred. I thought back to when the fox was telling me about how she needed to help Kokoro. While I couldn't remember the exact words, it was something along the lines of stopping the men from doing her harm.

Well, they surely couldn't hurt anyone in their current state. I had a sneaking suspicion I knew who was responsible for their deaths.

As if to cement that idea, from the forest behind me I heard the unmistakable laughter of the fox, close enough to send goose-bumps down my arms. Grimm pricked his ears forward, honing in on the direction the sound came from. He let out a warning chuff.

"What was that?" Nic asked, looking around.

I made a choice not to alert him to the fox. I couldn't say why; my gut simply told me to keep it to myself. "These woods are full of wildlife. It was probably a jay."

Grimm apparently couldn't wait to go investigate. He let out another chuff and ran straight into the underbrush by the side of the road.

"Grimm!" I yelled after him. He took no notice. I began to follow.

"Woah, woah, woah, are you crazy?" Nic said, running over to try to stop me. "There might be a killer on the loose. You can't just go running off into the woods!"

I scoffed. "I'll be perfectly safe with Grimm around. Stay here. I'll be back." Without waiting for more admonishments, I turned and made my way through the bushes after Grimm.

Nic did not follow.

Once I was a safe distance away, I shimmered down. "Grimm! Where are you?" I called out as I tracked his scent through the wild growth.

I sensed her before I saw her, that potent magic infiltrating the air around me. I pushed my way through one last bush and found myself in a tiny clearing. At the far edge, Kitty sat daintily in front of Grimm, who looked down on her with interest. I must have interrupted a conversation between the two canids. Kitty turned her head in a smooth motion to watch my entrance.

"Well, hello again, Cousin," she practically purred.

"Kitty. Why are you here?" The old resentment resurfaced, although it was tempered by the new knowledge I had gathered since her absence.

"Just telling your handsome friend how handsome he is." Kitty stood and began a slow saunter around Grimm, who looked uncertain as he stayed still to allow the fox her perusal. His tail gave a couple of thumps on the forest floor.

I wanted to roll my eyes. She was playing the seductress again. "What about the four dead men out there on the road? Was that you?"

"Oh yes. How kind of you to notice."

"*Why* did you kill them?" I asked in my nicest tone. She would not get under my skin. Not this time.

Kitty stopped her sauntering to stare at me with her unnaturally intelligent slitted eyes. "It's simple. Those four men were the right hands of Inaba Ebiru. They did his bidding for his business, and they also helped him keep his wife in line. And when I killed Ebiru, they each swore to avenge his death. But they targeted Kokoro, not me. An oversight perhaps, using her body to kill him. Regardless, I promised to save Kokoro. Their deaths were necessary. And there are still more to go before my vow to deliver Kokoro into the palms of freedom is fulfilled."

I flicked my tail. "Right. Well. I suppose I didn't understand *how* you'd be keeping her safe from those particular men. I figured prison or something. But I can see you are more of the vengeful spirit sort. Carry on?"

She bowed her head. "So kind of you to give me permission."

"Listen, Kitty. Why didn't you tell me that Kokoro's life was in danger because of you? If I had known that a failure to help her could end in her death, I might have reacted differently to your request."

The fox cocked her head to the side. "Oh, but I did. You simply chose not to listen. Sometimes an ego can block the path of words to our hearts. What difference does it make if Kokoro's death comes at the hands of men like the ones on the road, or from my inaction? The result is the same. But it is no matter. You chose, and now we must forge our own journeys. I can guarantee something, however. Our paths *will* cross again soon, Cousin. Grimm," she cooed, sashaying up to the dog and giving him a small lick on the chin, for which he stood statue-still, "let me know if you would like to switch partners for a spell. It could be ... illuminating."

I bristled at her tone, but Grimm merely said, "I'm good, thanks."

"Suit yourself." Kitty gave me one last look before darting into the surrounding brush and out of sight.

Grimm seemed to come out of a spell. "Is it just me, or is she frightening?"

I continued to watch where she had disappeared. "Frightening is not the word I would use. But she's something, all right." I gave my head a brisk shake. "Come on. Let's go back to Nic."

CHAPTER 17

We decided to leave the bodies in the MC, but pushed the vehicle to the side of the road so that ours could pass. Nic was in a rush to get over the mountains, and neither of us had the energy to do anything else with the corpses. He assured me it would be fine to leave them as they were, as someone else would eventually stumble upon them and dispose of them properly. This inaction on my part made me feel like a slimeball, but I trusted his words.

Kitty's assurance that those men had been up to no good did something to assuage the guilt I felt over simply leaving their corpses. While I had initially not been able to trust her, something had changed inside of me. What with Fleurette's affection toward the woman, and Gavin's harrowing new information about fox possession, I was now Team Kokoro all the way. Even if that meant turning a blind eye to the blatant murder performed by the magical fox. That creature was not afraid of leaving a wake of carnage in her path, apparently. She was a vicious, bloodthirsty animal, and in a way, it made me feel better about the human she was possessing and protecting.

And so, we continued our journey through the mountains, albeit a little greener around the gills, perhaps.

The gray sky gave way to autumn darkness soon enough. By six in the evening the headlights were our only source of light. By seven, Nic let out a beleaguered sigh.

"I think we need to call it a night," he said. "I'm exhausted, and I need to eat."

"Fine by me," I agreed. I needed to get out and stretch my legs.

As soon as a decent pull-out spot appeared, Nic parked the MC. The storms that had plagued our trip during the day had luckily moved on, but they had left the area soaked with rain. Each drop glistened in the light of the headlamps as we fished out sandwiches for dinner from the supplies in the trunk.

Grimm took his sandwich gently from my hand and trotted off to eat. I began to follow, scouting for a log or rock to rest upon while I ate, but realized that every surface was soaking wet. It may not have bothered the dog, but I was not looking forward to a damp behind in this body, so I clambered back into the interior of the cab, and Nic followed suit. As starving as we were, we focused on our food, the only break in silence coming from our individual chewing. I had no idea what was on Nic's mind, but mine? Mainly just one thing.

"Where are we sleeping?" I asked abruptly. If he thought we'd be sharing another bed, he had another think coming.

Nic swallowed his bite of sandwich before replying. "Um, I brought a tent. I assumed we'd be camping out at least a couple of nights on this trip. It's big enough for two people—"

I suppressed a groan.

"But you can use it if you like. I'll sleep in here."

Oh. "Are you sure?"

He rubbed the back of his neck. "Sure. I assumed I'd be the one in the tent when we still had the wagon, but the tent is roomier than this MC, so you should share it with Grimm."

"That makes sense. Thanks, Nic." I stuffed the last bit of sandwich in my mouth and opened the vehicle door, ready to set up the tent.

"Oh, are we doing this now?" he asked with uncertainty.

I looked back at him in the dim interior of the MC. "Sorry. It's been a long day and I'm exhausted."

"All good, all good," he assured me as he opened his own door.

He got the tent out of the back, and together we set it up next to the MC. It was a small white thing, waterproof, I noted with gratitude, and just large enough for two people to lie side by side. Or as the case was, a person-slash-cat and a large dog to lie together.

Once the tent was set up, there was one last thing I wanted to do before turning in. "Nic, can you find my mirror?"

Nic paused. "What mirror?"

"My message mirror. You told me you stashed it in the trunk after I left it in the stable. I wanted to check in with Lyle to see how Humbert is doing."

"Did I say that?" Nic scratched his chin, thinking. "I was so out of it this morning, after the night we had."

I nodded, a bubble of irritation growing in my chest. "Yes, you did. Can you find it, please?"

Nic turned and began rooting around in the trunk. After a few minutes without results, I joined his side and began searching for it myself.

Five minutes after that, Nic said, "I'm sorry, Cressida. I can't seem to find it. I thought I put it in this bag, but it's not there."

"Keep looking," I urged.

Another five minutes slipped by. The two of us had searched every single bag. The mirror was not there.

Nic was chagrined. "I am so sorry, Cressida. I could swear I put it in here. It must have slipped out before we left the inn."

I pursed my lips in frustration. "You don't happen to have one on hand, do you?"

He shook his head. "Sorry."

I frowned. "What about the one you had at your house?"

He threw up his hands. "I don't have it. I must have left it at home."

I opened my mouth to argue that I had seen him place it in his pocket, but he seemed so incredibly sure that he no longer had it. Arguing over whether or not it was on his person would accomplish nothing. More than anything, I wanted to yell at him for losing my only link with Humbert, but I tried to keep my cool.

Nic must have noticed my agitation. He reached out and rubbed my shoulder. "Hey," he said soothingly, "I'll make it up to you. I know those things aren't cheap. Forgive me?"

His touch calmed me down. Of course, he didn't mean to misplace my mirror. After the brouhaha with the werewolves, and the lack of sleep it caused, it was only natural for mistakes to be made. I couldn't hold it against Nic.

"There's nothing to forgive," I replied, forcing myself to smile. "It was an accident. Last night was crazy. It's fine."

All the while, Grimm followed this exchange with questioning eyes. I watched him for a few seconds before turning to Nic with a defeated slump. "Well, I guess I'll turn in, then."

In the tent, I waited until Nic turned off the headlights of the MC before shimmering into my cat form. I did not wish to broadcast that transformation through shadow play.

Grimm must have been waiting patiently for this because he instantly accosted me. "Cress, I've been thinking."

I stretched and began a quick groom of myself. "What about?"

"About last night. I stayed up later than you, going over some things in my head."

"Like what?" I paused my grooming, focusing on my partner.

"Like ... why wouldn't Nic tell us about his powers? It seems like something important to know beforehand."

"Oh. Well, why didn't I tell him about *my* powers? Because it's my secret to keep. Besides, it's obvious that he's ashamed of it."

Grimm let out a soft growl. "That's another thing. You keep defending him. Twice today, I watched you get angry at Nic's actions. And twice, instead of justifying your anger, instead it just ... dissipated."

"What, you expect me to hold a grudge?" I lowered my ears.

"Frankly? Yes. I know you, Cressida. I can read you like people read books. You tend to hold on to your anger and let it go slowly. Not all at once like an untied balloon."

"Are you saying I have anger issues?" My tail flicked from side to side.

"I'm saying that's just how you are." Grimm pawed at the space between us. "Yes, you have a temper. I've seen it flare up many times during this trip, and yet you just let it go whenever it's directed at Nic."

I crouched back, away from the dog. "Here we go. Is this another jealousy issue?"

Grimm stood, insulted. "Are you really throwing that in my face? The answer is no. Not a bit. I can tell you are not interested in Nic. And I feel like I was justified to feel jealous the last time with Gavin, seeing as how you acted on your attraction."

"It was one lousy necking session!" I retorted, letting my tail fully lash. I sat on my haunches. "Emphasis on the lousy, in case you needed that reminder."

The big lug tried to pace in the tent, but mostly marched in place with agitation. "Be that as it may, let's not pretend that you are immune to jealousy, either. I see how you react when Kitty flirts with me."

"Because the fox likes to get under my skin." I snarled. "I'm only worried about her using you to hurt me. You can be such a dense hairball sometimes."

"Well, I can be concerned for you *without* being jealous, despite what you imply. I was only trying to tell you that something is different about you. But, judging from the name-calling and feline stubbornness you are currently exhibiting, I can see that you aren't willing to be mature about it."

"I can't believe you are making a big deal out of this, you fat-headed mop!" I hissed.

Grimm tucked his ears back. "I can't believe you aren't making a bigger deal out of it!" he retorted. "Have you forgotten that we were attacked by werewolves last night? Werewolves that had no business being werewolves at this moon phase?" He turned to the opening of the tent. "Speaking of, I think I'd rather stand guard outside in the cold and the rain than be in here with you right now. You can dig your heels in and call me names all you want. It doesn't change the fact that something is off, and we'd best be alert for it. Think about that. Get some sleep."

"You'd rather be outside in the cold than in here with me? I don't need guarding, Grimm!"

"Cressida, you are a walking disaster sometimes. Guarding you is the least I can do. Let's not forget the mess you found yourself in the last time I wasn't around." Grimm stared at me, his eyes glinting in the dark.

"It was a mess I was making my way out of on my own just fine, thank you very much," I retorted with another tail lash.

Grimm snorted angrily. "Whatever you need to tell yourself. But hey, if you think you can handle everything on your own, maybe I should just leave."

"Well, go on, then! Nobody's stopping you!" I yelled at his backside.

Grimm did not bother to get the last word in. He nudged the flaps of the tent aside, squeezing out without another word and leaving me alone, holding onto a grudge, just like he said I usually did.

I may have gone to bed angry, but the edge wore off quickly. I tucked in, just my small cat self on a rollout sleeping mattress, wondering when Grimm would finally come back inside. But my feline pride wouldn't allow for me to go and get him, knowing that he was justified in the things he said.

Instead, I fell asleep from pure exhaustion, and had a similar dream to the previous night, where an unseen figure stalked me through the ancient woods, the path before me ending in whiteness. The humanoid shape loomed nearby once again, all but hidden by a barrier. It wanted in. It wanted me.

I awoke with a start, noting that the quality of light filtering through the white tent had shifted to an early morning dimness. If my eyes weren't deceiving me, I had slept through the night. I stretched my legs, feeling a definite and unusual chill about my small body. It was an odd sensation, I realized, but I couldn't pinpoint why. Not until I actually looked at my surroundings.

Grimm was absent.

His great body always kept me warm at night, like a black shaggy comforter. But there was no sign of him, not even a dent in the bedding to indicate he had been here.

My mind flipped to last night: the argument we had, his abrupt departure from the tent. I knew that directly after he and I parted ways, he had stationed himself outside of the structure, because I could hear him shuffling about near the doorway. He had still been there by the time exhaustion had pulled me under. But I also had expected him to come back inside halfway through the night. We always cuddled together. Besides, he knew I couldn't stay mad at him for very long. He meant too much to me.

At least, I assumed he knew that.

I shimmered, regaining my human form to go and see if he was still asleep outside of the tent. Folding back the flaps, I poked my head out.

It was still decently dark, but the sky was gray with the beginnings of a gloomy fall day. It was more than enough light for me to scan my surroundings. And my eyes saw no sign of a shaggy black dog.

"Grimm?" I called out softly, hoping that he had simply wandered into the nearby trees to investigate something. I crawled out of the tent, hugging myself to keep the sudden chill from invading my body.

I called out a couple more times, but there was no response. After the fourth shout, I heard one of the MC doors open behind me.

I swiveled to face Nic as he got out of the vehicle. "Have you seen Grimm?" I asked without preamble.

Nic stopped short. "I assumed he was with you last night."

I shook my head, fear beginning to grab ahold of my chest. "He ... was restless last night. I think he was worried about more werewolves. He seemed to want to stand guard in front of the tent."

Nic ran a hand through his unkempt hair. "I'm sure he's around. Does he wander?"

I bit my lower lip, thinking. "Sometimes, yes. He often hunts for himself when we travel."

Nic snapped his fingers. "Then I'll bet that's where he is. I can't imagine sandwiches are all that filling for a big beast like that. We'll just give him a little time to come back. Come get some breakfast while we wait."

I was worried, but what Nic said made a lot of sense. Grimm did often wander far away, arriving back at the wagon after as much as an hour sometimes.

I ate breakfast and we broke down the tent, stowing everything away. By that time, the sky had lightened considerably, and Nic was anxious to get on the road. But Grimm was still missing.

Now the fear gnawed at my belly like carnivorous caterpillars. "Grimm!" I called out, hoping he would hear me. I walked out to the road, where perhaps the break in the trees would allow my voice to carry even farther. "*Grimm!*" I yelled as loudly as I could.

Only a Steller's jay answered me with a mocking screech.

I looked down at the ground, trying to rein in my bubbling emotions. My eyes caught on something: mud near the road's shoulder. Three large canine footprints were left behind. They pointed in the direction we had already traveled.

But hey, if you think you can handle everything on your own, maybe I should just leave. Grimm's last words besieged me. Could he truly have been serious?

Even then, I refused to give up. He could have chosen to depart only moments before I got up. He could still come back.

Nic allowed me to scream my partner's name for the next ten minutes before he finally placed a gentle hand on my arm.

"Cressida, we need to get going. I'm sure Grimm is fine; he probably decided to leave on his own."

Tears streamed down my face as I nodded. In my heart, I knew the truth.

Kitty's words came back to haunt me. *I know Grimm is incredibly loyal to you, and you don't deserve his devotion.*

I hadn't deserved his devotion, and I finally managed to push him away.

Grimm was gone. And it was all my fault.

CHAPTER 18

I was not a pleasant companion that morning. Nic dutifully drove the MC through the thick forest and all I did was silently cry and stare out of the window. The road conditions still had not improved, so the going was painfully slow. And yet, I couldn't find it in myself to care.

Grimm had left me. That was all that mattered.

I should have seen it coming. I knew that Grimm had been incredibly unhappy when I chose to work alongside Gavin last March, passing up him, my real partner, for a temporary one. But I thought I had patched things up after the dust had settled.

Grimm had assured me he wasn't jealous of Nic. After I had time to reflect upon our argument last night, I believed him. After all, I had no interest in the man as a romantic partner, not like I had, in retrospect, with Gavin. But perhaps Grimm had been lying to me. Or to himself.

I assumed Grimm was loyal to a fault. He had never given me a moment's pause before, even despite our issues last March. I should have known not to take that loyalty for granted.

The damn fox Kitty had even warned me about how I didn't deserve Grimm. And she knew everything, I was beginning to understand.

I was an idiot.

I stopped crying three hours into the journey. Nic looked over at me, a pitying smile on his face. "Chin up, Cressida. We're about to crest the peak, and then it's all downhill from there. You'll get your first glimpse of the ocean today."

I frowned. "The ocean can stuff it."

He chuckled at my sullen statement. "Of course it can. Listen. Animals are fickle. I once had a bird, a lovely little budgie that my father bought for me on one of his trips. I was rather lonely, you see, since both of my parents worked a lot. My mother didn't even live with us, so I rarely saw her. My budgie was a pretty little green thing I called Fay. Her wings were clipped when I first got her, and she was very tame. She would perch on my finger or my shoulder any chance she got. I took her everywhere with me—any room of the house, and outside in the garden—and she dutifully stuck by my side. And then one day when we were outside, she realized her feathers had grown out and she could fly again. She took off into the sky, and even though I yelled after her and begged her to come back, I never saw her again. It broke my little eight-year-old heart."

Despite thinking my eyes had been fully wrung of tears, they prickled anew with a fresh batch as I thought of little kid Nic losing what he thought was his best friend. "I'm sorry."

Nic waved the sentiment away. "The point is, I thought my love was enough to keep Fay with me. But it wasn't. Grimm saw an opportunity for freedom, and he took it."

I choked on a sob.

Nic reached out and grasped my hand. I let him, seeking some sort of physical comfort. "You still have me," he said.

I didn't say anything. Replacing Grimm with Nic was not a trade I would have willingly done. But, not wishing to hurt Nic's feelings, I only squeezed his hand.

We reached the peak of the mountain range shortly after, and then began our descent. At first, the view was blocked by trees, trees, and more trees, but as the MC slowly chugged downhill, a perfect break in the tree line materialized that allowed us to see for miles.

It wasn't much, but off in the distance I could see a thin, gray line on the horizon.

"Is that ...?" I began to ask.

"Yes," Nic confirmed without needing the full question. "The ocean."

For the first time that day, my heart pounded with something other than sorrow: a deep curiosity, a thrill of the unknown.

Before I could explore that feeling further, the MC's engine stilled, ceasing its constant drone, and the vehicle rolled to a standstill.

"Why did you stop?" I asked Nic.

He shook his head, perplexed. "I didn't. I lost power."

MCs ran on free energy, same as the electric lights. I shared a look with Nic. Another outage?

Nic undid his safety belt and opened his door. "What are you doing?" I asked him.

He got out, turned, and bent down to frame his head with the door opening. "I'm going to see if I can find what's causing the drain," he said. "Care to join me?"

I hesitated. I could sit in this MC by myself and hope it restarted, but then again, if the driver was absent, a working MC was still useless. The other option was to get off my sad and sorry butt, move some muscles, and get my mind off Grimm. When I pitched it that way, the choice was obvious.

"Fine," I agreed.

Nic and I wandered off the road to the left, an arbitrary direction chosen by the lawyer. Oddly enough, there *was* a path here; it was no more than a defunct deer trail, but it served well enough to break the dense foliage at the side of the road. Still, the vegetation was thick here. Waxy salal leaves brushed against my legs with every step I took on the path.

As we followed the trail, I began to hear a hum, reminiscent of an MC's engine. At first it was so slight that I thought my ears were ringing, but the farther we traveled away from the road, the more persistent it became.

I finally placed a hand on Nic's shoulder to halt his step. "Do you hear that?"

He frowned and froze to listen, craning his head to the side. "What is it that I'm supposed to hear?" he asked after a pause.

"An electrical hum. You can't hear it?"

He shook his head. "No, but I believe you. Why don't you take the lead and follow the noise?"

An excellent idea, I thought. He moved off the path enough to allow me to pass, and then we continued our walk.

The humming persisted and grew in strength the deeper we ventured. I was just feeling the urge to cover my ears from the intrusive sound when our path opened up, ending in an old, human-made clearing. I dared not venture out into this open space in case someone was around. Besides, I was rooted to the spot with trepidation.

A giant metallic tower took up the center of the clearing.

It was at least twenty feet high, with a strange ball-like appendage at the very top. And it was definitely what was responsible for the horrific hum.

"What *is* that?" I whispered.

Nic placed a hand on my shoulder. I wanted to shrug it away, but I stayed still. "It must be one of those antennas I told you about. From Tyonoshima," he answered, his voice sounding awed. "I'll bet that's what is gobbling up the free energy in the area. Even I can hear the hum now."

"*That's* what is causing the blackouts?" I asked. "But we must be miles from the inn. Surely it can't be drawing that much energy."

Nic didn't take his eyes off the metal tower. "Maybe there's more than one."

"But for what purpose? What could they possibly need that much electricity for?" If this truly was the work of the ACF, I doubted it was for a worthy purpose. But my mind blanked when I tried to think of what the massive amount of energy could be feeding.

Nic didn't answer me. He instead began walking toward the antenna.

"Nic, what are you doing?" I hissed at him, worried that bad guys would leap from the bushes at any moment, despite the evidence that we were alone. This tower had made me paranoid.

He waved me over to follow him. "Relax, nobody is here. I want to see if there's a way to shut it off."

I refused to move away from the brush line. Nic ignored my petulance, focusing his attention upon the technological monolith. He reached out a hand. The tower made an angry thrumming noise.

"*Stop!*" I yelled before he could touch it. My vivid imagination dredged up abhorrent images of Nic being fried to a crisp by the sheer electrical output.

Luckily, the scene stayed only in my mind, for Nic heeded my warning. He turned to me, a strange smile playing upon his face. "This thing is absolutely packed with energy. It *has* to be what's causing the blackouts. And look, over there." He pointed. "There's a small shed."

I followed his finger with my eyes. Sure enough, there was a small outbuilding perched at the far edge of the clearing. Its wooden construction blended in nicely with the surrounding woods.

Nic came back over to me and tried to take my hand. I politely resisted. "Come on," he wheedled. "Let's see if there's something in the shed that will shut this off. Then, hopefully, we can be on our way again."

"Are you sure?" I asked, my voice small.

Nic smiled, flashing his dimple at me. I relaxed. "Sure, I'm sure."

The shed resided on top of a secured crawlspace, so there were three steps to get to the solid door, which we found unlocked. But it was quite dark inside. No windows. I shivered despite myself and hung back from the space.

Nic peeked his head in. "I'm going in. You can stay out here."

I nodded, the trepidation still anchoring me to the spot in front of the steps.

Nic opened the door fully and walked in, looking for some sort of illumination.

The door slammed shut behind him.

"Nic!" I shouted.

His voice came to me heavily muffled. "Cressida, did you close the door?"

"No! It shut on its own!"

He let out a swear word I could barely make out. "Can you open it?"

I bounded up the steps and grabbed the handle. Try as I might, it would not budge. "It's stuck fast!"

Nic tried the door from his side as well, but he had no luck either. I began to panic.

"Cressida, see if there's a … switch … or something around the shed. It's getting hot in here and I'm having trouble breathing!"

Oh, hairy hairballs. I ran around the perimeter of the shed, seeking some sort of entryway or anything that might magically open the door again. The only thing that was possibly accessible was a small door at the back of the shed's crawlspace.

I fell to my knees and opened it. Instead of an open crawlspace spanning the area of the shed, the door opened to a shaft, like I had seen for ventilation. Perhaps there was a way to at least vent the shed to temporarily help Nic.

"Cressida, help! It's getting bad in here!" He sounded desperate.

"Hang on, Nic! I think I found something!"

It would fit a small person, but I wasn't taking any chances with becoming stuck in that shaft as a clumsy human. A smaller body was the way to go. At least for a quick look in there, I surmised.

I transformed and raced into the shaft. The walls were smooth and metallic, but otherwise unremarkable. I kept going.

A wall of metal shot up from the bottom of the shaft in front of my nose. I jumped back in terror, raking my back against the roof, and ramming into a second wall that must have risen behind me. In utter panic, I pinged off the walls of this new mini room like a stray bullet. I could no longer think clearly, but instinct told me to do whatever was necessary to get out of this prison.

Meanwhile, Nic, above me, began yelling for me with increasing distress. There was no way for me to answer back; the shaft's new dimensions made the space much too small for a human.

I crouched, panting, and tried to think. Tried and failed.

A flash of purple invaded my vision.

"Sleep."
And then, nothing but the abyss of oblivion.

CHAPTER 19

C old. I was so cold.

I opened my eyes.

Metal bars surrounded me.

I clumsily jumped back, pushing myself into a corner and crouching to make myself as small as I could. I wrapped my tail around me, an inefficient safety blanket considering this nightmarish episode.

Where was I?

The cold metal at my back dug into my spine, and the floor's chill seeped into my paw pads. The only area of this cage that held any warmth was in the spot I had recently been sleeping.

My toes felt funny. I thought it might be due to the freezing metal, but my feet had been in cold spots before. This oddness seemed to sprout from the tips, where my claw sheaths resided. I picked up my right paw, flipped it over, and extended my claws.

Each claw was trimmed down to the quick.

In horror, I checked my left paw, only to discover the same treatment. And—yep, my back claws were all dull nubs as well.

I had never once had my claws clipped. I took pride in my natural weapons and kept them neatly sharpened at all times. Now, they were so short that the edges ached where the quick was too exposed on some toes.

A new emotion, that of righteous anger, added to my over-whelming fear. I looked around. Yes, I was truly surrounded by bars, in a kennel that measured sixteen inches wide by twenty inches long, at my best guess. It was only tall enough to allow my feline form to stand without ducking.

There would be no shapeshifting while I was in here. I'd prob-ably break my legs or my back even trying it out.

All four sides of the cage consisted of the same sturdy bars, but a blanket had been draped over the top of the enclosure, blocking my ability to see past the barriers in any direction except the very front, which, upon closer inspection, appeared to be the door.

I studied this next, creeping forward on silent paws. The bars were barely wide enough to snake an arm through them. Perhaps I could unlatch the door and escape that way. The latch seemed simple enough; the crude design would stymie a mundane cat, for sure, but whoever put me in this cage knew they weren't dealing with a mundane cat. There was a lock on the latch.

"Double drat!" I said to myself.

Looking out of the front bars, I surveyed the room I found myself in. It was the size of a bedroom, with walls the color of burnt orange, and dark wood floors. Bookshelves lined the wall across from me, but they were largely empty. In fact, the room itself was mostly devoid of furniture, save for a rather ominous table in the middle of the room, a stand next to the table upon which rested several surgical instruments, and a secretary desk and rolling chair in one corner.

And my cage, of course. I assumed the kennel was resting upon something, because my view was elevated above the ground. But from my vantage point, I could not see what it was.

"Ah, awake at last, I see."

The voice startled me anew and sent me into the far corner once again, my ears folded back in distress. I knew that voice.

Gregory Elkins strode into view, looking more or less the same as he did the last time I saw him. Silver hair, manicured beard, striking blue eyes. Even his suit exuded style and class. A silver fox, by anyone's definition.

But I was aware of the rotten soul that the perfectly groomed exterior held.

He crouched a few inches to view me fully. I growled, a thin threat even to my own ears.

He ignored my vocalization. "You've been asleep for more than twenty-four hours. My magic sometimes has that effect. A pleasure to see you again, Miss Curtain." He chuckled. "Of course, you look a bit different than I recall. More furry." He smiled widely at his joke.

I hissed.

His smile rearranged into a tight-lipped grimace. "No, if I had only known exactly what I had that last time, things would be very, very different. But it wasn't until you had already escaped that Althea informed me of my mistake. By that time, of course, you were long gone."

I refused to take my eyes from the man, and my ears were as flat as they could go. Another growl sounded in my throat.

"Cat got your tongue?" Elkins quipped. "My apologies for the one-sided conversation, my dear. But this is the form we need you in. I'm not taking any chances in allowing you to carry out your side of the discussion as you would see fit. You see, six months ago I wanted to wring your little neck." His cadence turned angry with a hint of a growl as his face morphed into a terrifying scowl. Then his features turned pleasant again. "But as it stands, there's a new plan for you. Otherwise, you'd already be dead. Alas, I was outvoted."

A door opened off to my right. Elkins straightened.

"Ah, Doctor, Althea. Good timing. Our little patient is awake, and as feisty as ever."

Another male form walked into my sight range. He was too tall for me to see his face from my corner. And behind him came Fleurette's mother.

I was unlikely to forget her face, as similar as it was to her daughter's. Althea had changed, though, since I last saw her. She had deeper wrinkles on her pale face, and a more haggard countenance than I remembered. Her long platinum hair was tied back in a braid that traveled down to her mid back. She hunched her shoulders and did not make eye contact with anyone. She looked like a woman who had given up on the joys life could offer.

The man that had entered with her responded to Elkins. "Good news, sir. When would you like to proceed?"

Elkins bent again to peer at me, like a child at a zoo. I wanted to scratch his eyes out, but I neither would have been fast enough, nor would my claws have done the trick in their current state. "Tomorrow morning. Will that be sufficient time?"

The other man bent to join Elkins in watching me. My eyes widened and my ears perked forward for the briefest of moments, disbelieving what—or who—I saw.

Dr. Orcutt, his small glasses still perched on his fatherly face, gave me a sad smile. "I'll have everything necessary by then, sir."

My heart sank. Dr. Orcutt had been so helpful, so kind back at the inn. Was it all a lie?

Elkins straightened and clapped the veterinarian on the back. "Good man, Orcutt. I'll have Althea help you with the surgery as well. Isn't that right, Althea?"

She nodded automatically, still refusing to lift her gaze. "Of course, Greg."

Elkins gave me one last examination, the glee of having me here evident in his twinkling eyes. "Miss Curtain, believe me when

I say that it's truly a pleasure to see you again." He gave me a significant look and then left the room.

Althea, in the background, finally lifted her head to look at me. I still crouched in the corner, fearing for my safety. I had no clue what to expect from the woman. When we first met, she had planned to kill me on the spot, but she changed her mind just as suddenly and let me go. This meeting was just as unpredictable.

I expected her to say something, but after watching me cower for a minute, she shook her head and left without a word, leaving me alone with Dr. Orcutt.

Orcutt still stared at me, wide-eyed with wonder. Now that he was the only person left, I tracked every movement he made, refusing to even blink. I may have trusted him once, but clearly I had been a fool to do so.

He cleared his throat when I refused to settle. "Cressida, it's hard to believe it's actually you. I'm ... sorry for the subterfuge. You seem like a nice lady. Cat. Whatever. But sacrifices must be made in order to create the world we are striving for. Annie Coddle's return will be worth the pain, I assure you."

Pain? I did not like the sound of that.

"It's a simple operation, really. I've performed it on numerous cats. And dogs. And I'll make sure you are asleep for the surgery. You won't feel a thing until you wake up."

I really did not like the sound of *that.*

Orcutt looked abashed. I couldn't tell if it was because he truly was sorry for me, or if he felt self-conscious having a one-sided conversation with a cat.

Anyway," he continued, "your sterilization is absolutely necessary for the start of the new order."

Sterilization? I *definitely* didn't like the sound of that.

Orcutt gave me one last smile. "Get some rest, Cressida. Your spay will happen in the morning."

CHAPTER 20

I knew I had been in sticky situations before. I had nearly died when Annie tried to fry me with lightning a year ago. Six months ago, I was imprisoned and shot at by fireballs. And I'd faced death a second time in the form of drowning when Grimm and I had been stuck in the flooding prison basement. But somehow, this was worse. Facing the impending loss of my uterus really took the cake.

I was already cursed to never fall in love with a man. But even with that knowledge, I had held onto a string of hope that the curse would be broken and I could bring a child into the world to continue the legacy.

This surgery would take away all traces of hope. Without my reproductive organs, I was thoroughly screwed.

And if there was no hope for me, there was no hope for my world.

I paced in my cage, checking every nook and cranny for some weakness in the kennel design. I tested the strength of the bars to the best of my ability, no small feat given the limitations of my feline body. The metal seemed secure, despite my hopes of finding a flaw.

I began to go over options in my head. Could I shimmer and somehow move through the bars? Other than my record of shimmer holding while under attack from Annie, my next best effort of holding my shimmer was five seconds. From my calculations, it would be long enough to relocate myself to the outside of my cage, but there lay the problem: I had never tried to move myself while I was holding the shimmer. I wasn't sure it could be done.

Which led to my second option, which would be the default if no other option presented itself: morphing into a human while still in the kennel. I pushed on the ceiling to see if I could burst the seams if I transformed. The cage held fast, which gave me no data, but I kept the idea as a last-ditch effort. Even if I did egregious injury to myself, it was better to be crippled in some way than to be sterilized.

Throughout the hours of my imprisonment, Dr. Orcutt kept coming in, sometimes to fiddle with papers at the secretary, other times to take stock of his instruments and drugs. Still other times, he sat in the rolling chair and just watched me. I hunkered down during those moments and did nothing, hoping to make myself as boring as possible. Unfortunately, he seemed fascinated with me. I realized I was a bit of an infamous celebrity around here. He certainly acted as if he were star-struck, despite still planning to take away my reproductive organs.

Near dawn, I was so exhausted that I began to drift off, despite my best efforts not to.

The nap did not last long.

My cage jostled, jarring me into full wakefulness. Opening my eyes as wide as they could go and flattening my body, I took a quick look at my surroundings. A person stood directly in front of me, wearing a long red wrap dress, her blonde hair still trailing over one shoulder in a braid.

Althea.

She bent down, allowing me to see her face. Her sullen and cowed disposition was gone. Instead, her expression was one of slight amusement, her red lips perked up in an almost-smile, her eyes dancing.

This was it. It must have been time for my surgery. It was now or never to save myself. I worked up the nerve to shift. Unfortunately, my nerve was in hiding.

While I battled with my wills, Althea had the gall to wink at me, throwing me off my game completely.

I hissed in response.

Undeterred by my hiss, Althea picked my kennel up by a handle I couldn't see. The blanket fell away, revealing the entire room for my perusal. As my visual access to the whole room expanded and Althea angled my cage toward the door, Dr. Orcutt walked in.

I was about to bite the bullet and shift, but a glance at Orcutt's face gave me pause. He looked confused.

"Althea? What are you doing?" he asked the woman.

Perhaps it wasn't surgery time, after all, if Orcutt wasn't prepared. I decided to hang tight and see how this played out.

"Greg has requested the cat's presence. I don't make the rules, Carl. I just follow them."

Dr. Orcutt rubbed his chin. "Odd. Mr. Elkins never said anything to me about this."

"Would you like to ask him about it?" Althea asked, her voice tinged with anger.

Orcutt put his hands up in mock defeat. "No, no. You go ahead. The boss knows what he's doing."

Orcutt swept to the side of the room, allowing Althea to pass through the door. I swayed with each step she took, and I darted my head to take in new surroundings. The hallway we were in was large and long, with doors to my right every few feet. Although the color scheme was different, it reminded me of Deerhorn Manor, where I had first met Elkins. This in and of itself was enough to send me into a fresh spiral, both metaphorically and literally, as I twirled about in my cage. What if I had been asleep long enough for them to take me all the way there?

But no, I reminded myself. Fleurette had scoped out Deerhorn Manor after the events of this spring. It had been thoroughly boarded up, with no sign of activity ever since. This must be Elkins' new digs.

Althea took enough twists and turns to get me thoroughly lost. She said not a word to me during this time but concentrated on walking. Now that I thought about it, she seemed to be in a bit of a hurry. She must have been worried about showing up late to wherever Elkins was holed up. It must have been important to him to see me again before the operation.

I could have tried my risky shifting attempt again, but I decided to bide my time. Instead, I simply darted my head this way and that, until a flash of orange grabbed my attention.

I focused on the object, intrigued.

It was a tail. A fox's tail, to be specific, curiously emerging from Althea's backside through her dress. It swished slightly against the fabric as she walked.

My brain sputtered at the sight, trying to come up with a plausible conclusion as to why Fleurette's mother might be growing a fox's tail from her posterior. I finally grabbed upon something, as implausible as it was.

"Kitty?" I asked, bewildered.

Althea, or whatever was carrying me, stopped, as if she could actually understand me, despite the difference in species. She looked behind herself, as if looking for the tail. As soon as she spotted it, she straightened and rolled her eyes in exasperation. Then she turned to the nearest window, rushing my cage over to it.

"It would appear I am out of time. This way," she said. Her voice sounded odd, a curdled milk version of Althea's voice.

She placed my cage down and I heard her open the sash. A blast of abnormally salty air breezed in, and a strange, distant yet pleasant rolling roar filled my ears. My cage was once again lifted, and the lock fell off.

I was eye level with what used to be Althea. It still bore a resemblance, but the once-blue eyes were now an unnatural coral color, and the pupils were vertically slitted. The creature smiled cunningly at me. "We're on the first floor. Jump down and take a left. There's a spot under the stone wall that has been dug out. Meet me on the other side."

With that, the Althea-thing opened my cage wide and tipped it at the open window. I had no time to react as my feet slid on the bare metal and I slipped out. My paws briefly touched the wood of the window ledge, but momentum carried me forward and I fell six feet to the cold ground.

Instinct took over as soon as I overcame the shock of my change of circumstances, and I scuttled along the building's exterior to the left-hand side. As soon as I encountered the corner of the building, I made a beeline for the stone wall in front of me, hiding under a bush for a moment to catch myself up. Only once I had calmed down sufficiently did I start to skirt along the wall, looking for a space to squeeze under.

Ah, there it was. It was tight, but a cat's body was made to compress when necessary. Seconds later, I was free on the other side of the wall, a bit dirty from the soil but otherwise unharmed.

The sonorous roar I had heard at the window was louder on this side of the wall. I looked ahead of me and froze. Beyond low-lying shrubs and down a gentle slope was a wide expanse of flat, white sand, and beyond *that* was a sight I had never witnessed before: the ocean.

The thin gray line I had spotted before the MC had died did not hold a candle to the magnificence before me. The crash of waves sent a shiver up my spine, but the sensation wasn't terrible. It was thrilling.

"You took your time," the fox commented from behind me.

"Gah!" I jumped, aligning my whole body to face her. "Kitty! Don't sneak up on me like that. How did *you* get here so fast?"

She positioned her vulpine lips into a semblance of a grin. "Walls cannot hold me. You have not been paying attention."

My heart began to decelerate now that the threat had passed. "You saved me," I stated. "How?"

Kitty opened her mouth in a silent laugh. "Oh that? Just another trick I can do. Kitsune as old as I am can temporarily change shape. It is rather difficult, so I am unfortunately unable to hold the form for very long, as you could see."

I eyed her. "So, you didn't possess Fleurette's mother as well?"

Kitty snapped her mouth shut. "I can only possess one human at a time. To relinquish Kokoro now would spell her death. I would lose a tail."

"I suppose I should be grateful that your unwillingness to lose a tail is keeping her safe from harm. So, you mimicked Althea. Why not just let Kokoro out to save me?"

The fox spun in a circle, agitated. "Two reasons. One, Kokoro's nakedness would be a distraction. I can only tuck *her* away when she gives me bodily control, not her clothes. In that department, Cousin, you have the distinct advantage. And two, I have kept Kokoro tucked away for so long that I fear she is greatly weakened. You saw how she was after I relinquished her the last time. It is no different this time around. She would submit to unconsciousness the moment I let her loose. And that would be no help to either you or I."

"Well, thank you. For the rescue. I couldn't foresee getting out of that one in one piece. Although you could have warned me it was you."

Her eyes sparkled in the dim light. "Oh, but I did."

"You did?" I asked with skepticism.

"I believe the action of winking is a universal notification."

"Oh. Well, coming from Althea, it only made her come off as unhinged and psychotic." I cocked my head at Kitty. "I suppose since she was you, it still comes off as unhinged and psychotic. Anyway, there's something I'd like to say to you."

She watched me with curiously luminescent amber eyes. "Yes?"

I swallowed. "I've given it some thought since I saw you after your ... revenge killings. I'm ... sorry. For, you know, being too hasty making a judgment about you the first time we met. I should have given you a chance. If not for your sake, for Kokoro's. And Fleurette's. As I mentioned before, I didn't know about what would happen if you failed to help Kokoro."

"One path winds around and around the mountain, and the other leads you straight up to the peak. Either way, you will reach the summit," she stated, sitting on her haunches.

I blinked.

Correctly interpreting my silence for incomprehension, she said, "There is still time to help. Not all is lost. Now come."

She began walking away.

"Where are we going?" I asked her.

She stopped and swiveled her head around. "Do you see behind you? If you wish for death or bodily alteration, please, stay here. They will find you eventually if we linger."

I shivered and turned around to look despite myself. The building I had escaped from was a rather large house, brilliantly lit up against the dark of predawn. It was less grand than Deerhorn Manor, but still oozed with a misplaced grandeur that only the ultra-rich could pull off.

Ahead of me, Kitty disappeared into the shrubs that grew thickly on the banks. Her words still thrummed in my head. I followed her.

The ground underneath my feet grew pliant and sandy as we trekked through the underbrush. Eventually the bushes thinned out and opened onto an environment that was as foreign to me as the moon: the beach.

It was still mostly dark out, but the sands glowed white in the moon's light, and each wave that crashed upon the beach was laced with a magical glow. The sound was unlike anything I had ever heard; it reminded me of a living, breathing leviathan, careless of what it might eat and timeless as the world itself.

Perhaps that was why I held it in such thrilling esteem. It was a predator, like me.

Kitty turned to me. "This way, Cousin."

She motioned with her snout to skirt along the edge of the first dune. I dutifully followed, but curiosity got the best of me. "Where are we going?"

"Your friend and Kokoro's cousin are being held in the house next door."

The words did not make sense at first. "My friend? Fleurette? And Gavin?"

"Yes."

"Wait." I stopped walking, my pulse pounding. "Fleurette and Gavin are in trouble? How? What happened?"

Kitty turned to me in a swirl of orange. "There is more than one threat upon this stretch of coastal land, unfortunately. The house next door is owned by a Mr. Santorum. He is an ally of Elkins."

The name was not familiar. I wondered who he might be, and what his connection to all this was. And then another thought popped into my head. "What about Nic?"

The fox regarded me without blinking, as if she were searching for an answer. As far as I could tell, that was exactly what was happening: the fox using her omniscience to seek the truth. Cooly, she answered, "He is also in this general vicinity."

That actually made me feel better. I didn't know what had happened to him after I was captured. For all I knew, he could have died in that shed. I was glad to learn that wasn't the case.

Kitty resumed walking. My mind swirled with all this new information. "So, what's the plan?"

She did not stop walking this time. "*My* plan was to release you from custody. I have done that."

"Wait, hold on." I sprinted to catch up to her. "What do you mean? You don't know how to get them out?"

"Why is it up to me? They are your friends, not mine, after all."

I flattened my ears. "Because I'm not the one with amazing powers! I have no clue how to navigate any of this!"

The lights of another house above the bluff came into view. Kitty glanced up, stopped, and stretched with a wide yawn.

"Oh, Cousin," she replied. "How little you know."

Now my tail lashed with irritation. "Thank you for rubbing it in my face."

She ignored my barb. "Let us revisit your claim that you have no amazing powers. You alone are the only thing stopping Annie Coddle, a supreme witch, from reentering this world. You alone are guarding millions of lives that would otherwise be snuffed out by Annie's vision for her rule. Does that not make you incredibly powerful in your own right?"

I glanced at my front feet, half-buried in the sand. "Well, that isn't exactly what I was referring to. I mean, all I can do is change from cat to human and vice versa. How am I supposed to stop her, when she is so close to getting what she wants?"

"Ah." Kitty closed her eyes, lost in thought. She opened them and met my gaze with a cunning glance. "The future dances before me on many legs. I cannot tell you which will trip and which will be sure-footed, but for a word of advice. Great power must be met with great power."

"What in the blazing blue furballs does that mean?" I growled, exasperated by the fox's cryptic statements.

"You are more powerful than you know, but you will need strength in numbers. A swarm of bees can defend the hive against a bear when a single bee's sting fails."

I breathed deeply. "Why do you keep saying that I'm powerful? You still haven't explained that."

Kitty opened her mouth wide, a jubilant yet quiet whine escaping. "You do not believe me? Let me show you."

"Show me what?" I asked.

She licked her lips; the movement was almost hungry and made me nervous. "Your greatest strength."

CHAPTER 21

My greatest strength. I couldn't possibly fathom what the fox was about to show me.

She did not let me hang in anticipation for long, though.

"I want you to transform into a human," she told me. "And then, pick me up in your arms and revert into a cat."

I blinked. "Um, Kitty, I've only taken one other lifeform into my interdimensional pocket before. I'm not sure what it will do to you."

"You lack imagination and brains at times, Cousin. Why do you think I asked you to do this? I'm going to show you exactly what is there."

I flicked an ear. "I could have done without the insult. Are you sure about this?"

She leveled her gaze at me. "Trust me."

I didn't, not fully anyway. Still, I was curious about what she had to show me, and so far she had not demonstrated any concrete proof that she was lying to me.

I shimmered. Now I towered over the fox, who sat complacently and looked up at me with half-lidded eyes.

"Okay, then," I said to her, reaching out my arms with trepidation. "Here we go. Don't bite me."

Kitty lolled out her tongue as if laughing at me. I bent down and carefully picked her up, one arm under her front legs and the other scooping up her hind end to lift her off the ground. She cuddled into my arms, oddly content at being held.

Despite the nagging feeling that I was holding a living bomb, her fur was soft, and I enjoyed the sensation of snuggling her, I had to admit.

"Ready?" I asked, even though I knew she was. I supposed the question was more for me than her.

I transformed.

Every single time I had performed my transformation during my life, I had gone from a solid feline or human body to an energy state, and then finished as the opposite physical body. I expected this time to be the same. I expected to be looking out of my feline eyes with a fox tucked into my pocket.

I also expected to be standing on the sandy dune at the Oracune beach as the sun rose behind me, with the timeless ocean stretching out into the distance under the newly full moon. Instead, I opened my eyes to an alien sight.

I stared into an eternal blackness with tiny pinpricks of colored light that appeared to be an infinity away, reminiscent of stars in a night sky. I looked to see what I stood upon, only to realize there was nothing beneath my feet. I apparently floated in this abyss, untethered but supported as if I had become suspended in cosmic jelly.

I thought I was in my feline form, but as I looked at my paw, it flickered and became a hand for a second before reverting back. "What?" I said aloud, in my human voice.

"Welcome, Cousin," Kitty's voice reached my ears from above me. I looked up.

The kitsune was no longer just a fox. She was huge, a constellation of her own in this odd not-sky. Her orange fur undulated like flames, giving off the occasional flare of red, yellow, green, and purple. Multiple tails, like brilliant large candle flames, billowed in a fan behind her, twisting this way and that. I tried to count them, but only got up to seven before becoming confused and giving up. Her face looked like a fox still, but her eyes were fiery pink, glowing with the power of gods, and her snout stretched longer, with lips that curled into a true smile. She was terrible to behold, but I held no fear for her.

I now understood why someone would worship her as a god. She was incredible.

"Why do you look like that? And where are we?" I could no longer tell if I spoke human speech or if I spoke the universal animal language. Perhaps it was neither or both at the same time.

It didn't matter because Kitty understood me regardless. "When I am upon a mortal plane such as your world, I must conform to your mortal boundaries of existence. I am not truly a fox, but I appear as one because that is how mortals see me. This form is closer to how I truly look, because here I can be free of mortal restrictions. Same as yourself."

"And 'here' is ...?" I nudged.

"A simple question. You are in what you call your interdimensional pocket."

I experienced a pause in mental activity. "How is that possible?"

"I made it so. Your brain is simple but contains the necessary functions to do great things. I merely flipped a switch, so to speak." She blinked her luminous eyes slowly at me.

I frowned, or at least experienced the sensation that I was doing so. "Does that mean I can now come in here whenever I wish?"

The kitsune lashed her tails, rippling them about like streamers in the wind and sending a shower of yellow and green sparks into the void. "Yes and no," she replied with her usual cryptic way. "If, while you transform, you focus hard enough, you will send yourself here. But without a guide, you run the risk of getting lost. I would advise against traveling away from this point by yourself. Your pocket is quite big."

"I noticed." I shivered at the thought of losing myself in my own pocket. "Just how big is it?"

"It is its own universe." She stretched her legs out, like a galactic hug.

It was a smidge overwhelming, to say the least. "Oh."

"So you see, Cousin, you are more than what you thought you were. A being that unwittingly carries a whole universe in her pocket is a powerful being, indeed."

"I suppose so. So, when I become my cat self, do my clothes just stay here? Floating in a universe?"

"So to speak, yes."

I thought about it some more. "You said that a person can get lost in here by themself. But what about my mouse, Lucky? Why didn't he go careening off into space?"

"The mouse was in your clothing's pocket when you changed shape, yes?"

I nodded, or at least I thought I did. "Yes."

She yawned, shooting pink flecks of space spittle into the void. "Then, he stayed in the pocket while in here. He was safe, since he stayed with your clothes."

"Got it. My mouse was in a pocket in my pocket. Makes sense."

She shrank and floated down to my level, becoming more foxlike, although her fur stayed like fire and her eyes still glowed pink. Her tails grouped together, like the petals of a closed blossom, with a strange bulge as if they held onto something.

"Cousin, I have another reason to show this power to you. It is a favor I seek."

"A favor?" What could this awe-inspiring god-like creature possibly want from me?

Her tails opened, the flower blooming. In the middle, a shining orb emerged.

"What is that?" I asked, unable to tear my eyes away from the shimmering ball. It was roughly the size of a small apple, and it glowed with unearthly light, looking like a miniature star, although it did not hurt my eyes to behold it. Rather, I had a hard time tearing my gaze away from the object.

"This is my *hoshi no tama*."

The words were completely foreign. "Your what?"

Her tails worked independently to move the item amongst them with precise contact juggling. I was reminded of a man I once saw moving a coin from finger to finger. "My fox ball. Also known as a star ball, or a fox pearl. It is, in essence, my power."

"Your power?" I repeated, as I watched the pearl swirl from tail to tail. Both the ball and its graceful movement were mesmerizing.

"Not all of it, mind you. But the bulk of the power I have gained with each new tail. When I have obtained my ninth tail, my *hoshi no tama* will allow me to ascend to the heavenly planes, from whence I came."

"I don't understand."

"Kitsune are like familiars, Cousin. Neither lifeform is native to this world. Familiars are called here by witches, and for my people, this place is a bit like a prison sentence. Once upon a time, I misbehaved, and so I was sent here. Only by doing acts of good can I once again return home."

"I see. Well, what was the favor you wanted of me?"

The fox pearl lifted of its own accord and floated over, pausing in front of me. "I seek to keep it here, temporarily," Kitty explained.

I wanted to touch it, but I dared not. "Here? In my pocket?"

The fox bowed her head in acknowledgement. "I fear that I have kept it too close to my human host, and it has in turn weakened her faster than I'd intended. I need to hide it for a time, so that she may regain her strength. If I leave her body in such a weakened state, she may die, and even if I finish the task of helping her, I will not receive my tail."

I studied the orb. "Will it weaken me?"

"No. Your magic, if anything, will strengthen while you hold this in your pocket."

"Well, alright then. You can keep it here."

Kitty nodded. "Many thanks, Cousin. Now, come. It is time to return to your world. Mortals who dally in here cannot comprehend the magnitude and can quickly lose their minds."

I didn't like the sound of that. "Lead the way."

Kitty rushed to me in a gliding motion. I thought she meant to settle into my sometimes-arms, but her first touch melded with me instead. I gasped at the contact and closed my eyes.

I opened them to the sound of the crashing waves, the smell of the tangy saltwater carried by a cold wind that ruffled my fur, and the prickly sensation of sand between my toes. Kitty's face, once more a normal fox's, peered at me from a few inches away.

I jumped back a fraction, my heart pounding. I fought off a momentary bout of dizziness. "Woah, that was a trip."

Now that I was back in the physical world, and the woozy feeling had subsided, I felt ... amazing. Strong. Powerful. It made me suspicious.

"Say, Kitty," I said. "Your pearl. Is it able to affect me even though it's in my pocket?"

The fox threw her head back in a vulpine laugh, although again she kept the volume down. "The *hoshi no tama* can indeed amplify your prowess, even from another astral plane such as your pocket. It is that powerful."

"Sweet Freya," I muttered. If this was what it felt like to be a kitsune, it was a heady experience. No wonder she acted so full of herself. "Well, shall we go rescue some people?"

Kitty bowed her head in acquiescence. "We shall."

CHAPTER 22

The plan was set: step one, walk up to Santorum House. Step two, figure out a way to get inside. And step three, get my friends and get the hell out.

Okay, it wasn't much of a plan. Winging it was apparently my specialty.

Kitty and I used our petite size to slink up undetected to the beach house next to Elkins' manor. It appeared that no one was yet awake, given that most of the lights were off and everything was silent. We crept up onto the weather-worn back deck, avoiding the wooden chairs that faced the ocean. I peered through the glass window that served as a back door.

"Kitty, how do we get inside?" I asked her.

No answer.

"Kitty?" I turned to look for her, but she was gone.

The latch clicked from inside the door. I whipped my head back around to see the fox through the glass as she finished nosing the lock of the door open. She looked at me pointedly.

I transformed just long enough to open the door, walk in, and close it behind me, finding myself in a cozy breakfast nook. A lavish kitchen greeted me to the right, a peninsula sectioning it from the nook.

Back in cat form, I asked, "How did you get in here?"

Kitty gave me the long stare she undoubtedly reserved for conversing with incompetent people. "I've told you; nothing can contain me. Walls, doors, iron bars. I go where I please." She looked smug at this fact, but she also seemed off. Her eyes had lost some of their unearthly sparkle, and she slumped where she sat.

"Great. Good for you. Are you okay?" I added this last question because she swayed on her feet when she stood up.

She shook her body unsteadily. "I am finding myself winded. Without possession of my pearl, I am in a weakened state. I must rest soon."

"Rest? If not having your pearl is so hard on you, why did you give it to me in the first place?"

She regarded me. "Because that is the way it must be. I already explained this to you. I can't kill Kokoro, for that would be disastrous for all, including myself. Better to get her away from my *hoshi no tama* so that she can easily recover."

Her reasoning did not make much sense to me, but it was out of my paws. "Okay, then. Is there anyone else around? Any servants we might bump into?"

Kitty cocked her head to the side, considering. "Santorum is here, but he still sleeps. He sent his servants away before obtaining his captives. The servants are merely employees, and not a part of his inner circle. He instead relies upon Elkins for any staffing issues. And he was supposed to play host and employer to Inaba's people, but I have dispatched them."

"Right, the vehicle full of dead guys," I snidely replied. "Well, thank Freya for small favors. Now, where to?"

She padded down the hallway on silent feet. "This way."

The fox led me to a set of stairs heading down. I puzzled over this; a basement at a beach house? That didn't seem like the usual construction, considering how close we were to a massive body of water. But then again, given the size of this monstrosity, the owner could afford more bells and whistles than the average person.

At the bottom of the stairs another hallway beckoned. Kitty made a beeline to one door. She turned to me. "This is where Fleurette is being held."

Wasting no time, I shimmered and grabbed the doorknob, eager to release my friend.

My hand rattled the knob. "It's locked."

Kitty yipped at me quietly. I looked at her and reverted in order to speak to her.

"Of course it's locked," she chided. "Don't be so impulsive. Give me a moment. My energy has been depleted faster than I originally estimated. I will go and unlatch this lock for you, but then I need to rest. But go ahead and become human again. And be prepared."

I did as she bade. In the time it took me to shift, she disappeared. But I heard movement on the other side. And then the lock disengaged.

I opened it, expecting to see Kitty waiting for me. Instead, I caught a naked Kokoro in my arms as she fell forward.

In hindsight, this was what I was supposed to be prepared for. Oops.

"Oomph!" I uttered as the weight of her body hit me.

She was not fully asleep, but incredibly weak. Her eyes fluttered as she tried to grasp my arms. "Cressida," she mumbled.

I grunted with the weight. Kokoro was taller than me, and the difference in height made holding her up awkward. I shuffled forward, hoping she could keep her footing.

Luckily, a couch lay to the right of us inside the room. I carefully guided her limp body to it and plopped her down. She fell onto the couch like a sack of bricks.

With Kokoro no longer impeding my vision, I had an opportunity to survey the room. There wasn't much to it, other than the couch, a small table on the opposite wall, and a single wooden chair in the center with Fleurette tied upon it.

"Fleurette," I breathed, rushing over. She appeared to be asleep. I shook her arm. "Fleurette!" I put more volume into her name.

"She's been spelled," Kokoro chimed weakly from the couch.

Of course. Elkins was around. I should have foreseen this.

I rushed over to Kokoro. "Is Kitty in there? I need help!"

Kokoro flopped her head forward in an attempt to hold it straight. I placed my hands on her cheeks to help stabilize her.

She worked to keep her eyes open. "My fox is oddly drained. I had fallen asleep a while ago; I have no memory of the past few hours. What happened?"

I pursed my lips together. "Her pearl was beginning to kill you. She gave it to me for safe keeping."

"Her *hoshi no tama*? It is dangerous for a kitsune to be away from it for too long. It must be why she was forced to give me my body."

I looked her over, quickly skipping over certain parts of her anatomy. "But you look better than you did the last time you came out of a long fox period. She must have been right; the ball was having a negative effect on you."

She sighed. "Whatever is happening, my fox is in no position to help. She says you must do this yourself."

I frowned. What could I do? I could only shapeshift.

Unless ...

I still felt the boost of power Kitty's pearl had granted me. Perhaps I could harness that power and borrow a little magical juice from it. It was worth a shot.

I walked back over to Fleurette, who still sat in the chair, her head slumped over with her mass of wavy curls hiding her body like a curtain. Her arms had been tied to the chair with her hands resting on the knobs of the chair arms. I grasped the hand closest to me.

"C'mon, Fleurette," I said softly. "I need you to snap out of this."

I focused on our connected hands, visualizing a healing energy flowing from my soul, down my arm, and into her body. As far as I knew, I was making this up, but I could swear our hands grew warmer as I envisaged this.

After thirty seconds, I felt unusually depleted of energy. I was about to give up, admitting that my half-baked idea held no merit, when Fleurette moaned.

"Fleurette?" I asked, her name on my tongue tinged with hope.

Fleurette bobbed her head up a fraction, letting out another moan. She raised her head fully, her eyes squinted shut. "Cressida?"

"Hey!" My happiness at her awakening was palpable.

From the couch, Kokoro added her own joyful, if exhausted, greeting. "Fleurette, I am so happy to have found you again."

"Kokoro?" Fleurette seemed to gather strength from her presence. "Are you okay? Oh—you're needing clothes again."

Kokoro waved a heavy hand of dismissal. "A most unfortunate side effect of *kitsunetsuki*. Fox possession. But I am well. Tired, but well. My fox has just relinquished control to me. I shall be fine shortly. I just need a little rest." She leaned her head back and closed her eyes.

Fleurette breathed a sigh of relief. "Thank Hecate for that." She tried to raise her hand, but her arms were still tied down. "Why am I tied down? Where am I?"

"I believe we're in Oyster Bay, on the coast. The Serenic Ocean is just outside. Elkins is next door. I recently had a lovely time there. This house belongs to a Mr. Santorum."

"Santorum?" Fleurette asked. "Rafferty Santorum?"

"Well, I don't know what his first name is—wait, how would you know it? And why is the name Rafferty so familiar?"

She sighed, letting her head fall forward slightly. "Rafferty Santorum is Gavin's father," she replied.

My first instinct was anger. Had Gavin led Fleurette into a trap for his own benefit? But then I recalled how much he had seemed to despise his father. He was most likely innocent.

I focused my righteous, if displaced anger, on tackling Fleurette's bindings. When the knots proved too tough for my fingers, I reached into my boot and extracted the knife to saw through the ropes.

"Be careful with that, Cress." Fleurette warned me.

"Cool it, Mother," I replied with a mature manner befitting my age. "The charm's gone. I had to kill a werewolf the other night."

"A werewolf?" Fleurette exclaimed with alarm. "What's the date?"

I did some quick mental math. "It's the morning of the 19th."

She blinked in confusion. "But that means *tonight* is the start of the full moon."

A rope snapped after careful sawing. "Yes, Flo, I know how the moon works. And trust me, I was just as confused as you are now. But it was clearly the night of the 15th that we were attacked. And they were definitely werewolves."

"The 15th? That's the night we were captured."

I moved over to her other arm. "What happened?"

Fleurette shook her head. "Nothing spectacular, I assure you. We had been going slow, checking all the areas we thought the fox might have passed through. We spent the first night in Kousa, so we did not make it very far at all. The day of, we had been making our way to the coast, through the mountains. We were going to call it a night soon, I recall. Gavin was driving, and it was dark out, so I'm guessing it was around eight? Eight-thirty? Whatever the time was, Gavin's MC suddenly lost power. We coasted to a halt and sat there in the dark for about five minutes, wondering what we should do. And then Gavin said he saw movement in the bushes, and a purple light flashed at us. And then I lost consciousness. And I've been asleep ever since."

"Purple light? That's Elkins to a tee. But holy hairballs, you've been asleep for close to four days?"

Fleurette screwed her closed eyes up. "Yes, and judging by the way my bladder is screaming at me right now, I believe it."

I doubled my efforts to release my friend. Finally, the last rope frayed and broke.

Fleurette stood, rather unsteadily. "Ah, that's better."

"Happy to help."

Fleurette surveyed the room. "Where's Rupert?"

I frowned. I had forgotten about the crow. "I haven't seen him."

She whipped her head around, her eyes large with fear. "He didn't find you? After I was captured?"

I sighed. Rupert had confessed to me the last time I was in a pickle that Fleurette had spelled him with a means to track me down no matter where I was. It came in handy, for sure, although it was odd to consider I was a crow's homing beacon. "Nope."

She scrunched up her lips. "I was hoping he had escaped to warn you. How did you know to come here, then, if not for Rupert?"

"I was making my way here with Nic—he's a lawyer working with Babcock, but don't worry, he's on our side. He asked me to help him take down Elkins shortly after you left. We got attacked by the werewolves that first night, and then the second night I lost Grimm, and—"

"Woah. You lost Grimm?" Fleurette's alarm ratcheted up a notch. "What do you mean, you lost him?"

I looked at the floor, defeated. "We got into a fight. He stayed outside to guard my tent, but he must have had enough of my crap because he left in the middle of the night."

"Oh, Cressida." Fleurette wrapped me up in a hug. I didn't want to get emotional, but a couple errant tears leaked out despite my best efforts.

I let go of her. "It's okay," I tried to convince myself and Fleurette. "It's better he left before this craziness started. See, I was captured myself by Elkins the next day. So was Nic. In fact, Nic's somewhere around here, and once you and Kokoro and Gavin are safely away, I intend to find him and rescue him as well."

Fleurette gave me an inscrutable look. "This Nic fellow. Do you have any ... feelings for him?"

I rolled my eyes. "I do realize I made out with the last man I took a trip with, but it's not a pattern, thank you very much. No, I trust Nic, and I think he's a nice guy, but that's it."

Fleurette held out a placating hand. "Okay, okay. I just wanted to check. There's still a curse to break, you know."

"Don't remind me. Look, we should get out of here. I still need to find Gavin. Is there anything here that we can use to clothe Kokoro?" I motioned my head at the nude woman behind us, who had passed out on the couch.

The room was too barren to have anything of use. Instead, Fleurette unzipped her down jacket, took it off, and walked over to Kokoro on the couch. Tenderly, she propped the woman forward and slid the coat over her shoulders, carefully threading her arms through the sleeves. Kokoro groggily assisted, but seemed like she was too tired to care about much of anything at the moment.

"Kokoro, it's time to go," Fleurette calmly told her. The other woman grumbled but stood up shakily. The jacket was long enough to cover her bits, but just barely. Still, it was better than nothing. The Oracune coast may have had a more temperate climate than on the other side of the mountain range, but it was still much too cold outside to be frolicking about sans clothing.

Fleurette wrapped an arm around the other woman to help steady her. She nodded her head, a signal that they were ready.

"Right," I said as resolutely as I could. After all, I still had no plan, a mostly naked exhausted woman, and another with a close-to-bursting bladder. Still, appearances were important. I squared my shoulders. "Let's go."

"And where, might I ask, are you planning to go?" a new voice demanded from beyond the door.

I jumped and turned in time to see an older man block the entrance. He wore a satin robe over pajamas, apparently having just woken up. In one hand he held a tin bucket. He smiled, an expression that glorified his lips but did not reach his eyes, which glittered with malice.

I took a guess. "Rafferty?"

He laughed. I once again was drawn to his mouth. His jawline and lips were incredibly similar to Gavin's, even if the resemblance stopped there.

"You should address me as 'Mr. Santorum,' Miss Curtain. Manners do matter. And sneaking about attempting to steal my guests is not nice manners. You've been missed over at Mr. Elkins' place."

"What have you done with Gavin?" I demanded.

Santorum's brow wrinkled into a frown. "My wayward son is none of your concern," he told me sharply. "He's safe, though. We are trying to bring him back into the fold before tonight's festivities. He's a willful child, though. I suppose I only have myself to blame."

"For the lack of love and support you showed him growing up? I suppose so," I growled.

Santorum ignored me, looking beyond me with an expression of yearning that almost humanized him. "Gods. You must be Kiroko."

"Kokoro," I corrected automatically.

He ignored me. "So, it's true. The fox *did* spirit you away after you murdered my business associate. You look so much like Motoko, it's almost painful to look upon you."

Motoko was Gavin's mother, and Kokoro's maternal aunt. She was murdered many years ago, much to Gavin's heartbreak. And despite his statement of how painful looking at Kokoro was, his open salacious leer said otherwise. I was only thankful that Kokoro was no longer naked.

But I refused to broach that subject. Instead, I focused on the first useful tidbit of information he had granted us. I narrowed my eyes. "Business partner?"

Santorum shot me a pitying glance. "Of course. Tyonoshima is rich in magic-infused metals, perfect for our needs. But that's enough out of you. I need to let Gregory know where you're at. Ladies, stay put." He made to close the door but stopped and turned back around. "Oh, I nearly forgot. Here." He flung the bucket at me. I caught it reflexively.

I stared at it, and then at him. "For sandcastles?"

Rafferty rolled his eyes. "Bathroom." He sneered. He pointed at Fleurette. "I imagine this one is close to bursting by now. Enjoy."

"Cressida, move!" Fleurette yelled as she quickly began positioning her hands into special configurations. I knew a hastily made attack spell when I saw one, and I also knew that Fleurette could pack a wallop when she was suitably motivated. I flung myself to the side as Fleurette released the spell at Santorum.

Nothing happened.

Fleurette looked at her hands in confusion. "What ...?"

Santorum smirked, completely unfazed. "Aren't you a feisty one? But your mother dosed you with a nulling potion while you slept. That's right, baby doll; your magic is kaput until tomorrow, I'd say. Nice try, though."

"My mother?" Fleurette's voice was small, lost.

"Can't wait for the family reunion," Santorum called out as he shut the door, this time locking it from the outside.

CHAPTER 23

I t was clear we weren't making the daring escape I had envisioned after all. With the finality of the lock clicking, Fleurette guided Kokoro back to the couch, and together, they sank into it, with Fleurette's arm still around the other woman.

I was not about to give up, however. I briefly considered trying to borrow magic from Fleurette to somehow break us out, but I had refused to allow Fleurette to practice this technique with me—I had no clue if it truly was borrowing or outright stealing and I wasn't about to hurt my friend—but I concluded that with her powers temporarily nullified, it wouldn't work anyway. Instead, I paced the room, looking in every nook and cranny, searching for any tiny means of escape. After all, the two other women may have been too large to fit through most tight spaces, but I had an advantage in that department.

Alas, my searching turned up exactly zero escape routes. No windows, no vents. Just the solid door that was clearly locked.

Wait a minute.

Kitty didn't let a locked door stop her. Could it now be the same for me?

I shimmered down and scoped out the door. It was solid, yes, but I decided not to let that stop me. Instead, I visualized myself on the other side of the door, no barrier in between ...

I was standing in the hallway, on the other side of the door.

I blinked, honestly surprised that my idea worked so easily. I hadn't even felt the transition.

"Cressida!" Fleurette cried out through the door.

I shifted, shushing her the moment I had human lips. "I'm here. Not so loud."

"How did you do that?" she asked, incredulous. "One second you were there, and the next you weren't!"

"Fox powers. It's a long story."

"Can you get us out?"

I studied the door and was dismayed to see a padlock keeping it securely shut. "I need a key," I relayed through the door. "Hang tight; I'm going to go see if I can find Gavin and Nic."

"Be safe and get out of here at your first chance! Don't worry about us," Fleurette said in her motherly tone.

"Like hell I will," I muttered, easing away from the door.

"What was that?"

"Nothing! See you soon," I said as loudly as I dared, and then I took my cat form for ease of subterfuge.

This time as I padded through the house, I felt incredibly alone now that I no longer had Kitty by my side. I would have laughed if I were in human form; I actually missed the vexatious creature. That damn fox had managed to weasel her way into my good graces, after all.

But without her leading the way, I wasn't sure where to go. It was a good thing I came equipped with some excellent tracking apparatuses. While I was used to being in a more natural environment while utilizing my gifts, this time I'd go hunting in a modern setting.

I kept my ears alert for any nearby footsteps. My eyes scanned for movement. And I put my nose to the greatest test.

My feline olfactory sense was nowhere near as keen as Grimm's—a pang shot through me in thinking about him; at least he had escaped this particular nightmare—but it could still detect specific smells much better than my human nose could. And there was one scent I was looking for: a sweet and spicy musk.

I had gotten to know it quite well six months ago, so it was easy for me to single it out once I caught the scent.

Gavin's smell led me up a set of stairs to where I surmised the bedrooms were. And there: the third door on the right simply swam with his bouquet.

There was another lock on this door, so I had even more evidence that Gavin was being kept within. It was time to try my new trick again.

I paused, though. What if he saw me when I breezed through the door? What if I had to shift in front of him?

What if *not* risking my secret gave the bad guys the upper hand? That last question sealed the deal for me. It was better to possibly expose myself to Gavin than potentially doom us all. I readied myself for another blink through the door, come what may.

I was in luck. The room I found myself in was empty of any people. But I took a moment to gawk at it. It was huge, with a lavish four poster bed, ornate dressers, a desk, and an attached bathroom, from which came the sound of running water. I surmised Gavin was in there.

I quickly transformed and began walking forward.

And promptly tripped on the rug.

"Who's out there?" Gavin's voice resonated through the closed door. He sounded angry.

Before I could say anything, the bathroom door flung open, revealing a shirtless Gavin with a toothbrush dangling from his mouth. He began to storm out, muttering, "I told you before—"

He stopped at the sight of me, his mouth falling in a wide enough gape that the toothbrush fell to the floor, forgotten. "Cressida?"

I gawked at the toned abs on display, willing myself to look at his face instead. I might not have been romantically interested in him anymore, but I could still appreciate a fine physique.

"Surprise," I said, but didn't get another word out before Gavin crossed the room and flung his arms about me in a crushing hug.

"How did you get here?" he asked once he let me go.

"I heard you were in trouble," I replied, sidestepping the *how* portion. "You have toothpaste on your face."

Gavin grinned and ran back into the bathroom, emerging seconds later with a clean face and a shirt that he buttoned as he strode back over. "I'm probably in a better position than Fleurette," he admitted ruefully. "At least I'm not in the special basement dungeon. My father has decided to keep me in this room until I fall in line."

"I just saw her. I tried to rescue her, but I failed." I paused. "Kokoro's here now, too."

Gavin blanched. "Is she okay?"

I nodded, but waffled a hand. "More or less. She's weak, but she'll bounce back. What about you?"

He barked a humorless laugh. "Just fine and dandy. Elkins put me to sleep, same as last time, and I woke up here. Without any of my items, including my pocket watch." He frowned. "And my father's been in a handful of times to harass me into joining his cause. He's as big of a bastard as I remember."

"What has he told you?" I asked, intrigued.

Gavin frowned. "My father has taken up with the ACF. I had no clue he was a part of this, I assure you. I mean, I've known since I was young that he's been into some shady shit on some level or another. It's part of the reason I decided to walk away from him and his money." He shook his head. "But this is just bonkers."

"Bonkers? How?" I pressed.

He seemed at a loss for words momentarily. "That Annie Coddle character you told me about? Well, he's helping bring her back. And he claims it's happening tonight."

"Tonight? This is bad." I paced about the room. "Did he say how, exactly, they plan to do this?"

Gavin shrugged. "No. I'm not allowed the pertinent details or freedom until I've agreed to be a good son again."

I gave him the side eye. "Were you ever a good son?"

Gavin grabbed his chest, faking a shocked expression. "Why, Cressida! I'm hurt by your insinuations!"

I smiled wryly. "Sure you are. The way you told it back on the train, you were your mother's son through and through."

"I still am. So I guess that means I'll be living out the rest of my life in this room."

I sighed. "At least it's spacious. And you won't have to come into contact with Annie. Seriously, what is wrong with these people? Why do they want to bring her back?"

Gavin looked me in the eye, serious once more. "From what I could piece together, Annie Coddle is old. Like, really old."

I nodded. "She took an immortality potion about five hundred years ago. I saw her once. She doesn't look half bad for a woman in her mid-five-hundred-and-forties."

"Rafferty told me *why* she took the potion in the first place."

"Go on." This was a part of the story I did not know.

"Annie Coddle wants to make herself into a god."

I stared at him. "You're kidding."

He seemed on the verge of laughing. "I wish I was. She thought this world was lacking a definitive deity, and so she decided to make herself the ruling god here. And probably expand to other dimensions as well."

It all clicked. Dr. Orcutt had made a mention of a new world order, which at the time made little sense. "These whackos are helping her in order to be on her good side when she comes back?" I surmised.

Gavin nodded. "Exactly."

I rubbed a hand down my face. "Ohhh, this is bad. Say, um, Gavin ... did your dad tell you anything else? Like, I don't know, the reason why she hasn't come back yet?"

Gavin looked at me with narrowed eyes. "Nothing specific," he replied. "But he did say there was one last problem to tie up before it could happen. Why do you ask?"

"No reason." I scanned the room again, avoiding Gavin's gaze. At least he could no longer gain definitive proof I was lying.

His raised eyebrow told me he could accurately guess at my dishonesty, although he made no mention of it. "Well, I'm sticking to my guns. I want nothing to do with this debacle. I can joke, but he can't keep me imprisoned forever."

An idea flashed in my head. "Gavin, I have a better plan. Tell your father you'll join the cult after all. But maybe don't call it a cult to his face."

"What? Are you insane?"

"At times, yes. But listen; you can get a better inside scoop, and be safe from harm as an 'insider.' And in the meantime, I'll work out a way to get you out of this mess before tonight."

"Are you sure about this, Cressida?"

I shook my head. "You should know by now that I'm never sure of anything, but perhaps that's why I keep landing on my feet."

Gavin smiled fondly at me. "You do surprise me. One of these days you'll have to tell me how you got involved in all this tomfoolery."

"Yeah, I have that feeling too."

He stuck out his hand. "Very well. I'll join the bad side. For you."

I shook on it. "I'll try to make it worth your while."

CHAPTER 24

With Gavin now in the room with me, there was no way I could use the fox's trick for leaving without having to explain way too much. That left one alternative.

Gavin's prison room had a two-paned picture window on the far wall. I nodded my chin at it. "Does that window open?"

Gavin followed my gaze. "It's stuck fast. The latch won't budge. Besides, how would you get down?"

I walked over to it, assessing. Perhaps a touch of fox magic could loosen it up. "Don't worry about it. I have my ways."

I placed my hand on the latch, forcing energy into it as I pulled upward. At first nothing happened, but then, like a stubborn jar of pickles, the window popped open an inch.

Gavin stared. "I've been trying for ages to open that window. I must have loosened it for you."

"Either that, or I'm just stronger than you," I answered with mock smugness.

He began to issue a retort, but I placed my hand over his mouth. "Quiet. I think I hear someone coming."

My ears had detected the muffled staccato of shoes on the hardwood floor of the hallway. My escape was now or never.

Gavin couldn't yet hear the footsteps, but he knew how keen my hearing was. He quickly opened the sash of the window for me, the pane sliding up easily, before backing away to give me access. I poked my head out. There was a narrow roof encircling the second floor, so I at least had a place to plant my feet once I was on the other side of the window. It would do.

I crawled out feet first, until only my head remained inside. Before I could fully extract myself, Gavin grabbed my face and pecked me full on the lips. It was over before I had time to react, but my chest gave a small throb, warning me of my curse. Once I broke from my stupor, I gave him a narrow-eyed glare.

"Sorry," he said, although the wry grin on his face implied otherwise. "It's for good luck. Be safe out there. Don't break a leg."

I returned the grin, forgiving his transgression. After all, if not for my curse, I probably would have enjoyed the interaction.

I pulled my head away from the window and quickly moved to the side, out of view of the room. Just in time, too. A sharp rap came from Gavin's door as he pulled the window shut. From my hiding spot, I heard the door creak open, and the voice of Santorum ask, "Gavin? Are you awake, son? Have you given it some thought?"

Now's your time to shine, Gavin, I thought. And he did not disappoint. As I carefully moved away from the window and transformed into my cat self, I heard him begin his conversation. "Actually, Father, yes, I have. You make some excellent points and I think I will take you up on your offer after all ..."

The view from this section of roof was lovely, as it looked out over the gray ocean. But in terms of finding a way down, it offered none. I rounded the bend off to the right.

This side of the house faced Elkins' monstrosity. While the two properties had a good distance between houses, there was not much in the way of natural screens. The grounds between the estates held a variety of bushes and beach grass, as well as the occasional ocean pine, but otherwise the view was undisrupted.

I would have to be very careful in my maneuvering in order not to be spotted by anyone who happened to look out the window at the wrong time.

Of course, this excellent line of sight worked both ways. I paused my roof traipsing as a vehicle pulled up to the beach manor. Two men got out of the front of the MC, went to the back, and dragged a third man out.

I squinted to try to improve my sight. This third man appeared to be unconscious at first glance, but then I realized he was tied up and unable to move without the assistance of the other men. Still, the figure hung his head limply as he was dragged into the building. His sandy blonde hair shone briefly in the morning sun.

Nic.

I should have been looking for a way to save Fleurette and Kokoro. But Nic was in this mess partly because of me, and it looked like he needed my help in this moment just as much, if not more, than the two women.

Once the activity had stopped at the other house, I renewed my efforts to get off the second floor roof safely. I found a downspout that allowed me to get a little lower before jumping. I still fell ten feet, but the ground was sandy, and my body expertly landed so as to minimize the impact.

I sprinted across the windswept terrain, right up to the side door that Nic had disappeared through. I breezed through the door with ease using my borrowed powers and followed the sound of angry shouting coming from a room off this main hall.

At the door, I paused.

"Where is she?" Elkins yelled with a booming intensity. The question was followed up with a sharp slapping sound.

Nic answered in a pained, yet angry voice, "Go to hell!"

My blood boiled. Nic was in serious trouble. The awful sounds emitting from this room took me back to another time when a friend was being tortured for information about me. Just as I had stepped into that room without thinking to save Gavin, my sudden need to put an end to Nic's torture caused me to shimmer into human form. I prepared to step into the room without a plan in place.

The cold metal of a knife pressed against my throat.

"Are you really this stupid?" a woman's voice hissed in my ear. "You were gone and free, and yet you walked right back into the lion's den."

I stayed perfectly still but craned my eyes as far over as I could. It was enough to get a glimpse of pale skin. Althea, then. And this time she was the real deal.

She adjusted the blade so that any wrong move would slice the skin.

"I can't let my friends suffer," I said.

She almost laughed. "No? Well, I would say that's very noble of you, if it weren't so incredibly stupid. You've used up all my goodwill cards in this game, kittycat. I'd almost feel sorry for you, but you brought this upon yourself."

With those words, she opened the door and pushed me inside, shutting it swiftly behind me.

It was dark in here, a single candle being the room's only source of light. I frowned at the drastic change in illumination, waiting for my eyes to adjust with impatience. From the small amount I could see, however, I knew I didn't want to be in this room.

Elkins, a few feet away from me, turned and stared at me with wide eyes before his features settled into a smug expression. Beyond him, Nic sat tied to a chair, his head lying low.

"Well, well, well, Miss Curtain," Elkins crooned. "You do have a flair for timely entrances. You're just the person I was looking for." His hand began to emit a purple glow.

I called upon Kitty's magic to bolster me, unsure if it would work, but hoping it would be enough. Elkins threw his magic at me, hitting me squarely in the head. I swayed, suddenly exhausted, but held onto consciousness. Within seconds, the tiredness faded to a dull weariness, and then my energy fully bounded back. I glowered at Elkins.

"So, it's true." He sneered. "The kitsune gave you her star ball. It's the only way you could have fended off my somnification. Very well." He approached me menacingly. I shrank back, but the door stopped my retreat. He raised a fist. "Give it to me."

"What?" I asked.

"The fox's power. You will hand it over."

"Why do you want it?" I asked, stalling for time.

"It belonged to Inaba. He kept it in his pocket until the fox stole it. I want it back."

I laughed. "I'm pretty sure the fox's power belonged to the fox in the first place. Do you really think I'm just going to hand it over? You can't be serious."

"Would you like to see how serious I am?"

I stood my ground. "Try me."

His fist came faster than I expected, rocking my head to the side as a sharp pain exploded in my left cheek bone. I took a couple of seconds to process what had happened. I cradled my throbbing skin as I turned back to glare at the man. And then I carefully reached down to extract the knife from my boot.

Elkins guessed what I was up to and swiftly pinned me against the wall, grabbing both of my wrists. I fought back, trying to wriggle out of his grasp, but he was surprisingly strong for an older man. With precision, he transferred both of my trapped wrists into one of his much larger hands, reached down, and fished the knife out of my boot. He tossed it to a corner of the room and then let me go.

I pushed him with all my strength and tried to run to the corner to retrieve my weapon. But Elkins grabbed me from behind in a crushing bear hug.

"I can see you have no concept of self-preservation," he rasped in my ear as he squeezed me until I gasped. "You're just lucky that I can't kill you right now or the kitsune ball would be lost forever."

He continued to squeeze, threatening to break ribs. I wanted to shout insults at him, but I could no longer properly breathe.

Nic did shout insults at him, but Elkins ignored him.

"But from what I've gleaned, you've always seemed more interested in preserving your friends over your own life. Let's put that to the test, shall we?" He dropped me. I fell to the floor, gasping and trying to take a full breath through my bruised ribs.

Elkins approached Nic and, looking back to make sure I was watching, punched him squarely in the face. Nic's head rocked back as he groaned in pain.

"Nic!" I yelled hoarsely, still on my hands and knees on the floor.

"Will you give me the ball?" Elkins asked, his tone heated.

"Don't do it, Cressida!" Nic called out.

Elkins hit him again, this time in the stomach. Nic tried to double over with a low groan of intense pain.

"Now, where did I throw that knife? Perhaps I could put it to good use," Elkins mused aloud as he searched for my fallen weapon.

The bastard was right. I couldn't stand seeing people I cared about get hurt.

The older man located the knife and retrieved it. He began advancing on the wheezing Nic. I had no doubt in my mind that he would kill Nic in front of me if I continued to hold out.

I couldn't take it anymore.

"Stop!" I yelled before Elkins could touch Nic with the knife. "You can have it. Just don't hurt him anymore!"

Elkins straightened his shirt. "You have my word," he said smoothly, once again the debonair gentleman he showed to the world at large.

I hesitated. "I—I'm not sure how to get it."

Elkins tsked. "I suggest you figure it out." He placed the knife against Nic's forearm and pressed down. "Tick tock, young lady."

I gave it some thought. How was I to extract the pearl from myself? I reflected on what Kitty had done to me. She told me I could access my pocket now that she had shown it to me. It was time to test it out.

I stood, closed my eyes, and began the process of transformation. But instead of willing my feline shape to emerge, I told myself to enter the interdimensional pocket instead. I opened my eyes.

The vast void surrounded me, and directly in front of me was the shining orb of the kitsune. It still beckoned to me with its pearly splendor. I felt so amazing with it in my possession. And it was important to Kitty. Could I really give it up?

But Nic would die if I didn't give it to Elkins. It was better to ask forgiveness than permission from the kitsune. She would understand. And if she could steal it back from one man's pocket, she could do it again.

I grabbed it, marveling at its power one last time, and then brought myself out of the shift.

Surprisingly, I was still human. I had never stayed in static form while shimmering. But I had no time to dwell on this anomaly. I held the ball in my right hand.

Elkins had approached my position while I was in my pocket. He snatched the ball before I could comprehend another course of action. "Thank you, Miss Curtain," he said, studying the orb with great delight as he brandished my own knife in my direction. "Nic, you can stand up now."

I frowned, confused by this last command.

From the other side of the room, barely illuminated by the candlelight, Nic stood, the ropes that had seemingly bound him falling to the floor.

He rubbed his chin, wincing. "Ouch. You didn't have to hit me that hard."

Elkins shrugged. "I had to make it believable, son."

CHAPTER 25

Oh no. Elkins had just called Nic "son." Perhaps he meant it in the kindly-older-man-talking-to-a-younger-man way.

Nic glowered at Elkins. "Whatever, Dad."

Well, there went that theory.

My mind reeled. Dad? Son? I almost couldn't comprehend what was happening here, but the answer was too obvious.

Elkins must have been watching the figurative floor drop out from underneath me. He chuckled. "Nic, go have your mom patch you up. Cressida and I are going to have a little chat."

Nic moved toward the door and opened it. He stopped as soon as light spilled through and looked over his shoulder. He scrutinized me, sending me a pitying look when he met my eyes.

"She needs attention as well," he pointed out.

Elkins grunted in annoyance. "She'll keep, don't you worry. I'll have her fixed up before tonight." He handed the glowing fox pearl to Nic. "Give this to Althea. She knows what to do with it."

Nic lingered for a couple more seconds, staring at me. Then he shut the door, his footsteps receding down the hallway.

I felt numb. Nic was not on my side. He never was. And I had just royally screwed myself.

And Kitty, for that matter.

Elkins ushered me to the chair Nic had previously occupied. I sank into it, uncaring of my surroundings. The fight had left me.

"You're probably feeling confused and betrayed right now," Elkins said. "After all, how could you have known that Nic is my son? We don't have the same last name. But I can assure you, he is indeed my progeny. I just changed my surname recently. It's a thing I do every thirty years or so."

"What are you talking about?" I asked, uncomprehending.

Elkins pulled up another wooden chair and sat across from me, as if we were two friends having a relaxing conversation. "You see, Cressida—I can call you that, right? My real name is not Gregory Elkins. It's Gregor Hoterson. Well, at least that's the surname my mother came up with for me. My father didn't have a surname, so we had to improvise."

"Who was your father?" I asked in an almost-whisper. My curiosity had gotten the best of me, despite my circumstances.

"My father was a very important Fae lord. His name was Hyotur, and he had the power to visit other worlds, in which he would often lead the Wild Hunt. He was a giant of a Fae, with antlers growing from his head."

"You're Fae?" I asked weakly.

"Half-Fae. My father soon fancied himself akin to the god Cernunnos and fashioned a new title to fortify that vision: The Elk God. In some dimensions, his name was bastardized into Herne the Hunter. But Cernunnos was angry with Hyotur for taking the spotlight away from him. Gods can be jealous like that. And so, around five hundred years ago, the Fae Council made my father a criminal at Cernunnos' insistence and shipped him off to a dimension they had recently decided to use as a prison."

Things were starting to add up, and I wasn't sure I liked the implications.

"My father was one of the first to be placed on this prison world. But he was not the only being living there. You see, unbeknownst to the Fae, there was a woman who had been stranded there for about thirty years by the time my father showed up."

I felt sick to my stomach. "Annie Coddle."

Elkins made a hum of appreciation. "You do catch on quick. Annie and Hyotur hit it off immediately, and quickly fell in love. And I came along very soon after that. Yes, Cressida, Annie is my mother."

"But how?" I stammered. "If that took place five hundred years ago, then—"

"I am four-hundred-and-seventy-three years old."

"That—that's old," I remarked. "How is that possible?"

"Good genetics?" Elkins quipped, but the joke fell flat. "Hyotur was Fae, and so he was practically immortal. And my mother is fully immortal, as you well know. I, sadly, am not. I do age, but at a much, much slower pace, as you can see. People assume I am in my sixties. Given this rate, I can expect to live another two hundred years at least."

"So, you've been here for hundreds of years?" I asked.

Elkins nodded. "Humans can be a bit touchy about nearly immortal men, so every so often, I either change my name, or pretend to be my own descendant. I had been a Hoterson for many years, having revisited the name in the late 1800s. I was tired of claiming to be my own grandson, so I decided a change was needed, about ten years ago. Nic had the opportunity to change his surname to Elkins, but he chose to keep it as is."

"If you were born in the prison world, how did you get here, then?"

Elkins looked sad for a moment. "You've been there. You know what that place does to magic."

"It sucks it up like a sponge," I replied.

"Yes. Many Fae die within a matter of months of being placed there. Some last longer, if they are powerful magic users. My father lived five years in that desolate place before succumbing."

I didn't whistle in appreciation, because I didn't want this windbag to know I esteemed anything that came out of his mouth. But still, I knew what a toll the siphoning of magic had on Fae folk.

"Despite the constant loss of magic, my father helped my mother engineer a storage crystal, and he tried to sink as much of his magic into it as possible. His hope was to allow us to escape before he died.

"But it wasn't enough. After his death, my mother tried to figure out how to make the magic stretch enough to open a portal for us both. She failed. In the end, when I was twelve and my own magic began to manifest, she sent me alone. She worried the place would eventually kill me, same as my father.

"So, I waited. I figured out how this world works and learned to survive it through my teenage years. I studied business and worked my way from the ground up. After thirty years or so, I faked my death and willed everything to a new persona. Eventually, I amassed a fortune, and with Mother's help, I began the long search for your kind in order to allow Mother to return."

I recalled a snippet of conversation I had overheard at Deerhorn Manor: something about not being able to contact his mother. "You communicated through the crystal, didn't you?" I asked.

He nodded, then set his mouth into a fine line of distaste. "I did, until you destroyed it. I had a fragment of the crystal, you see. It allowed us to talk, like any communication crystal. But it took Mother a good number of months to reestablish the line. By then, you had destroyed the Addelboro facility and fled."

"I'd say I'm sorry for that, but I'm really not," I drawled.

Elkins' knuckles turned white as he tightened his grasp on his chair. We may have been holding a civil conversation, but I could tell that his amiable persona was wearing thin. It begged the question.

"Why are you keeping me alive? You don't like me, and killing me would solve all your problems, wouldn't it?"

He flexed his jaw. "Every single thing I've done over the years has been to release my mother from prison. Your death would have been much celebrated even before you destroyed her crystal. But once I learned that Mother had lost all of the magic she had spent centuries collecting, we were forced to change plans. I still would like to kill you, in all honesty. But there's something stopping me."

"What's that?"

The door opened abruptly, making me flinch with the unaccustomed light.

"Me," Nic said, butting into our conversation. He walked over to me, sinking down to be at my eye level, his back to his father. His face was back to pristine, with no hints that he had been abused.

"Cressida, I'm so sorry for the lies. Everything I did was for your best interest. I convinced my father to spare you, because ever since I saw you at the Equinox Ball, I've been enchanted with you. I've spent the last six months trying to find you so that I can get to know you. My intentions were good. Please, forgive me?"

The pure loathing I held at his deception slowly melted away with each word he uttered. By the time he asked for forgiveness, I wanted to give it to him, but a small part of me, the obnoxiously stubborn part, held out.

"I'll think about it," I replied.

He smiled, his charming dimple making an appearance. "That's all I ask. Now, come. Let's get you patched up, and then we can have some breakfast."

I carefully brushed my fingers along my battered cheekbone, the pain from the gentle touch almost too much to bear. "I don't want to be healed," I said, digging my metaphorical heels in. "But I *would* like to eat something."

"Are you sure?" he asked, his eyes flashing with pity. "It looks painful."

"I'm sure."

"Very well. I'll get us some breakfast. You wait here. Father, for the Hunt's sake, turn some lights on in this room!"

"Watch your tone, boy," Elkins growled. "She's still a prisoner even if you've tamed the beast."

I said nothing. Despite his treachery, Nic still made me feel safe. I still trusted him. But that exact feeling? I could no longer trust it. My cheek throbbed, and for some reason, it was important to me to keep this pain as a memento, lest I lose myself completely.

CHAPTER 26

After a quick breakfast, I was largely left alone for the rest of the day. Nic promised that no harm would come to me or my friends, and so if I needed some feline time I would not be whisked away to surgery. According to him, being spayed was officially off the table. I still trusted his word, so, as soon as I was locked into my windowless room, I immediately transformed.

My feline cheek throbbed just as much as my human one had, but I carefully cleaned around it with wetted paw. I thought I would settle down for a nap, but my mind was a whir of activity, and no amount of lying in a cat ball with my eyes closed would put it to ease. Instead, I put it to work, ticking over the events from the last couple of days. The more I thought about this trip to the coast, the more I felt like a complete, played fool.

I should have clawed Elkins' eyes out when I had the chance. But my claws would not have gotten the job done in their current state, I surmised dolefully as I inspected them. Still, a good mauling may have done wonders for my spirit, even if it wasn't fully effective.

He probably would have killed me, however. I was walking a thin line, despite Nic's assurances.

A knock on the door broke my reverie.

"Cressida? I'm coming in," Gavin's voice filtered through the door.

I quickly transformed into my human body as the lock clicked and the door slowly opened. Gavin peeked inside, saw me, and swiftly entered and shut the door behind him.

"Why is it so dark in here?" he asked. I had been given a small lamp to light the room, but I currently had it turned down low, since there wasn't much to see.

"I was trying to nap. And failing miserably. Hang on," I said, turning the brightness up.

Gavin winced at the sight of me, as soon as he could properly see. "Ooh, your cheek."

I shrugged. "A little memento from Elkins. I'll be fine. But what are you doing here?"

Gavin seemed agitated. "What am I *doing* here? You threw me into the crazy end of the pool, Cress! What have you gotten me into?"

"Slow down, Gavin." I walked over to him, guiding him to sit in the chair Nic had pretended to be strapped to. "What's going on?"

Gavin was at a momentary loss of words. He studied me. "Rafferty came to my room after you left, and I told him I was willing to join the ACF. He then took the time to explain what's happening. Only, it makes no sense! Make it make sense, Cressida."

I had a sinking feeling I knew where this was going. My heart rate sped up in anticipation. "Okay, Gavin," I said, my voice calmer than I felt. "What exactly did he tell you?"

Gavin put a fist under his nose as he gathered his thoughts. He looked up at me. "Okay, bear with me. Annie had a cat—a familiar—that cursed her to the prison dimension, and ever since there's been a cat in this world that keeps Annie from returning. And somehow you are also keeping her from returning, because

Rafferty mentioned that Elkins wants to kill you. So, what am I missing?"

I could lie my butt off. I could spin an elaborate tale to explain my presence and still keep my secret to myself. But in this moment, I was too tired to try.

It was time for that moment of truth.

I sighed deeply, emptying my lungs with the weariness of a long-burdened secret keeper. "He wants to kill me because *I* am the cat that is keeping Annie from returning."

Gavin stared, unblinking at my statement. "You," he stated.

"Me."

He let out a laugh. "So, both sides are certifiably mad, then. Good to know."

I shook my head. "No, really. Gavin, remember when I told you I had big secrets to keep for the good of the world?"

His eyes narrowed. "Yes ..."

"Okay, well, here we are. The fate of the world is crumbling around us, and guess why that is? I'll give you a clue: I've been captured by the ACF."

"But you're not a cat, clearly." He gestured at my body.

I blew out a breath. "Did your dad say the part about 'the cat that walks as a woman?'"

Gavin nodded. "When he said it, I got the mental picture of a cat in high heels and a dress, wearing makeup as it walked about on two legs."

I rolled my eyes. "Of course you did." I placed a hand on his shoulder, readying him, readying myself. "Look, just don't freak out, okay?"

He lowered his brows. "Freak out about what?"

I closed my eyes. "This." I shimmered down into cat form and opened my eyes to look up at Gavin.

He jumped away from me, nearly overturning the chair in the process. "What in hell—Pita? *Cressida?*"

I mewed at him, perking my tail jauntily and raising a paw for maximum cuteness.

He shook his head in disbelief. "No, that's ... that's ..."

I transformed back. "Hard to believe?" I finished for him. "Well, it's true. I'm the cat of prophecy. Sorry I couldn't tell you before."

He stared at me. "Your hair finally makes sense." He had been of the opinion that I dyed those two black streaks in my hair, until I set the record straight for him this spring. "Who else knows?"

"Not many." I began ticking my fingers. "Fleurette, Lyle, Fal, Wren, hmm ... your cousin. My dad. Oh, members of a secret society know."

"Elkins?" he supplied helpfully.

"Yes, Elkins, his *son* Nic, Althea, Dr. Orcutt, your dad, apparently ..." I was already up to eleven fingers, not even counting the numerous members of GOGS. This was becoming more people than I liked to admit.

Gavin finished the list. "And now me."

I gave a quick nod. "And now you. I'd truthfully like less people to know. But I assume I can trust you with this knowledge, right?" I gave him an imploring look.

"I should have known there was something about you. And cats. Always cats!" He gave me a once-over. "It suits you, though. Thanks for finally telling me. Your secret's safe with me, although I don't see how it's relevant, considering everyone here already knows."

"If we get out of this alive, it'll be more pertinent," I replied. "And I fully intend to get out of this mess alive. Things just got a little ... messier than I had anticipated."

"I heard you waltzed right back in here. Not your finest move."

"No, it wasn't," I replied ruefully. "I thought I was rescuing a friend. You know, like last time I saved someone from torture." I waggled my brows at him. The motion made my cheek ache. "Can I still count on you to be our eyes and ears on the Annie side?"

"What, you don't want to get out of here right now?" he asked.

I shook my head. "Not without Fleurette and Kokoro. Unless you already sprung them?" I added with hope.

He pursed his lips to the side. "No such luck. Rafferty has them locked up tight. I'm not even supposed to be in here talking with you."

I slumped my shoulders. "Then, we bide our time. Or I will, at any rate. If you want to bag out, I'd understand."

He threw up his hands. "Escape on my own? No. Not without my cousin, and your friend, who is a lovely person, by the way. And you. I can't leave you to save my own skin. You once put yourself in danger to save my life. I'm returning the favor. I can't let a *cat* show me up."

I smiled with relief. "Thanks. You're a good guy, Gavin."

He returned the smile as he stepped toward the door. "No, I'm not. I'm a baaad guy, remember?" he said with a wink, before slipping out into the hallway.

CHAPTER 27

Once again, it was just me and my thoughts for a few solid hours.

At five, Nic opened the door, and I shimmered into my human form with the intent to chew him out.

He got the first word in though. "Cressida, did you get some rest? I've come to collect you for dinner. We have guests, as well."

He sounded genuinely concerned for my wellbeing. I was still determined to hash out some things with him, but the need to bite his head off once again receded. I only nodded and walked out of the room with him by my side, my head held at a proud angle despite the pain I experienced.

Nic led me to the formal dining room, complete with a grand table bedecked in the standard white tablecloth and a setting at each chair. Large silver cloches sat in the middle, keeping dishes of food warm.

My eyes focused immediately on Fleurette and Kokoro, who sat side by side at the far end. Kokoro now wore a simple gray tunic, the rest of her body hidden under the table. Both women also wore grim expressions. Fleurette blanched when she saw me, focusing on my battered cheek.

Across from them sat Rafferty and Gavin, the former gazing at Kokoro with obvious interest and the latter looking somber at my entrance. I met his eyes briefly, but I looked away, not wanting to draw attention to our connection. After all, he was in the enemy's camp now.

Elkins—I refused to think of him by any other name—was also present, sitting at the head of this bizarre little dinner party. On his right, next to Kokoro, sat another man whom I recognized.

"Babcock!" I sputtered.

Mr. Thomas Babcock, esquire, rose from his seat at my utterance, his round belly threatening to dislodge his place setting. "Miss Curtain. I was told you were here. How nice to see you again."

I scoffed. "I wish I could say the same."

Nic nudged my arm. "Manners, Cressida."

I scowled at him.

The last person was Dr. Orcutt, who was seated on Fleurette's right. He nodded his head at me in muted greeting. I did not return the favor.

Four of Elkins' goons stood about the room, guarding the ways out and monitoring the prisoners. I recognized them from the inn's dining room as the group of men who had sat against the far wall.

Althea was conspicuously absent. I would have thought that as one of Elkins' cronies, she would have been a shoo-in for this affair.

Nic guided me to sit down at the nearest end of the table, opposite his father. He then situated himself next to Rafferty, on my right. As soon as we sat, a servant appeared and began removing the cloches and dishing up food for each person.

I studied the food when it was placed before me: bloody sirloin, sauteed greens, and roasted baby potatoes. It looked delicious, but I had no appetite. I picked at the meat with my fork, gathering up the will to eat.

Freya only knew if I would need the extra strength this meal would give me tonight.

Meanwhile, every single seated person was silent, the tension in the room growing to suffocating levels.

I couldn't take it any longer. "So, Nic, are your family dinners always this delightful?"

Nic, taking a drink of water, choked.

"Miss Curtain, did no one teach you manners?" Elkins interjected. "With your position, you should know not to speak unless spoken to."

"I'm a little foggy on the rules, Gregor," I responded. "Perhaps they got knocked out of me today."

"Come now, Gregory! She is the guest of honor, is she not?" Rafferty butted in with enthusiasm.

"Am I?" I asked. I looked from Orcutt to Babcock, sweeping over Elkins and skipping past Gavin to settle on Rafferty, who smiled widely at me.

Babcock cleared his throat. "Technically speaking, none of this would be possible without her."

"And what about all of you?" I asked. "You are all guests at this table. Surely that means you are all bootlickers—I mean, executives of tonight's occasion, whatever it may be. I have a good guess for each of you. Gregor, you're easy; mama's boy."

Elkins narrowed his eyes at me before glancing around the room. Nobody else uttered a sound.

I flew a hand up to my mouth. "Oops, was that a secret? Was I not supposed to blurt out that you are Annie's son?"

Elkins glared at me, his polite facade wearing ever thinner by my digging. "It was not exactly common knowledge to all, no."

Orcutt said quietly, "It certainly explains a couple of things. Sir." He tacked the honorific on as an afterthought.

I stifled the giggle that threatened to explode out of me, "Well, let's continue my guessing game, shall we? Orcutt, you were two seconds away from removing my uterus. I've heard that's not happening anymore. Now you seem sort of redundant. Rafferty—"

"Mr. Santorum," the older man corrected me.

I rolled my eyes, making sure the gesture was on full display. "Right. You were responsible for the towers, were you not?"

Rafferty nodded, pleased. "The towers will be essential for tonight. They will channel the free energy to where we need it most. And the fox pearl; thank you for giving it back to us. Inaba had taken it from the kitsune a few years prior. With it, he was able to grow his empire in Tyonoshima. And the Kitsune could do nothing about it as long as he kept it in his personal possession."

I flinched. Poor Kitty, being without her power for so long. And now she was missing it again, because of my stupidity.

Rafferty gave a small shake of his head. "It was a blow to learn that Inaba had been killed, and the pearl was missing. It's our engine, after all. The towers and machinery were all designed around using it, so not having it would have completely screwed us. But, things worked out in the end, after all."

Kokoro looked stricken at this news. Kitty must have been fuming within her.

I felt sick to my stomach, but tried to keep up my flippant demeanor. "Yes, well, there's that. Babcock, I have no idea why you're here."

The portly man swallowed, uneasy at my glib behavior. "Legal channels, Miss Cressida. I'm here to ensure the validity of Annie's claims."

"Of course, how stupid of me," I commented, brandishing my fork. I decided a slight change of topic was needed. "Is it true that you're bringing Annie back to make her a god?"

Someone dropped their silverware onto their plate with a clang. The sound reverberated for a second.

"Who told you that?" Elkins asked, glaring at Nic.

Nic shook his head in an "it wasn't me" gesture.

I grinned, pleased to cause a little chaos. "A little birdie told me. My question is, are you all out of your minds?"

Orcutt spoke up, "My dear, other worlds have a patron god or gods. This realm has simply borrowed from other dimensions. We feel it would be a boon to have a god of our own."

"This world has been in balance for millennia," I countered. "The current system works. Annie is a mound of disastrous dung just waiting to cover this world in a layer of her filth."

"Are you always this cavalier when your friends' lives hang in the balance?" Elkins asked as he speared me with a glower across the way. He began stabbing his potatoes with more force than necessary, probably imagining them to be me.

I flattened my lips. "Do they, though? I've still not been informed about what the plan is. You could be taking us on a lovely little stroll to a freshly dug pit, for all I know."

"Cressida, I told you; you won't be harmed," Nic reiterated politely.

I rolled my neck, popping a couple vertebrae. "Me, no. Fleurette and Kokoro? Maybe. How am I to know they will be safe no matter what?"

Elkins sighed heavily. "As long as you cooperate, no harm will come to them."

I wished I had Gavin's watch for the second time today.

Rafferty, who had been swilling a glass of red wine like it was the antidote to poison, added, "I'll give you some reassurance, girlie. I'll keep them safe. I'm throwing my hat in the ring for the Tyonoshimese girl."

His statement was met by silence all around. Even the scraping of utensils against plates ceased. Gavin finally broke it. "Ew, Father. That's your niece."

"Only through marriage," Rafferty replied as he heavily stared at the woman in question. Kokoro tried to hide under her inky hair. Her discomfort weighted me down.

Trying to ignore the fetishizing that was taking place at the other end of the table, I addressed Elkins. "I've hazarded a guess about your cronies' reasons for being here. But what about me? Just what is it, Gregor, that you would have me do tonight?"

Elkins settled his gaze upon me, a calculating stare. "Tonight is the full moon before Samhain. The Hunter's moon. We will be connecting our world with Annie's world. And then you will invite her in."

"Over my dead body!" I shouted.

Elkins kept his cool. "Well, my darling girl, if that is the way it must be. But we've already established that you don't flinch over personal bodily harm." He pointed to his own cheek to remind me of the swollen bruise on mine. "The well-being of those you care for is another matter. Therefore, I have constructed an insurance policy, if you will, in the form of people that appear to be near and dear to you. These two women are just the start, I assure you. A visual reminder of what will be at stake, should you decline your assistance. But I can give you my guarantee: you do what I say, and you and your pals will be untouched. But if you refuse, I will personally end each one individually while you watch. Only after I am through with them will it be your turn."

I believed him. My rage over his statements was a caged tiger, contained but never docile. He had the upper hand. I would keep the cage shut for a little longer.

"Fine. You win, Gregor. Although so far, you haven't shown me that you are capable of murdering anyone."

"It's true that my somnification isn't strong enough to kill anyone. Yet. That's why I sent my son to do the dirty work."

I frowned. "Your son? Do you have another one hanging out in the eaves or something?"

Elkins shook his head, never breaking eye contact. A smile as slight as a reed in wind breezed across his features. "I only have the one son," he said almost gleefully.

Stricken, I looked at Nic. "Is this true?"

Nic looked ashamed, and, dare I say, annoyed with his father for spilling the beans. "Yes."

"That was why you were in Knobby Hill," I surmised, heat spreading into my face. My inner tiger roared. "Maurice."

"It wasn't my idea, you must believe me, Cressida," Nic pleaded. He placed a hand on my forearm. "I was only following orders."

My anger fizzled. Of course, Nic was just a pawn in all of this, same as me and everyone else at this table.

Kokoro narrowed her eyes as she watched Nic's interaction with me.

"Cressida, I promise you that all will work out. You'll see. Just please don't be angry with me, okay?" Nic continued to work his case. Every word made so much sense. It *would* work out; I believed him.

"Very well, Nic," I said, and took a bite of cold steak. Despite the excellent cut, it felt like rubber in my mouth.

Elkins dabbed his lips on a napkin and stood up. "Well, this has been a charming evening. Ladies, gentlemen, I must get ready. Dr. Orcutt, why don't you accompany me and escort the ladies here to their quarters? And then meet me outside to assist our other guests." He left before the other man could give his assent.

Dr. Orcutt went to help Fleurette up from her seat with a hand on her arm. Fleurette flinched away. *"Don't touch me,"* she hissed, speaking for the first time this evening.

Orcutt held up his hands before making a shooing gesture with them. Fleurette and Kokoro locked hands as they were ushered out of the room. But at the door, Kokoro stood her ground, turning to look at me. I cocked my head to the side, puzzled.

"Cressida!" she yelled to me while Orcutt and another goon began pushing her and Fleurette out of the room. "It's Nic! He is completely yellow!"

That's all she got out before she disappeared behind a door.

I glanced at Nic, puzzled by what she said. He shrugged, not understanding either. He wasn't yellow, of course, although he had blonde hair. Nor were his clothes yellow. What had she meant? What else could be yellow?

And then it hit me: the memory of Kokoro telling us that she saw magic as colors. Fleurette was mostly green; I was white. And Lyle had small specks of yellow from his natural charisma.

Yellow. Mind magic.

CHAPTER 28

Dinner was clearly over, now that the master had stepped out. Rafferty and Gavin took their leave, the latter shooting me one last concerned look before exiting. It was just me and Nic left at the table.

I turned to Nic. "So that's it, huh? Mind magic?"

Nic looked puzzled. "What are you talking about?"

"Oh, come off it!" I hissed. "You've been messing with my emotions this entire time."

"Is that what that woman was blathering about?" Nic asked, his tone becoming heated. "Fine. You want to know? I'm a kharismorph. I can control emotions in other people. And I have to say, you have given me quite a workout."

This whole time. Every instance when I'd gotten annoyed or angry with Nic, the feeling had simply evaporated. Grimm had been right. I was being magically controlled and I had been oblivious to it. I wanted to cry at my ignorance.

"Come on now, Cressida, it isn't all that bad. Surely you can't be mad at letting go of your anger."

Now that I knew what to look for, I could feel it. His magic wriggled its way around in my brain, chasing away the anger like an oily yellow worm. It still worked too, except deep down I held on to the kernel of rage, my sleeping tiger, never allowing myself to forget what caused it.

"You're right. I *am* angry a lot. Maybe I have a lot to be angry about. But it *is* nice to let it go," I replied with false cheer.

"Good girl," he praised. I forced myself to keep the scowl off my face.

"Did you really kill Maurice?" I asked, a heavy weariness settling over me at the overall hopelessness of the situation.

He nodded, but took no joy in the motion, his face solemn. "And the others. Father would find them through his dreams, pinpoint their locations, and send me out to do the final task. He claims he's been working on offing people in their dreams himself, but he doesn't seem to have it mastered yet."

"Poor guy," I deadpanned. "So, you've lied to me from the start? You said you weren't a killer."

He squirmed at my grilling. "I don't like to think of myself as a bad guy. I'm only doing this to release my grandmother."

"Your grandmother, the most malicious witch this world has ever known? The one that began culling magical folks to cut down on competition? The grandmother who delighted in tormenting the local populace with never-ending dancing spells and purposefully killed crops with snowstorms in summer?"

"She's still family. Isn't family important to you? And besides, that was a long time ago. Completely circumstantial. What if *your* ancestor imprisoned her out of spite and not out of duty like your sycophants spout?"

I pinched the bridge of my nose at the hypocrisy I was hearing. There was no point in arguing with him. "Sure. Let's just agree to disagree. Where are we going?"

Nic led me past the room I had previously been stored in. "My MC," he replied, gripping my arm with enough extra force to be on the edge of pain. "It's time to get to the site. And Cressida, for the love of the Hunt, please behave yourself."

His magic tugged at me, making me want to please him. I obediently allowed myself to be led outside and into the front seat of the same MC he had borrowed back at the inn.

"This is yours?" I iterated.

He turned on the head lamps against the dark of fall and pulled out of the generous driveway. "Yes, it is."

"Now that my rosy glasses have fallen from my face, I'm viewing the happenings over the last few days in a different light. Let me recap and see if I've missed any tricks. First, I noticed some familiar faces at dinner tonight. I remembered them from the inn. They were there to keep an eye on things, yes?"

"More or less."

"I'm going to go with more. And the werewolves; they were with the goons too. The attack was planned out. They targeted Humbert on purpose, didn't they?"

Nic gripped the wheel. "They weren't supposed to go after you, though. But werewolves, even those who have been magically enhanced to change sooner than the full moon, aren't exactly known for the stability of their minds."

I took a deep breath. "That's why you killed the one Grimm and I had captured. You were worried he'd spill the beans."

Nic said nothing. I took his silence as an affirmative.

I pressed on. "This MC just happened to be waiting there for us to use. And Dr. Orcutt was also staged there, to 'help' Humbert, but more importantly to get a good look at me. No wonder he seemed so excited to meet me. And the Tyonoshimese men?"

Nic blew out a breath. "I knew they were there too. They were looking for the fox. For the woman it possessed, more specifically."

I studied him. "Their deaths rattled you, didn't they?"

"Can you blame me?" he asked, glancing my way. "I wasn't expecting to come across their corpses. Rafferty had told me that they were a ruthless bunch, but the fox cut them down like stalks of wheat."

"She's nothing to trifle with." I tapped my chin with a finger. "What about the tower we came across?"

"What about it?"

"You knew it was there, didn't you?"

Nic flexed a hand on the steering wheel. "Yes."

"And you knew why the power kept cutting out. So, your 'mishap' at the shed was all staged?"

Nic nodded reluctantly. "Dad needed you to be in cat form before you were knocked out. We set it up in advance to capture you under the shed. He predicted you would do anything to help me if you thought I was in danger."

"It sickens me that Gregor knows me so well," I muttered.

Nic shrugged. "He was right though, wasn't he? Just another reason why you're my unicorn."

I hated that nickname but kept it to myself. "So, this whole trip was a study in how to isolate me. First you took away my horse and transportation, and then you conveniently 'lost' my only form of communication, and finally ..." I choked up, unable to finish as I thought through the implications.

Grimm hadn't left me after all.

I didn't know which warring emotion held more sway: happiness that he would have stuck around, or sadness that he too fell prey to this scheme.

Nic summed it up for me. "Your dog was dangerous. I got a firsthand look at that during the werewolf attack. We took the opportunity to take him out when he served himself on a silver platter that night."

"Did you kill him?" I whispered, not wanting to hear the answer, but needing to know. A tear leaked down my cheek.

Nic pursed his lips, thinking over what to tell me. "He's been asleep. Dr. Orcutt wants to study him. He's our resident werewolf expert, and he helped with the creation of the enhancing serum. Orcutt was over the moon to get his hands on Grimm. Lycanhunds are so rare that their magic is not well understood. His blood may be useful in developing new potions and spells, especially for further augmentation of super-werewolves."

"He's alive?" I barely believed my ears.

"As long as he behaves himself, yes. It's a big maybe, though. He seems rather unstable."

"Only to jackasses who want to harm me," I muttered.

Nic either didn't hear me or ignored what I said. He reached over and placed a hand over mine in my lap. It took all my willpower not to pull away.

But then I no longer wanted to. His touch felt safe, comforting. My anger at the situation dissipated.

"Don't worry. All will work out as it needs to," Nic assured me.

I believed him.

CHAPTER 29

The ride lasted two hours. Nic had driven away from Oyster Bay and inland into the dense coastal forest. We encountered no other vehicles for the bulk of the ride, but near the end of the trip, another MC drove behind us, shining its lights into our back window.

Nic pulled off the main highway, slowly driving us down a tight dirt road. The forest was practically primordial here, with lichen dangling from giant limbs like tattered lace. I was macabrely reminded of funeral shrouds.

Nic parked in a small turnout from the dirt road, where two other vehicles already waited, empty of passengers. The MC behind us also parked.

"Looks like we're fashionably late to the party," Nic mused.

I said nothing, but my pulse hammered with unspoken anxiety.

Nic picked up a lantern and got out, rushing over to open my door like a true gentleman. He pulled me to his side, once again grasping my arm in a possessive manner. I looked over at the other MC as Rafferty and Gavin climbed out.

"The gang's all here," Rafferty declared with his usual dollop of buffoonery. It made me wonder how Gavin could have turned out as suave and self-assured as was—or at least pretended to be.

Speaking of Gavin, he stared at me with unhidden worry. I gave him a subtle headshake. *Play your part*, I willed at him.

He looked away.

Nic took the lead, holding up the lantern with one arm while gripping my wrist with the other. A small break in the shrubbery indicated the start of a path, and he eagerly pulled me along it. Huckleberry bushes and salal lined the trail, with crowding ferns brushing against my legs with every step. It had rained recently, and the leaves deposited enough dew to leave wet marks on my thighs as we traipsed past.

The march seemed never ending, but in all reality lasted fifteen minutes. And then the path ended, widening onto a clearing that held a large rectangular building in the center. The windows were lit up in an almost inviting manner after the trek through the dark woods. But I did not want to go in there. Foreboding struck me immobile.

Nic tugged at me, noticing my reluctance. "Almost there."

I closed my eyes as I took a deep breath, fortifying myself and trying to calm my pounding heart. And then I gave in to Nic's insisting tug and entered the building.

The slow humming of machinery met my ears the instant I entered. It seemed to be coming from one side of the open room to my left, where one of the short walls was taken up by a variety of technological apparatuses.

Having satisfied my need to find the source of the hum, I focused on the room as a whole.

It was filled with people.

Elkins stood closer to the machinery, with Althea standing behind him. She seemed shrunken in upon herself, hiding her face with a sheet of platinum hair, a stark contrast to the first time I had met her, when she acted as wrathful and proud as an ice goddess.

Babcock stood near Althea with a folder in his arms. I almost snickered at the thought of him handing the papers to Annie upon her return and saying, "Please sign here ... and here ..." It was too bad that the dour mood of the room sucked most of my levity dry.

The same goons that monitored the dinner party hung out toward the back of the room. Across from the wall of technology, stood my friends. I was dismayed to see not only Fleurette and Kokoro, but Lyle, Fal, and Wren. They appeared to be unharmed, but their eyes shone with undisguised fear.

Kokoro and Fleurette grasped each other for comfort, as did Fal and Wren. Lyle stood apart, but his eyes stayed trained on the woman that was his long-lost wife, his expression one of anguish.

Meanwhile, Dr. Orcutt also loitered in the background, guarding a large black dog with yellow eyes.

"Grimm," I breathed as I took a step toward him.

Nic jerked me back. "Not now, Cressida," he warned me.

Grimm flicked his ears down and licked his lips anxiously. But he was smart enough not to barrel over to me. He knew what a sticky predicament we were in. I only smiled worriedly at him, to let him know I was okay.

Meanwhile, Rafferty and Gavin squeezed past us into the room. Elkins saw them and motioned for the two to stand next to Althea. Once they were in position, he smiled broadly at everyone, including the prisoners.

"Friends, family, tonight is the night. For years you have toiled ceaselessly to do something momentous. Tonight, we will bring our matriarch back."

The thugs in back applauded. Orcutt and Babcock smiled. Rafferty clapped his son on the back.

"Over one year ago, my mother and I had been working on a way to allow her into this world. But disaster struck." Elkins glared at me. "She lost her stored magic, and the worst part was the fact that communication was halted between us. I had no idea what had happened. But time prevailed. With Rafferty Santorum's expertise in combining magic and technology, as well as his knowledge of Tyonoshimese lore, we were able to come up with a new plan.

"Inaba Ebiru, may his soul be at peace, had taken a *hoshi no tama* from a kitsune many years previously. With Rafferty's help they devised a way to harness the power of the fox in order to open a gateway between my mother's world and this world.

"Our new plan was simple in concept. We needed a location to open a gateway. The reality was much more complex, however. To open a gateway, we required more magic than all of us combined possessed." He paused and scanned the crowd, as if making sure we all hung on his every word.

"All the dimensions in the universe are interconnected in some way. Natural doorways exist between certain planes, and can more often be found upon Samhain, when the Veil is at its thinnest. However, the full moon before Samhain has its own magical properties. Dr. Orcutt established that with his research into modified lycanthropy, and Althea was able to test his research in the real world.

"Thanks to Dr. Orcutt and Althea, we have discovered two unique geographical locations to facilitate our task at hand. Both sites unsurprisingly are sacred to the Memory Keepers, our Indigenous brethren. One location is far from here, worshiped because of the natural and permanent thinning of the wall between worlds in that location. Practically a doorway in and of itself. This will be the site of the new gateway between worlds."

So that was how it was going to happen. Elkins was about to tamper with a magic older than time in order to force a rift between worlds.

Elkins continued his speech, "A thinning between worlds was a bonus to us, but still not enough to make the gateway a possibility. But upon this spot, the second sacred site, we have discovered that magic is naturally amplified. This was where we built our marvelous machine, as you see before you. A modern miracle of technology." He stepped back to give his technological miracle a loving pat.

"And what does it do, you might ask? My friends, this machine will amplify the already amplified magic, making our power go from tenfold to one hundredfold. And it does that with the use of free energy.

"The machine needs more electricity than we are ever allotted at one time, however. Much, much more energy. So much more that we had to channel it from half of the region. And that is what the towers are for. They have been set up to collect the abundance of electricity and send it to one of the two places. The free energy they gather boosts the natural magic and enhances its power.

"Even then, it would not have been enough. But with the addition of the fox pearl, our engine for this machine, we will finally have enough magic and power to open the gate."

I scowled once again, thinking of how I was tricked into giving up the most important piece to this whole nightmarish situation.

"Lastly, thanks to Mr. Babcock, we have secured both sites for our use, effectively shutting out the Memory Keepers from these places."

I pursed my lips. The Memory Keepers, the original inhabitants of Vinland, were revered. They would not be pleased with Elkins for taking over their sacred spaces for such a task.

"And now, tonight, all our hard work is finally about to pay off," Elkins continued. "It was touch and go once we lost the kitsune power," Elkins chuckled as if it had been a playful farce, "but we got it back in the end. The gods have smiled upon us in this endeavor, folks. It is clear that we have been blessed by them, and that they intend to welcome Annie Coddle into the Universal Pantheon."

I snorted at this high-handed statement.

Elkins ignored me, as fired up as he was. "By combining the sacred location, this Hunter's moon, and the marvels of modern technology, we will now open a permanent doorway between my mother's realm and this one."

Elkins turned to Fleurette's mother. "Althea, ready the lights." His tone brooked no argument.

Like a dog who had been whipped, she sprang forward. Althea uttered no words, although she stole a glance at her daughter with eyes large and glassy. She moved her hands, producing a small orb of glowing light, like a will-o'-the-wisp. She fanned her hands out, and the wisp moved away from her, traveling to a far corner of the building. She repeated this action several more times, until wisps lined the walls.

Elkins stationed himself by the machine. Muttering some magical words, he pulled down a lever. The contraption hummed ever louder, as if revving up. The lights flickered overhead.

"And now, the fox pearl. Althea!" Elkins barked.

Althea bent and picked up a wooden box at her feet. She opened its lid, revealing the shimmering light of the fox pearl.

Elkins picked it up out of the cradle of satin it had been resting upon. He reverently swung his arms around to the machine and fit the orb into a socket in the contraption.

The room's lights went out immediately as the machine consumed all the nearby free energy. Althea's wisps did their job well, however, keeping the space bathed in a pleasant low glow.

The engine began to roar with the amount of electricity it had. I saw the star ball spin and glow brighter.

Kokoro groaned, clutching her midsection. Fleurette wrapped an arm around her for comfort.

I cringed. Kitty must have been in pain. This could kill Kokoro.

"It's working," Elkins marveled. He turned to me gleefully. "Only one last thing to do. It is time for your sacrifice, Miss Curtain."

CHAPTER 30

I stared blankly at the man.

"My sacrifice?" I repeated, puzzled.

Elkins frowned. "Yes, you silly git. You must allow Annie Coddle back into this world. The surest way is for you to willingly give your life for the cause."

"I never agreed to that," I countered.

"Miss Curtain, you seem to be under the impression that I care what happens to you and to the people you love. Listen, it's this simple. Either you cooperate, or ..." he walked over to the other side of the room and grabbed Wren's arm in an iron grip. Fal stepped forward to protect her, but Lyle held him back. Elkins marched Wren back to me. He held her around the waist, practically lifting her off the ground. He glared at me defiantly. "I *will* begin practicing sacrifices on your friends. Starting with her."

I stood immobilized, panic flooding me. I had set out on this journey initially to protect Wren, and now her life was once again being threatened. Wren's eyes spilled over with silent tears as she looked at me. There was no way I'd let this monster harm her.

"Well now, hang on," Rafferty exclaimed. "If we're going to start culling people, I want to call hands off on this one." He strode over and grasped Kokoro by her neck, forcing her upright and away from Fleurette—who glared at the man but made no move to stop him— and up against his front as he wrapped his hand around her throat. "I want to keep her."

Even Elkins looked disgusted by Rafferty's declaration. "Very well, Rafferty," he said.

Rafferty was the cat who got the cream at that statement. He stroked Kokoro's hair with his free hand. Kokoro squeezed her eyes shut, a pained expression upon her face. She dared not double over again while Rafferty held her, however.

Fleurette narrowed her eyes at the man. If looks could kill, he would be ablaze by now. But she was helpless to assist Kokoro. Instead, she sought comfort with Fal and her father, holding their hands and finding strength in familial contact.

Grimm also was a study in barely restrained agitation. He now spun in place, his ears fully back, and his lips quivering with the desire to show his teeth. Orcutt had him on a leash, I realized. The veterinarian held the end in a tight grasp but allowed my partner an ample length of the tether. He seemed prime to tug at the leash if Grimm did more than his agitated spinning.

If Orcutt thought the leash would stop Grimm from doing what my partner desired to do, the man was delusional. He may as well have tied Grimm up in a layer of spider silk, for all the good it would do.

I surveyed the room, the wheels of my mind spinning in mud as I sought the purchase of any sort of plan that would at least get my friends to safety. But I couldn't grasp a solution. It was too much. All I wanted to do was punch the smirk off Elkin's urbane face.

That wouldn't help anyone, but it would sure make me feel better.

My feet began to move of their own accord, advancing on Elkins to give him a taste of my wrath. Nic, assuming I was about to give in and sacrifice myself, grabbed my hand and pulled me back.

"Wait. You don't have to do this. There's another way," he said.

"And what would that be?" I asked, my usual scowl plastered on my brow.

"Allow her in. Denounce your claim to the legacy. And stay by my side." Nic held my hands in his, not to keep me there, but for the pleasure of my skin against his.

"What are you saying?" I asked, not fighting his small physical act of affection.

"You don't have to die. You can be mine for the rest of your life."

"Nic," I said quietly, his magical charisma softening me. "I can't love you."

"I know, but I can make you feel like you do. And I can talk Grandmother into reversing your curse. At least then you could feel some natural affection for me. It would be a fulfilling life."

He gripped my hands harder in desperation. I could feel myself falling into the depths of his earnest blue eyes.

Beyond him, Grimm let out a warning bark.

"I may not have been truthful about everything, but you really did enchant me when I first laid eyes on you. Your dress, your posture, your face," he declared, rubbing his thumb over the top of my hand in soothing passes. "I knew I had to find you. Mom even gave her blessing. She told Dad to allow me this happiness. You were meant for me, Cressida. My unicorn."

Nic's declarations of affection tugged at my heart. That last strand of stubbornness refused to let go, however. "Nic, I don't know ..."

"You will want for nothing, Cressida. I will grant your every wish. You would become a part of Grandmother's family. As her granddaughter-in-law, your status in the new world would be as high as you could get. You would be revered by all." He took a step forward, closing the gap between us.

A low growl filled the room. It was background noise. Only Nic mattered.

I could see this life as he described it. To be waited upon hand and foot, my every desire met. No more fighting for my right to live. No more living in fear. It sounded ... lovely.

But.

"What about my family?" I asked, my voice breathless.

"They'll be safe, I can promise you that. Please, Cressida. Don't throw away your life. Let me love you."

Nic leaned forward, intent on kissing me. I could allow that. It would be nice.

A ragged roar filled the air, finally tearing my attention away before our lips could touch. Dr. Orcutt cried out as Grimm turned and jumped up on him, clamping his jaw around the veterinarian's shoulder. Orcutt folded under the weight of the dog with one last howl of agony. The leash slipped from his fingers as Grimm gave one final vicious shake to his shoulder. Grimm let go and set his sights on Nic. He raced toward us, snarling in rage.

Nic straightened. "Oh, enough of this," he said with contempt. He turned toward the approaching dog with silver light leaking from his fingers.

"No!" I yelled as soon as I understood.

Nick fired off the silver light, hitting Grimm just as he leapt to attack.

Grimm yelped and rolled to the side. He whimpered once and then was still.

"No!" I screamed, my horrified gaze riveted on the unmoving dog.

"There," Nic proclaimed with satisfaction. He positioned his fingers on my chin, turning my head away from the sight of Grimm's still form, once again intent on kissing me.

He had just promised me he'd keep my family safe. He lied. Deep inside of me, the tiger broke its cage.

"*How could you?*" I seethed at Nic, taking a step back from him. Any illusions of positive emotions—comfort, attraction, trust—were irrevocably broken.

Nic must not have realized that yet. "Cressida, that dog was a menace. Look at what he did to Dr. Orcutt." The veterinarian was still on his back, panting in pain as his shirt turned red with blood. Nobody moved to help him, a testament to how little the ACFers cared for each other. Nic shook his head, changing his expression to one of false sympathy. He gave a small, pitying smile at me as his magic tried to worm its way back into my good graces. "Vicious mongrels should be put down."

"You're right," I said, stepping toward Nic again. His face blossomed into a full smile, his dimple making another appearance. The smile turned to confusion as I grabbed Nic by the wrists, clamping down hard. I narrowed my eyes on him. "They should be."

I shimmered.

I focused on my pocket. As soon as the comforting void greeted me, I put all my attention on Nic, who floated in front of me, tethered by my grasp on his wrists. He looked around himself, fear making his eyes widen.

"Wha—" he began.

"Goodbye, Nic," I interrupted as I let go of his wrists. With a final hard shove on his chest, I sent him flying away from me.

Nic let out a scream as he careened away from me, his hands reaching out to grab something, anything, as he traveled farther away. I savored the panic he exuded as he grew smaller, until he finally disappeared into the inky blackness.

I resumed my human form.

The place was in an uproar.

The goons had surrounded me while I was gone, but I was fine with that.

After all, I had one other trick up my sleeve.

My hands glowed with stolen silver light that I threw at one, two, three, all four of the men in quick succession. They crumpled as soon as the magic hit their chests.

I sought out Elkins next, only to see the backside of him as he hobbled determinedly out the door, with Wren clutched tightly to him. I couldn't pursue, because there were still more threats in the building to take care of first.

As soon as Elkins was gone, I turned to Althea, expecting her to be my biggest threat. But her attention was elsewhere. She released a different magic, aiming at Orcutt, who had gotten to his feet and was about to brandish a knife at Fleurette. He let out a yell and dropped to the ground. Once she had taken care of him, she walked backward into a corner by the machine, crouching down onto her heels and making herself as small as possible.

Babcock was behind me. The portly man seemed frozen by the sudden carnage. He made to flee, but Gavin strode up and punched him squarely in the face. Babcock dropped like a water balloon.

Gavin made eye contact with me after knocking out the lawyer. I gave him a head nod toward the machinery. His face displayed his apprehension, as if he could not believe the mayhem that was happening in front of his own eyes, but he once again proved to be unflappable. He casually strolled over to the machine and plucked the fox pearl out of its socket.

The machine gave a chugging cough. Sparks flew out of the empty socket as the overhead lights tried and failed to flicker back to life.

"Thanks," I yelled to him.

Gavin winked in response.

There was one last person standing on the opposing force: Rafferty Santorum. I thought I might take him out with Nic's stolen power, but I was worried about hitting Kokoro, who was being used as an unwilling human shield. Besides, I felt like I may have already used up the magic on the goons.

I wasn't afraid of the old lech. I began striding toward him.

Kokoro suddenly cried out in his arms and arched her spine. I stopped my march, trying to make sense of what I was seeing. She screamed, a thin, reedy sound. Her open mouth filled with light, and an energetic form flowed out and landed at her feet.

The form coalesced into the kitsune within the blink of an eye. The fox gave herself a brief shake, and then looked around. Before anyone could react, she whisked over to Gavin, took the orb from him, and pounced directly upon Rafferty, who had dropped the limp and unconscious Kokoro to the ground. He had time to let out a single scream before falling over. It was difficult to discern what Kitty was doing to him, but whatever it was, it left him as unmoving as Dr. Orcutt nearby.

All this happened in the periphery of my focus, however. Because in the middle of this pandemonium, there was only one thing I was wholly fixated on. Grimm still lay on his side, motionless.

As soon as Rafferty toppled, I rushed over to my partner and fell to my knees in front of his belly. I removed the leash from around his limp neck and cast the despised object away from us. "Grimm," I said, hoping he was still okay. After all, Nic did not hit him with a concentrated amount of magic.

Perhaps he only slept.

I placed a hand on his chest, checking for the rise and fall of breathing. No movement. Panicking, I reached under his back leg, groping for his femoral artery to check for a pulse. It was there, but barely.

"Fleurette! Fal! Lyle!" I called out, my voice cracking.

Gavin placed a hand on my shoulder. "They aren't here. They ran out to chase after Elkins, since he has the girl."

My chest heaved. "I need them. He's dying. Please, go find them!"

He squeezed my shoulder. "I'm on it."

I heard the back door open and slam shut while the machinery still coughed and groaned. I ignored it all, refusing to look away from Grimm.

A tear dripped down my nose and landed on his black fur as I buried my fingers into the soft tufts. I felt something nudge my arm and managed to rip my eyes away from Grimm's prone figure long enough to see what it could be.

Kitty. She looked glorious, her fur shining with an almost fiery quality, and her eyes aglow with a coral backlight. She had all her tails on display, and they writhed about behind her like fluffy snakes. She made a questioning yelp.

I transformed.

She looked uncertain. "He is not long for this world."

I hissed and lashed out a paw, claws out, into the air between us. Her words angered me. "Then *do* something."

"I cannot. He suffers from no mortal wound. It is a trauma to his soul that dooms him."

"I can't fix that. I—I don't know how."

"Then," she lamented with a soft sigh, "all is lost. I will be one tail short."

"*What*? You should have your tails. You separated from Kokoro." I glanced at the woman, who was no longer unconscious and starting to sit up. "You obviously didn't kill her when you left her body, which means you succeeded in helping her. That was your ninth tail. Isn't that what this is about?"

Kitty sighed again. "Yes. Kokoro is now safe. All the men who would do her harm are dead, and I have accounted for her future happiness by pairing her up with her heart's mate. But I admit, Cousin, I have lied. I only had seven tails. I now have eight. But I need one more."

"Unbelievable. My best friend is dying, and you want to talk to me about chasing tails?"

I couldn't listen to her anymore. I resumed my human form and rechecked Grimm's pulse.

It was gone.

"No," I whispered, scrambling to find a different spot on his inner thigh. "No," I repeated louder, not wanting to believe what my fingers were telling me.

I dug my hands into his shaggy black fur over his unmoving chest, grasping the strands with desperation. "Grimm. No. You can't do this to me. I need you," I sobbed, allowing more tears to drop from my eyes onto his body.

My mind spun uselessly. As I burrowed my fingers down to his still-warm skin, images of our intertwined lives sprouted up, one after another. Our first meeting, when Grimm nearly died of malnutrition, and I nearly died at the hands of a serial killer. The instant connection we had after we saved each other. The two of us deciding to be business partners. Hunting together. Cuddling every night together. Grooming each other. Heartfelt fights. Playful teasing. A life of contentment.

In every memory, good or bad, Grimm was there. My partner. I realized it now: my life did not start until I met him.

And now he was gone.

Any thoughts of my future vanished, a puff of smoke blown away by a careless wind.

All that was left inside of me was a ragged despondency.

I fell forward, hugging his still body to me. "You can't leave me, Grimm! You just can't. I can't do this without you. How can I?"

My tears soaked his ebony fur as I clung to him, pleading with my words, my heart, my soul. All my memories raced like pictures through my mind.

"Please, Grimm," I choked out, one last attempt at beseeching death. "Please. You mean everything to me. *I love you.*"

Those three words hung in the air.

I gasped. Time stopped as a heavy weight fell from deep inside of me, a mending of what had once been grievously harmed. The hole left in my soul from the curse healed over, replaced and forged with a new piece of soul that was both foreign within me, but as familiar as the dog it belonged to. I could feel a fragment of my own soul detach and transfer to his, mending the damage Nic's magic had done to him. Despite the loss of this segment, I still felt completely whole.

Soulbond.

Fleurette had said once that there were two types of soulbonds: one created unnaturally and unethically, and one created from pure love.

Love.

I loved Grimm.

Grimm, who wasn't a man.

The last traces of Annie's curse echoed hollowly in my head. "*I curse you, Descendant of Glivver, that from this day forward, and for the rest of your life, you will never fall in love with a man. Without true love, the line of Glivver will die with you!*" With that last iteration, the voice vanished, and the words faded from my mind, no longer etched upon my soul.

I had broken the curse.

More importantly, Grimm stirred underneath me. I let out a hitching gasp of a laugh, and then quickly morphed into a cat.

I sprang to his prone head, placing a paw on his cheek. "Grimm? Grimm, are you okay?"

"Cressida." He sounded woozy, weak, but blessedly alive. "Say it again."

"Say what?"

He was still too weak to lift his head. He gave me the side eye, a skill he had mastered during our time together. "That you love me."

I rubbed my forehead forcefully into Grimm's jaw, following it with my whole body. "I love you, Grimm."

He delicately flopped his tail on the floor. I could feel his happiness like the vibration of a bell in my soul. "I love you too, Cressida."

CHAPTER 31

"Ahem."

I lifted my head from Grimm's cheek to glance at Kitty.

She looked ... different.

"Kitty?" I asked. "What's happening?"

The kitsune was no longer a red fox. She was a pure white creature, with a brilliant otherworldly glow about her, the same shine as her fox pearl.

And she was beginning to levitate.

In my periphery, Kokoro stood and walked closer.

"Cousin. Thank you," Kitty said.

I cocked my head to the side, confused. "For what?"

She answered serenely, "Do you remember when I told you I had lied to you about the number of tails I had? It was because as soon as I learned about your existence and your curse while crossing the Serenic Ocean, I decided that helping *you* break the curse was my last good deed."

"Me?" I practically squeaked. "Why didn't you say anything?"

She narrowed her fully coral eyes at me. "If I had told you I was relying on you to ascend, it would have ended badly. Especially at the beginning of our acquaintanceship. The legs of the future were clear on that point. No, I needed to make you realize that you loved Grimm without any hints. I did try to make you jealous to assess if your stubborn ass could see that the solution had been in front of you all along."

"*That's* why you kept flirting with Grimm?" I asked, incredulous.

She dropped her head slowly in a serene nod. "I had no intentions to mate with him. Mortal dogs are not appealing to me, and I knew he was not interested, either. But I had to nudge you somehow. Regardless of your obstinate nature, you broke your curse. And you gifted me my last tail. Thank you."

"Oh." I picked through the minor insults to find the good in her comments. "You're welcome."

"Also, you should know that you now deserve Grimm's devotion. Well done."

A small weight lifted from my psyche. Her words from earlier in the week had apparently been gnawing at me. "Thanks."

She studied me, calculating. "Before I go, I would like to grant you one last favor, if I may."

"Um, sure. What do you have in mind?"

She pointed her nose at me. "The human in your pocket. I do not recommend leaving him in there."

Right. Nic. In all the hoopla, I had forgotten about him.

"Yes. How do I get him out?"

"Shift. I will find him."

I did as I was told. The fox dove at me as I shimmered and lost form. I did not hold the shimmer, instead transforming into my human self. But Kitty had already done her work.

Nic sat on the floor in front of me, his eyes wide but unseeing as he gibbered to himself and shook.

Kitty had been right; most mortal brains were not equipped to deal with the vastness of my pocket. In the short amount of time he was in there, Nic's mind had clearly broken. Even after the deceit and torment he had put me through, I felt a modicum of guilt for that.

Althea, forgotten in the corner of the room, cried out and ran forward, wrapping her arms around the man as he shook and drooled. Her blue eyes—the same color as Nic's, I realized—squeezed shut as she held him with affection.

Another puzzle piece snapped into place.

The door behind Kitty burst open, revealing Fleurette, Fal, Lyle, and Gavin. They stopped short once they caught sight of the two people in the middle of the room, and then they fixated on the ephemeral fox.

Kitty now floated four feet off the floor, her body perpendicular with the ground. Her nine white tails made a perfect fan under her. She gracefully moved her head toward Kokoro, who watched her with tears glistening in her dark eyes. Although the fox did not speak as a human, her speech flowed into our heads. "Kokoro, thank you for allowing me to help you."

Kokoro made a small bow. "The honor is mine, *Tenko*."

It took me a moment to remember what that word meant. I recalled Kokoro telling us just days prior, although it felt like a lifetime ago. *Tenko*. Celestial fox. The honorific was fitting.

"Fleurette," Kitty called out. Fleurette moved forward, gazing in awe at the heavenly fox. "I have come to know your generous heart. There is room for the love of another, yes?"

Fleurette nodded slowly, her eyes staring at Kokoro for a beat. "Yes."

"Excellent. You will be in good hands, then."

Kitty fixed me with a stare. "Cressida. Remember what I told you."

I nodded, resolute. *Great power must be met with great power.*

Kitty began to fade into a wash of shimmering motes, her ascension nearly complete. "In almost one thousand years, I have never encountered a group of people like yourselves. Thank you for allowing my help, as I am most grateful to be able to return home again."

Once the last of her words ceased, she was gone.

The apparent spell she had cast upon us all ended. Immediately I noticed the unhealthy rumble of the infernal machine, which now also belched puffs of smoke and large sparks of fire.

"That can't be good," I remarked.

Althea, still cradling Nic on the floor, looked up at me. "Get them out of here, cat."

"What about you?" I asked. She did, after all, help us in our hour of need.

She gazed at Nic. "I can't leave my son. I will make sure this machine does not survive."

Fleurette stepped forward. "Mom ..."

Althea looked up at her, her eyes wide and apologetic. She fished into her bodice and tossed something at Fleurette, who fumblingly caught it.

"Go," she said to Fleurette. "Please. I can't lose both of my children."

"Althea?" Lyle's voice was pained.

She only closed her eyes in shame.

The machine made a grinding roar, spewing a shower of sparks into the room with a puff of dark smoke. The entire building shuddered.

Althea held out her hand, willing the machine to stay together with her powerful magic. "Go. Now! I can't keep it contained for much longer!"

"This is not a drill!" I yelled. I ran to Grimm's backside and tried to push him to his feet. Grimm scrambled to sit up but lacked the strength to get his legs underneath him. Gavin and Lyle ran over to help me. Since the two of them were physically stronger than me, I moved out of the way. Together, they lift-ed Grimm—Lyle at his front half and Gavin in the rear—and rushed for the door with the large beast.

With Grimm off to safety, I herded Fleurette, Kokoro, and Fal over to the same exit. Fal fled the building readily. Fleurette paused near her mother.

"Why?" The single word came out choked, a desperate cry from a long-buried child.

Althea hung her head, even as her body shook with the effort of her magic. "I'm sorry."

"Fleurette," I said, eyeing the increasing amount of smoke in the room, "we need to go."

She nodded, took a hold of Kokoro's hand, and marched resolutely out of the room.

I was the last to leave. I turned and looked over at Althea and Nic. The floor near the machine had caught fire, and the flames licked up the side of the ailing instrument, which continued to chug with a dying heartbeat.

"Are you sure?" I asked Althea.

She nodded, her face shiny with perspiration. She broke off her magical containment spell, looking down and stroking Nic's cheek with motherly affection.

I turned and ran.

I made it to the edge of the clearing before an enormous explosion pushed me forward. I landed in a clump of salal, the wet leaves holding me up and the branches jabbing painfully into my flesh. I turned my slightly suspended body, shielding my eyes from the incandescence of the flames. The entire structure was ablaze.

I would have been worried for the surrounding forest if not for the frequent drenching it got.

"Cressida!" Fleurette yelled from down the path with a note of hysteria in her voice.

"I'm here," I called out, groaning as I tried to disentangle myself from the salal.

She and Lyle came running up. Fleurette reached out a hand to help me. "Thank Hecate. I thought you were still in there."

"I'm fine." I winced as a twig poked my bad cheek. "Well, I'm alive, anyway."

"I suppose that's more than others can say," she said, her gaze on the conflagration. She stepped back from me before I was completely free from the bush. She held something in her fingers, rolling it around with a lost expression on her face. I squinted to see what it was. A crystal, glinting in the firelight. The last gift from her mother.

Lyle grabbed my shoulders, finally righting me. A stern expression uncharacteristically graced his face. "Why didn't you tell me about Althea sooner?"

I opened my mouth, but only made gasping noises. My words seemed to be trapped in my throat.

Fleurette looked at me quizzically, and then her face smoothed. "Right," she breathed out with exhaustion. "Cressida, I release you from your promise."

My throat opened once more. "I'm so sorry, Lyle! I wanted to say something, but—"

"But I accidentally spelled her with an unbreaking promise. It's my fault, Dad. Don't be cross with her. I didn't want you to know," Fleurette explained.

He watched the inferno. "And now it's too late to do anything about it."

Fleurette watched with him. "How could she do this?"

I put my arm around her back, a feeble attempt at comfort. "It was her choice," I said softly.

"It was all her choice." Fleurette studied the crystal. "At least that's what I'm expecting this to tell us." She sighed and carefully pocketed the object.

Lyle clapped her on the back in fatherly affection. "Sweetheart, I need to go check on Grimm. Will you be okay?"

She nodded. "I'm going to stay here for a while. Make sure the fire doesn't get out of hand."

Lyle made a noise in his throat. "Don't let this eat at you. Remember, we still have Wren to think about." He walked away before anything else could be said.

I had almost forgotten about Wren, which made me feel instantly guilty. "She's still missing? You didn't find Elkins?"

Fleurette clenched her jaw. "That slimy weasel managed to make it all the way back to the MCs. Fal had nearly caught up with him, but Elkins sleeped him."

"Wait, though. I saw Fal in the building. How did you wake him up?"

Fleurette half-chuckled. "Gavin, of all people. He slipped some drunk-me-not potion under Fal's tongue. It worked like a charm."

I nodded. "We learned the hard way about the effects the potion had on somnification. But, Wren—how do we find her?"

Fleurette shook her head. "I'd say we use Grimm, but he can barely hold his head up. Don't worry—" I must have had a look of consternation on my face. "He's weak, but he'll live. Dad is going to give him a thorough check over, and I'm sure Fal will help in any way he can. His healing powers aren't as effective on animals, unfortunately. He learned that when he accompanied Dad to the inn to fix Humbert."

Ah, yes, another lost companion of mine. "Is Humbert okay?"

"Yes. Apparently, Dad and the kids stayed at the inn for the entire day, and by the end they had Humbert on track to fully healing. But then that cad of a veterinarian came back that night and captured them all. As far as I know, Humbert is still at the inn."

"I can't believe I actually liked Dr. Orcutt when I first met him," I said. "But he turned out to be just another weak-minded sycophant." And now his corpse burned away in the shell of that building, along with Althea, Nic, Babcock, and four other men.

I shook my head to clear it of these morbid musings. "We should go. The others might be waiting for us."

Fleurette slowly tilted her head in negation. "You go. I want to stay and watch it burn."

"Nah," I said, sliding up next to her. I put an arm around her waist in a half hug. My friend needed me. "They'll know where to find us."

CHAPTER 32

The structure only lasted another hour. Fleurette refused to leave the site while the embers were still hot. Despite the damp conditions, we worried about the fire gaining a second life and spreading to the nearby trees, which would be disastrous. A sacred site such as this warranted more respect than a man-made ecological calamity.

It had been over twelve hours since Fleurette last tried to use her magic. She tapped into it again, delighting in the trickle of power she felt come to her fingers. It wasn't the deluge she normally experienced, but the weak and sluggish herbal affinity was enough to ferry water from deep roots up to the surface, dousing the remaining embers and setting our minds at ease.

Only the foundation and a few charred beams remained when she was finished. Once more, I was awed by her power, even as muted as it currently was.

When we finally walked the path back to where the MCs were parked, we only found Lyle, Kokoro, and Grimm.

"Gavin took Fal to see if they could find Elkins and Wren," Lyle explained.

Satisfied with that answer, I rushed over to Grimm, who was now strong enough to lie on his haunches. He wagged his tail and licked my face when I bent down to hug him.

I broke the hug and stroked his face, feeding our souls with contentment at being reunited. His euphoria radiated from our bond, warming us both.

"Aw," Fleurette cooed. "He's so happy to see you. How did he survive, though? That was some dark magic that hit him. Am I right, Kokoro?"

I glanced at Kokoro, who confirmed with a nod. "Nic's magic was mostly yellow, like I said before, but I saw a blackness within him as well. Dark Magic. Same as with your mother. That magic was meant to kill."

I huffed out a breath. "He did mean to kill Grimm. My partner was the only thing in Nic's mind that stood between him and me. But Nic didn't account for how I'd react to his actions. He underestimated one thing."

"What's that?" Fleurette asked, intrigued.

I smiled. "My love for Grimm."

"Well, of course you love him! You've been practically inseparable since you partnered up. You—" She stopped and looked at me, her eyes widening with dawning comprehension. "Did you figure it out?"

"Figure what out?"

"The curse. Grimm. You just said you love him. Annie never specified what type of love the curse would block. She only thought about romantic love, not the deeper love between two souls."

I shrugged, playing coy. "Well, then, yes. I am free of the curse."

"I knew you could do it!" She clapped her hands together. "It's a wonder the curse wasn't broken sooner. Although, if you, a stubborn cat, failed to see what was in front of you for the last two years, I can imagine the curse kept ticking away, even though the answer was right there the whole time." She shook her head. "Why didn't I think of that?"

"Because it makes no sense," I replied, my happiness dampening. I gazed into Grimm's eyes, his own full of the same love that I held for him. I smiled sadly. "I'm still in the same mess I was with the curse, even though I've found my true love. Our difference in species still separates us in a major way."

She waved away my statement. "Cressida, have you not learned anything? You broke a curse. The universe wants this for you. We'll figure out a way around this barrier as well. Have faith." Fleurette placed a hand on my back with a comforting touch.

"If you say so," I said. "But to answer your first question: for all intents and purposes, Grimm died. But, somehow, we soulbonded and that saved his life."

"Incredible," Fleurette breathed. "A soulbond is something not just anyone can do. It takes an enormous amount of love to commit such a thing. For you to have saved Grimm in this way, it means he truly is your soulmate. Cressida, you really are a wonder. A bumbling wonder, but a wonder nonetheless."

"Thanks," I responded dryly, but my smile consisted of nothing but warmth.

Grimm finally regained enough strength to stand around midnight. Gavin and Fal were still gone, but we felt it prudent to stay where we were in case either they or Elkins showed up while Grimm was still incapacitated. Fleurette and Kokoro had gone into one of the MCs to rest in the backseat together, while Lyle and I kept my partner company.

I took advantage of this slightly stressful interlude to get some quality cat time in. I groomed Grimm's ear as he explained what had happened to him.

"I was so angry at the whole situation, Cress. I trusted Nic, but I didn't trust what was happening to you. It wasn't jealousy, either. I fully admit, I *was* jealous as hell when you were off with Gavin. This was more … unease, I suppose, at how you were acting."

"You were right to be suspicious, though. Nic was a kharismorph. He was controlling my emotions. Yours too, from the sound of it."

He licked the side of my head, engulfing the entire area with his large tongue. "That makes sense. So, that night. I was annoyed. I was a little hurt—"

"I'm so sorry," I butted in, my guilt eating at me for how I had treated him.

"Love, you needn't apologize. I understand why things went down like they did. I place no blame on you. But as I was saying, hurt, annoyance, and yes, suspicion led me to leave the tent. The werewolf attack was still fresh in my mind. I figured being outside and alert would at least help put me at ease, knowing I was protecting you."

"What did I do to deserve you?" I asked dreamily as I started to purr.

Grimm snorted. "CC, you know I'm willing to lay my life down for you, ever since you rescued me. I suppose now I know you'd do the same for me."

"I just brought you back from death, didn't I? But sorry, I keep interrupting your story. Go on."

His chest heaved with a sigh. "So, there I was outside the tent. I stood watch for some time. How much, I have no clue. You know that time is a concept I have little grasp of."

"I do."

"I was beginning to get tired, so I thought perhaps I'd go back into the tent. But then I heard a noise farther down the road, from the direction we came. The moon was visible above me, so I worried about more werewolves. I went to investigate. I turned a bend in the road, and suddenly, there was someone standing in front of me. I growled in warning, but he only laughed. I decided it was best to rush back to wake you, but a light flashed from his palm and I instantly lost consciousness."

"Was it purple?" I asked, caught up in the story.

"The light? It looked blue to me. I can't see purple, remember?"

"Oh yeah. Sorry."

He flicked his ear. "Anyway, there's not much else to tell. I was asleep for a long time, I think, and then I woke up in that building. Lyle and the kids were with me. And that doctor fellow. And two of the other men. I knew we were in trouble, based on how Lyle and the kids were acting. I thought that perhaps I could take down the men that held us and go save you. But Lyle told me to be good. So I waited and didn't fight."

"You are an extraordinary beast, Grimm."

"Thanks. But when you showed up, I began to lose the will to sit still. And when Nic began bending your mind to his desires, and you began to reciprocate, I ... I just snapped."

I rubbed my forehead on his cheek. "Grimm, when I woke up to you being gone, a part of me died, thinking you had left me."

He nosed my fur softly. "I would never leave you, Cress. Not willingly, anyway. I will always stand by your side, no matter if you have two legs or four."

I was about to respond, but Fleurette flung the MC door open with a flourish, crawling out quickly.

"I got a message from Fal!" she declared, waving her message mirror in the air. I shimmered up, not wanting to miss this. The four of us humans crowded around the mirror.

"AT THE SANTORUM HOUSE. WE THINK ELKINS IS NEXT DOOR. COME OVER HERE TO DISCUSS WHAT TO DO."

We wasted little time appropriating the largest vehicle to take us back to the beach house. As much as I did not want to revisit that place, I would do anything to get Wren back. And, I had to remind myself, Rafferty was no longer there. The threat was gone. If anything, it was Gavin's house now.

We pulled up after an uneventful trip. The two houses shared a road access, but luckily, the Santorum house was the first driveway, so we did not have to advertise our arrival by driving past Elkins' beach lodge.

Fal met us at the MC, having heard us pull into the driveway. "We're pretty sure that the car Elkins used to escape is parked outside of his house right now," he said without preamble.

Fleurette's mirror buzzed. She jumped at the sensation and pulled it out.

"Oh, Cressida, look at this," she said.

I peered at the mirror in her hand. "I HAVE THE GIRL," it read. "I WILL ACCEPT A TRADE FOR THE CAT. OTHERWISE YOU WILL NEVER SEE HER AGAIN."

It was not signed, but we all knew who sent the message.

Fleurette glanced worriedly at me. "What should we do?"

I thought about it. "Elkins wants to get his hands on me so that he can kill me. I'm sure of it. So, going over there won't be an option. He'd sleep me instantly, knowing him, and kill me without taking any more chances."

"But what about Wren?" she countered.

I drummed my fingers against my lips. "I have an idea. Do you have full access to your magic again?"

She settled her gaze on the nearest plant, a tuft of beach grass growing by the front door. She walked over and touched it.

When she had put out the fire with the root water, it had taken all her effort and several minutes to accomplish the simple task. This time, within seconds, the grass grew taller and the color changed from winter beige to spring green.

Fleurette smiled widely. "Yes, my block is gone, thank Hecate."

"Excellent. Can you put me to sleep in my human form? But in a way so that it doesn't affect my ability to dream?"

She frowned but nodded. "I think so, yes."

"Hand me the mirror."

Fleurette passed the object to me. I got to work on the message. "CAT HERE. I WILL NOT GO OVER THERE. YOU'LL HAVE TO FIND ANOTHER WAY TO GET YOUR HANDS ON ME."

I could practically feel his frustration as he messaged me back. "I WILL END YOU."

"IN YOUR DREAMS," I concluded with a smirk.

He messaged one last word. "PRECISELY."

I handed the mirror back to Fleurette with a chuckle. "Come and get me, then, you putz."

CHAPTER 33

I dream-walked through the ancient woods. The sun barely touched the earth due to the denseness of the foliage above me. The path I followed was crowded on either side once more with the variety of forest berry bushes and ferns. It felt incredibly familiar to me.

When I came to the clearing with the wooden building, I knew why.

Apprehension filled me as I entered the structure. The last time I had seen this place, it had been dark, and only the blackened remains of a few beams still stood upright, like the charred skeletal ribs of a dragon.

But the inside was not the single room bedecked with wooden timbers and the infernal machinery at one end. Instead, it was ... nothing. Whiteness. A blank slate.

I looked down at myself to check that I still held my human body. It was imperative, although I couldn't quite pinpoint the reason. Something to do with meeting someone? Whatever the case was, I caught sight of my human hands and my dove-gray vest. As on edge as I felt, this soothed me to a degree.

"There you are."

Elkins' smooth voice flowed over my back, bringing goosebumps to my arms.

Oh, yes. Now I remembered why I was here. The dream snapped from fuzzy sensations to a more lucid quality.

With the burgeoning of realness, my heart sped up. I spun around, my eyes wide with fear. Elkins stood a few feet away, looking as dapper as always in his suit, but his eyes held an intensity that caused my body to tighten, a coiled spring waiting to bounce away.

"Is Wren okay?" I asked, wanting to get that point out of the way.

Elkins smiled, showing off his perfect white teeth. "The girl is fine. I wanted to keep her as a backup plan. Despite what I led you to believe, I wouldn't have actually disposed of her so quickly. A projectionist is a wonderful tool to have in one's arsenal."

"She's a person, not a tool. Unlike *you*," I spat. "What took you so long to get here?"

"What a mouthy thing you are. I wonder what my son saw in you. He was so sure he could tame you in the new order. His little cat on a leash." He ambled around me, as if I were encased in an invisible bubble. "You know, I've tried to enter your dreams before, but I could never quite do it."

"I figured. I saw you loitering around the outskirts of my dreams a couple of times. It must have been my feline brain that kept you out."

He pursed his lips as his eyes narrowed. "Yes, I had the same conclusion. I've never tried to enter an animal's dream before. I felt like I was getting very close to entering yours, but it shouldn't have been this easy. Why is that?" His question sounded calculating in tone.

I tapped my chin. "Hm. Maybe I invited you here. Maybe I wanted to have a chance to speak to you without being put to sleep or killed."

"That's incredibly unwise of you to make such assumptions about my ability to kill through dreams. What makes you think I can't?"

My pulse leapt. "Nic told me you couldn't. It's the reason you sent him to do away with the people you dream-stalked, rather than getting your own hands dirty."

"Nic's killing magic and my sleep magic are of the same kind, young lady," Elkins drawled, still circling me. "It's just a matter of magical strength. There is only a small difference between sleep and death, after all."

I made sure to keep facing him as he walked. "You admit that your son was stronger than you?"

Elkins' face twisted into a scowl. "Stronger, pah. My son may have had a more concentrated form of my magic, but in the end he was weak. I saw how you sucked him away like it was nothing. It was the single most disappointing action I've ever witnessed. I knew there was a reason I staved off having kids for the last four hundred odd years. For all his power, he was useless."

"That's terrible," I remarked. "I may never get the chance to have a child of my own, but I would love her no matter what her powers—or lack thereof—may be. Children are not just extensions of the parent, nor should they be treated as such."

He stopped walking. "Are you quite finished proselytizing to me? I assure you, your remarks make little difference in my life, just like my child made little difference. In fact, I'm rather glad Nic is out of the picture. I gave that boy too much leeway in certain matters."

"Such as?"

"Such as keeping you alive. I do believe he used his kharismorph ability to convince me. Ungrateful brat. But I'm not tied down to his wants anymore. As a matter of fact, I think I'll finish this now."

He took a step forward.

"Wait!" I yelled, holding out a hand and matching his momentum with a step backward. "You can't hurt me here. It's just a dream."

He laughed. "Whoever made you think that way, Miss Curtain? You aren't looking at a dream version of me; I am here in this dream with you. If I am real, my actions are real too. My magic allows for dream behavior to become physical. I'd been practicing on Althea once she outlived her usefulness. It took some trial and error, but a hard pinch to her upper arm in her dream translated to a sore bruise in real life. I may not have been able to kill those people a month ago, but practice now makes perfect."

He lunged at me, catching me off guard. I screamed and tried to run, but his hands clamped down on my throat, ready to squeeze, and yet he didn't. I froze.

"You creatures really are weak, especially in your dreams," he remarked coolly.

I decided to push my luck. "At least I got the upper hand in the end. Your machine is gone, destroyed, taking your cronies with it after you fled like a coward. And I stopped your scheme of opening the gate."

Elkins laughed cruelly. "Is that what you think? Oh, Cressida, how sad for you."

I paused, my brows forming a knot. "What?"

He gave me a smile of pity. "You didn't stop anything, my dear. The gate opened. Not enough to allow Mother through, but enough to allow magic to leak into her world. It's only a matter of time before she finishes you all. All you've done is delay the inevitable. We've won after all, my girl."

No. This couldn't be! We had destroyed the machine that powered the gate. Had we really been too late?

Elkins chuckled at my demoralized expression. "I'm going to savor that look on your face for the rest of my life. And now, it's time to end you so that I can finish bringing Mother fully into this world, with your little friend Wren's help. Goodbye, Miss Curtain," he said, readying his hands to choke the life out of me.

Despite my unfeigned terror, I laughed. He frowned at my unexpected reaction.

I wasn't going to give up that easily.

"Goodbye, Gregor," I responded, placing my hands on top of his arms and gripping down hard.

He gave me a look of utter confusion.

And then I shimmered.

I accessed my interdimensional pocket, smiling when the darkness of the vast void greeted me. Elkins startled at the change of dream scenery and let go of my throat, craning his head about with wide eyes. I gave him a push away from me, watching as he tumbled into the unending space until I could no longer make out the mien of horror upon his face, and then I left the pocket.

The dreamworld was the same as I had left it, only now I was the only person here.

It was a rather nice dream after that.

I awakened, refreshed. But I startled in alarm when I opened my eyes to find four people staring at me.

"Personal space," I grumbled. I rubbed my eyes, unaccustomed to having hands while waking. "What time is it?"

Fleurette checked her watch. "It's three in the morning. Are you well?"

I forced my brain to do the mental math. I had only been spelled to sleep about half an hour ago. Dream time was strangely slow.

"I'm fine. But Elkins told me we might not be for long. The gate's been opened a bit, just enough to allow magic to trickle through. But at least I did what I set out to do. I think. Did it work?"

Fleurette shook her head. "I don't know. How can we tell?"

My mouth opened to respond, but there was a knock on the door. The sound made us all start with nerves.

Fleurette cautiously tiptoed to the door and peeked through the peephole. Then she let out a nervous laugh and undid the lock. She flung the door open.

It was Wren. She looked exhausted, but unhurt. She walked into Fleurette's waiting arms.

Fal rushed over to add to the hug. "Wrenny! You're okay! How did you escape?"

Her reply was too muffled from having her face mashed into Fleurette's sweater, so she extracted herself from the embrace. "It was surprisingly easy," she said to the room, a big smile gracing her face. "Elkins had put me to sleep, but then I woke up and found him in the same room as me, which was *very* creepy. But he was also asleep. So, I snuck past him and got out of there. There was no one else at the house to stop me."

A smug smile blossomed on my face. "We should go over there to be sure. But I have the feeling that nothing in this world is going to wake up Gregor."

"Why do you say that?" Wren asked, intrigued.

I grinned wider. "The man you and I saw in our dreams wasn't a facsimile of Elkins, it *was* Elkins. Or his consciousness outside of his physical body, at any rate. Elkins explained to me that his brand of magic made what happened in dreams real. He was about to kill me in my dream, but I got the best of him using his own magic against him. I shoved his consciousness deep into my dream self's interdimensional pocket. The man in the house across the way? He's just a shell now."

"Woah." Wren ran to me and gave me a crushing hug, which I returned with pleasure. "Remind me never to get on your bad side, Cress."

"What can I say?" I replied wryly. "Pockets are a woman's best accessory."

CHAPTER 34

Of course, everyone wanted to verify that Elkins was indeed out of the picture. We made our way over there, tromping inside like we owned the place.

Wren led us to where she had last seen Elkins. Before we even got to the room, however, I heard a shrill, yet muffled voice emitting intermittently from the locale in question. If I were in cat form, my ears would have been angled forward to catch every last sound. But as it was, I tried to keep my curiosity in check until I could discern exactly what was causing the noise.

We found Elkins right where Wren said he'd be: in a chair, slumped over, eyes closed. Initially, he looked dead, but Fleurette easily found a pulse, and he breathed the deep respirations of a sleeping man.

"It's true," Fleurette said on a relieved exhalation. "One more enemy vanquished. Good job, Cressida."

"Way to work his magic against him!" Wren cheered with the enthusiasm of youth.

I smiled and shrugged. "I—"

The faint voice interrupted me. "Gregor! Gregor, where are you?"

I looked at Fleurette. "You heard that too, didn't you?"

She frowned and bent toward the comatose man. She reached into the pocket of his trousers, extracting a small shard of crystal. It glowed faintly.

"Let me see that," I said, holding out a hand. Fleurette obliged. I held the crystal, letting it warm with my body heat. I recalled the last time I had used a communication crystal, six months ago, at the Information business in Dogwood. At that time, I had been making an outgoing call, but I assumed receiving a call would be the same type of mechanism. So, I freed my mind and thought carefully about opening the communication channels.

"Annie?" I spoke.

Silence. Then, "Who is this?"

It was her, alright. I suffered through over a year with that voice etched into a curse upon my soul not to recognize it.

I decided to have a little fun at her expense. "Annie, babe, don't you recognize my voice? I'm hurt, really and truly. It's your kitty-cat booboo."

"*You!*" she snarled, although the gravitas was lost through the tinny connection. "What have you done with Gregor?"

"Gregor's going to take a nice, long nap for the next two hundred years or so, so I'm sorry to say he won't be able to answer any more calls from you, mommy dearest. He did try to talk me into inviting you here for tea, but I'm declining that invitation."

Wren's eyes bugged out at me. I gave her a wink while I listened to Annie Coddle rage.

"You scaramouch! Cow-handed besprawler! Carbunkle!" I couldn't understand a word she said, but the inflection of her voice made the meanings clear as day.

I laughed, hoping it would further incite her fury. "Annie, darling, I'd love to stay here and listen to you spew insults at me, but it's late. I'm going to go ahead and turn this crystal to 'silent,' just as soon as I figure out how. Unless, that is, you'd like to tell me the whereabouts of the gate?"

"You just wait, you feline bladderbag! I'm going to make your life so miserable that you'll *have* to let me into this world. You'll either be dead, or wish you were!"

And that was enough of that. I merely thought about severing the connection, and Annie's voice instantly ceased.

All eyes stared at me, wide and unblinking. "What?" I asked with fake innocence.

Gavin cleared his throat. "Do you think it was wise to egg her on like that?"

I smirked. "Annie's going to do what Annie's going to do, no matter what. I was half hoping she'd go into an apoplectic fit and burst a vessel, but that would be too much to hope for. Anyway, I doubt she can do anything at the moment."

Fleurette wiped the bemused expression off her face. "No, but if what you say is true about the gate being opened, we may be in for a rough time. We'll have to make it our priority to find its location and stop Annie for good. I fear our world won't take the strain indefinitely, otherwise."

I held up the crystal. "What should we do with this? I sort of want to smash it underfoot, but it might come in handy in the future."

Fleurette flattened her lips, then nodded in agreement. "Give it here. I'll put a sealing spell upon it, so she won't be able to reach out to us. But we can call her, if need be."

I readily agreed to this, passing the object to my witch friend. She placed it in the pocket of her skirt and patted it to make sure it was in its proper place. "Thanks. I'll work on this as soon as we get back to Gavin's beach house. Fal, would you be able to lend me a hand when the time comes?"

Fal grinned. "Of course. I'm always up for learning new spells, Fleurette."

"Well then!" She clapped her hands together. "I say we give this place one last search before getting out of here. I already informed GOGS about what's happened, and they'll be sending out some members to investigate this whole mess. Someone will need to care for Elkins for the rest of his days as well. I want to be doubly sure that the house is empty, and there are no new surprises waiting for us. Dad, why don't you take the kids to inspect this main floor. Gavin and Kokoro, check the second. Cressida, Grimm, and I will take the top."

We moved out accordingly. Fleurette found a staircase and soon was leading me to the next set. As I climbed the stairs to reach the third floor, I said to her backside, "I'm surprised you wanted to be paired with me. I thought this would be the perfect opportunity to get some alone time with Kokoro."

Fleurette stopped her ascent and turned to look at me. She seemed almost troubled.

"I figured the cousins haven't had a chance to get to know each other. This would be a good opportunity to allow them some bonding time. But also …"

"Yes?" I coaxed. It was unlike Fleurette to be so recalcitrant. She was normally excellent at speaking her feelings.

She struggled to find words. "I—I don't know if Kokoro even likes me. Like that. She was thrust into a terrible marriage, barely escaping it with her life, and I'm worried she won't want to start any relationship, let alone one with a woman."

"Is that the mind game you're playing with yourself?" I replied with a huff. "The 'what if she doesn't like me' game? You sound like a teenager."

"I feel like one, too," she admitted. "Cressida, I've never gotten a chance to have a real relationship. What *if* she doesn't like me?"

I squinted at her with one eye. "Okay, first. She flat out said she wasn't interested in men. Now, granted, she could be asexual, but chances are high that women are on her list. Second, Kitty explicitly said that she felt Kokoro was safe now because she had found the perfect mate for her. In case you were too thick-headed to understand at the time, she was talking about *you*. And third, suck it up and ask her. What's the worst that could happen?"

"Abject humiliation," Fleurette responded without missing a beat. But she smiled fondly at me. "You break a curse and find your true love, and you become a fount of dating wisdom. But you're right. I'm just nervous."

I absently rubbed the top of Grimm's head as he leaned his weight into my side. I considered her words. "As you have every right to be. Now, can we please get out of this stairwell? I'm tired of craning my neck up to look at you."

Fleurette rolled her eyes and sighed dramatically, but continued up the staircase, with me behind her and Grimm bringing up the rear.

The third floor was mostly unremarkable, save for a small room near the back of the house. This location had clearly been inhabited by a magic user, based on the notebooks scattered on the desk, the drying herbs dangling from the ceiling, and the various miniature bottles sitting on shelves. And ...

"Rupert!" Fleurette exclaimed, rushing over to the brass bird-cage in the corner of the room, where the familiar crow unhappily sat. He gave a feeble squawk as we entered the room.

Fleurette opened the cage and gently grasped the bird, pulling him from the perch and out the cage door before cradling him to her chest like a tiny, feathered baby. "Oh, Rupert, what did they do to you?"

He only nuzzled into her, letting out small sounds of happiness.

I paged through one of the open notebooks while Fleurette became reacquainted with her corvid friend and Grimm prowled about the room, cataloging the various scents. It appeared to be a journal of sorts. I stopped flipping the pages and read an entry:

10/14, 9am: Having extensively studied the research of Horten Gelbert (circa 1890), and with Carl Orcutt's insistence that his studies of werewolves were sound, I was convinced I could enhance the stamina of the lycanthropy disease with a simple serum. Today, it was finally ready. Greg's trio of werewolf employees had allowed me to collect vials of saliva at the last full moon (a dangerous undertaking, but Carl kept them as subdued as possible in their werewolf form, and only one person was killed in the process). I also charged a bowl of water under the Harvest moon, knowing that this particular lunar event would be more powerful than others. Over this last month, I steeped the saliva in the moon water, and added aconite, mandrake root, and mugwort. Every night at midnight I performed a ritual over the concoction to bring out the strength in the werewolf saliva. I have just injected the three men with the serum. If it works, they will be able to turn into werewolves much earlier than otherwise. Of course, we will need to supplement the magic with energy from the towers to boost the transformation. Greg plans to send them out to intercept Nic on his journey…

"Holy Freya's feet," I muttered. "Um, Fleurette? Come take a look at this."

Fleurette joined me at the desk, reading a few lines from the book. Her mouth set in a firm line. "That's my mother's handwriting. This was her room. Let's gather all of these up," she said with determination. "Perhaps there's something in these we can use."

Since her arms were full of crow, I took the task upon myself. It was only by happenstance that I looked behind me when Fleurette wasn't paying attention, and I witnessed a look of utter misery upon her face as she viewed the very last room her mother had ever slept in. I turned back around, giving her the privacy to grieve in this small way.

CHAPTER 35

I should have heeded Annie's warning with more gravity after all.

After the search turned up nothing more past our discovery of Rupert's incarceration, we headed back to the Santorum house. It was closing in on dawn by now, and a deep weariness had affected every single member of our strange party. So, our first order of business was to sleep. We all hunkered down in various bedrooms and slept soundly with the exhaustion of a traumatic shared experience.

I awoke at ten in the morning to snow covering the ground and flakes still falling rapidly.

Mind you, it was mid-October. Snow may have been a normal occurrence in other parts of the country at this point in the year, but the Oracune region, and especially the coastal area, had a temperate climate that hardly ever saw snow even in the coldest months.

It was unsettling, to say the least.

As I stared out of the sliding glass door at the snow-covered beach, Fleurette joined my side, a steaming mug of tea in her hand and a blanket wrapped around her shoulders.

"So, it's begun," she commented.

A puff of a laugh escaped my mouth. "So soon, though? I thought she'd need time to gather her magic together."

"I imagine she got a good deluge of power as the gate first opened. Perhaps our destroying the machine slowed it to a trickle. Still, this is not good. Annie wasn't kidding around when she said she would make our lives miserable." She took a sip of her tea, ruminating. "We need to head back to Knobby Hill. There's nothing more to be done here."

When we told the others, Lyle, Fal, and Wren agreed with the decision to leave after breakfast. Gavin stated that he needed to take the time to put his father's affairs in order and chose to stay at the coast for a bit longer.

"I don't care a lick about the fortune I'm set to inherit," he joked. "But if I can turn this weight of money around and use it for good, it's motivation enough to start the process."

Kokoro was oddly silent about the whole thing, neither agreeing to go with us nor to stay with Gavin. It clearly weighed upon Fleurette, but she kept her distance from the Tyonoshimese woman, much to my dismay.

After the number of times that they shared a bed, held hands, and told each other intimate secrets, I was shocked at the reticence of those two. Even Kitty had made it sound like it was a forgone conclusion.

I decided to take the matter into my own hands at breakfast. The eight of us sat around the table, with Grimm at my feet and Rupert carefully perched next to Fleurette. We dug into a veritable feast of bacon, eggs, fried fish, and biscuits—all food that we found in the kitchen. There was no sense in letting it go to waste.

I waited until everyone had full plates and were busy filling their bellies before I began my meddling.

"So, Kokoro, how does it feel to be a free woman?" I asked casually.

She paused her fork midway to her mouth, then set it back down on her plate, the bite uneaten. "Odd," she finally said. "I had gotten used to having the fox inside of me. Now that she is gone, I feel incomplete. I am sure I will get used to her absence with time."

"Yeah, I miss her too, surprisingly enough," I agreed. "But now that she fulfilled her promise, what are your plans?"

"I am unsure," she began, her tone stilted. "I do not wish to travel back to Tyonoshima. My old country is filled with nothing but bad memories. I would like to stay in Vinland, but I do not have a home to go to."

Gavin swallowed and said, "Kokoro, you can stay with me for a time. Although I only rent a room from the Hunters' Guild. I can't keep you at the dormitory once I'm back in Knobby Hill. I suppose I could set you up in an apartment in town, though, if you want."

"I'm sure Fleurette would be happy to have you live with her," I suggested.

Fleurette cleared her throat. She shot me with dagger eyes once I looked her way. Addressing the gathering, though, she said, "I would be happy to share my home, although Kokoro may find that it's a bit too soon."

"Too soon for what?" I asked innocently.

Fleurette speared me with another glance. "She may not enjoy the cramped quarters the cottage has to offer, *Cressida*."

"But you can just share a bed, can't you?" I asked, still keeping up with my innocent act.

Gavin spluttered into his coffee. Fleurette stood, nearly knocking her own mug off the table with the ferocity of the movement. "Kokoro, can I speak to you in the hallway for a moment?"

Kokoro nodded and daintily set down her napkin. The two women stepped out of the dining room, into the hallway outside.

"Cress, what has gotten into you?" Lyle hissed at me, albeit with a small twinkle in his eye.

"Shh," I whispered back, pointing to the closed door. "I'm trying to listen."

Everyone fell silent at that. I doubted anyone other than myself or Grimm could hear the conversation behind the door.

The perks of having catlike hearing.

"I'm sorry about what Cressida said. I hope she didn't make you uncomfortable," Fleurette said, her voice muffled.

Kokoro answered, "Oh. No. Not exactly."

"Listen, Kokoro. I'm not sure if I've made it very clear. I like you."

"I like you too," Kokoro said immediately.

A pause. And then, "I want to make sure there isn't a language barrier thing happening. I am not attracted to men. I like women."

A small laugh sounded from Kokoro. "I understand that perfectly well. I thought there might be something wrong with me when I was married. My husband was nice to look at, and many women were attracted to him. Even before I knew what a horrible person he was, I was not attracted to him. I have discovered I … also like women."

"You do?" Fleurette asked with an unsure tone.

Silence. I assumed that Kokoro nodded.

"Do you like … me?" Fleurette asked next.

Another silent pause. And then Kokoro answered with a very quiet, "Yes."

"I know we haven't known each other for very long. And I know you just got out of a terrible relationship and may need time to heal," Fleurette said with hesitancy. "I don't want to move too fast. But when we are both back at Knobby Hill, can I take you out on a date? When you are ready?"

"I would be honored," Kokoro said.

I grinned broadly and picked up my fork. "They're coming back in," I whispered to the group. They all followed suit and began eating noisily again.

Fleurette and Kokoro walked hand in hand back into the room before separating to sit at their individual seats.

"It has been settled," Kokoro said, beaming. "Gavin, I will take up your offer of an apartment in Knobby Hill. Thank you."

Fleurette, who also smiled radiantly, looked over at me and narrowed her eyes. "Why are you grinning like that?"

"I just really like this bacon," I answered innocently as I took a big bite.

We left after breakfast. Gavin lent us two vehicles in which to drive back over the coastal mountains. Fleurette, Grimm, Rupert, and I piled into the first MC, and Lyle drove with Fal and Wren. He planned to take them straight back home, whereas Fleurette was taking me to the inn to collect Humbert.

By the time we left the beach house, the snow had stopped, and it slowly melted with the lack of freezing temperatures. Fleurette seemed relieved.

"She's already used up her magic, I'm guessing," she said as she carefully drove. "Weather magic takes a lot of oomph. I think that was her idea of a tantrum. Hopefully, it will be a while before her next attack, whatever it may be."

I stayed silent, watching the landscape slowly lose its white mantle. Behind me in the back seat, Grimm let out a sigh. Rupert, also in the back seat, ruffled his feathers and looked miserable. He still had not fully bounced back from his imprisonment.

As Fleurette approached the coastal mountain range and we began climbing in altitude, I swiftly learned that the road Nic had driven me on was *not* the main artery over the mountains. Once he and I had left the inn, he had turned off the highway onto a much older road that had been long since bypassed for a newer, more direct route. I had been too sleep-deprived to notice.

More trickery on his part to separate me from my life in general.

The new road took us to the inn in record time, even with us going slowly due to the snow that still fiercely clung to the ground in higher altitudes. The speediness of our return trip was a good thing too, because I was anxious to reconnect with my horse employee. Even though I trusted Lyle when he said he was in good shape before they were forced to part, I still worried.

My fears were unfounded, however. Humbert greeted us with a delighted whicker as soon as he caught the scent of me. The stable boy on duty told me that he been treated well, despite the odd circumstances in which the horse had found himself abandoned. When I offered to pay for the boarding, the innkeeper himself proclaimed that I had taken down two of the werewolves myself, saving countless lives, and that was payment enough.

Humbert's wounds had healed nicely. He bore four long scars on his flank, a memento of his fight that would stay with him for the rest of his life. All the smaller nicks and bite wounds had fully healed. Lyle and Fal—and Dr. Orcutt, I begrudgingly added—had indeed done a marvelous job of nursing the old horse back to health. He was in good spirits too, clearly ready to get out of the stall and get back to work.

Work. With Elkins out of the picture, could *I* get back to my job?

I broached the subject with Fleurette after we hitched up the wagon and were back on the road home.

"I'm not sure," she said cautiously. "I think GOGS meant well when they had you go into hiding, but honestly, it didn't change anything. You still got captured by the ACF. Annie is now an immediate threat. I have the feeling that until we find where the gate opened and figure out how to close it to stop Annie, it's going to be an all-hands-on-deck type of situation. And as far as I'm concerned, that includes you."

"Will GOGS agree with that?"

She chuckled. "GOGS has been my life. But the society has taken a beating these last couple of years. If the council can't see through their hubris, it may spell the end of GOGS. But the point is, no matter whether they allow you to return to work or not, you may not have time for bounty hunting if my predictions about Annie's tricks come true."

"Listen. As long as I get to *do* something, I'm okay with it not being bounty hunting per se," I replied. "Just please don't sideline me again."

"You have the knowledge and the skills needed to help us through this challenge. If GOGS has an issue with that, I think it will be time to go rogue," Fleurette responded.

The rest of our trip was completely uneventful. Humbert pulled into Fleurette's drive a few minutes past eight that same evening, and we reconnected with Wren and Fal, who had beat us home by a few hours.

Lucky squeaked with pleasure as soon as he saw me. I picked him up off the back of the love seat.

"Oof, you feel much heavier than I remember, little buddy."

Wren rolled her eyes. "We left in such a hurry from Lyle's place that we simply dropped him off in the kitchen with food available. The little monster decided to take full advantage and helped himself to the pantry while we were gone. Lyle wasn't impressed."

I laughed, cradling my mouse in my hand. "You cheeky little punk," I chided playfully.

We fell back into a semblance of routine the next day. The kids had already missed a lot of their classes, so they were begrudgingly sent to school. Fleurette puttered about, trying to fulfill Samhain orders that had been neglected, but I could see her heart wasn't in it.

When I discovered that she was instead poring over her mother's old journals with an air of despondency, I decided I'd had enough of her moping about.

"It's time, Fleurette. Go tell your dad to come over and see what is on that crystal."

She sighed, slumping where she stood. "I know. I just ... I worked so hard to stop the pain she caused. I don't want to feel it all over again."

I placed a hand on her back. "How does not knowing make you feel, though?"

She smirked. "Terrible. I want to know, but I don't want to know." She straightened, resolute. "The word 'want' isn't good enough. I need to know. I deserve to know. Okay. I'll send for Dad. But only if you're there too."

"Me?" I stared at her askance. In my mind, this was a very personal issue. I never would have dreamed of inviting myself along. "Why?"

Fleurette sighed and clasped her hands together, fiddling with her thumb like it was a worry stone. "She went from being a

GOG to an ACFer. Everything she did in her life was somehow related to you and your family, whether positively or negatively. You also deserve to know the inner workings of my mother."

"Fleurette, I'd be honored."

She met my eyes. "Thank you. Shall we?"

CHAPTER 36

Lyle wasted no time in walking over, as I had predicted. The kids were not due to be home for a couple of hours, so we parked ourselves in the sitting room. Lyle took a chair, Fleurette and I stationed ourselves on the love seat, and Grimm rested at our feet. The seating arrangement made for an intimate gathering, with the three of us leaning toward each other. Fleurette took the crystal out of her pocket, her hand shaking ever so slightly as she studied it.

"A simple enough dictation spell," she murmured. She said a word under her breath, making a series of three sharp gestures with her fingers.

The crystal glowed with a dull white light. Fleurette placed it on the low table in front of her.

Althea's voice, small and tinny, sounded from the crystal.

"Hello, Fleurette. And, if you're listening, hello, Lyle. I've recorded this on the night before the full moon. The cat has been in our possession, but she still sleeps. I saw you as well, Fleurette. I know it's been ... let's see ... twenty-four years since I last saw you, and my, how you've changed, but I would have recognized you no matter your age. I'd like to think seeing you was what made me decide to say all of this, but I don't want to lie to you. Not anymore, at any rate. It was the cat, the lynchpin of this whole thing, that spurred

me into action. I don't know what's going to happen tomorrow, but it could go either very badly, or infinitely worse.

"In the likely case that I don't get the opportunity to speak to you in person, I want this to be my last confession. It will not exonerate me, even if my death awaits, but I think I can go to my fate easier if I at least get the chance to explain things to you. So here goes.

"Fleurette, I'm not a good person. I'm sure you've come to that conclusion all on your own, and I don't blame you. But it started much sooner than me leaving you. It started with my own childhood.

"You see, I resented my parents. They were both GOGs, and they didn't shy away from that fact. As you know, the first families to take up the mantle of guarding Glivver passed down that responsibility to their children, and from then on it was always expected of offspring to follow in their parents' footsteps. I know that some people keep the society a secret from their children until they reach an age in which they can join, in an attempt to give them a normal childhood. I wasn't given that opportunity.

"I suppose that I resented GOGS, because I was forever playing second fiddle to the Society. When I reached puberty and my magic began to grow, my parents were incredibly excited. But not for me, as a person. They were excited by what my powers might do for GOGS. They instantly began training me for a slot.

"I didn't want to join! But they never even asked what I wanted. If I broached the subject, they would tell me that I was expected to join, that it was my birthright, because outsiders were hardly ever invited in, for fear of 'contamination.' AKA, spies, you see.

"No, I wanted to travel. I wanted to study with the great masters in Yuroba, the old country, and perhaps become a grand witch! I had the talent for it. I could have easily had a familiar of my own, even when I was just eighteen. My powers were that great already.

But, no. I was destined to spend my time in a dusty old society, practically hidden away from the world.

"I began to fight with my parents. I was angry. I wanted to live my life the way I wanted to."

I took a deep breath upon hearing these words. How often had I felt the same way? Before the insanity of the last year, before Annie Coddle had swept into my life, all I had wanted was as normal an existence as possible, with no legacy looming over me. A life in which I got to do what *I* wanted to do. I actually empathized with Althea in this moment.

"It finally came to an ugly head when I was twenty-one. I was once again railing against becoming a GOG. The argument became incredibly heated, and I—I snapped. I lashed out. But instead of using words, I accidentally used my magic.

"I had no idea I was capable of such a thing. But I felt such intense rage, and, yes, hatred for my parents. And it boiled out of me in a silver haze that hit them. And they died."

I blinked, shocked. Perhaps I had less in common with Althea after all. As much as my mother annoyed me at times, I never wished her bodily harm.

"I never told anyone what happened. It was *an accident. But it was one that I couldn't fix. So, I lied and said I didn't know how they died, that I had found them that way. But through all of that, I had an intense guilt over what I had done.*

"The only silver lining was the thought that I was finally free to do what I wanted. I prepared to travel, even going so far as to contact one of the masters who lived in Vitalia at the time. But, no. The council of GOGS swiftly initiated me, given the vacancy my parents left. I was stuck, a cog in a wheel I had no desire for. But they were so happy to have me, that I grinned and bore it.

"They quickly shunted me to a backwater area, due to a lack of representation there. I was used to a ... more urban atmosphere, I

guess, so Knobby Hill was a little stifling at first. The only bright side was the local veterinarian, whom I found to be sweet, charming, and very loveable."

I glanced over at Lyle, who sat statue-still, his face devoid of emotion while he listened to his long-lost wife.

"Lyle, you gave me some beautifully bright spots in the haze of my sullen existence. I did love you. It's why I married you. I know you always thought it strange that I, a highly talented witch, would settle for a mundy, but please believe me: your lack of magic was a huge selling point to me. I didn't think GOGS would want you.

"But once again, I was wrong. Even without any magic of your own, they welcomed you with open arms. And when Fleurette was born, I worried about her being doomed to repeat my horrible childhood.

"Fleurette, it was clear to me from the start that you would be gifted. I didn't need to wait until you were of age to know this. The amount of times I'd peek at you out in the garden, talking to plants, touching them just so, and they'd respond. Even if it was just a slight perking up of a leaf, or a bloom lasting longer than it should have. I knew. Plant magic from your grandmother, Betty, with a healthy dose of more powerful magic from me.

"I tried my best to enjoy my life, I really did, but the old hurt and resentment started to trickle in as the years passed. Lyle seemed so enamored with being a part of a secret society, and he couldn't contain himself with our daughter, so soon enough she knew about it too. But unlike me, she was excited by the prospect of being a part of GOGS one day. It only made me feel like more of an outcast in my own family. The itch to travel resurfaced with a vengeance.

"And one day, I met someone. He was older, but suave and self-assured. He could see my frustration and offered a release from it. He told me it wasn't right for a witch of my standards to rot

away in a backwater burb. He was the epitome of everything I wanted.

"And he was also the 'enemy,' as I soon found out. At first, I balked at continuing to see him, but he told me of his mission to save his mother, and how they were planning for a better future for this world. He said I had been indoctrinated my whole life, and what did I have to show for it? He could help me utilize my powers for a greater purpose.

"I didn't mean for it to happen. I swear. But I had been so beaten down by the 'good' side at this point. His offer was so very tantalizing. Even then, I held off. I had a family. I couldn't do this.

"And then I found out I was pregnant. And I knew, I knew, it wasn't Lyle's."

Next to me, Fleurette gripped the throw blanket of the loveseat in a tight fist.

"There was no way I could pass off a fully white baby as Lyle's child either. Fleurette may have been much lighter than his skin tone, but it was still clear that she was of mixed race. This baby would have been a dead giveaway of my infidelity. So, I did the only thing I could think to do: I left with Greg. It was better to leave with my dignity intact, I figured. And now, I was at least free to travel and live the life I had always wanted.

"And yet, the guilt grew."

"Good," Fleurette muttered.

"My biggest regret was hurting you, Fleurette. And Lyle, although I honestly had fallen out of love by this point. But my daughter, I didn't want to abandon you. If you had only been like me, I would have taken you along. But you were too much of a daddy's girl."

A tone of resentment crept into Althea's voice in this last line. Her demons ran deeper than I could have guessed.

"Despite the guilt, I enjoyed being free for the first time in my life. Nicomedes was born, and while I wasn't exactly thrilled to care for an infant again, I did it with grace. Luckily, Greg was rich, and I had help that time around from nannies and servants.

Greg doted on me while Nic was young. But when Nic was still a baby, Greg asked me to be in charge of a new project that was farther away. I thought, "Travel? Yes, please!" and so I took the opportunity. And I spent the next twenty-one years at Addelboro Correctional Facility. Part of that time was served while the prison was still functioning; we simply rented out the cattery from the wardens. Under the table, of course. The wardens delighted in padding their pockets. And many of them ended up joining our cause. Plus, the cattery was in a section of the prison that hardly anyone went to. A win-win situation.

"After the facility went bust, there were a few months where we hardly operated down there. Local tours happened upstairs in the wake of the scandal, but I remained below with a few cats, keeping up with perfecting my cat call to find the descendants, and having food delivered to me in the dead of night when no one was looking. To keep anyone from discovering us, I placed a spell on the area that would make anyone who was unaware of our presence incredibly fearful if they approached the door. Rumors of ghosts and hauntings soon surrounded the prison. It was enough to keep everyone away.

"Greg was working hard to buy the facility outright during this time, and he managed to do so in less than a year. Then, we simply stopped the tours and pretended that the place was empty. But I'm sure your cat has filled you in on all of that.

"At first, I was happy with the assignment. I was doing something so anti-GOGS it filled me with a twisted sort of pleasure. And, although it took an extraordinarily long time, we did catch one of Glivver's descendants. So, it wasn't a complete waste of time.

"But I was also lonely. Greg came to visit, frequently at first, but less and less as the years went by. I hardly ever saw Nic, to the point that he seemed like a stranger every time he visited. Not only that, but he acted more and more like Greg as time went on. He was being molded by his father to fit a perfect vision of the heir. I no longer felt like a mother to him. I was just stuck in a damp dungeon of my own making.

"Not only was I in charge of the cattery, but I also served as a spy of sorts. You see, I have the ability to scry upon people I have a relationship with, just as long as I also know where they are residing. I used this power to check in with various members over the years, to investigate if they knew where the cat's whereabouts were. Greg demanded weekly updates, hoping to find her sooner than later.

"I spied on many GOGs, Fleurette, except for two. I never once looked in on you or Lyle. I couldn't bear to. I felt that as long as I left you alone, I wouldn't be reminded of the terrible thing I had done to you.

"The years passed, and none of the GOGS were ever seen shadowing a cat. Greg began to get angry with me, even though I was doing the best I could!

"And then the stupid cat came waltzing into the dungeon of her own volition. I couldn't believe my luck! Here I had spent years of my life stuck in this pit searching for her. Greg was happy to keep me there until I died. When it began to flood, I rejoiced. And when I ran across the cat in the hallway, I thought that the gods had finally smiled upon me.

"And then I saw the necklace. My necklace, the one you now own. And I knew. I knew you were this cat's guardian. I knew that the reason I had never found her was because she was with the two people I refused to scry upon.

"And I knew I had to do whatever possible to protect you. So, I let her go.

"Greg was of course in a terrible rage after the destruction of Addelboro. He was incredibly angry that he'd had the cat just under his nose the whole time, and that she had gotten away. His love for me had cooled years ago, but he had never been cruel to me. Now, though, he began to torment me. Pinches in my dreams. Barbed words meant to wound. He demanded that I take action by helping him kill off the members of GOGS one by one, in the hopes that it would flush the cat out of hiding. I had no choice in the matter. I began giving him names to satisfy him.

"I tried to stay as geographically far away from Knobby Hill as possible, in order to save you. These were older members, the ones I had remembered from my parents' time, and my time with Lyle. But I messed up.

"I didn't remember Maurice, but his father was a member I recalled from my time with GOGS, and Maurice happened to live with his father. When I scried upon the home, I saw a girl there as well. I told Greg of my findings with this house. He became unusually excited when I described the girl, Wren. I didn't recognize her at the time, but she was a Rambert, a family I had spied upon before, and someone whom Greg was familiar with as well. He decided to kill Maurice and, knowing that the cat had a connection to the girl, targeted her next in order to draw the cat out from hiding. Simultaneously, Nic had gained an interest in the cat, and together they figured out her general whereabouts.

Greg was ready to kill the cat the first chance he got. But Nic had caught sight of her in her human form at the Equinox Ball, and he seemed smitten with her. I decided to try to keep the cat safe by suggesting an alternative plan to Nic, that if she willingly joined us, Annie could still be free. Nic ate it up. Greg reluctantly obliged.

"I tried my hardest to keep the two of you safe from harm. And I'm not done yet. Fleurette, the gate between worlds must not be opened. I see that now. I've wasted my life fighting for the wrong side. The machine used to power up the opening of the gate must be destroyed. I will do what I can to stop it.

"Fleurette, I have a lifetime of regret. I've wronged you too many times. I can never expect you to forgive me. I can only hope that you perhaps understand me better. And above all, you should know that even though I'm a terrible person with a diseased soul, I believe from the bottom of my heart that I've done one good thing in this world: I gave it the gift of you. I am so extraordinarily proud of you, my daughter. And I love you.

"I am so very sorry."

The crystal went silent.

We all stared at it in shocked silence, each of us coming to terms with Althea's confession.

I placed my hand over Fleurette's and gave it a little squeeze before standing and moving over to Lyle. He stood with shaking legs. I touched his shoulder with careful sympathy. He nodded at me and joined Fleurette on the sofa, where the two of them leaned into a heart-wrenching embrace. Fleurette's shoulders shook as she sobbed into her father's shirt. Quietly, Grimm and I slid out of the room, giving the father and daughter time to grieve the woman they had lost all over again in the solitude of their shared trauma.

CHAPTER 37

Ten days later, I helped Fleurette set the table for the special Feast of the Dead. It was four in the afternoon and the kitchen was abuzz with activity as Wren stirred the squash soup, Fal prepped veggies for a salad, and Kokoro chopped sweet potatoes for her dessert. She also had a lovely fish already in the oven, which I personally was excited to eat.

Kokoro had arrived back in Knobby Hill five days prior. Gavin had been true to his word and rented out a small apartment in town, above a bakery. It was a two-bedroom place, and he decided to vacate the guild's dormitory to live with Kokoro when he was between jobs.

Ever since her arrival back to the area, Kokoro had come over daily to be with Fleurette. They were disgustingly cute together: cuddling on the couch, holding hands on walks, or when keeping each other company while they worked on individual projects.

Kokoro claimed to be an artist when we first met her, and now I knew she wasn't joking. Lyle gifted her with watercolor paints as soon as he heard of her creative side, and Kokoro took to them with aplomb. Fleurette was now the proud owner of a stylized portrait of herself; the serene face had a touch of Tyonoshimese influence, the hair was a cloud of curls swirling about her head, and the body was surrounded by an explosion of green, with wisps of other colors dancing about the painted figure. It was breathtaking.

Kokoro did not stay over once within the last five days; however, I could tell she was reluctant to go each night. They claimed they were taking things slow, but I could see right through them. I predicted Kokoro would move in with Fleurette within four months.

Gavin, on the other hand, had been completely absent. Kokoro explained that he was taking time to set up the apartment and move his things over. He had declined our invitation to our Samhain celebration. I tried not to take it personally.

It was entirely possible that he needed some time away from the craziness that was my general life. Especially now that he knew my secret. I didn't blame the guy.

As I passed forks to Fleurette to place on the table, I counted the settings. "You have too many places set," I remarked.

Fleurette looked at me. "Do I?"

I held up my free hand. "Me, you, Kokoro, Fal, Wren, and your father. Plus, the seat for the dead. That's seven. You have nine."

"Are you sure that's all who are showing up tonight?" Fleurette asked with a secretive smile on her face.

A knock sounded on the door.

"That would be Dad," Fleurette said as she continued to add the utensils to the table. "Be a dear and answer that, will you?"

I rushed out of the dining room and through the kitchen. My black pointed hat—a staple of the Samhain tradition— sat on the side table near the door. I placed it on my head.

"Blessed Samhain!" I greeted as I flung the door wide, inviting in Lyle. And then I did a double take.

There were two people standing behind him. They both beamed at my stunned expression.

"Mom! Dad!" I exclaimed as the three people entered the cottage. Mom swooped in to give me an uncommonly crushing hug.

"Oh, Cressida, how I've missed you!" she murmured into my shoulder. I hugged her back with the same ferociousness.

"Mom, you look amazing," I said as she squeezed me. It was true. She rarely donned her human form, and every time she did, she had worn the same shapeless dress, not caring about her appearance. But now she wore a new ensemble of flowing pants and an aubergine sweater that actually showed off her figure. Her multicolored hair, longer than mine, was artfully worn in a fishtail braid.

She straightened and looked me in the eye. "You still don't know how to stay out of trouble, do you?" she asked me, but her mouth turned up at the corners, belying her seriousness.

Roger, my father, stepped up and placed a warm hand on my back. "Now, Belinda. Let's not forget where she gets that trait from."

I let go of my mother to hug him. We barely knew each other, so my hug was more perfunctory, but it still felt right.

"As far as I'm concerned, Roger, it was from you. I certainly have never been kidnapped before," Mom said wryly.

He let go of me to turn and, with a cunning smile, he planted a kiss on her lips.

It warmed my heart as much as it soured my stomach. "So, you're back. When did you get here?"

My dad straightened from the kiss. "Just this morning. As soon as GOGS told us the mysterious killings had stopped and that we could come out of hiding, we made arrangements. It took us six days to travel. And no, we will not divulge where we were."

I nodded, raising my eyebrows. "Fair enough. Where will you stay, though?"

Lyle, forgotten in the sitting room, cleared his throat. "I've invited them to stay with me. At least until we can finish their cabin."

"Cabin?" I asked with a puzzled frown.

Mom took over the dialogue. "Well, we certainly can't live in the barn! Lyle has graciously gifted us with a small parcel of his land out back, away from prying eyes. We plan to build a little home for just the two of us. That way, we can still be close to you."

I turned to Lyle with wide eyes. "That's amazing! Lyle, how thoughtful."

He ducked his head with a shy grin. "I miss having Belinda around. Even though her job has been successfully given to another cat. I'm sure she doesn't mind so much, though."

I gave him a quick hug, my hat skewing to the side in the process. I laughed and straightened it back out. "Well, come in! Dinner will be in about an hour."

As soon as the food was ready, we all piled into the dining room, a rather cramped affair with that many people. At the far end of the table was the place setting for the deceased, with a special oversized plate, bowl, and goblet. All the food stayed in the kitchen, and we took turns dishing ourselves large portions. Before sitting down at our seats, however, we approached this special place at the head of the table and scooped a small amount from our plates onto the dead's setting. Even a sip from our own glasses was poured into the goblet.

We each wore a pointed hat as was tradition, and ate our meals in near-silence to honor the people that had passed before us.

After Kokoro's *daigaku imo*—candied sweet potatoes—had been consumed, we retired into the sitting room to digest with hot spiced cider made by Wren. I took the opportunity to inform my parents on what had happened earlier in the month.

Including, with a small amount of hesitancy, the discovery of my feelings for Grimm.

They sat on the loveseat side by side. I happened to be across from them in the wingback, with Grimm stationed next to me in a stoic sitting position as I rubbed his ears. My mother's eyes turned slightly steely as she glanced from me to Grimm.

"Grimm? The *dog?*"

My dad put a hand over hers, as if to temper her.

I needed pacification as well, given how much her tone of voice made me bristle. "Yes, Mother. The dog. My business partner. My best friend. The one who has repeatedly saved my life. It may be a strange arrangement, but we are soulmates. He is the one, and if you don't like that, your disapproval will change nothing."

Grimm licked my hand. I took a breath to soothe my nerves while I waited for my mom's reply.

She laughed brightly, a response I did not expect. "Oh, Cressida. You've always had such a spine of steel, especially when it comes to your loved ones. Never change."

"What?" I asked blankly.

She grinned at me and cuddled even closer to Roger. "Leave it to my daughter to never do things the traditional way. If Grimm is your true love, he's your true love. It's never been done before in our family, but then again, Annie's never tried to come back before either. My only concern rests upon the fact that you can't … ahem … consummate the relationship."

That last line hung in the air for a beat. "Ew, Mom," I finally said. "Nor do I want to. I'm not sexually attracted to dogs. I love *Grimm*. Not his looks."

Fleurette, seated near me on one of the table chairs, butted in, "We are well aware of the … dilemma, Belinda. Cressida still must bring a daughter into this world. Once we figure out the whole Annie thing, it's next on our to-do list."

"And speaking of Annie," Mom continued with a small grimace, "have there been any other magical incidents since the snowstorm?"

Fleurette once again took the lead on this conversation. "No, there has not, but GOGS has been informed, and we are on the lookout. We don't actually know what Annie is capable of, but we are taking her threats seriously."

Mom nodded as she stared into space.

Fleurette stood. "The witching hour approaches. Fal, let's get that bonfire started."

Fleurette and Fal had stacked a bonfire earlier in the day behind the cottage. Now, all of us joined hands around the carefully placed pile of wood, as per my friend's instructions.

I blinked in confusion. "But Fleurette, the bonfire still needs to be lit."

It was completely dark out, with only a small light from the crescent moon far above. Nevertheless, I could see the wry smile on her face. "Oh, ye of little faith. I've been working on a little something, with Fal's help. I've laid down a simple spell on the unlit pile. With all of us here, we are going to light it with magic. You all don't need to do anything; just keep your hands connected. Fal, are you ready?"

"Ready."

Fleurette began a low chant, the words nonsensical to me, but they were edged with a magical sharpness. Fal joined the chant.

My arms began to tingle. I shivered at the sensation. Looking over at Mom on my right, I could tell that she felt it too.

The two witches increased the speed and volume of their chant, and the sensation spread through my body. On a final shouted syllable, Fal and Fleurette stopped, and the energy that had been building around the ring of humans poured out onto the pile of wood, which burst into a pleasant flame with a whoosh.

My eyes were dazzled by the sudden conflagration. Fleurette grinned broadly.

"Worked like a charm," she exclaimed. Her face grew more serious. "Friends and family. We are here on this Blessed Samhain to pay tribute to the people in our lives that have passed from this plane. May we hold them in our hearts, and then let them go."

"I'll go first," Wren chimed in, her face somber in the dancing light of the fire. She took her felted hat off, holding it in her hand. "Maurice, thank you for being the best teacher I ever had. I release you." She mimed throwing something into the fire.

Murmurs sounded around the ring as we all offered our blessings to her words.

Next in line, Fleurette stared into the fire. "Mom. Althea Williams. You did some terrible things in your life, but in the end, you saved mine and the lives of the people I loved." She took a deep breath, her voice catching as she threw a handful of air into the fire. "I forgive you, and I release you. Be free, Mom."

My own heart was heavy as Kokoro went next, not forgiving her deceased husband or his cronies, but releasing them all the same. This was her first Samhain, as Tyonoshima had their own special day of the dead in their culture. It was similar enough to Samhain that she felt at ease adapting her cultural practices to this holiday.

Around the circle we went, until it was my turn. I reflected upon the people who had passed, and finally settled on what I would say.

"Nic, I wish things had been different for you," I began. "Fleurette is like a sister to me, and too late I learned that she actually *was* your sister. You could have used your power for the benefit of people, but with your parents and upbringing, you didn't have a chance. I'm sorry for how everything turned out. Nic, I forgive you, and I release you." I mimed throwing a handful of something into the fire, and then wiped a tear that had fallen from my eye.

Across the way, Fleurette gave me a sad smile.

Much later, after Lyle and my parents had left, Kokoro had kissed Fleurette goodnight at the door, and the household had gone to sleep, I curled up in a contented ball against Grimm's shoulder on the loveseat, a feeling of gratitude swirling through me. My canine companion leaned his massive head against me, creating a warm and comforting cradle.

I should have been exhausted, given the late hour, but the festivities from Samhain still gripped me. Instead of sleeping, I stared out at a light that had been left on in the kitchen, casting a soft glow into the sitting room.

My mother's face when I told her about my love for Grimm flashed through my mind, causing a nugget of discontent. "You don't think it's weird, do you?" I asked as I flexed the claws on one paw, pleased with the new growth they sported.

"I'd have a better grasp on the weirdness factor if I knew what 'it' is," Grimm responded.

"Us. Soulmates. I can feel your emotions sometimes, even when I'm human. I couldn't do that before; could you?"

Grimm snorted softly. "You are always there with me, Cress, even when we are apart. I thought I was good at reading your emotions before, but now I'm a champion. And yes, I can tell that your mom got to you yet again. Knock it off. It doesn't matter if a cat and a dog being forever linked by love is weird, it only matters that it happened."

"And what if we can't find a workaround for the whole 'consummation' thing?" I asked, hating the word even as I said it.

Grimm raised his head to nose me affectionately. "You know I love you, right?"

"I can feel it in my soul."

"You should also know that I don't find cats or humans particularly attractive."

I lowered an ear. "I'm not going to take offense to that. Dogs don't get my motor running either."

"Well, I'm still here, because I can't imagine not being with you. Our love goes beyond the physical, my love. We were meant to be."

"I love it when you call me that," I remarked. "Just never call me a unicorn."

Grimm chuckled in his canine way. "Deal."

The light in the kitchen blinked out. I raised my head, listening for any signs that Fleurette had turned it off.

The house was silent.

My hackles raised as Grimm sent out a bolt of agitation through our new bond.

"You don't think ..." I began to say.

"I do," replied Grimm. He began a deep growl in his throat.

Fleurette's bedroom door banged open and she hurried into the sitting room. "Cressida, are you awake? Something is happening!"

I jumped off the sofa and shimmered. "We already figured that out. What do you know?"

Fleurette brandished her message mirror in her hand. "A GOG closer to Dogwood sent out an SOS, concerning the sudden appearance of an enormous water construct that rose out of the Willmaunt River and walked into the outskirts of the city. People are in a panic."

The light in the kitchen turned back on. Fleurette's mirror buzzed.

She looked at it, her eyes widening with horror. "Oh. They just wrote that it deconstructed quite suddenly."

"Anyone hurt?" I asked as I walked over to her.

She ran a hand down her face, the bags under her eyes evident. "Probably. They said the creature was so massive, it flooded the entire area with a huge wave when it collapsed."

"How much magical talent would it take to make such a thing?"

"A lot. More than I have."

We locked eyes.

"Annie," I stated with conviction.

Fleurette nodded grimly. "She wasn't kidding when she said she was going to cause havoc in this world. I need to leave for an emergency GOGS meeting. I imagine Annie used up her power reserve for a number of days yet again. Now is the time to get ourselves prepared!"

I glanced down at Grimm, whose yellow eyes shone with determination. We may have won a battle against Elkins and the ACF, but there was still a war to fight.

But at least I now had one strong weapon on my side.

Love.

ACKNOWLEDGMENTS

What an amazing thing it is, to write a book! And *Chasing Tails* gets the distinct honor of being my first book that I fully wrote as an already published author. *Unfamiliar Territory* took me around ten years to write, and *Relative Truths* took me about a year. But this one? I finished the rough draft in four months.

I'll admit, this manuscript was harder. I'd had so much of the first two books mapped out in my head before I started. But for *Chasing Tails,* I only had the beginning and the end. The in-between bits I made up as I went. But it came together beautifully once I got in my groove.

Since publishing my first book, I have gained a small following, and these people really help to keep me going! So, to Jennica, Jennie, Susie, Eileen, and anyone else who has written to me to tell me how much they love my stories, thank you from the bottom of my heart. *You* are the reason I chose to become an author, and your support means the world to me.

Tina S. Beier, thank you for being a joy to work with! I truly thank the stars for finding you when I did. Your editing skills are much valued, as are your sweet notes and genuine love for Grimm. Sorry/not sorry I made you cry in this book.

Thanks go to Cynthia Ley for her proofreading skills, and to Nanci Remington for the final check before this book got pushed into the world. You two are amazing, and I appreciate you.

I am continually in awe of my cover designer, Angelee van Allman, not only for her art skills, but for her kind and generous heart and her ability to offer me an alternative view on my writing while she beta reads. Angelee, I hit the jackpot with you! And much appreciation to my other beta reader, Rachel, who thankfully pushed me to finish this book in time for her birthday, giving me a solid deadline that I would have otherwise ignored. Thanks for being there for me, friend.

A special thanks goes to the country of Japan for being a huge inspiration in this particular book. I heavily borrowed from their lore of the kitsune, although I did give my own personal spin to this supernatural creature. I do hope I represented this mythology in a respectful manner. Honestly, Kitty has been one of my favorite characters to write, and I'll miss her. If Kitty has piqued anyone's interest in kitsune, I urge you to read some books of Japanese mythology to learn about the real deal.

I wanted to take a moment to acknowledge my family and how much their support means to me. Matt is my rock and has been incredibly supportive in all of my endeavors, going so far as to alpha read for me. My daughters have been incredible about giving me my writing time willingly, and they are my mini cheerleaders. My parents have also been a great support, allowing me to vent any frustrations or share my triumphs over the phone. The same holds true of my in-laws, although they get to hear about my book highs and lows in person. And my aunt Carolyn's pride in me has really helped to push me forward on this journey.

I give my last thanks to all of my readers. Each time that I see that someone has bought my book, or recommended me on social media, or given me a follow, my heart swells. You are what makes all of this worth it. You are supporting a dream. And I appreciate this so, so much. You've made it three-quarters of the way through *The Familiar's Legacy*. Are you ready for the final chapter in Cressida's story? I know I am.

ABOUT THE AUTHOR

R. Lindsay Carter wanted to be a zookeeper when she was a girl. Now, she is content to stick with her small menagerie at home, which includes her supportive husband and her two daughters. When she isn't in the throes of writing, you can find R. Lindsay creating art, reading, gardening, ignoring household chores, and otherwise lounging about, usually with her lap taken up by her dog and/or one of her three cats. Born and raised in the Pacific Northwest, R. Lindsay happily lives in Oregon.

BOOKS BY R. LINDSAY CARTER

The Familiar's Legacy:
Unfamiliar Territory
Relative Truths
Chasing Tails

CONNECT

Follow R. Lindsay Carter for all the latest news!

Social Media:

https://www.rlindsaycarter.com

https://www.facebook.com/rlindsaycarter

https://www.instagram.com/author_rlindsaycarter

https://www.tiktok.com/@author_rlindsaycarter

Newsletter:

https://www.rlindsaycarter.com/newsletter/